# The Presence of Grace

4/1/01

# *The Presence of Grace*

## a Holden Grace novel

## Daniel R. Surdam

To John + Amanda,
Here's hoping that this is the first
of many Holden Grace novels. That
way, Peggy + I can buy a house
on Kiawah Island, and you guys can
come and visit. I expect you guys
to be my Boston, Notre Dame and
Philly reps. Spread the word and
spread the joy that is "Holden Grace."

Daniel Surdam

ISBN: 0-75960-722-2

This book is printed on acid free paper.

1stBooks - rev. 1/4/01

For Margaret,
*who has endured and believed*
*for every second.*


*And many thanks to*
*Paul Cammilleri, who provided the*
*design and illustration of the cover,*
*and Mom and Dad.*

## *Chapter 1*

You would think that an eventful day for a private detective would consist of more than thoroughly reading an article from the early morning *Syracuse Post-Standard* about a survey of college women and what they found attractive about men. But, at this point on a Friday morning in the middle of one of Central New York's classic ninety-plus degree heat waves in August, this was a big event. Why? Because I fit the description given by the candid coeds. That, and maybe the phone seemed like the ringer was shut off and the door failed to yield a knock. Where were the Girl Scouts pedaling cookies when you needed them?

Ah, but how those young college ladies described me as their ideal attractive man did plaster a sly grin on my face. So what if I was fifteen years older than they were? They certainly seemed intelligent enough, and damn if I didn't feel better knowing I could still flaunt a couple of attractive qualities. They liked smiles, some stubble and big, beautiful eyes. I'd be sure to put all three to work the next time I visited the Syracuse University campus. I could only hope the young coeds didn't mistake me for someone's parent. I made a note not to visit the Hill during Parent's Weekend. Shrewd.

Then again, no one could accuse me of looking all of the thirty-plus years I had lived. I did my best to keep in top physical shape, working my five-foot-eight inch, one hundred seventy-five pound frame hard. You don't take care of business and you can forget about a seductive smile from an attractive young coed, let alone a second glance from her mother. Unless, of course, you possessed my winning charm and razor-sharp wit. But, then again, I had to work them as hard as my body. Trying to keep together a complete package takes work. Serious work. Probably more than the results achieved.

I tossed the newspaper on my large pine desk and laughed at my musings. At least I could entertain myself on a slow day. I was getting good. Too good. I stared at the closed door to my office and read the reversed words on the frosted glass to myself.

"Holden Grace. Private Detective."

Still sounded good. I rolled my eyes from the door and scanned the office that I had occupied for a few years. The second-story Holden Grace headquarters was situated on West Fayette Street in beautiful downtown Syracuse in a district known as Armory Square, an upscale, yuppie hangout with microbreweries, hip nightclubs and chic restaurants. It didn't used to be that way. The building that I set up shop in once housed a leather goods store, but the economy turned all that pigskin belly up and when I moved in, my office overlooked a parking lot where the attendants stashed the customers keys in the driver-side visors. Faith in mankind. Didn't last long. Developers ripped up the lot and decided to replace it with fashionable condos. Part of the master plan to turn Armory Square into the affluent little slice of city that Syracuse deserved. I missed being able to see the actual Armory itself, an archaic, yet strong foothold of the past that once hosted Syracuse Nats games and has since been renovated into a science museum. At least they didn't turn it into condos. I always wondered where the new residents of the place across from me parked, now that all those parking spots were laid to waste. But I did have to be thankful. This office sure beat my old one down on South Clinton Street where traffic passing by was the best scenery.

I sat back and decided to critique my surroundings, a ritual that I seemed to go through all too often lately. While the Armory was the place for pretentious jerks to hang out, it wasn't the place for elite businesses to plug in and get popular. That was Franklin Square. Another recently renovated area reserved for hotshot radio stations and ad agencies where the rent soared as high as some of the egos. Maybe I belonged there. Then I caught sight of a silverfish scurrying across the floor and that snapped me back to reality. Just as well, I couldn't see myself in a ponytail with my nose buried up some client's gold-plated ass.

The walls were painted a neutral beige. I had originally thought about a nice, soothing flamingo pink in an effort to match the vistors' locker room at some Big Ten conference football school's facility implemented to transform high-strung college animals into tea-serving, quilt-knitting sociable types with no desire to pummel the opponent. Maybe that would work on my clients. Highly unlikely on both counts. The only results I could expect from pink walls were a desire to throw up and plenty of grief from my clients. Therefore, the neutral beige.

I had stripped and waxed the hardwood floor, bringing it back to a look of respectability. A fashionable Oriental rug, which was a gift from a close lady friend, covered much of the floor space in front of my desk. I had enough taste to adorn the walls with some decent artwork including a Holden Grace original entitled *Timber Crappie*. I could very well have plastered New York Rangers, Yankees, Knicks, Jets and Syracuse University sports paraphenalia all over the place, but they had their place in my desk. I was never sure why they were there.

A pair of rustic green leather armchairs fronted the desk which was equipped with an executive dart board, a miniature basketball hoop, a phone, answering machine and a few scattered papers (besides the morning newspaper) for effect.

In the drawers were my Glock, the obligatory bottle of booze, in this instance a bottle of Jack Daniels, my sports schedules and ridiculous amounts of office supplies such as staples, tape, paper clips (I always thought paper clips were more an annoyance than anything else. I wondered who put them there. Couldn't have been me. No way.), envelopes, labels, writing and copy paper and everybody's favorite, a hole punch. I'll admit to putting the punch in the drawer. I liked something that could turn plain old typed pages into neat little members of a binder. That was order. A binder. Not flimsy, useless paper clips. I made another note to get the paper clips the hell out of my desk.

So far a productive morning. Two notes to myself. One not to visit the SU campus on Parent's Weekend and the other to eliminate those damned paper clips. Make that three notes. Find out who supplied those irritating twisted bits of metal to me.

The highlights of my office had to be those things I could turn to when I needed to think, blow off steam or simply screw off. I had a Aiwa stereo rack system, a small Sanyo refrigerator, a basketball hoop and a well-worn heavy bag.

Since I was a music lover and played the guitar, the stereo was a necessity. Certain moods always called for specific musical interludes, and for me, it was almost always rock. Classic bands such as Rush, the Doors, the Stones, Black Sabbath and modern kick ass stuff that included Pearl Jam, the Stone Temple Pilots, the Offspring and other bands that only the young twenty-somethings were supposed to appreciate. Hell, my CD collection had Rebecca Timmons, Tori Amos, Frank Zappa (who was an absolute genius) and a wierd collection of Tiny Tim covers, so I figured I transcended the label that any demographic hungry music rep wanted to pin on me. Music is a daily part of life.

The refrigerator always housed a variety of beverages -- juice, sparkling water and, of course, some serious suds. I prefered to keep some Bass Ale, Fosters and Becks on hand, but my thin wallet normally didn't allow those pleasures, so I had to settle for Rolling Rock or some Molson, and when things were really tight, I'd grab some PBR's and be happy that I could snatch up a cold one when I wanted. The same friend who gave me the Oriental rug questioned the sensibility behind keeping beer in the office, but I told her that it was a matter of will power. That just because it was there didn't mean I had to crack one open. But I could understand her concern.

My four-foot tall basketball hoop was tucked in a corner and allowed fifteen-foot jumpers from behind my desk but, unfortunately, did not offer any baseline shots. And my jumper from the left baseline has always needed work. The price you paid for small office space. That hoop came in handy. When

I'm on a thinking binge, firing up a few shots always helped me along. Also, my clients tended to find it charming, although they always seem to refuse a quick game of one-on-one. Home court advantage, I guess.

The heavy bag predominantly worked as the opposite to the junior hoop. When I found myself frustrated by a case or situations, I usually took to the bag with an exuberant fervor. If the combinations I threw and the sweat I worked didn't spawn any clever ideas or solutions, at least I always felt better afterward. Sometimes it only takes a simple tool to save a little sanity.

There was also a four-drawer coffee-brown metal filing cabinet planted against one wall, neatly filled with alphabetized files on every case I had been involved with through the years. On the exterior, when a person glances at my desk, they may grasp a perception of disorganization, but that's just the surface. It's only my desk top, for God's sake. When it comes to important details, everything has a proper place. So what if I hadn't dusted my office in weeks? Didn't mean things weren't in order.

Yeah. I guess I was satisfied with the look of my office. The only thing it needed besides air conditioning was a client. I mean, it wasn't like beautiful, buxom women with wads of fifties bulking up their Gucci purses were kicking my door in with their pumps for my business. This was Syracuse. I shouldn't be greedy. A beautiful woman asking for directions to the Carousel Center, the city's big mall, would wax a smile on my face. I'd settle with a lost dog case right now. For two hundred a day plus expenses, I'd be happy with a lost dog case.

It wasn't even noon yet, but the thermometer was pushing ninety and the humidity was stuck at its redundant ninety-plus percent. My short-sleeve button down Arrow shirt did its best to perform a skin graft with my back. Once again, I forgot to bring a fan from home, but that wouldn't do much good, just pushing hot air from here to there. Someday, that air conditioning. Probably in December. I bet they had AC in Franklin Square. It

*Daniel Surdam*

was too hot to don the gloves and work over the heavy bag, so I fished my plastic basketball from my bottom desk drawer and decided to work on my jumper. I turned on the stereo and drilled my first long-range bomb. Michael who? My next shot rimmed out just as the door burst open.

## *Chapter 2*

Startled by the sudden intrusion, I quickly stepped to my desk like a point guard driving to the rack and pulled my pistol from my top drawer and set my sights dead center on the chest of my guest. The problem was, if this someone was looking to fill me with a a lot of lead, I most likely would have been too late to my weapon. Not that I had too much to worry about. But that still made note number four. I just hoped I'd remember to write them all down. Note number four -- when playing hoops in the office, keep the piece close at hand. I was lucky. The party crasher was a buddy of mine.

"Jesus, Holden, put the gun down," said Mick Allen, as he shut the door a little too hard for my liking.

Mick didn't look good. The color was drained from his face and the dark semi-circles under his eyes indicated little sleep the night before, or for as much as I knew, a few days. Generally, Mick was a good looking guy. Six-one, one-ninety, short styled brown hair, those chiseled features and green eyes that drove a lot of women to the edge. Not all of them, but a lot. Compared to me, he was the bigs and I was Triple A at best, but today he just got demoted to the rookie league.

I set the Glock down on my desk and shut off the stereo.

"Sorry, Mick. Jesus, you look bad. I got a feeling this isn't a social call," I said.

Mick nodded then headed straight for one of my leather chairs and dropped down into it like a man on his last legs. He buried his face in his hands. Was he going to cry? I thought I'd jump in before he had a chance.

"What the hell's going on?" I asked.

"I need a drink."

Not the answer I was searching for, but I could work with it. I dug out the half-full liter of Jack Daniels, stepped around my desk and handed it to Mick. I didn't bother having any glasses around, since I'm usually the only one taking hits from the bottle. Besides, the alcohol would eradicate all of my germs, right? Mick took a two-gulp swill from the bottle and held the crutch tightly around the neck. He winced slightly as the bourbon registered in his tender stomach. Mick never was much of a drinker, and it certainly showed now. Before he spoke, he tipped the bottle back to his lips and swallowed. Again, he made a face only a mother could love.

"Take it easy, Mick," I said as I sat on the corner of my desk.

"Fuck it, Holden. I could use a little numbness."

I snatched the bourbon from his hand and set it down on my desk.

"You gonna tell me what's goin' on? It's a little early to get juiced up, don't ya think?"

Mick looked around my office, most likely to gather his thoughts and not to enjoy my decorative skills. Although, his eyes did linger on *Timber Crappie* longer than anywhere else. At least the man had taste. I always thought that. Mick was a good guy.

We'd known each other about eight years. I first met him as a softball teammate for a roofing company in a highly competitive slow pitch league in Skaneateles, a quaint little village that I called home about twenty-five miles from Syracuse. The village was situated right at the north end of Skaneateles Lake, one of the famous Finger Lakes, and had the distinct look and feel of a tourist town. But one thing, it was a nice place to live. And, the softball was serious. Mick had been an established player, and it was my first year with the team. I had played a few years on another team but was recruited as an attempt to build a softball dynasty. The guy who ran the team, Mike Doyle, was someone I grew up with, someone whom I had always competed against in the sandlot, the school yard and in high school. He remembered the good old competitive days and decided to nab me as an ally instead of having me continually leave his team in fits over how to stop me. Not that I was Superman in softball cleats. My biggest asset was that I played harder at shortstop on every play than most guys in the Major

Leagues. Of course, why bust your ass when you're making seven figures and have a guaranteed contract? I was no stranger to the dirt. Sometimes to get things done, you had to get dirty. Not the dirty kind of dirty, but the clean kind of dirty. I carried that over to my line of work, when I finally figured out what I meant.

Mick wasn't thrilled with my arrival on the team at first, as was the case with a couple of other players. I represented a threat to their nicely controlled world of recreation. The players that knew me personally pretty much liked me. Come on, how could they resist? But Mick, he was a hot shot left fielder with a cannon for an arm and a flare for the spectacular. I always thought he needed to carry a jar of Grey Poupon to go along with all of his hotdogging, but he was good. And as the season progressed, and the blowout victories piled up, Mick warmed up to me and we became good friends, as well as league champs. It was just a matter of time before my winning personality won him over. Yeah. Right.

He eventually tried to hook me up with his younger sister, Rachel, who I had never met. Being the smooth guy that I am, I declined repeatedly. Didn't want to mess with a friendship. That and there was no way I'd chance a blind date. Too many of those went up in flames, and then you're back to the friendship thing. When I did meet Rachel, I was impressed. She was an absolute knockout and an exceptional athlete on top of that, but she hadn't even turned twenty yet. Too bad. We never became an item, be we did become good friends, up until last year when she left Skaneateles and headed to Burlington, Vermont. We lost track of each other as time passed, mostly because I was lousy at returning calls or letters. Then she suddenly came back a few months ago, and we had seen each other a few times, but never kept steady contact. She had changed. Or so I thought she had. Maybe I did, but I doubt that since I had always been an overgrown kid. Still was. Rachel Allen. I missed her friendship. Maybe I'd work a little harder at staying in touch.

9

I looked at Mick. For a guy as usually steady as Mick, except when he knocked back a few too many, he looked devastated. That was the word. Devastated. I had no clue what Mick's next words would be, but the chill along my spine educed a feeling of anxiety.

"Rach is missing. I think she might have killed herself," he blurted out.

"What? Hold on a minute, buddy. This doesn't sound like you or her."

"I know. I know. But you saw how she's been lately. Not the same..."

"But to whack herself? Come on, Mick. What's goin' on?"

"I... we... we had a business meeting the other night. To talk about selling the sporting goods store. There's been offers. Since we're partners, we had to talk. I mean, I just couldn't figure her out lately. Ever since she came back, ya know? She called and canceled at the last minute. We rescheduled for a breakfast meeting yesterday morning."

I handed him back the bottle of Jack. He took a hit, winced. His mind had to be spinning from the booze. No way Rachel would do herself. Or so I thought. Maybe Mick knew something. He continued.

"She never showed. Never called. Nothing. That was yesterday morning. I mean this was business, Holden. You know how she felt about money."

"Yeah. I know. She used to talk about rolling around naked in it. And I thought that was just in the movies."

That one made Mick snort. I always knew the right things to say. I grabbed the bottle from him and drained about a shot. I made it a practice not to imbibe before noon, but I guess right now I was subscribing to the camper's philosophy -- it's always noon somewhere. The liquor did a little mamba in my stomach before settling down. I needed to have a little more than Designer Protein and skim milk for breakfast to handle these early lunches of bourbon.

Mick pushed on. The J.D. had really loosened his tongue. I was hoping for a liitle more concrete info about Rachel's sudden hiatus from society.

"I called her place a million times. Left messages. Call me, Rach. What's up? Nothin'. No calls. I went over there. No answer."

"You don't have a key?"

"Well... yeah."

The Jack was starting to weave its turn-your-brain-to-slush magic on Mick. He was slurring his words, and taking a little more time to compose his sentences. So, he decided he wanted a little more of that ole Kentucky prestidigitation and took the bottle from me. He drained a bit, swallowed, tipped the bottle back and gulped even more. The once half-full liter was pushing empty. It looked like I'd have to set up a meeting with my favorite discount liquor store sooner than expected. Mick closed his eyes and leaned his head back. With his one hand that wasn't holding the bottle, he rubbed his face. It looked like he was making sure all of his facial features remained. A few more ounces of my friend Jack would have him checking to see if he could still walk.

He sighed heavily and opened his eyes. They were the eyes of an old, broken, beaten man, not of my buddy Mick's. Christ, he was thinking the worst, and he knew Rachel better than anyone, but to ice herself? I wasn't convinced. He gathered himself enough to pick up where he left off.

"Yeah, I have a key, but ... but..." He searched for the words that were probably a lot simpler to grasp than he knew.

"It's her place, ya know. Her privacy. I didn't wanna bust in and maybe... I don't know. I thought maybe she'd call me. And maybe I didn't wanna go in. See her, ya know... just... oh, Jesus..."

I tried to help. "Mick, maybe she just took off. Like you said, and I've noticed, she hasn't been herself. She's got stuff on her mind. Come on, she's always been pretty strong-willed. She needed some time away."

11

*Daniel Surdam*

"But I called her, H. We're tight, ya know. Fuckin' tight. I gotta look out for her, ya know?"

He looked right at me. Into my eyes. And that's when his tears welled up. Call me cold-hearted, a Neandrathal, not a 21st-century kind of guy, but I hate to see a grown man cry. And believe me, many women, especially the close ones, have had their share of comments about my lack of tenderness in this area, but I feel that you don't have to open up the flood gates to feel emotion. Although, I do admit that I became misty on a couple of occasions -- when Dennis Byrd of the New York Jets overcame his terrible spinal injury to walk again and the same for Reggie Brown of the Detroit Lions. Right now, I understood that Mick was suffering, but he was assuming a hell of a lot. In fact, I would rather see a grown man puke all over his car hood from a heavy night of drinking than see one cry. Of course, in Mick's case, I might see both this morning.

"Holden." Mick fought the tears. He was winning. "I want you to find her. Find out what happened. If anyone can find the truth, it's you."

His words melded together as the Jack Daniels kept kicking into his weakened system. He handed me the near dead bottle of booze.

"Sorry 'bout that," he managed to say. I wasn't sure if he meant drinking as much as he did or the near breakdown into tears. He knew my opinion about the latter.

"No problems." I got up and stashed the bottle back in its proper place and turned back to Mick. He was weaving a little in his chair.

He asked, "You'll take the case, right. I can handle the fee. I jus' want the truth."

"Mick, I don't think it's a case..."

He interrupted me before I could finish my thought.

"Dammit, H. You knew her." The tears were making a comeback. "Chrissakes, aren't you sick of chasin' after lost dogs and spyin' on unfai... unfaith... cheating, goddamn spouses? You can do this for me, can't ya?"

12

His words came out like he was talking underwater. I had to really concentrate to hear every syllable. I would let the insults about my occupational foibles as of late slide this time. There hadn't been a German Shepherd I'd failed to locate yet. K9PI. Maybe my new vanity plate. That or ICU. Then again, some people might confuse me with a doctor on that one.

The scenario did leave me with an unsatisfied feeling gnawing inside my head and in my gut. Mick knew Rachel better than I did. He would be the one to know if she might have done something as crazy as taking her own life. To me, it seemed as if she had a lot going for her -- young, smart, attractive and a head for money. But maybe it was more like a craving for money. She had once told me that one of the reasons she left Burlington was because things weren't working out for her financially. And she meant working out big. In Skaneateles, she could establish the sporting goods business with Mick and focus on her future. She never elaborated on what exactly that future was. I assumed it included raking in the dough. But despite her lust for cash, she was a great kid. And although I hadn't seen her for a month or so, I had always intended on giving her a call and asking her to join me for some dinner and drinks at the Blue Water Grill on the lake. Hopefully, I'd still get the chance.

If, for some crazy reason, she did whack herself, I wanted to know what forced her to the ultimate final act. People call many things the final act -- a game winning point, retirement, marriage, divorce and, of course, death. Personally, I look at suicide as the final act. Not just the death itself, but the desperation and the disrespect so often linked with taking too easy of a way out. Death may be a final moment associated with a living being, but suicide is a final act. A closed curtain of failure. A last sour note. A washout of all that could have been good in that life.

Mick stared at me with his tear-filled, half closed eyes. The guy was really hurting and had turned to me to help him through this. Finding the truth about Rachel was the main reason Mick was sitting, drunk at eleven o'clock in the morning, in my office, but he was also there to lean on me. The guy had no family to turn to besides Rachel. His and Rachel's parents had died in an automobile accident six and a half years ago on New Year's Eve. Now his only real family member was missing. The more I thought about the circumstances, the more I needed to check into things, even if I discovered that Rachel had committed the final act. Mick deserved to have a friend stand by him, and by agreeing to poke my nose around a bit, I knew he'd feel better. Before Mick cut me off and belittled my sleuthing talents, I planned on telling him that it probably wouldn't hurt to ask some questions. I just didn't look at this as being a case. And now, I was certain I wanted to ask questions. I wanted to find Rachel. Period.

"Okay, listen, Mick. I'll check into this."

The world seemed to lift from his overburdened shoulders.

I continued. "But if she ran off with some zillionaire to Monaco, you're gonna feel awful stupid."

He gave me a half grin and nodded. I think speaking at this point took a little too much effort.

"I'm not worried about my fee..."

"But..." he interrupted.

I waved my hands. "We'll settle up anything later. Maybe a case of Fosters. Right now, this is what we're gonna do." I sat on the edge of my desk. "You're gonna go home, get as sobered up as possible. I'll meet you in the Sherwood tavern around two. We'll grab some lunch and talk a little more. Fair enough?"

Mick agreed. He raised up from the chair a little unsteadily, but made it to his feet. This was the first time he stood since busting into my office and draining most of my Jack Daniels. It had to be tough to get his legs. It reminded me of a line from some obscure song -- "Don't vacillate in the wind or I'll kick your ass over." Nice. I had a penchant for recalling odd things. Wasn't that part of my job? Mick shook my hand and thanked me, then made his exit a little less dramatic than his entrance, especially when he stumbled into the closed door. Thankfully, he had a short drive home, but I should've called him a cab. Note number five -- when you send a buddy out of your office drunk before noon, don't let him drive.

I could only hope that my unofficial investigation would proceed quickly and smoothly, with simple answers and a sister who turned up in one piece. Of course, I've learned through the years never to assume that even the simplest of cases on the surface will fall into place and wrap themselves up as neat as a Christmas gift with a little white bow.

In the last half hour, it seemed as if the summer heat decided to pay special attention to my little corner of the world. I slid the Bush CD *Razorblade Suitcase* into the stereo, snatched up my miniature basketball and threw up an air ball. Not just an air ball, but a hot air ball. I needed a little more release right now than shooting a few hoops.

"Bag time," I said.

I had planned to stop home and shower before meeting Mick for lunch anyway, so I might as well blow off some steam and soak my clothes thoroughly. I dug my Everlast 4302's out of my desk, slipped them on and introduced myself to the heavy bag with a right cross.

## *Chapter 3*

I had stopped home and enjoyed a revitalizing shower after a solid fifteen minutes on the bag. The drive from my office in Syracuse to my house in Skaneateles took about twenty-five minutes, and I relished the air conditioning in my maroon Jeep Grand Cherokee. As I cruised west on Route 690 to Route 695, then onto 5 West and south on Route 321 to Skaneateles, I mulled over Rachels' disappearance. Mick still didn't give any good reason why Rachel would commit suicide. Hopefully, he'd be a little more cognizant when we met for lunch.

I changed into a white golf shirt that had Joe's Roofing embroidered on the left chest in dark blue stitching, a pair of khaki lightweight Dockers and a pair of Nike Air cross trainers. I either looked like I was ready to step right onto the PGA tour or just looked like every other yuppie running around Skaneateles. At least I felt comfortable with the look, unlike the pot-bellied, I-think-I'm-too-sophisticated-to-dress-this-way but still-will-to-get-the-image guy around town. I was equally at ease in a pair of coach's shorts and a t-shirt; a pair of Levi's, flannel shirt and Timberlands; some dressier Dockers, a Van Heusen with a silk paisley tie; or a good old penguin suit. I looked good and felt comfortable in most anything. I sported the wardrobe that suited me and me alone. No thongs. No sandals. No slippers. No bright pink. No pajamas. The ladies in my life loved that last one. Had to be because of my independent spirit.

The drive to the Sherwood Inn from my house took about five minutes, north on Mill Road, across Seneca Turnpike onto Fennel Street into the village. A right onto Jordan Street, then a quick right at the main light downtown onto West Genesee Street. I've noticed that almost every city, village or town in New York had a Genesee Street running through it somewhere. Who knew that the Rochester brewery had so much influence around the state? I parked in the large lot behind the establishment and entered through the back door, which leads directly into the tavern. The central air smacked me right away. It was a little too cold. What were they trying to do? Keep the stiffs at the bar from rotting?

The Inn was established in 1807 and perched like a hungry gray monster across West Genesee Street from the north end of the lake, reputed to be one of the purest in the world. I hoped that Rachel Allen's body wasn't polluting it right now. The locals wouldn't be too pleased. I'm sure if her body came bobbing to the surface somewhere, they'd pass a law that made it illegal to drown yourself in the pristine waters of the lake. You see, Skaneateles was big money -- new and old. Million dollar homes along the shoreline were common. That's where a lot of the new money took up residence. The old money occupied the majority of the three-story houses in the village. Big money also meant political posturing. If someone with substantial clout wasn't happy with something, a phone would ring and actions were taken. The ironic twist about beautiful Skaneateles was that there certainly were plenty of middle class denizens to round out the census numbers, including a lot of farmers and Holden Grace. It all made for an interesting mix.

The Inn had seventeen antiquaited hotel rooms that took up the second and third stories. The first floor housed the tavern, dining rooms, various conference rooms and the semi-stuffy lobby. The owner did a pretty good job of keeping the place up, considering it was probably crumbling at the very foundation. But wasn't that part of the charm of an antique? The flaws that made it stand out and give it character? If the general public got a behind the scenes look at the White House, they'd see plenty of defects brought about by time. Hey, old is old. You can't change that.

The Sherwood did an ample job of catering to the hordes of summer tourists and the upper crust of the community. I wondered why they let me in. Probably because I always snuck in the back way. Hell, could have been my winning attire. I'm sure I could really pal around with the boys as they took a day off from the country club to make an appearance in the village.

"I say, Biff, ole boy, but I love what you've done with the pleat in your Dockers. And the upturned collar really gets it done. Say, let's be fashionable and order up a round of Chardonnay. With a Jose Cuervo chaser and a Bass Ale draught." Okay, so maybe I didn't quite fit in with Biff, Binky, Bomber and the boys. Just as well. My name started with an "H," and I preferred a good bottle of Cabernet Sauvignon with some serious backbone over a Chardonnay.

Now, don't get me wrong. I don't think that every guy who drives a BMW, lives in a four thousand square-foot home and lists his favorite hobbies as polo and yachting are arrogant chumps. Some people are the genuine article, with or without affluence. I'd like to think that if the monetary gods smiled on me in the future, I'd stay the same charming asshole that everybody either loved or hated. I doubted that I'd ever find out, but a person can dream. It just seemed to me that I'd run into too many rich types physically softer than kneaded dough, with receding hair lines, double chins, thick glasses and not a whole lot of consideration for other people. And the kicker? They all had gorgeous wives. I just couldn't figure it out. It was like a Picasso painting. I don't know, maybe it was the big bulge in the designer pants. The one with all the plastic.

The tavern was quite dark for a shining August afternoon and quite full considering the lunch crowd should have scattered by now, but the tourists loved to congregate at a fashionable watering hole and eatery, leaving their screaming children behind at the summer rental cottages along the lakeshore, to hobnob with the village's finest. Or so they hoped. John Walsh had been known to grace the Sherwood, as well as James Taylor, Alec Baldwin, Woody Harrelson and Tom Cruise. What about the presence of Grace? A sure fire way to increase the table turn and boost alcohol sales. So what if it would be gray-haired widows wondering if I was named after William Holden. I was.

It wasn't just the tourists escaping their offspring who jammed the bar and tables. Many regulars and locals flaunted their wares before, during and after the lunchtime crunch. The dining room, which was across the lobby from the tavern, was pretty much empty. The lunch crowd always filled the tavern, and the dinner throngs sat themselves down for some fine continental cuisine in the dining room and the front porch where they could look wistfully out at the lake, their view occasionally distracted by semis rumbling down Genesee Street, also known as Route 20, on their way to Route 81 and that great big world out there. Actually, the constant presence of the eighteen-wheelers had caused quite an uproar, as they used the route through Skaneateles as a shortcut. The main concerns involved their travel south along East Lake Road, a somewhat winding country road that offered fantastic views of the lake and the homes. It just wasn't paved with the truckers in mind, and that battle continued. One skirmish that the village came out victorious on involved the military hauling nuclear arms right through Skaneateles. Questions arose regarding the safety of the drinking water, since the lake not only served as Skaneateles' source of water but also quenched the city of Syracuse, should disaster strike. Good questions. No more nukes.

The tavern bar was to my right and stretched maybe fifteen feet, then took the standard ninety degree turn, this one to the right, and met the wall. Behind the bar, a large oil painting of a dark and uninspiring horse scene drew a patron's initial gaze. I would have preferred a dazzling brunette posed tastefully on a bright green golf course, with sunlight streaming down, touching nature's fire to each blade of grass, from the fairway to the green. But, who was I? I know I was someone who was repulsed by the existing painting. Remember, I'm an artist, so I can critique. Twenty-five tables, or so, covered the floor of the tavern, with a wall dividing the space. A constant murmur from the feeding crowd played in tune with the strangely rythmic pattern of silverware against china. Housewives bragged of new jewelry. Out-of-state residents raved about the quaint village. Businessmen slung their horseshit. And regulars bitched about the excess crowd.

20

It was around one forty-five, and I was lucky enough to find two empty stools near the elbow of the bar between a ruddy-faced guy working on a Manhattan and a guy who looked like he got caught in an explosion in a paint factory. While I had the chance, I staked my claim. The bartender, who Mick and I played ball with, noticed me and gave me a nod as I planted myself next to Mr. Paint Swatches. He quickly made his way over to me wearing his standard Sherwood Inn blue broadcloth button up, busting at the seams. Jess was a dead ringer for a younger George Clooney and probably a better actor. He was a body builder and had about as much fat on him as in a bag of pretzels. He stood five-ten. Weighed in around one ninety-five. His skin was paper-thin and he sort of reminded me of Ray Bradbury's *The Illustrated Man* with his veins ready to bust through the epidermal layers that scarcely held them back. Anyone looking to stick a needle in Jess would hit the bonanza.

"Hey, buddy. How ya been?" he asked.

Softball season had ended a couple of weeks ago, and I hadn't seen Jess since we captured another title.

"Not bad, Jess. Still walkin' and talkin'"

"Probably too much as usual."

"Can't screw with fate."

"You got that right. Bass Ale draught?"

It was more of a statement than a question. I nodded my approval.

"Menu?"

"Nah, I'll wait. I'm meetin' Mick," I answered.

"No problem."

Jess headed to the taps and expertly drew my beer in a pint glass and set it in front of me with a square cocktail napkin. The ale looked like a vial of amber nectar and tasted the same.

He proceeded to instinctively empty ash trays and swab up wet spots on the bar.

"Keeping busy, I see," I said between sips.

Just then, an elderly gentleman in a gray herringbone three-piece suit at the other end of the bar called Jess by name and

21

waved his empty Manhattan glass. What the hell was it that people liked about drinking a Manhattan besides the name? I looked at Red Cheeks to my right, and he seemed down right pleased with the taste of his. No thank you. I'd rather drink a vinegar cocktail to cut my cholesterol.

Jess said, "Gotta love it." He whisked down to the thirsty customer and started mixing his magic.

I always found bars, taverns, or whatever you wanted to call them a fascinating gathering place on days like this. To sit back and look at the people hiding from the sunlight like vampires. I had to ask Jess how many Bloody Mary's he served during the day. Of course, here I was, sitting at the bar, savoring a Bass Ale when I could be out playing eighteen holes at Dutch Hollow or maybe hanging out at my office waiting for nothing to roll into my lap. But I was here for a specific reason, to help Mick and to stuff my stomach. So, two reasons.

I felt a tap on my left shoulder. I turned and looked into the bloodshot eyes of Mr. Paint Swatches, who I believed to be a regular. He looked to be fifty-five or so, but chances were he was only in his forties. Now, there was no way that this guy had a beautiful wife.

"You're lucky to find a stool here today," he said unsteadily. The stupid grin on his face warned me of some followup sure to make me want to defenestrate the poor bastard. It wouldn't take much, but I couldn't afford to replace one of the Sherwood's windows.

"Usually you get that when Leo over there's passin' gas."

He pointed to Red Face and snickered at what he thought held some humor. I failed to smile. I failed to understand why he would even attempt conversation with me. But what he didn't fail to do was overstep the boundaries of good taste, let alone any taste at all. As he chuckled to himself and turned his attention back to his beer, I saw Jess look at me and offer an apologetic shrug. Hell, it wasn't his fault. I don't know how Jess could slop drinks to idiots like this day in and day out. I knew I couldn't do it. But Jess had the personality for it. He was patient, good natured, soft spoken and his bulk didn't hurt either. And he pulled in some serious tips, especially during the summer. Right now, my mood did not dictate juvenile attempts at humor by a guy dressed in plaid shorts below the knees, high white crew socks, sandals and a bright pink and turquoise golf shirt. He was immediately guilty of breaking many of my dress code rules, except for the white socks. I wore those while playing ball and dressing casually. Otherwise, the guy was a wardrobe nightmare.

I knew I should have ignored him, because before too long, Jess would have been scraping his face off the bar anyway, but I was in no mood to have an important conversation with Mick about Rachel with Ernest Goes to the Sherwood Inn sitting next to me.

"Hey, Patches the Clown."

He lifted his head and looked at me.

"Yeah, you." The tone in my voice was not friendly.

"Oh, whatsa matter, pal? No sensa humor? Jesus Christ, what a tightass."

He slurred the last line quietly to himself as he turned away. Then, as he somehow comprehended the accidental pun, he started giggling. Softly at first, then more noticeably until his entire body shook.

The last straw. I looked at Jess. He cringed, because he had a pretty good idea about what was coming next. I reached out and grabbed the guy's stool underneath the seat and pulled him toward me. Before he knew what the hell was going on, I spun him until his back faced me. I grabbed the back of his pretty pink and turquoise shirt near the collar and lifted him up, wrapped my right arm around his neck and applied a little pressure. Not too much, because I didn't want to hurt him. I released his shirt, reached across his head with my left hand and cradled his face with my palm under his chin and my first two fingers pressed under his eyes. If he made a move, I could hurt him badly. The man wisely made no move.

I growled into his ear, "I know you think you're Skaneateles' answer to Jay Leno and Ralph Lauren rolled into one, but not with me. Not now. Not today. Not ever."

He squeaked out a word that sounded like "okay" and I relaxed my grip. A seat had cleared at the other end of the bar, and he was happy to make a beeline for it. I could hear him letting whomever would listen that I was a fucking lunatic. A touch of truth to ameliorate my image. But, come on, Mick's situation had me upset.

The episode had unfolded so rapidly that very few of the patrons realized it had even taken place. Only those close to the bar took notice, and since I dispensed of the little rodent quickly, they turned their attention back to themselves and their own little worlds of greed, self-absorption, deception and whatever other pieces of their lives that kept them going.

I drained the last few ounces of my draught, and before I set the glass back down, Jess was there with a refill in a fresh glass.

"Ah, yes," I said. "It always pays to have friends in the right places."

Jess gave me a wink and said, "On me."

I toasted him and took a healthy slug of ale, rolling the liquid around in my mouth like a fine red Bourdeaux. I didn't have enough opportunities to savor a really good bottle of red, so I practiced my technique with a magnificent brew. Hell, to me, the Bass was comparable in many ways to a great red.

Mick appeared to my left looking much better, dressed in gray shorts, a polo shirt and a pair of Reeboks. Unlike me, he had entered through the front door. Probably wanted as many people as possible to see him pull up in his Mercedes and make his grand entrance. Either that or he just found a nice parking spot out on the street. Mick did okay financially, as evidenced by the beautiful piece of German engineering he drove. He owned a lot of real estate -- apartments, houses and land, and was a partner with Rachel in a sporting goods store in Skaneateles. He pretty much let her handle everything. I wondered who was taking care of it right now. He slapped me on the shoulder and slid onto the stool recently vacated by my colorful pal and pulled out a Marlboro Light and lit it.

"You're looking better," I said.

He exhaled a large blue-gray cloud of smoke away from me. "Took a nap. Didn't think I'd sleep at first, but when I hit the sofa, bam. Out."

"When you gonna quit that nasty habit?"

"How 'bout the day you ever get married?"

"Guess you'll be smokin' a long time." I held up my beer. "Add another vice to the list?"

"I don't know. After this morning... Oh, shit. What the hell. One, I guess."

"Jess, another Bass."

He nodded and drew the ale.

"Couple of menus, too," I added.

Jess brought the beer and the two menus over. He slid an ashtray over to Mick.

"Hey, Mickey, how ya been?"

"Good, Jess. How 'bout you?"

"Can't complain."

"Still liftin' hard?"

"Every day, buddy. I gotta get you and Holden in the gym with me sometime. Course, you gotta quit those cancer sticks sometime, too."

"You guys are worse than my sister. Ya know..." Mick stopped.

Jess jumped right in, because he didn't know a thing about Rachel being missing. He was just making conversation.

"Hey, Mickey. So, how is Rachel?"

"She's good. Real good."

"Well, you tell her, it's nice to have back around. Tell her she's gotta stop in and see me sometime, huh?"

"You bet, Jess. You bet."

I was getting hungry. "If you girls are finished being social, think we could hear the specials?"

Jess rattled off a few items -- Yankee pot roast with red potatoes, baked scrod, stuffed breast of chicken with vegetable medley, and shrimp salad over a bed of greens.

"Uh, Jess. I got a question."

"Shoot."

"Just what is the vegetable medley?" He started to answer me, but I at least was kind enough to finish my thought. "I mean, do they do Motown stuff? Or maybe some Elvis?"

He threw his dish rag at me. "Smart ass." I tossed the towel back.

Mick was laughing. It was a good sight. "One of these days, your questionable wit is gonna tweek the wrong person."

"Come on. Me?"

"Yeah. You."

"No, I mean, me, with questionable wit? Please, Mick. You of all people."

"Yeah. Right."

Jess decided it was time to return to work, so he asked, "You guys need a coupla minutes to order?"

"Yeah. You know me. One plate's not enough," I said.

"All right, but when I come back, just don't ask me what that chicken's stuffed with."

Jess headed toward the other end of the bar to ply his skills on two young, tanned beauties, who had just entered from the back way. Hey, what do you know. I wasn't alone in my inconspicuous entrance. I'd have to use that to my advantage when I struck up some captivating conversation after Jess failed to impress them.

Mick sipped his ale. We opened our menus.

"Okay, Mick. Rachel's missing. First question. You fill out a missing person's report?"

"Hell, no. Not when I got you."

"All right. So, I take it you don't want me to make a lot of noise about this? Keep it low profile?" He nodded. "So, who's lookin' out for the store right now? And do they know anything?"

26

"Nah. Danielle's got the store under control. I just told her that Rachel was taking a few days off. She's got her own key. She's responsible."

"So, Mick. Come on. It's me. Why the hell do you think Rachel would do it?" I kept my voice low. "You haven't convinced me. You gotta be holding out on me. The store's doing well, right?" He nodded again. "She leaves Burlington to come back home. She's here a few months. Store's doing well. Then she suddenly decides life sucks and bang, she cuts out? Ain't Rachel. She wouldn't do this to you, let alone herself."

Mick didn't answer. I didn't know if that was because he didn't know what to say or he didn't know how to say what he should have been telling me. I used the break to look over at Jess and nod. He stepped up with an order pad and a Granby Construction pen. I always recognized the pens, because they were bright chartreuse with black lettering which read "YOU'RE ALWAYS BUILT BETTER WITH GRANBY." Clever. Really must appeal to the housewives looking to remodel. I wondered if the same slogan pertained to the buildings. Curtis Granby was a bigshot real estate and construction mogul who resided on the east side of Skaneateles Lake. He spread his influence where he could in order to spread his affluence when he could. I wondered if he had insinuated himself on Jess personally or to the Sherwood Inn. My guess was the Sherwood. Jess looked at me.

"I'll go with the shrimp salad on greens and a turkey club."

"Some of that sissy stuff to counteract the club, huh?" Jess was getting back at me for the medley crack. He wrote the order and turned to Mick.

"Turkey club is fine."

"Hey, Jess. How about some rolls, huh?"

"Would I forget those, Holden?" He took our menus and my empty glass and headed to the kitchen.

Mick said, "Rachel's just been actin' different lately. I can't really put my finger on it. She just wasn't herself. Moody, I

27

guess. Maybe she was concerned about the offers for the store. I don't know."

"You said you had a meeting about it?"

"Yeah. Carl Hendrix had made us a pretty damn good offer. But I think the idea of selling it appealed more to me than Rach. The store was her thing. She really wanted to make it big as a business person."

"Follow in her brother's footsteps?"

"More like wipe 'em out. She was hungry to succeed. To have power and money."

"Still doesn't make her a bad person." Without a cadaver, I liked to talk about someone in the present tense.

Mick fished out another smoke and fired it up. "Yeah, I know," he said. "This has just got me all screwed up. I'm worried about her." He flicked his ashes. Some people, when they smoked, let the butt burn down more than smoke it. Not Mick. He allowed little tobacco to go to waste.

"You went to her place, but didn't go in?"

"Right."

"Her car there?"

He paused. Thought. The wrinkles formed in his forehead. "Actually, yeah. Yeah it was."

My stomach growled. Loud and angry. Jess returned with another beer for me and looked at Mick, who shook his head.

"Ya know, chances are I'm gonna have to get kinda personal. Like with ex-boyfriends, close friends. Like that."

Mick nodded again. Hey, I was an expert at making people respond to me. Behind us, the tavern stayed unusually busy. To our right, a verbal outburst between a somewhat attractive, if not a little plump, redhead and a spike-haired guy with considerable bulk broke out. From the conversation, he seemed displeased by my presence.

Mick started to elaborate on his nod, but I held up my hand to silence him as I studied the bellowing behemoth with the flat top. I heard some four-letter expletives spew from his less than educated mouth as his lady companion cringed more from embarrassment than anything else. The more I studied, the more I recognized. This beer-bellied, pseudo-iron pumping moron had been bedding down with the wife of a client of mine a few years back. I didn't think he made the chic Skaneateles circuit. And I thought I could hang out without even an eyelash flickering. I suppose it was hard to keep my fame in check.

"What's up, H?"

I barely heard Mick's question. I concentrated on the couple, especially the guy. I remembered that one of his pleasures with the wife, now the ex-wife, was slapping her around. He had once said that she liked the rough stuff. Bullshit. Don't hit a woman unless she's ready to blow your head off. Bad habits die hard, and with a head case, even harder. I never had the satisfaction of tangling with him before, and I wasn't about to shy away from a confrontation now. My mood dictated an ass kicking. I was real hungry and one of my best buddies was pretty shook up.

She reached her hand out to him, and he shoved it away. Violently. He pushed his chair back and stood to face where Mick and I were sitting. Jess kept a careful watch on the situation. He knew that one-on-one I could handle most guys, so he left this predicament up to my judgment. I always appreciated that about him.

He did, however, in this instance, take the first step toward pacification. Probably didn't feel like cleaning blood up off the floor.

"Why don't ya take it easy," he warned the angry patron in his calm way.

The guy looked at Jess. "This ain't with you, pretty boy. I juz wanna have a word with Gracey here."

He turned back to me. "Ain't that your name, sweetie? Gracey? Remember me? I sure the hell remember you."

Mr. Kind stepped toward me aggressively. I slipped off my stool and faced him, looking very amiable.

"I believe the name is Eldon? Am I right, Eldon? Now that's a mean name." I drew out the word "mean." "Now who

29

the hell would name their child Eldon? Unless maybe they just figured they'd grow up to slop around in pig shit all their life. That what you do, Eldon? Play in pig shit all day?"

Eldon lunged at me with a sloppy, slow right hand, which I blocked easily. I knew the punch was coming when Eldon started flexing the fingers of his right hand. Instead of delivering a solid blow to his overly protruding jaw, I dropped down to his overabundant stomach with a crisp right hand. I didn't know if I was striking flesh or gelatin. For a guy with big shoulders and arms, he seriously let his gut go to hell. Suppose you don't need to be in shape to terrorize women.

I surprised Eldon with the punch, and he doubled over just enough to let me rock his jaw with a right cross, followed by a left hook as he was reeling back on his toes. The punches I threw were of the heavy variety, where I really threw my weight and turned my body into them. I knew I'd be icing my knuckles later.

Eldon tumbled back into his own table, which, strangely, was now empty. Gee, I hope that wasn't his sister. I grabbed him by the front of the shirt and yanked him to his feet. Eldon was no panty waste, though, and recovered enough to throw a knee at my groin. Fortunately for me and the ladies in my life, the blow was not a direct hit and lacked a lot of force. He tried another right that I blocked. I'd had about enough and drove a right into his chin as I held him with my left hand, then set him down gently in his chair. I'm a caring, thoughtful pugilist. He slumped over. I leaned my face to within an inch of his.

My voice was low and serious. "That case was finished business once. And this little episide closed the chapter for good. Understood?" I could throw cliches as well as right hands.

He nodded weakly.

"Good. Now I've got lunch to eat."

The innkeeper, a tall, lanky Richard Benjamin lookalike, neatly dressed in blue slacks, a blue dress shirt, a red power tie and blue blazer, had made an appearance, and Jess was busy smoothing things out with him. The patrons on hand had really gotten their money's worth -- lunch and entertainment. Maybe I should sign a contract to perform daily. Meanwhile, Eldon dropped a wad of cash on his disheveled table and skulked out the back way. Should have known. He'd be lucky if his date had evened waited for him. If she had any sensability, she'd be long gone. Unless, of course, Eldon drove. And most likely a Trans Am or Camaro. Then, she'd be stuck.

I hopped back on my stool as if nothing had happened and turned back to Mick who was shaking his head in absolute amusement. If anything, I provided Mick a slight diversion from his concerns. Jess gave the innkeeper a reassuring pat on the back and ushered him from the tavern back to some staid office, I imagined. I wondered who of the two was really the boss.

Jess shouted over, "Lunches comin' up, guys." He headed to the kitchen.

"Holden, why's it every time we're out somewhere, your fan club comes out of the woodwork?" Mick asked.

"Maybe it's the autographed photos I send them of me in my BVD's. The women love it, but the guys get jealous."

"Jealous of what? How white your undies are?"

"I do use bleach, ya know. And mountain fresh fabric softener. Maybe I should start sending out scratch and sniff photos."

"Just don't be bending over."

"It's good to see you haven't lost your sick sense of humor."

Jess delivered our lunches. The shrimp salad was adequate and the club was a club. I made it a point to devour the rolls. I had, after all, asked for them, and they were actually one of the highlights of the lunch. Mick actually finished his meal. I was a little surprised. The Bass Ale was left for dead, though. Too bad. He filled me in on the names of Rachel's friends. At least the few he knew about. She didn't have many. I didn't know whether to be surprised or not. The boyfriends were even fewer. That I could picture. Rachel had selective tastes. One name that I'd be sure to check was her most recent Gary Howard, whom

Mick fixed up with Rachel. Mick said they dated a few times but that was about it. He'd be getting a visit from me soon. Mick also provided me with the key to her apartment and the names of a couple of neighbors. I had her old address in Burlington. A road trip might have been in order. Depended on what turned up in lovely Skaneateles. Hopefully, Rachel, alive and well.

Mick was gracious enough to pick up the tab. Part of my expenses, he told me. We said good-bye to Jess. I told Mick I'd be in touch, and he exited the way he came, and I slipped out the back. Unnoticed. The two gorgeous women whom I planned on impressing were long gone. The floor show chased them off, I was sure. My next step was to check out Rachel's apartment. Then, I'd get in touch with Mr. Gary Howard. I thought about stopping by and seeing my old college roommate and Skaneateles village cop, Wade Reynolds, just to touch base, but I promised Mick I'd keep this low profile. Good luck when I started questioning people. But I knew if I needed an ally, Wade would be right there, because not only was he a good cop and an old college buddy, he was a good guy.

It was time for the digging to begin, like a rat in a landfill, turning up some lousy smelling trash. I was always impressed with my work, and for some reason, I felt this one would rank right up there. Not that I had a hell of a lot of experience chasing down missing persons, but this one had a rank aroma, speaking of ranking right up there. The day was young, and I had some work to do.

## *Chapter 4*

When I walked out of the inn, the blast of hot air nearly sent me back to my bar stool and my frosty glass. But I thought about Rachel and Mick.

It was nearly four when I swung out the Sherwood's back parking lot and onto Genesee Street heading east. The village was bursting with people, lining the sidewalks, looking at the overpriced shops or just walking around and acting important. It was rather ironic how many of the locals cursed the presence of so many tourists when it was their bucks that pumped a hell of a lot of revenue into the place. Something like biting off more of the horses ass that feeds you and you can chew. Rachel lived in a fashionable sandblasted brownstone condo above a row of shops that overlooked the lake. Rent wasn't cheap, but the digs were impressive. She liked opulence and was willing to pay for it. I wondered where all of her money came from. Maybe she never ate. To get to the parking area for the condos, I turned right into a small alley that went under and behind the brownstone. The parking spaces were all individually assigned, and there was Rachel's '92 Black Saab 900S tucked neatly into her designated area. I pulled my Jeep into an empty space next to it, most likely reserved for some tight ass who'd throw a fit when he or she came home from the office after banging somebody on their desk. Fine. Let them try to have it moved. I pulled my Glock out of the glove box, pulled my shirt out from my pants and slid the gun in my holster, then lowered the shirt, untucked, over the piece. When I met Mick at the Sherwood, I didn't exactly feel a need to be packing. I was a hell of a lot more comfotable when a gun butt wasn't digging into my side. But now, who knows what I might encounter? No sense in taking chances. I could always point it at Mr. or Ms. Parking Space and make them jump into the lake if they started getting rough.

I locked up the Jeep and checked out Rachel's car. The doors were locked. Everything seemed fine. No congealed pools of blood on the seat. No messages scrawled on the windshield in crimson. No note that said, "I'm in the Caribbean with a handsome rich man named Spenser. Be back soon. Ciao for now. Rachel." Just a car, parked in its proper place staring out at the lake and the mansions and country club on the opposite shore.

By looking at the front of the connected brick buildings that housed the twenty-something shops that ran the stretch from the main traffic light where Jordan Street intersected with Genesee Street east for a few hundred yards until the green grass of Thayer Park put an end to the commercial real estate, one would never even recognize the backside. The whole scenario reminded me of a seaside Mediterranean village with the multi-leveled residences in multitudes of architectural styles and colors hovering right on a magnificent body of water. I kept my eyes scanning for some dark-haired, young Italian beauty wanting to fill me full of her pasta. No such luck. This was literally a one-eighty from the front facade, and I could imagine how certain individuals may have found the appearance on this side an eyesore, but something about it appealed to a sense of realism that defied the other side and the clean streets, the just-so shops and maybe the illusion that existed over there. The moment placed me in a print by a local artist of this view from quite a distance south, where the buildings all along Genesee Street make a statement of character. A signed copy of the very print hung in my house. The view was distant, yet spoke volumes. At least to anyone with a good imagination.

I used Rachel's keys to let myself in the back way of her building and headed up a flight of stairs two steps at a time. The upkeep was immaculate. It looked like dust bunny hunting season was in session year round. If Elmer Fudd could only have such luck. The richly carpeted floors were tasteful, the walls a clean looking eggshell with an occasional painting hung with care and the lighting was good. Very important when returning from Lord & Taylor with an armful of packages. I found Rachel's apartment and thought how damn lucky she was that she could score a place like this as soon as she returned to town. Luck or fate? I thought I felt eyes on me as I let myself in.

Nice. Very nice. This was my first foray into Rachel's abode. In fact, I don't think she ever invited me. Upon looking at it, I figured she didn't want me to mess it up. Shiny hardwood floors. Cathedral ceilings. Contemporary furniture in warm earthtones carefully arranged. Artwork appropriately placed. No clutter. No useless knick knacks to collect dust. The apartment itself was large and open and a little warm. The AC certainly hadn't been run for awhile. I entered into an expansive living area. They don't call them living rooms anymore. Too common sounding, I suppose. They were either living areas or spaces or great rooms. This one had a balcony to the left and windows that let the southwestern sun stream in to mingle with the tiny particles of dust floating ceaselessly in the air. No matter how clean you kept a place, there was no escaping the dust. Rachel had a twenty-seven inch color television on an entertainment center that also held a VCR. A stereo rack system was against one wall along with contemporary looking CD holders. Pretty bare bones. A few scattered pictures of Rachel and her family, with old friends, at least I assumed, and I had even made my way into one or two. There was a stepper in one corner and an exercise bike in another.

Further ahead was a breakfast bar/countertop that separated the living area from a modern, well-laid out kitchen with beautiful light oak cabinets and what was probably laminate flooring. Expensive, but worth the price. I had some of the stuff in my house. No dirty dishes. No coffee in the coffeemaker. I looked in the refrigerator and found that I was in the ballpark about Rachel's eating habits. Some skim milk, juice, yogurt, cheese, a few fruits and veggies, and that was about it. No leftovers. There was, however, a bottle of Moet & Chandon White Star and a bottle of Salmon Run Johannisberg Riesling chilling on their sides. The freezer contained unground coffee beans (she shouldn't do that, because the cold removes the oils from the beans), some of those health conscious frozen dinners, a few packages of boneless breast of chicken and frozen vegetables. I noticed she didn't have bagfuls of meat scraps and other waste items in her freezer like I did. The reason I didn't toss that stuff in the garbage was because I didn't have a garbage disposal and I didn't want my trash to smell like something died, because it did. I don't know, I always thought it was a rather hygienic idea. Freeze all that crap before the bacteria festered away like a maggot on, well, rotted flesh. I poked around in the cabinets and drawers and found silverware, pots and pans, non-perishable food, flashlights, candles, matches -- all the stuff you'd expect to find in a kitchen. No notes. No hints or clues as to where Rachel might have gone. I was careful not to disturb anything in case she returned and panicked because she thought some low life had come in and rummaged through her things, maybe looking for a pair of panties or other intimate apparel. I'd be sure to avoid her underwear drawer if at all possible. I could picture the scene, "Sorry, Mick. Couldn't find a clue, but Rachel sure has some nice lacy Victoria Secret's stuff." Yikes. A right to the chin for that one.

There was an oak table with matching chairs in the ample dining area. A Waterford crystal vase with gold trim filled with a bright collection of summer flowers rested in the middle. Some of the petals, however, had fallen off and others were starting the decaying process when life ebbed away and death was not far behind. I smelled the discolored water. A little rancid. It hadn't been changed for a couple of days. I picked up the vase and returned to the kitchen where I changed the water. No sense in allowing an early demise to something holding such beauty. I carefully set the vase back, making sure that no water spilled onto the oak, and moved onto the other rooms.

The condo had two bedrooms and one and a half baths, with the master bath directly connected to the master bedroom suite in the very back of the apartment. I checked out the half bath first.

It smelled nice, and I noticed one of those plug in deodarizes in an outlet. I suddenly felt like one of those snoopy people who raid someone else's medicine cabinets to find out more about them. But, like I've always thought, what the hell do they expect to find? They could check mine anytime. They'd find hemorrhoid cream, hydrocortizone, deodorant, toothpaste, some of those teenage zit pads for my oily forehead and a slew of other things you'd expect to find in anyone's bathroom. Tough luck, no prescription meds. I still had to check Rachel's. Nothing. I knew that eventually I should dig through each waste basket, or at least give a cursory glance, but held off in case something else jumped out at me. What exactly, I didn't know. At the least, something tangible like a written note about a flight, a person, an alien abduction.

At this point, all I knew was that Rachel had been missing since at least yesterday morning, her car was still around and there was no sign of a struggle or illegal entry.

Onto bedroom number one, which Rachel had set up as an in-home office with a multi-media computer system organized on a large corner computer desk, telephone, answering machine, file cabinets and books neatly stashed in large, solid, and expensive hardwood barrister bookcases. I figured she had an e-mail address and surfed the Net. Two components of the modern world of which I had little use for. I understood the major benefits of both. With e-mail, you could almost instantly contact someone across the world, and with the Internet, you could find virtually any information at any time. It was at your fingertips. Certainly well-intentioned advances, but out of hand. Whatever happened to the art form called letter writing? And how about privacy? They're more computer hacks out there than hacks sitting behind the wheels of taxis. Sure, you could always steam a letter open, but why worry now when everyone has e-mail? Not that I was the greatest at letter writing, with my tendency to procrastinate, but that was part of the institution. The anticipation of the reply. The waiting until someone picked up the damn phone to find out where that letter was. And the millions of scope heads surfing their lives away on a computer screen was pathetic. I recalled the days of actually getting up off your ass to research a subject for a school paper, or to shop, or to participate in meaningful conversation, or to play sports. It was all too much and made too much too easy for too many people. Sloth was certainly creeping up on the Seven Deadly Sins meter in my book. How soon would the day come when we merged with computers? The thought made my stomach turn, and I know it wasn't the Bass Ale. Rachel's diplomas from Syracuse University adorned the wall -- the B.S. and M.B.A. The room was almost sterile, certainly all business like, maybe with the intent of no distractions. Again, there was order. I looked at some of the books lined up on the shelves -- textbooks from college; hardcover and paperback novels, but not the romance types, the more thought provoking creations, even if some were of the horror and detective genre; self-help books regarding relationships and how to succeed in business. I decided to check out this room last. It was just so damn impersonal. I had a home office in my house, complete with multi-media computer, but the room had so much character, so much clutter. It was comfortable.

At the end of the apartment was the master suite -- a large bedroom at least twenty by fifteen with another balcony to privately catch the gentle sound of lapping waves and the stimulating odor of being so close to a body of water. There was a queen-size bed with ornately carved posters and a headboard against one wall. Damn, Rachel sure did well for herself. She had a huge dresser against another wall. I felt sorry for the movers on that one. I knew Victoria was in there. Waiting. Tact. That's all it took. Tact and being professional. That is, if I deemed it necessary to investigate. For such a large bedroom, Rachel had very little to fill the space. The bed. The dresser. A nightstand with a lamp, telephone and clock radio. A wicker love seat. A television. Once again, more nice artwork on the walls. The master suite also came with an expansive walk-in closet and the master bath.

I checked out the closet first. Full of clothes and shoes. What seemed like top of the line clothes and shoes. There was also luggage neatly stacked away in a corner. So, it didn't look like she hopped a flight out of town somewhere. Everything looked almost too neat. Too perfect. A few empty hangers, but I accounted those to dry cleaning.

The master bath was roomy, of course. Why break the theme of the rest of the place? The floor couldn't have been Italian marble, now could it? There was a free standing sink with a classical looking medicine cabinet above it, a whirlpool tub with separate shower, a large mirror with ample counter space and a linen closet. I banged the knuckles of my right hand when I opened the linen closet, and that instantaneous pain accentuated the constant ache from earlier. I noticed slight swelling after I cursed at the closet door. Maybe next time I'd use my irreverent humor to diffuse a situation. Right. I found a whole lot of nice towels, sheets, wash clothes and feminine products. The medicine cabinet held the usual, except for a couple of stand out items -- some massage lotion, half gone and a tube of odorless arthritis cream. Interesting combination.

I felt little trickles of sweat beading up and running their ticklish course down my back where they deposited themselves at the waistband of my boxers. I thought about cranking up the air conditioning, but I wouldn't be much longer. I stepped back into the master bedroom and out onto the balcony. The air hadn't cooled down much and the humidity wanted to keep grading out with straight A's by staying near one hundred percent. The view was very impressive. To the left, you could check out the curve of the lake and the eastern shore where it coiled off from Thayer Park. To the right was Clift Park filled with sunbathers, Frisbee tossers and those brave enough to plunge into the frigid waters of the lake. While not the deepest of the Finger Lakes by a long shot, Skaneateles Lake certainly ranked as one of the coldest. Even in the hottest stretches of summer, like now, the water would still remain in the low sixties. My anatomy hurt just thinking about the sudden temperature change from the air to the water. Just before the park, a long pier extended well out into the lake. About fifteen years ago, the pier was a deteriorating mess and dangerous for anyone to traverse, so a decision was made to spruce it up. It received a complete makeover with an attractive brick walkway, lights, a circular viewing area at the end and railings to keep the drunks from Morris's across the road from falling in and becoming a pickled meal for the trout. Now, hundreds of people each day walked out to the end, leaned on the railing and gazed out at the blue water. I had spent a few evenings at that spot, fishing for rainbow trout that moved into the shallows and fed on the tiny mysis shrimp that ventured from the cold depths after the sun set. I could think of worse places to spend time than at the end of that pier. Others had the same idea, as the traffic was steady. Past Clift Park, the shoreline curved to form the west side where, if you followed it for a couple of miles, you'd encounter many estates and the Skaneateles Country Club, of which I was not a member. I could smell the Blue Water Grill, which was only a couple of hundred yards to my right. The Blue Water was the only restaurant actually on the water in Skaneateles, with a multi-tiered deck out back right next to the outlet. I frequented the place. Of course, I was friends with the owner. Traffic sounds floated up to the balcony as if from another world. I could see how someone would want to live here, even when the monthly rent check was probably more than twice my mortgage payment. I checked my watch. Nearly five. The diners would be filling up the many eateries in town soon. I still had to investigate Rachel's home office, and I wanted to talk to a neighbor or two before I headed home to fire up my grill, so I cut short my sightseeing foray and made a beeline to the room, making sure I relocked the door to the balcony first.

Where to begin? How about the answering machine. Mick had said he left a bunch of messages for Rachel yesterday and today after she failed to make their breakfast meeting on Thursday morning. Sure enough, the light was blinking like Rudolph's nose on speed. I hit "play." The calls were all numbered in sequence on a digital readout. They were all from Mick, except one from her friend Amy, who Mick had told me was Rachel's closest friend. She wanted to work out. No threatening ransom call. No disgruntled lovers.

Time to find out who she called last, and with my luck, it would be the Chinese takeout place down the road. I picked up the phone and punched redial. It rang three times in my ear when a woman answered.

"Hello?" The voice was a little tipsy, but she didn't sound Oriental. She didn't give the name of a restaurant either. Maybe it was time for a little luck.

"Oh. I'm sorry. I think I have the wrong number." God was I ever a good actor. If the detective gig didn't pan out, I could see myself starring with Brian Bosworth in some touching melodrama where we did a lot of questioning about life's cruel twists and cried a lot.

"That's okay," she said in the tone of voice that meant this short conversation was about over. She sounded young, in her late twenties or early thirties, and attractive, but I learned you could never rely on that one. Just take a look at the sexy sounding sirens on radio. That's why they're in that medium, because they have the faces for radio and not television. Every once in a while though, sensual is as sensual sounds.

I wasn't through with her yet. "I'm from out of town and my buddy told me to call him when I got here. I just wanna make sure I got the number right. What number did I dial?" I tried to sound as unthreatening and as much of a weary traveler as possible. It worked. She gave me the number, and it was a Skaneateles exchange. I snatched a pen up from Rachel's computer desk and scribbled the number on my hand. Adapt and overcome. I told the kind woman that it must have been my mistake dialing, because the numbers were different and thanked her as I hung up. Finally, a little bit of light at the end of the carpal tunnel. Maybe. The phone immediately rang. It appeared that somebody didn't mind spending their seventy-five cents on star sixty-nine. I saved her the change and ignored the ringing. I sat down at Rachel's desk and went through her drawers. I found nothing out of the ordinary, but did discover her daily planner or organizer or whatever the on-the-go masses called it these days. I knew of many people who said they couldn't make it through the day without theirs. In fact, they had gone to seminars that taught them the proper way to organize their time and fit it all so perfectly in the hallowed pages between the fashionable binder. Talk about trapped. Organization is one thing, I should know, because I do like order, but some of these people were hooked on their planners like a narcotic. I flipped open the busybodies' bible and thumbed to the current week. Wednesday's meeting with Mick was penned in. Thursday's wasn't. I turned back the pages, noting general appointments like for her hair or the dentist. Then, I found what I presumed to be a hastily scrawled note on a Monday afternoon a few weeks back that simply read "Dr. Russell, 4 p.m." Could've been nothing, but every other entry had been neat and more detailed such as her dentist appointment. It said what, with whom and when. Same with the hair. So, who was Dr. Russell? And why was he or she so different? I tucked the binder under my arm and decided that it was time to find a neighbor hopefully willing to shed some light on Rachel's disappearance. Hell, all I had to do was smile and they'd open up to me like a steamed clam. Preferably not a spoiled one. I looked out at the parking lot before I left the apartment to make sure my Jeep hadn't been towed. Still right where it belonged, in someone else's parking spot.

## *Chapter 5*

I knocked on the door directly across from Rachel's, waited a minute or two, then headed up the stairs. I tried the place directly above Rachel's. Maybe they were the type of neighbor to glue their ear to the hardwood floor and listen for perverse noises to complain to others about yet personally enjoy in their own company. The door opened a crack. Come on, this wasn't the Bronx. A face peeked at me, and I couldn't tell if a male or female body was attached to it.

"Yes?" A wispy voice asked. Still couldn't tell.

"Hi, I'm with the Bureau for Beautification of Condominium Hallways. Wonder if I could have a word with you about the status of this building."

"Excuse me?" The door opened a few inches more. Okay. It was a woman. No, a man. Definitely a man. I caught the glimpse of an Adam's apple.

I pulled out my creds and flashed them, along with a very trustworthy smile. "I'm a private detective. Just gotta coupla question about Rachel Allen. Standard stuff."

"Is she in trouble?" The door slowly kept inching open. I felt like I'd have to dangle some candy pretty soon to gain entrance.

"No. Like I said. S.O.P. For business purposes."

"So, she's not in trouble?" He seemed disappointed in an overdramatic way.

"No." Could I be any clearer? "I'll just be a few minutes, then I'll be outta your hair. Honest." The comforting smile. Bang. I was in. The door opened full, and I stepped into another world.

No wonder I had trouble defining the gender of this timid tenant. He had long, different lengthed blond hair, wide blue eyes and sharp little features in his face. He stood maybe five-four and couldn't have weighed much more than one hundred twenty pounds, and that was probably being generous seeing as he had on a baggy pair of paint-stained overalls and nothing else. He moved very fluidly as he turned from me when I entered. If Rachel's place was sophisticated and simple, this place was a scene from a carnival. Hard to believe that both apartments had the exact same layout. Everywhere I turned, strange and bright paintings assaulted my eyes. The furniture was a hodge podge of contemporary, traditional and what looked like leftovers from when the circus came to town and thrown about the place in no order that I could figure. Drop clothes covered the floor where Sweet Pea worked, and that pretty much was everywhere, and the place was dark. Open some blinds for Chrissakes, it's summer. Of course, it didn't look like he made it out into the sunshine too often, unless he wore about a two hundred SPF. I bumped into a strange mass of clay set upon a table that I assumed was one of this guy's pieces of "art," and easily steadied it before it had a chance to meet a welcome death on the floor below. Sweet Pea jumped toward me with a look of dread sculpted on his tight face.

"I got it. These are shortstop's hands." He didn't seem comforted by the reference. And I think he was seriously doubting his judgment about allowing me to enter his sanctuary of sideshow artwork.

"It's just that that piece means a lot to me."

"Sorry. I'll try not to be a bull in a china shop, all right?"

"I'd appreciate it. By the way, I'm Rex Steinman, and as you can probably tell, being a detective, I'm an artist. And you are?"

I had closed the door and we stood in the living area.

"Sorry. My bad. Holden Grace." I stuck out my right hand and he shook it. He had a pretty strong grip. I respected him more already. Some guys, they could be six-eight, three hundred pounds and when you shook hands, it was like grabbing a dead fish. When I meet somebody, I give a firm handshake. I do it with everyone, including women, because, to me, it's a sign of respect. None of those limp-wristed, grab-my-tender-fingers Marv Albert-type handshakes. How could you call that a handshake when you're just touching their fingers, and who the hell knows where those fingers have been? On the rare occasion that happens, I swear, I feel like I should kiss their hand and genuflect.

"So, you have a few questions about the lovely Rachel?"

"Yeah."

"Would you care for something to drink? I have bottled water, tea, coffee, beer and probably some scotch around somewhere." He walked now as he spoke, toward a table covered with acrylic paints and a couple of chairs that actually matched. He motioned to one of the chairs and moved to the kitchen. I sat and placed Rachel's day planner on the table in front of me. At least he had the common sense to crank the AC. He grabbed himself an Amstel Light and looked at me.

"No, I'm fine."

"Suit yourself." He popped the cap and took a pull from the bottle and moved back to the table and sat. This guy moved. He didn't walk. "So what would you like to know?" He set the beer down on a dry paint-smeared palette and noticed the day planner. "You need a pen to take notes?" He assumed it was mine.

"Nah. This doesn't call for that." I paused a bit and looked right at him. "Clearly, you know Rachel." Enough wasted time.

"Beautiful girl." Girl? How old was this guy? He looked twenty-five.

"Just neighbors? Or friends?"

"I keep to myself. Oh, I'd run into her once in a while in the hallway, which I believe you were quite concerned with earlier, and we'd exchange the usual pleasantries."

"How long you lived here?"

"About ten years."

"Nice apartments. Great view. Right in downtown. Rent's a little much though, huh?"

"What's that have to do with Rachel?"

"I need an idea about how much she shelled out. You know, as part of her monthly expenses." I didn't know how much longer he'd buy into the business bullshit, if he ever did.

"Why don't you just ask her?"

"She's not around. But I bet you knew that."

"Maybe. I don't pry."

"So, c'mon. Give me at least a ballpark on the rent."

"I'm locked in at twelve fifty. I don't know about Rachel." He drained a few ounces from his beer. Somewhere in the apartment, a clock chimed the bottom of the five o'clock hour. That's when I realized how quiet it was in there. I know that when I did anything at home, especially trying to paint, I needed music turned up. When I was in Rachel's apartment, I hadn't noticed a single sound from above. I couldn't even tell if Rex owned a stereo.

"That's a good buck. You must do all right."

"I sell well in New York. The City." Like I would confuse it with perhaps a new line of weight equipment from York Barbells. Artists.

"Rachel must do okay for herself then?" I figured since Rex had been living here ten years and payed twelve fifty, the chances were pretty good that Rachel had to squeeze out even more.

"I wouldn't know."

"Fair enough." My gun was poking me in the side, and I adjusted for it. I had a pretty good feeling that Rex knew that Rachel hadn't been around for a couple of days, and I wanted to press that issue. But could I be tactful? Before I could try an approach, the phone rang.

"Would you excuse me?" He bounced up from his chair with minimum effort and glided over to the phone.

"Sure. I'll just keep myself entertained. Mostly trying to figure out how the hell you get paid for creating some of this crap in here." Of course, I was practicing being tactful, so I said it very low. It wouldn't have mattered. Rex completely shut me out as soon as he answered his call on a cordless phone. I stood up to stretch my legs as Rex engaged in conversation with someone named Danny. He seemed quite enamored with the person on the other end of the line. I watched as he made the conversation a performance piece. His free arm flailed about, gesturing wildly as he spun in his bare feet on the hardwood floor. He looked over at me and gave me one of those "I'll be through in just a minute" gestures, so I sat back down and thought about how I'd proceed. Rex was in tune with his surroundings. He knew what happened in this building. Someone doesn't stay in one place for ten years and not become the resident expert on the neighbors. I flipped open Rachel's day planner and skimmed through the pages in search of what, I wasn't sure. I started going back in time. Since Rachel had only been back in Skaneateles for a few months, maybe it was a good idea to check out her Burlington appointments. I found a lot of the same -- neat, precise notes about normal, expected appointments, until I came across a weekend that had "The Sag" written and an arrow drawn from Friday through Sunday. Aha! A clue, perhaps. I was so good at my job. I would have bet my 1986 Ovation Collectors' Series guitar that "The Sag" meant The Sagamore Resort in Lake George, not too far from Burlington at all, and a very swanky joint indeed. It fit right in with Rachel's standards. Before I had much of a chance to gloat over my extreme sleuthing abilities, Rex hung up the phone and rejoined me at the table. I swear he was glowing. I thought only pregnant women did that.

"So where were we?" he asked like somebody who was completely preoccupied in his own thoughts.

I figured I'd stoke his fire, get him enamored with that great phone call, and maybe he'd be willing to share some insight about Rachel. If he had any.

"Must've been a helluva phone call," I said.

"Are you detecting right now, Mr. Grace?" He beamed.

"Not too tough to tell that whatever Danny had to say made you one happy guy."

Rex picked up his Amstel Light, knocked back the rest and set it down with an exuberant authority. "Know what, Mr. Detective? I'm a really fucking happy man right now."

"Do tell."

47

He floated back to the kitchen with the empty bottle, opened the refrigerator and pulled out two Amstel Lights. He looked over his shoulder at me, and I nodded. How many times can a guy turn down an Amstel Light and not expect to be kicked out of the host's home? He popped the caps, returned to the table, looked me squarely in the eyes and said, "I'm getting married."

My jaw dropped. I could only hope that he was so enraptured right now that he didn't notice. Some detective I was. I figured he was gay and that Danny was his significant other. Apparently "she" was. I told myself that sometimes I could really be the horse's ass. Why the hell did Rex have to be gay? Because he looked effeminate? Because he was an artist? Because he flitted about like a bee in search of honey? Obviously, he hit the apian jackpot. Should've known by the handshake. I recovered quickly though.

"Congratulations."

"Thank you."

"Kinda funny gettin' the thumbs up over the phone, isn't it?"

"Not that it's really any of your business, but Danielle, and I know you what you were thinking, is flying to Europe for a couple of months. Last week, I was in New York with her and popped the question." He accentuated the work "popped." "She didn't have an answer then, but she wanted to make a decision before she left, and she said 'yes.'" He toasted me with his bottle. We both drank.

"Well, Rex, now that your life is coming up roses, I'm sure you won't mind sharing a little insight on Rachel Allen." He scrunched his face up little a giddy little boy.

"I know you're full of shit about the business angle. I also know that Rachel hasn't been home since late Wednesday night." He was high on love, and I sure the hell was going to take advantage of it.

"Okay, Rex, I'll come clean. I'm looking for her. That's it. Not even gettin' paid for this one. So, what do ya think?" I enjoyed some of the Amstel. Thought it was a good gesture to the host. I did stop short, though, of saying "ahh" out loud when I swallowed.

"Believe it or not, Holden, I like you. And besides, you got a great name."

"That's awful kind of you, Rex. Now, how come you don't have some artsy fartsy name like Ashley or Adrian or something?" I never stopped amazing myself with my incredibly insightful repartee. I did make him laugh so that he choked on his beer. Score one for the private dick.

When he recovered, he answered, "I don't believe my parents knew my occupation when I was c-sectioned out."

"Got ya. And why am I not surprised you had to be ripped from the womb? You still like things dark." I pointed to the closed blinds.

Rex stared at me. He held the celebratory bottle of Amstel Light in his right hand. "But at night, when the world settles in, I'm wide awake, and the windows are wide open. I love the night. Always have. And that's how I know about Rachel." Yes. Enough of making a new friend. I wanted to start making some progress.

"What d'ya mean?"

"I do my best work at night. And Wednesday, I felt creative as hell. I was out on the balcony working when I saw Rachel leave around eight or so."

"Alone?"

"Yeah."

"That it?"

"Not quite. She came back late."

"How late?"

"Three."

"You were up?"

He picked up a stray paint brush and began twirling it between his palms. "Like I said, I work best at night."

"You're sure it was Rachel?"

49

"Let me see. A Saab pulls into her spot. A woman, fitting her description, gets out, comes into the building and enters her apartment. Hmm. You're the detective, you tell me."

Now I knew what people meant when they talked about tempermental artists. He flashed his three inch sable brush loaded with sarcasm and used me as his canvas.

"Sorry. Had to ask. So, she comes home at three and that's all you know?"

He smiled coyly, swished the last few ounces of beer around then downed it. "Not quite." He liked that phrase. "She left again."

"What time?"

"Not an hour later. But, this time, she didn't take her car." He saw my slight confusion. "And I haven't seen her since." He offered a wide smile. "Kinda strange, huh? Good thing I'm a night owl." He winked at me. I couldn't figure this guy out. In fact, I wondered if he wasn't just blowing smoke about his upcoming nuptials, but I really had no choice not to believe him on every count. Especially since things became much more interesting.

"Listen, Rex, I've been a thorn in your side long enough, so I got just one more question. Who owns this nice chunk of real estate you call home?" Maybe the landlord could offer up something.

"None other than Skaneateles' favorite taxpayer, Curtis Granby."

Looked like I'd have to give old Curt a call sometime soon and discuss his tenant. I made good on my word and didn't ask another question. Rex and I exchanged business cards. Of course, his looked like a fly swatted on the wall with its abstract design and colors and mine was straight forward -- name, office phone number and cell phone number. Less can be more at times. I wished him luck on his impending marriage and asked him if he'd be available for more questions should any come up. He said no problems and that he just might invite me to the big wedding shindig. I'd work well as a balance to all the artsy types that would be there. Could be interesting. I left the condos around six with a lot more than I came with, in need of some food and a Yankees game on the tube. My Jeep was still where I parked it, and I made it home in about ten minutes, twice as long as it usually took, as I fought the tourist traffic and pedestrians on my way out of the village.

## *Chapter 6*

I wheeled into my driveway, stopped at the end and got out to grab my mail. Across the road, my neighbors, a couple of younger guys who shared a house, were out hitting golf balls into a farm field as the owner's black lab, Alex, watched with keen interest. I shot them a wave, wrestled the pile of junk mail and bills out of my mail box and pulled the Jeep into my two-story two-car garage near the back deck and back door. I had pulled my Glock out and put it in my glove compartment for the ride home. I stuck it back in my holster and opened my door. Home sweet home. No outrageous art to worry about knocking over. No neighbors listening to my every move. No nooks and crannies to search for clues. Just my house, with a refrigerator full of beer and food, my guitars and a television waiting for the Yankees game. Of course, I still had some work to do tonight, but in the comfort of my home, it wasn't really work at all.

I tossed the mail on the kitchen counter and went to check my phone messages in the living room -- and that's just what it was, a living room. The house was small but open, which I preferred. From the kitchen, I could look into the living room and see the television, which was extremely important when I was whipping up dinner and didn't want to miss a game. A hallway ran vertically down the center of the house that led to two bedrooms, the bathroom (only one -- good thing a woman didn't live here) and the laundry room. Basic. Simple. All I needed. My weights, at-home heavy bag and sports gear were in the garage. As I cut around my sectional sofa to the answering machine, I figured that a handsome, single guy like myself was sure to have dozens of calls on a Friday evening. Or so I tried to convince myself. Two flashes repeated themselves. Better than a steady red eye staring at me and mocking me with its inactivity, unless the messages were from buddies looking to borrow money or my mom asking me why the hell I hadn't called in weeks. I punched play and Mick's voice was the first one.  He was just checking in, curious if I found anything that could help.  He told me to give him a call sometime over the weekend if I had the time.  I usually did.  The second message was from the female friend who gave me the Oriental rug in my office, Maggie, wondering what I was up to for the night.  Maggie was the best.  Confident.  An individual.  No games.  No bullshit about expectations.  We had great times together and appreciated the chemistry of those moments, whether it was playing eighteen holes of golf, shooting pool in a smoky bar, fishing for bass or unleashing incredible passion in every room in my house.  I knew this was a rare relationship, and I constantly thanked the relationship gods out there for Maggie.  We were buddies.  We could lean on each other.  But we also shared more, and we knew when the other neccesitated time for their own lives, whatever it involved, that was perfectly fine.  The individual counted most.  She asked me to call her if I wanted to.  Not when I had the chance, but when I wanted to.  Was she for real?  I often wondered if she would suddenly disappear as if she was an apparition or just a great figment of my imagination.  I had a few things to take care of, so I didn't return the call at that moment.  Perhaps later.  I knew she'd make alternate plans if she didn't hear from me.  An individual.  A strong individual.  Rare these days.

I headed back to my bedroom and changed into shorts and an FBI Academy tank top that I picked up in Quantico while attending a friend's graduation and returned to the kitchen and poked my head into the refrigerator.  I planned on marinating some boneless chicken breast for the grill, then checking out the phone number written on my hand, calling Gary Howard to set a meeting and looking for a Dr. Russell in the phone book.  After that, I planned on unwinding.  I removed the chicken from the fridge, along with some fat-free Italian dressing, Frank's Red Hot Sauce, dijon mustard, grated parmesan cheese and a beer, all the main ingredients for one of my many variations of marinade.  I plopped the chicken into the sink and went to work.  I minced some fresh garlic and dumped it into a bowl and added the refrigerated components of my concoction as well as thyme, basil and oregano and mixed it well. I tossed in the chicken breasts and put them back in the fridge to do their thing. With that completed, I inserted a Screaming Trees CD into my stereo, dug out my Skaneateles phone book and prepared to focus my eyes on a myriad of numbers bunched together, hoping that the one gracing my palm belonged to someone with the last name of Atkinson or Andrews or at least something in the B's at the very least. I sat at my kitchen counter with what was left of the beer I poured into the marinade and went to work. No luck in the A's. I wiped my eyes and continued. I recalled doing this as a teenager when I was looking to buy a car that was advertised in the local paper. I'd scan the telephone book until I found the name that matched the number and used that information to my advantage when haggling on the price of the car, because I always asked around about the owner and invariable found some weapon to use. I started young on my path to dealing with scumbags. By the time I reached the the G's, the beer was gone and I could feel my shoulders tightening up from the concentration. Thank God I wasn't far-sighted. I'd need a magnifying glass.

I got up, fished out another beer, stirred the marinade around the chicken and stepped out onto my back deck and just looked out at the stand of maple, dogwood, oak, elm, willow, and various fruit trees that were a couple of hundred yards behind the house. In full bloom against the clouds, which continually mutated from one form to another, they always filled me with calm. And, occasionally, I filled them with golf balls. I thought it was a fair exchange. I also started thinking about Rachel Allen and what I supposedly knew at this point. I knew that she was still around on Wednesday night. In fact, she went out, came back and then, for some reason, left again around three in the morning on foot, apparently with her purse. I knew that I was still looking for the Skaneateles number of the last person she called before stepping out. I knew she had a four o'clock appointment with a Dr. Russell on a Monday a few weeks ago. I knew she payed a lot for her condo. I knew she spent a weekend at The Sagamore Resort while she lived in Burlington. At least my sense of detecting gave me that one. I knew that Curtis Granby owned the building where she lived. I knew that I forgot all about the earlier notes I was supposed to make to myself except the one during Parent's Weekend on the Hill at SU. I knew that Rex Steinman wasn't what he appeared. So, who the hell was Rachel? Did I really know her? I thought she was a strong, goal-oriented woman with a shitload of reasons to go on living. But it seemed that little tainted bits were polluting the virtue of her image in my mind. But there was no note. No body. There was still no reason to think suicide. It was still very early. I needed to return to the phone book. I needed the name to fit that number. I toasted the tree line and went back inside and sat back down with my phone book. Damn good thing I wasn't looking for a Syracuse exchange.

I jumped back in with the H's and realized that the chances existed that the number was unlisted. I crossed my eyes for luck and continued. Then, there it was. Like matching up winning lottery numbers, and tonight's big winners were... Carl and Stephanie Hendrix. Now, that was, at the very least, interesting. Carl Hendrix had made a substantial offer for the sporting goods store, and that's what Mick and Rachel were scheduled to discuss. Carl Hendrix was also married to Stephanie Granby, Curtis Granby's daughter. In a small village such as Skaneateles, even small timers like me knew some of the social implications. So, why was Carl Hendrix the last person Rachel called? Mick said that Rachel wasn't hot on the idea of selling, so maybe she took it upon herself to tell Carl "not a chance in hell. Take your coin somewhere else, pal." Then she disappeared. I certainly added calling Carl Hendrix to my list of "to do's" over the weekend.

With step one accomplished, the time came to look for a Dr. Russell in the phone book. No Russell in Skaneateles. I knew that, so I went for the Syracuse book and flipped to the yellow pages under "Physicians." Once again, my detecting intuition impressed the hell out of me. There she was, a member of a Women's Physician Care Group. In other words, Dr. Amanda Russell was an OB/GYN. Okay, could have just been one of those dreaded annual gynecological visits, but, I added a phone call and a visit to her to the list.

The CD ended and I let the silence linger, mixed with the outdoor summer sounds of lawnmowers being pushed back and forth by homeowners not long home from work, children screaming with joy as the last days of their summer vacation winded down and resident insects reminding everyone within earshot that they were around for the long haul. I loved where I lived. I didn't need to have some resort on the lakeshore.

I still needed to call Gary Howard and set up a time to talk with him, so I found his number in the book and dialed away. He answered in two rings, slightly out of breath.

"Gary Howard, please," I asked politely. Had to be the comfortable ambience of my home.

"Speaking."

"Hey, Gary. This is Holden Grace, a friend of Rachel and Mick Allen. Hope I didn't catch you at a bad time."

"No. I just finished a run. What's up? Holden, right?" Probably a sales guy. He used my first name at the first opportunity.

"Well, I'm a private detective, Gary" -- turnabout was fair play -- "and I understand you and Rachel used to see each other not long ago."

"Yeah, just for a short time. Is everything all right?"

"Sure. I just wanna ask you a few questions. I represent the family with some possible sensitive matters." I figured this would sound more impelling to Gary than the line about business I used, unsuccessfully as I recalled, on Rex Steinman.

"No problems, but I'm ready to jump in the shower then head out for the night."

"How about tomorrow?"

There was a pause. "Tell you what. I've got a tee time tomorrow morning at seven-thirty at Foxfire in Baldwinsville.

I'm looking for a fourth. You're in if you want." He almost sounded like he thought he'd be putting his superior golf game up against my detective skills as a counterbalance. He needed some kind of edge, and it didn't come from anything to hide. It was simply a male code from his perspective on life. Someone should tell him that was a bunch of shit. Hopefully, I'd show him tomorrow from tee to green.

"I'll clear my calendar, even though it means canceling my manicure appointment."

He hesitated before answering, "Great. Then I'll see you around seven at the clubhouse. You know where it is, I take?"

"You take correctly, Gary. Look forward to it."

I hung up thinking that any time spent with Gary Howard would be nothing but a waste, unless I kicked his ass all around the course. But I wasn't making any assumptions, because I learned long ago from Felix Unger never to assume. I decided that was it for business. I'd contact Amy Simpson, Rachel's best friend, sometime tomorrow. I'd also call Carl Hendrix tomorrow. I'd deal with Dr. Amanda Russell on Monday. And I'd determine a few other details as the weekend went. Right now, it was time to kick back and enjoy the beautiful, if still a little too hot, summer evening. The Yankees game hadn't started yet, so I had time to bring one of my televisions out onto the back deck while I grilled my chicken. I called Maggie, but, as expected, got her answering machine. No problems. I grabbed another beer, flicked on the game and settled in for the night. I had an early appointment tomorrow anyway.

## *Chapter 7*

The redhead returned from the bathroom wearing nothing but a bright red beach towel around her. Her hair was pinned up with stray strands hanging about her face haphazardly. She wiggled her finger at me like I had been a very, very bad boy and she was ready to offer up the proper punishment. I frantically looked around the room for another way out and only saw the window that I'd have to leap through to salvation as an escape. I was too late to react as the redhead pulled the towel off in a bullfighter's motion. I froze in horror. Her three hundred plus pounds were revealed to me in their unending flaps and folds. I looked into her face, and it was Rachel. She said, "It didn't have to be this way." She slowly moved toward me. The shadows engulfed me.

Then the alarm kicked onto my favorite modern rock station and the nightmare was thankfully put to rest. I squeezed my eyes and read the clock to make sure. It read five thirty-five. Yeah, I was back to reality and an extremely happy man. Time for some golf and a score in the high seventies or low eighties at the worst. I had to admit that I wasn't exactly a morning person. In fact, there were very few reasons I actually liked to drag my ass out of bed before most of the common folk -- to participate in a sporting event, and that included golf, to go fishing, to follow a hot lead in a case and to have sex. Damn good reasons to me. Otherwise, I needed my beauty sleep, and if I slept until eight-thirty on a weekend morning, I had no reason to feel guilty. I never napped. I stayed up late quite often. And some days when doing that great surveillance work I'm known for, sleep was a rare commodity. Overall, I rarely broke the eight-hour mark in one night.

One incredible payoff of rising early, especially in the summer, was the utter quiet and calm that Mother Nature allowed. I soaked in as much as possible as I went out to grab my morning paper. Just that short walk was enough to pry my eyes wide open. Many times I had seen deer either in my back yard or across the street in the fields. They'd look at me with no fear and continue on their destination. One of the definite perks of living outside of the village.

As I read the paper, I boiled four jumbo eggs and prepared four slices of whole wheat toast. After five minutes, I determined the eggs finished, rinsed then quickly in cold water and set them to rest for a few minutes. When I had finished reading about the Yanks' extra inning victory over the New York Mets, I peeled the eggs, removed three of the four yolks and placed them in a plastic baggie to be frozen until removal to the local landfill. I spread a minute amount of real whipped butter -- no chemically induced margerine for me -- on the toast and ate breakfast. I allowed myself one egg yolk just because the yolk was hands down the best tasting part of the egg. Of course, there in lies the fat, cholesterol and sodium.

I showered and threw on a collared golf shirt and a pair of khaki shorts. Even though it was an early tee time, the shorts were a necessity, because the forecast was for another scorcher and I always played in shorts unless the mercury wasn't going to rise above forty-five or so. I snatched one of my two FBI hats from my rack, purchased the same time as my tank top, and headed to the garage where my clubs awaited me. I tossed them in the back of the Jeep and at six-fifteen I was on my way to Foxfire, a reasonably challenging course with the front and back nines each possessing a distinct personality and both wedged in between housing developments. The course had some sand, water, tight fairways and lengthy holes from the tips.

I pulled into the parking lot at six-fifty. At that time of the morning, the lot was pretty empty except for the hard cores who needed to step out as early as the course and Mother Nature would allow. I slipped on my Nike Air Apparent's with soft spikes, a requirement for most courses these days, and hauled my standup bag to the bag rack near the Pro Shop. I stepped inside and told them that I was with the Howard party. I was the first arrival. I liked that. The young guy behind the counter

60

motioned to coffee and donuts, but I declined, payed my fee and stepped out to the practice green where I was blissfully alone. Getting up early did have rewards. The dew was still heavy on the green from the humidity and each putt or chip I released left a fresh arc toward the hole. Some even led right into the heart of the cup. At times, I just stood looking around, admiring the greenness all around. I had always loved the aesthetic pleasures of a golf course, from even the roughest layouts to the Ocean Course at Kiawah Island. Each course had its own identity.

After confidently warming up my game on and around the green, I spent a few minutes loosening up, especially my back. I had seen too many guys hit the course cold and either play a terrible game or yank something in the process, and since I always gripped and ripped, being loose was key. As I was swinging my five and six irons together, a guy with a receding reddish brown hairline approached me. He wore long pants, an expensive looking golf shirt, Foot Joy golf shoes and held a black Greg Norman "Shark" golf hat in his left hand. His smiled showed a lot of very white and very straight teeth. He was about five-ten and wiry with a hooked nose and a finely trimmed moustache right underneath for added effect. I knew it was Gary Howard. He stuck out his right hand and introduced himself with a full hand-pumping salesman's shake. If I didn't have such good self-control, I would have presented him my Visa Gold and told him to charge ten of whatever he was selling. I decided to introduce myself instead and thankfully claimed my hand back.

"Gettin' nice and loose, I see." I could tell that Gary was very astute.

"Always a good idea," I said. I looked back toward the clubhouse and saw two Oriental gentlemen sitting together in a cart next to an empty one that had one set of clubs already strapped in the back. I pointed my six iron in their direction and asked, "Clients?"

"A salesman's work is never done." He shrugged. "So, you know Rachel?"

"Yeah. We've known each other for awhile."

"Oh yeah?" I knew what the tone of his voice meant. I ignored him. Besides, he invited me to play golf. I'd ask him about Rachel when I was damn well ready. Maybe on the back nine after I had beat him into submission with my awesome short game.

Back to golf. "We playin' from the tips?" I asked with a bit of a challenge in my voice. Gary Howard had not impressed me in the least, and I could see why he and Rachel never amounted to anything. I could, however, see how Gary and his right hand might be very intimate. I wiped my right hand on my shirt without consciously thinking about the action.

He stammered a bit. "Sure. Why not? Japanese aren't long hitters anyway, right?" He actually winked at me. Top of his class, this Gary Howard. Guess he never heard of Jumbo Ozaki. "How about some friendly wagering?"

"Nassau?" A Nassau bet in golf actually consisted of three separate bets -- the best score on the front nine, the best score on the back nine, and the eighteen-hole total.

"Between you and I?" His grammar lacked as well as his character.

"Yeah."

"Twenty bucks per?"

"Sure."

"And how 'bout five bucks a hole per skin for the group? My clients are already in." He jerked his head toward the two. Nice to see that he really looked after their interests. That sat quietly in their cart while he did his chest pounding routine with me. It was clear that he thought that Rachel and I had pounded the Posturepedic. Now he thought he'd one up me on the course. Hell, I could always use a few extra bucks, especially at the expense of some slicker-than-thou sales chump who never turned off the close-the-deal neon.

"Why not?" I returned his earlier wink.

62

"Great. We tee off in ten minutes or so. From the blues."
He returned to schmooze his short-off-the-tee clients, and I
returned to my loosening up.

After Gary introduced me to Yamato and Satoshi, who were
well-spoken and seemed well-humored, he gave me the honors.
The first hole covered nearly four hundred yards with a highway
running along the right side and trouble up near the green on the
left with some water. I promptly lasered my drive about two
eighty-five down the left side of the fairway. Yamato and
Satoshi let out a few "oohs" and "ahhs" as the ball took flight,
then high-fived me as the ball came to rest. Gary offered up a
subdued "Nice shot" and prepared to hit. He opened up and
sliced his tee shot about one eighty-five well to the right in the
rough. His clients then each outdrove him by fifty yards. Two
thirty-five down the middle isn't short off the tee in my book. I
hated to think that Gary underestimated his guests. I knew they
had game, from their drives and from the winks they each gave
me as we hopped into our carts to head down the first fairway.
At least we all had the sleepers cleared out of our eyes now.
Those first drives turned out to be a portent of the front nine.

Gary pressed too hard on nearly every shot and was
shanking all over the course. He was tearing up more turf than a
farmer on his John Deere. Yamato and Satoshi stayed smooth
and steady on every hole. Gary fought hard to keep a sense of
humor, because the golf game was small potatoes compared to
the business he was planning on squeezing out of his clients. It
had to be tough, because I had taken six of the nine skins and
fired a very respectable forty on the front side. Satoshi, whom I
nicknamed "The Toe," and not because he looked anything like
Lou Groza, shot a forty-three; Yamato, or "Mott the Hoople" to
me, came in with a forty-five; and poor Gary hobbled in with a
fifty. Or at least he would have hobbled in if we walked, which I
would have preferred. I was twenty bucks up on the Nassau with
Gary and had deposited one hundred and twenty in my pocket on
the skins. A good front nine, even if I had just one birdie.

It was around nine-thirty and the sun was really beginning to heat the course up as we pulled off the ninth green and headed toward the clubhouse before crossing the road to the back nine. Gary hadn't said too much while he was fighting with his game, and I decided not to press anything and hoped his game would come around enough to relax him a little. The Toe and Mott the Hoople were heading to the clubhouse for refreshments. They had a good idea.

"Want something to eat or drink?" I asked Gary as he drove. His face was a light shade of red, from embarrassment or the sun, I wasn't sure. "I'll buy." He actually smiled.

"Hell, that's the least you could do. Either that or shoot me now so I don't have to play the back side." Damn. Gary Howard was human. I can bring it out of anybody.

"Like I'd waste the bullet. Nine holes left. If you'd relax, you'd be all set. Look at The Toe and Mott. They're having a ball. That's gotta be worth something."

"Yeah. Jesus, I'm pressing. Ya know, I do love the game. And, believe it or not, I can play."

He looked straight ahead and drove to the clubhouse. We met The Toe and Mott there. I picked up the tab for four bottles of Gatorade, and we moved to the tenth tee. I had the honors and blasted another big drive. It faded slightly right though and flirted with the water, but I was safe. When Gary got up, he wasted no time over his ball and just took a nice cut. Straight, about two-fifty.

"Guess you've had your fill of bananas today, huh?" I needled him.

"Peels and all."

He put the head cover on his driver and hopped in the cart. I was driving. The Toe and Mott headed over to the woods on the left where they each hooked their tee shots. I decided that now was the time to throw out a few questions about Rachel, especially since I had done such a splendid job of warming Gary up. I took us over to Gary's ball and stopped the cart at a ninety-degree angle in the fairway while we waited for the lumberjacks to return from their logging trip into the woods.

"So, Rachel's brother, Mick, tells me that you and Rachel dated briefly?"

"Yeah. Briefly being the key word. We only went three or four times."

I knew that he knew exactly how many times they went out. There was no three or four. A guy remembers, especially when the woman was of the caliber of Rachel. My money was on three at the max.

"How long ago you guys date?"

"A few months ago. Right after she got back from Burlington."

"How'd you two hook up?"

"Met her at the gym. We were both workin' out with free weights and just started talkin'." He stepped out of the cart. There was a green and white post about four yards behind us on the right side of the fairway that indicated one hundred fifty yards to the middle of the green. Gary fished an eight iron out of his bag and swung it loosely. "I thought she was pretty amazing from the moment I met her."

"What you guys talk about?"

"At the gym?"

"Yeah," I said as I put my feet up on the dash of the cart and looked to the left. The Toe and Mott had given up on finding their wayward balls and decided to drop in the fairway. They should have hit provisionals from the tee. Oh, well. Neither one was winning this hole. I gave them the thumbs up, and they returned it as they prepared to hit their next shots.

"Goals. Physical. Financial. She seemed focused on what she wanted. Talked about making lots of money and being set for life. I really related to the financial angle. I never had much growing up. I put myself through school, and now I'm making a good buck. And I'll admit it, I want more. I thought we were a good match."

"Sounds like a dangerous one to me."

"What do you mean?" He sounded a little offended.

The Toe and Mott had hit, and now it was Gary's shot. He set up, waiting for my answer.

"You're too much alike. You'd end up killing each other out of sheer competitiveness. You'd start with the big stuff like careers and money until everything became the chance to one up the other. Right down to silly games like golf."

He took in my observation, then drilled his ball fifteen yards over the green.

"See what I mean," I said. "Just my talking about it gave you a shot of adrenalin. I know Rachel. She always wants to win. I get the same from you."

He stuffed the iron in his bag and got back in the cart.

"Obviously, things didn't work out anyway," he said.

I got out of the cart, grabbed my pitching wedge and walked over toward my ball. I turned back to Gary and asked, "And why not?"

He looked down. "We were too much alike."

"What was that?"

"All right. You're right. We were too damn much alike." He shook his head and smiled slightly.

"Thank you," I said, then promptly deposited my approach shot on the green. "I love this game, don't you? It's so relaxing." I slipped my club in my bag, grabbed my putter and started walking toward the green.

Gary drove alongside me. "But there was another reason."

"Really?"

"There was someone else. An older guy. With money, of course."

I stopped and gave Gary a serious look. "What makes you say that?"

"She told me. Maybe she figured it was easier for me if she said there was someone else. I don't know."

"She say anything about the guy?"

The Toe and Mott had finally gotten their balls onto the green and were waiting for us. The Toe yelled out, "Come on guys. Time is money. Mostly ours today, but there's plenty of holes left."

I got in the cart. Gary drove us to the green.

Gary shook his head in thought. "Not really. Just that she'd known him awhile. They had some differences to work out and he would take care of her."

"Sounds more like a boss/employee relationship to me. That's it? You said he was older."

"Yeah. Rachel mentioned 'more mature, cultured, refined.' Stuff like that."

"No name?"

He shook his head. "Just a quick once over of how great he was."

"Sucks for you."

"Tell me about it."

We finished the hole out and moved over to the eleventh tee. I still had a few questions, and I was sure that Gary had a couple for me, but I didn't want to compromise his business relationship with Yamato and Satoshi by talking about personal matters that included the disappearance of an ex-girlfriend in their company. Hopefully, they wouldn't hold it against Gary that I was such a smart ass with the nicknames I gave them, but they seemed to get a kick out of it. I decided to grease the wheels some more.

"Think you two could stay out of the woods this time?" I asked. "I mean, if you gotta go to the bathroom so bad, you should've done it in the clubhouse."

Mott the Hoople said, "Now that you have a sense of invincibility, I can take the rest of the skins. I can hear the trees calling your name, William Holden."

"And do you know what they're sayin'?" I asked rhetorically. "They're sayin', 'Don't hit it in here, 'cause you hit the ball so hard, it's gonna hurt real bad, unlike your Japanese friends.'" Everyone laughed. Even Gary. Then I drove it into the woods, and didn't they really love that one. It took a couple of minutes for everyone to recover so they could tee off.

The next few holes were uneventful, with the skins being spread around. I was still shooting well, but the others had picked up their games. When we had the chance, Gary and I spoke some more. He told me that he hadn't seen Rachel since they went their separate ways. Not even at the gym. He didn't harbor any ill feelings toward her. He did regret the fact that he never had the chance to get intimate with her. He eventually got around to asking me why I needed to know about their relationship. I eased his mind and told him that he was just a small piece of the puzzle in the backgrounds of Rachel and Mick. I asked him if he knew about the deaths of their parents, and he told me that Rachel did broach the subject. That was my investigative motive, I assured him. I guess he bought it. I found out that Gary sold semi-conductors on a worldwide scale. He spent a lot of time traveling and was good at his job. At least, that's what he informed me with his classic toothy grin.

I birdied the par-five eigthteenth hole to win the last two skins and finished the back side with a thirty-nine. Gary came in with a forty-two. Mott fired a forty-four, and The Toe carded a forty-five. Gary owed my forty more bucks for the back side and overall Nassau bet, and we calculated the skin amounts and divied the money up appropriately. Good thing I won, because I didn't carry a lot of cash on me. I said good-bye to Yamato and Satoshi, and addressed them as such out of respect. They told me they had a great time and were impressed with my golf game. I flexed my right biceps and told them it was all the pushups. Hey, I left them laughing. Gary told them he'd call them at their hotel about their dinner plans for later.

After Gary returned the key to our cart, I met him in the now crowded parking lot near my Jeep. I wanted to see how he felt about his short-off-the-tee clients now.

"Thanks for the game, Gary."

"Sure, Holden, no problems."

"So, how about those short hitters Yamato and Satoshi?"

"Okay. My mistake. I should know better. But I was busy flexing my manhood. Or trying."

"No shit. It's not always about winning, ya know?"

"Easy for you to say. You're richer today."

"But I had a good time. And that's how I approached it. I had business to take care of with you, but there was no reason not to enjoy the game. Look at The Toe and Mott the Hoople. They knew you saw your manhood being tested somehow, or at least in your own mind. You dissed them a bit at first, your own clients, but they still had a good time. They knew this was a game. Just a game. Frustrating as hell at times, but nothing more than a game."

He stuck out his right hand. I shook it. "I do apologize. And when you see Rachel, tell her I said hello, okay?"

"You got it."

"Great. Now I've got a coupla clients to apologize to. I did enjoy the back side, ya know."

"After eighteen holes with yours truly, how could you not? Thanks again for the game. Maybe another time? And don't give me a standard bullshit sure, no problems salesman's answer. You either want to play again or not."

"You're on. And I mean it."

"Drive safely. Stay out of the woods."

He hauled his Callaway bag and clubs over to his Infiniti Q45 and carefully lowered them into the trunk. I stashed my clubs and headed home. We had finished our round just before noon, when the blazing sun hung high in the sky and beat down on the poor souls just now teeing off. Even though we had rode, I still worked up a lather and needed a shower and some food to refuel for a gorgeous, if hot and humid, summer day. One of the great aspects of teeing off so early in the morning is that you have the rest of the day in front of you, if you have the stamina. I wanted to call Rachel's friend, Amy, to see if she would spare me a few minutes, and I also wanted to talk to Maggie to see what she was up to and Mick to discuss the Carl Hendrix offer a little more. Then I'd have to approach Carl Hendrix about the deal and why his number was the last one Rachel called. I also needed to find out more about this mystery man. Hopefully, Amy Simpson would shed some light on Mr. Philanthropic.

## *Chapter 8*

I headed south on Route 48, took a right onto Jones Road, drove underneath Intertstate 690 and turned left onto Van Buren Road. Just after I went under the New York State Thruway, I took the first left and was on my way over the back roads home to Skaneateles. I decided to call Amy Simpson from my cell phone, expecting only to get an answering machine or simply no answer at all. I had crossed Route 173 and was on De Voe Road when I made the call. Surprisingly, she answered on the second ring.

"Is Amy available?" I asked.

"Speaking." She didn't recognize the voice. She must have thought that I was a telemarketer and was probably silently cursing herself out with her admission of who she was. Personally, I had a pretty fool proof plan of cutting off the almighty phone solicitor. Not totally guaranteed, but pretty solid. I noticed that there was a slight pause and background yammering whenever a telemarketer called, so, if I didn't get an immediate response from the calling party when I said "Hello," I'd just hang up quicker than Gary Howard could close a deal. I presumed that if the call was important, the caller would punch my number right back in on assumption that there was some problem with the connection. Telemarketers never called back. That had to move onto the next number on the list. Very rarely did I ever hang up on someone whom I actually wanted to talk to, and thankfully, nobody who had only one chance of calling was ever left to hang out to dry. Yet. I had plenty of time to establish that first. So, that's how Amy could know I wasn't a phone solicitor.

"Hi, Amy. I'm a friend of Rachel Allen's. Holden Grace..."

"Oh, yeah, H." Her tone softened noticeably even from the single word she spoke before. I surmised that she had heard about me from Rachel. Thank God, it must have been positive. Not that I had any reason to doubt my image through Rachel's eyes. It's not like I ever had the chance to really screw up in the sack, thus becoming fodder for endless female bonding jokes from here to eternity. "What's up?" she asked.

Time for some more bullshit. Okay, Holden, sling away, buddy. "I'm checking into some personal matters regarding Rachel and her brother, Mick, on Mick's request, and I just had a few questions about Rachel."

"No shit? I thought you two were tight. Ya know, she once told me that if I ever needed someone to pull my ass out of a major fuckin' jam, you were the guy. Hands down. No questions asked. And now, you're comin' to me askin' questions? Ain't that the goddamn kicker. Wait'll I tell her. So what ya need to know, big guy?"

"I was kinda hopin' we could talk in person." I looked in my rear view and noticed a black Cadillac hanging behind me. I thought it interesting that a Caddy would be tooling around these out-of-the-way roads. Of course, I was almost to Route 5, which many considered a main road in Central New York.

"Tell ya what, H man. You play tennis? Rachel said you were an athletic guy."

"Yeah. I play."

"How 'bout we meet at Austin Park in about an hour? We whack the ball around a little and we talk. I'll bring the rackets. You bring the balls."

Amy Simpson was not a subtle woman. The Caddy stayed with me as I swung right onto Route 5 West, keeping a reasonable distance.

"All right. I'm in. But give me a little longer." It was twelve-fifteen. Austin Park was a reasonably large park in Skaneateles with softball fields, sand volleyball courts, tennis courts, basketball courts and a playground. They also had a picnic area and set the softball outfields up as soccer fields in the fall. "How's one-thirty sound?"

"Works for me. See ya then. I'll be the one with the big smile and the big forehand."

I hung up and checked my rearview mirror again, just in time to see a beat up Chevy pickup speed by the Cadillac and duck in behind me after we went through a traffic light where two lanes narrowed down to one. Drivers amazed me. It wasn't road rage. It was road stupidity. The maniac behind the wheel had a cigarette hanging between his lips and long hair beneath a dingy baseball cap with those God awful big, mirrored wrap around sunglasses. I could make out every detail since he was so close to me. He could have been a homemaker in a Ford Explorer with two kids strapped in the vehicle, a rich turd in a Mercedes with a bad hair piece or some young punk in a juiced up Camaro. They were all out there, making the roads an unsafe place in any weather condition, believing for some insane reason that they were infallible or, worse, immortal. Well, what about the other people? They didn't care. It was a world of me, me, me. I wondered where the guy now behind me could have been going in such a hurry only to have to ride his brakes as I kept my speed near fifty-five. One day, I was going to stop at a traffic light, get out and ask the asshole riding my tail, or chasing me as Maggie calls it, what they hoped to accomplish by gluing themselves to my rear bumper. Maybe today was the day.

I was approaching the intersection with Route 321 South that took me to Skaneateles, and it just so happened to have a light. As I neared the signal, it was green, but I slowed considerably as I moved into the left turn only lane hoping Mr. Pickup would be going my way. Ah, sweet fortune. He dipped right in behind me just as the light changed to red, and was promptly followed by the Caddy. A little parade. How nice. I knew the light was a quick one, and if I was going to probe this loser's driving mind, I'd have to act with haste. But I was too slow. I watched in my rearview as the driver of the Cadillac opened his door and unfolded his substantial frame out into the middle of the asphalt and strode to the Chevy. Mr. Pickup's driver's side window was rolled down and when the driver of the Caddy reached it, he never hesitated and drilled the guy with a fast right hand that rocked Mr. Pickup's head back and knocked the shades right off of his face and the cigarette out of his mouth. Cadillac Man glanced up at me, turned and got back in his car.

Meanwhile, the light had changed and I sat there for a few seconds to see if Mr. Pickup was coherent enough to drive. He shook his head a few times to clear the cobwebs, looked back covertly at the Cadillac and waited for me to move. A hell of a twist of events. I knew I could be mean and had a certain aura about me, but the Cadillac Man did not look like a customer to tango with. He was about six-two, two-twenty or so, hard to tell in his nice suit, and looked like a lifter. The kind of guy who'd juice up then go mental in the weight room. He had the aura. I bet he didn't hurt his knuckles on the guy's face. Now I kind of felt a twinge of sorrow for the guy in the pickup, because I hadn't planned on hitting him. I was just going to humiliate and debase him with my mastery of the English language. But, then again, maybe he got what he deserved and he'd think the next time he got behind the wheel. Of course, as the thought went through my mind, he flew around me heading down a hill on 321 with another vehicle coming at us. I braked so he'd get back in our lane without becoming the meat in a sheet metal sandwich. The oncoming car hit his horn and made a nasty hand gesture, but never slowed down. It was his space, goddammit, and he wasn't backing down. More road stupidity. I chocked up this move by Mr. Pickup to his fear of what or who was behind him.

The Cadillac stayed behind me, a few car lengths back, just cruising along nicely on a sunny Saturday afternoon as the Chevy accelerated out of sight. It was about ten more minutes to my house, and the Cadillac Man stayed with me the entire way, even off Route 321 onto Mottville Road, across Jordan Road onto Crow Hill Road and finally a left onto Mill Road. As I pulled into my driveway and stopped to check the mail, he slid by me slowly and kept on going. Strange. I memorized the license plate just in case. If he was on his way to Skaneateles, the easiest route would have been straight down 321 into Genesee Street right in downtown. If the guy was purposely following me, he had no qualms about me noticing. In fact, I'm sure that's what he wanted. And it's certainly hard to miss someone when they clock somebody else at a traffic intersection. Yeah, he wanted me to notice him.

## *Chapter 9*

Austin Park was a mecca for humanity in the summer, much like the village of Skaneateles, thriving with life even in the heat. Children's summer groups were being put through the paces by their adult supervisors; teenagers in-line skated on the asphalt path around the park; high school kids booted a soccer ball back in forth in preparation for the fall season, the playground overflowed with screaming children (most of them happily stretching their lungs); the hoop courts were full with either games or guys shooting around; and the four tennis courts were in use. I parked near the basketball courts, locked my gun in the glove box, grabbed my wide body graphite tennis racket and my bottle of All-Sport and headed toward the tennis courts, which were about a hundred and fifty yards away. As I passed the basketball games on my left, I recognized some guys that I played with on occasion. They were all shirtless, well tanned and playing some serious ball that had the old sweat glands working overtime.

A tall, lean guy with short black hair that was turning prematurely gray called out in between points, "Hey, H. The courts are full, man. Why'nt ya sub in here for awhile?"

"Gotta meet someone. Maybe later, Jazz. If your still standin'."

A teammate tossed the b-ball and hit him in the back of the head as a signal to get his ass back in the game. You lose a game, you lose the court. I walked around the south end of the tennis courts to the openings between the chain link fence on the west side. I noticed that three of the courts involved doubles matches. I watched briefly as they lobbed the ball back in forth in tired motions. They either played like that normally or the heat was wearing them down. I was surprised to see so much activity at the park with the world getting more and more obese as time moves on. It would have been a hell of a lot easier for most of these people to lay around in air conditioning eating ice cream and drinking Pepsi than be out working off the pounds. Of course, that didn't mean that later they wouldn't make a beeline for the freezer. Personally, I needed the aerobic conditioning. Since I disliked jogging, I needed to raise my heart rate and burn off the calories in other ways, and I did take in calories. I liked to eat, even though I was very impressed with my ability to avoid fat, cholesterol and sodium, and I liked a cold beer when I wanted one. At a hundred fifty calories or so in twelve ounces, those calories added up quickly. So, I played tennis, I worked out on my heavy bag, I played hoops, rode my bike, lifted weights. Basically, I stayed busy.

Before the exciting doubles action snapped my eyelids shut, I set my sights on a game of singles on the court nearest me. These two meant business. All out hustle. Solid shots. Making each other run from the baseline to the net and side to side. I could appreciate their effort. I wondered if Amy Simpson was as good as this woman who seemed to be getting the best of her male opponent. Then when she slammed a forehand winner down the line and she broke out in a wide grin, I realized this was Amy. I was in trouble. I could play. And I was no stranger to leaving my skin on the asphalt court, but she had game. After the point, which won the game, she thanked the guy for stepping in and told him that her real opponent was here. He gave me a wave, picked up his gear and headed to a cement slab and wall that was below the playground to volley alone.

Amy Simpson came over, took a hit from a bottle of Evian and thrust out her right hand. "I assume you're Holden."

I took her hand. Firm grip. "You assume correctly."

Amy Simpson was taller than I was. Around five-ten. Lean and in shape. She definitely put hours in at the gym. She had brown eyes and her long blond hair was pulled back into a ponytail. She either was blessed with a lot of natural curl, and if that was the case, she probably cursed her hair every day for it, or she put the curl in, in which case she probably cursed her straight hair every day. I was learning to be pretty good about the feminine mystique. Or so I thought. It was important to make an attempt to understand their point of view, because it was a hell of a lot different than the male species. She wore a sleeveless shirt with the Nike logo on it, a pair of Nike shorts and Nike shoes. I wondered if they were forking out for these endorsements. Then I realized that I was wearing my swoosh socks and swoosh shoes. Hey, at least Nike was the Goddess of victory. What was Adidas the Goddess of, huh? Or Reebok? Of course, I owned some of their goods, too. She was tan and attractive. In her late twenties. And as I recalled from our brief phone conversation, a bit rough. It showed with her language. Not rough in the physical sense. Not by any means. But rough, like, "Hey, I'm an individual who takes crap from no one. You'll either love me or hate me, and that's fine with me. I'm no princess. I'm no raving lunatic bitch. I'm just me. So, deal." Standing there, looking at her, I felt as if I were in the presence of one hellacious paradox. Like Callisto, since I had been thinking of Greek mythology, the beautiful nymph whom Zeus wagged the dog for and was zapped into a carnivorous bear by Hera out of jealousy. Beautiful, yet deadly. Especially on the tennis court. I wondered what juicy thoughts formed in her mind about me. Most likely how she was going to kick my ass and love it. But, I did catch her sneaking a peek at my pipes when we shook hands. If she was best buddies with Rachel, then she knew about me. She knew all of the exceptional qualities I possessed. Well, almost all, since we never consummated our friendship in the lustful sense, at least physically.

"Nice to see a man show up on time for a date," she said. She was right. She had the big forehand and the big smile. Slight overbite. Dimples in the cheeks. Smile lines. Wonderful.

"I'm like a pizza. Delivered on time or I'm free."

"Maybe you should've been late then." Her tone was enough to make me forget we were in a crowded park holding tennis rackets and a bottle of All-Sport that was ready to explode. Love or hate her? I loved her. I just had to remember that this was business. No cracks about eating the pizza before it got cold. No cracks about sausage or pepperoni. Besides, I liked to think that I was above that sort of juvenile symbolism that was blatantly obvious.

Instead, I played the Rachel angle. "Oh, you are Rachel's friend. I like you." I stressed the word "are."

"Why, thank you..."

"I just don't know if I'm a huge fan of your tennis game."

"And why's that?" The smile stayed in place. No way it was forced.

"Because it's too damn good."

"I could always lay back." Did she rehearse these lines? She must have been killer in a bar teeming with sharks ready to be bludgeoned by her sardonic commentary. They'd stand no chance, swimming around what they thought was easy bait only to be chewed up and spit out like bad haddock.

"Do that and neither one of us would play much tennis." The double meaning, I'm sure, was not lost.

"Well then, I won't hold back. If you don't."

"All's fair in love and tennis."

"A literary man. How intriquing. Ready to warm up?"

Hell, she was well past warmed up. I needed a fire lit under my ass to catch up with her.

"As ready as the tree that falls in the forest with no one around, and then thanked God for that." I set the All-Sport down and twirled my racket in my right hand.

"You are so cute. And distracting."

I'd have to use that to my advantage. I removed the cover of my racket and then realized I didn't bring any balls. Tennis balls. Thankfully, Amy was up to the task and had two cannisters of bright chartreuse Wilsons that she was busy retrieving from around the court left as reminders from her last victim. I stretched some, because the last thing I wanted was to pull a groin or hamstring and squirm around on the court in pathetic pain not able to ask the questions about Rachel that I needed to. When I was ready, I stepped out onto the court, confident that I wouldn't embarrass myself too badly. I instinctively looked over my right shoulder beyond the fence to the basketball courts to ensure that none of the guys I knew was watching. Actually, I didn't care too much, but it was just a reflex action, naturally surfacing from an extra shot of testosterone and adrenalin that flooded my Y chromosome brain.

Amy lobbed a ball over to me and I sent it soaring over the fence that divided the courts right into the middle of one of the doubles matches. Amy laughed heartily. No giggle. An all out belly shaker, if she had one. A belly, not a shaker.

She turned to face the fence and yelled out, "A little help."

A bewildered gentleman with a healthy gray mop surrounded by a white headband retrieved the ball and whacked it back over to us. I could see the women, who were battling the men, whisper to each other, their crisp, bleached white tennis outfits radiating purity in the afternoon sun. They reminded me of virginesque super heroines who disapproved of the malevolent forces just standing outside of the gates of hell, or in other words, Amy and me. With all the vericose veins weaving from ankle to thigh, they might want to worry about the evil forces under their skin. And why the hell weren't they at their club somewhere? Trading stories about tropical breezes and the four c's? Cash, Cadillacs, condos and the Caymans. Maybe they were wannabes. Or maybe they wanted to mingle with the masses as a reminder of why they loved having such wealth. I didn't care. I just knew I had to get my game under control. I needed to play with Fraulein Forehand in order to forge some conversation about Rachel. That or my ego needed it. I wasn't about to argue the point. I just needed to silence the laughter from the other side of the net at my inept expense.

"So, the object's not to see how far you can hit it?" Amy shook her head, still busting a gut. "And that big fence isn't the net?" More head shaking. "See, I thought it was us against them." I raised my voice so the foursome could hear me. "Listen, I'm really sorry." I was sincere. I didn't know if they believed me. "It shouldn't happen again." I waved my racket. They flipped me the obligatory salute and returned to their game. I asked Amy, "Do you have a cell phone here?"

81

She looked puzzled and her laughter stopped abruptly. "Yeah. Why?"

"We might be calling nine-one-one soon," I said as I craned my neck toward the foursome. The laughter overtook her again. All I had to do was keep this up and I had a chance to break that forehand into nothing more than a one-hand. If I could keep her laughing with me instead of at me, I had a shot.

Amy tried another lob over the net and I returned successfully this time, deep to the baseline on her backhand. I thought I'd test it early in the warm ups and hoped it was her weakness. She fired it back at me. Accurate, but with half the steam of her forehand. Okay. Mental note on that backhand. The volley continued for awhile until I stepped into a forehand and drove it into the tape. No question. This would be a challenge. But that was good. I didn't feel that it would be a crushing blow to my male ego if a woman defeated me. What it meant to me was that she was better. And if she did win, I could always ask her to arm wrestle. We loosened up for a few more minutes until I felt I was prepared to face her onslaught. One last volley determined the serve, and Amy won it. A nice, lubricating sweat had doused my body. It felt good as the droplets ran down through my buzz cut instead of hanging up in my hair, slapping me in the head and neck with its heavy wetness. I went to the closely cropped look a few years back for low maintenance reasons, and because it made me look meaner with my goutee, and at times like this, it provided more benefits. I could see that Amy had actually had an attack of perspiration while we volleyed. Nice to know that she was human.

Her first serve was deep toward the tee on my backhand. I shifted my feet, tossed the racket from my right hand to my left hand and returned with a lefthand forehand. Being naturally left-handed, it was instinct to switch hands when I played. I was a self-proclaimed ambidexterite, or ambidexterant, or whatever someone termed it, because I wrote, shot a gun, played pool, ate and, well, prescribed self-relief left-handed, but I also threw a ball, buried my three-point jumper, played guitar, played golf and threw my hardest punch right-handed. But I could interchange in times of necessity. My return bounced nicely to her forehand and away it went past me for the first point of the match. A portent of things to come.

I battled hard but succumbed six games to four in the first set. After I missed wide with a backhand to lose the set, we took a break to rehydrate and catch our breaths on the metal benches provided courtside. Smart design thinking there. Take a seat when it's cold and stick to the metal or plant it in weather like today and roast your ass. I drained most of my warm All-Sport. Amy had some more of her Evian.

"You're tough," she finally said. Nice to know she recognized my ruggedness.

"Well, I can do a hundred fifty pushups in a row."

"I meant your tennis game."

"Oh, that. Didn't think you'd notice while I was running all over the court like a dog on a long leash."

"Ah, but you chased those balls down like such a good boy. And you even returned most of them to me. Very obedient." Ouch.

"Oh, yeah. Wait til the match is over when I jump the net and hump your leg."

"Promises. Promises." She not only could play on the court but off of it as well.

"Speaking of promise. How the hell'd you get so good at this game?"

"I went to North Carolina on a tennis scholarship. Played first singles. Won the ACC my junior and senior years. Finished third in the Nationals as a senior."

"And it ended there?" I assumed it did since she was blasting balls by me and not Martina Hingis.

"Got tired of the goddamn pressure. The need to win. The need to fit someone else's mold."

"Coaches?"

"Coaches and parents. They wanted me to turn pro. My parents, that is. Thought I had what it took to compete. I just wanted to enjoy my life. Do what I wanted. Don't get me wrong. I love tennis. I love winning. But on my terms. I didn't want to go on the tour just to compete. No way I could beat the best. I'm good, but never was fantastic. I had lessons since I was seven years old. It grew tiresome. I had my life to live. It's not like tennis was the only thing I did in school. Believe it or not, I did get an education."

"You mean you didn't have to bat your eyes, tell the profs you were the tennis star and then get straight A's?" I wasn't serious and knew that Amy knew that. Or so I hoped. Otherwise, I could expect to get a Prince racket wrapped around my thick neck.

"This was North Carolina. Hoop heaven. Dean Smith. Remember? Besides, I don't think my married female professors would have fallen for it."

"How'd your parents feel about you baggin' the pros?"

Amy took another swig of her water, swished it around for a bit, then spit it out. The park stayed active, although the tennis courts had cleared except for two teenage girls who had secured a court kitty corner to where Amy and I were playing.

"At first, they were upset. My dad always wanted to play on the big circuit, but decided it was more important to be home with his family. My parents married young. So, he transferred the game to me. But when I explained my position to them, they understood. Surprised the shit out of me, too. Never thought they cared about what I wanted."

"Parents never cease to amaze."

"Yeah. As long as they're there."

She looked away for a moment, seemingly far away. Although Amy did her best to erect a nice brick facade to deflect the big bad wolf, she was still a caring person. On her terms, of course. Her seconds of reflection ended quickly though.

"Okay," she said, looking back at me with her game face intact. "Enough of this mental probing, trying to find a weakness. Back to the court so I can kick your ass some more."

She jumped up with a lot of energy. I pried myself from my seat.

"Ya know," I said. "I've had a long day. Up at five-thirty for eighteen holes of golf. And now all these laps around the court..."

"You're not giving up, are you? 'Cause if you are..." A disappointed look swept over her face like a dark cloud.

"No chance. Just workin' on my excuse in case, by some miracle, you continue to abuse me out here."

"Abuse you? Never. Use you? Maybe." She whacked me on the ass with her racket and sprinted out onto the court. I followed suit, just more slowly. At least the heat kept me limber.

Set number two belonged to me. I immediately traded in my serve and volley game for more trips to the net, which caught Amy off guard. Then, when she started working great passing shots, I returned to the serve and volley. Mix things up. That's the only way to keep an opponent of superior skill on his or her toes.

When we sat down after the second set, it was around three-thirty, and I was starting to feel the activity of my day. At least I didn't have to worry about any of my basketball buddies asking me to join them again. They had all left about an hour ago, most likely knocking back a few ice cold ones, just getting warmed up for a long night. Fine with me. I imagined they all got up around eleven o'clock in the morning after a very late Friday night down at Morris's, a local watering hole, or the Blue Water Grill. My All-Sport was gone, so I headed across the courts to the warm drinking fountain on the other side.

When I came back, Amy was tipping another bottle of her water toward her smiling lips.

"Ya know. I woulda shared," she said as she took a drink.

"Wouldn't want to give you my germs. Who knows where this mouth has been."

"I ain't afraid."

"Somehow, I didn't think you would be."

I sat down next to her on the bench, which was still intent on grafting to my legs. I was drenched in sweat and stripped my wet shirt off and tossed it on the side of the court. It made a funny "splat" noise when it hit. Not very attractive. Amy offered a glance at my naked torso. Not that I could blame her. I'm sure if she removed her shirt, I'd offer a studious gaze her way. I had brought another shirt with me but left it in my Jeep. That meant that Amy would just have to control herself.

Hazy clouds had moved in, obscuring the sun, giving hints of one hell of a storm brewing. When that cold front decided to tangle with this obstinate warm front that had been wearing out its welcome, the sparks were going to fly. I at least hoped it waited until I could grill some steaks on my deck. Then, if it wanted, the sky could light up like Las Vegas. I always loved watching lightning as it shot across the heavens at night.

As I stared out at the sky, Amy nudged my left thigh and said, "So, should we call it a draw this time?"

"Sounds fair," I answered with my gaze still fixed above.

"You're not having a heart attack or something, are you?"

I looked at her. "Me? This body is fine tuned, I'll have you know."

"Will you?" The tone in her voice and the look in her eyes said volumes more than her mouth. I needed to get on the subject of Rachel without totally shutting down the advances aggressively thrown at me. I knew it would constitute my utmost tact skills.

"Well, that would be something that Rachel never knew." Grace successfully negotiates the deep bunker with a masterful sand wedge.

"So I'm to understand. How come?" Her eyebrows lifted in curiousity.

"She's my buddy's younger sister." I started to put my racket away.

"Never stopped my brother's friends from trying."

"Some friends."

"You could say that." Amy twisted the cap back on her empty bottle of water, zipped the head cover onto her racket and stashed it into a carry bag.

"But, I bet his best friend was cool about it. Flirted some. But never went for it."

"Well..." She had the look of defeat.

"That's a real friend. Knew his boundaries. And respected you."

She laughed. "I never asked him if he respected me, but, yeah, he was cool. So, you're an expert on friends as well as on the court."

"Expert might be going a little too far."

"For which one?"

"Both. I try to know people. Part of my business."

"Ya know, I forget that you're a Private Dick."

"Most people don't after they've met me. Then they just shorten it to 'Dick.'"

"Shorten it, huh?"

She eyed my sweat soaked shorts furtively. It could've been incredibly easy to ask her if we could talk about Rachel at either her place or mine, but that would only lead me down a path I didn't need to tread right at the moment. I needed answers, and I had planned on calling Maggie later and asking her if she wanted to share my t-bones with me. But, I sure the hell had to muster up the willpower to think with my big head and not the little one. I smiled, shrugged my shoulders, stood up and stretched my legs as an excuse to put some distance between us. I wanted to steer the conversation back my way.

"So, since I'm a near expert on friends, and, a PI, mind if we talk some about Rachel now?"

She stretched her tanned legs out in front of her and folded her hands behind her head. The pose reeked of defiance. I guessed she wasn't thrilled with my self-control. She just might learn in the near future how good self-control can be in certain instances. I turned from her and faced one of the softball fields where a father and his children were whacking a tennis ball with an aluminum bat and circling the bases like Bernie Williams on a gapper to left-center field.

"Sure. Why not? That's why we hooked up anyway, right?"

"Reason number one." I turned back. The sweat was beginning to dry on my bare upper body. She held her pose. Then she smiled. I always break them down in the end.

"Okay. But before you interrogate me, I need some ID, mister. How do I know you are who you say you are? Hmm?" She was back with the sense of tease in her voice.

"It's in my Jeep. Guess you'll have to take my word for it."

"I suppose. And if I don't cooperate?"

I sat back down. Big mistake. "Sorry. I don't carry cuffs."

"Maybe I do."

"Amy, you don't need cuffs, my dear."

"True. Very true." She tucked her legs back in and brought her hands down to rest on her thighs. "So, just what is it you need to know about Rachel for these, uh, personal matters?"

Finally, down to business. "You and Rachel are close, right?"

"Yeah. We've been close friends for awhile."

"Talk to her lately?"

"Not since last weekend. I left a message this past week, but haven't heard from her. I figured she was gone on business or something like that. It's not like we talk every week, so I thought no big deal. She'd call me when she called me. Is everything okay?" She was actually concerned.

"As far as I know. Like I said, I need to check some things out for Rachel and Mick for personal matters. Not lookin' for anything specific."

"'Cause like I said to you on the phone, I thought you and Rachel were tight."

"Not so much these days. You probably know her better than anyone. So, what do you guys do together?"

"We used to hit the gym a lot. Play tennis. The shopping thing. Go out at night."

"Used to?"

"Yeah, well, lately, she stopped going to the gym. Stopped drinking. I hadn't seen her as much. She seemed, I don't know, preoccupied."

"She tell you why?"

"Unlike the male's concept of female friendship, we don't tell each other every detail in our lives. There's plenty of things I haven't shared with Rach, and I'm sure she has her secrets. We don't pry. If we want to talk, we'll talk."

"I take that as a no." She gave me an exasperated look. "Just makin' sure. Can't afford to assume. The last time I did, it made..."

"An ass out of you and me." We said the punch line together. "I'm a big *Odd Couple* fan too," she said.

"Ah, yes. Odd couples. Like Oscar and Felix. Elizabeth Taylor and that young construction guy. Hell, Tony Randall and his thirty-something wife."

"Don't forget Julia Roberts and Lyle Lovett. Or Bill Clinton and Al Gore."

"How 'bout Rachel? Know of any romantic links, say, out of the ordinary?" I had hoped to learn more about Mr. Older Rich Guy.

"She dated a guy awhile back named Gary..."

"Gary Howard."

"Yeah. They weren't a good match, though. She had also hinted about an older guy. Had money. Was gonna take care of her. Never met him. She only mentioned him a coupla times after nights out when she would beat off other guys. I just figured the guy was gay, married or died by now. I mean, come on, how often does a rich guy fall in your lap? Let alone not fucked up somehow, huh?"

"For me, never."

"Same here."

The family playing on the softball field had packed up and moved on. The father ready for a scotch and soda and central air conditioning and the kids ready for ice cream and more attention from the father. The black clouds kept rolling in angrily from the west, greedily stealing the last remnants of blue sky of an August afternoon. I loved summer. Spring was great. It symbolized new life, the end of usually nasty winters in Central New York, and the opening of fishing seasons, softball season and golf courses. But summer was unrivaled for throwing oneself into the full throes of life. If one chose, it could be nonstop activity. I thought about my day today and how it was still early. Four-plus hours of daylight left, if Mother Nature intended to let the light shine through, which, by the look of things, she didn't, and eighteen holes of golf and two hard sets of tennis already under my belt, with plans for grilling, maybe doing some chipping and then relaxing. And if we did get descended upon by a fury of thunderstorms, the lightning provided a natural show and the rain would allow me to go out and pick nightcrawlers just for the hell of it. I loved summer, but it was winding down quickly. Like life sometimes.

"Did you stay in touch with Rachel when she moved to Burlington?"

"We talked once in awhile. E-mailed each other. I took a road trip up there once for a weekend. Actually, not long before she moved back here. Nice place."

"Burlington?"

"No, the place she rented. Right on Lake Champlain. Big and open and classy. In a renovated builing. Don't know how she afforded it, but she always had a thing about living large. Like the place she has here. Right on the lake. Big. Expensive. I wish I knew where that girl got her money."

So did I, because it seemed like Rachel was either living over her head or supplemented her income in a way no one knew about. Something was sure the hell suspicious, and I couldn't help placing Carl Hendrix in the puzzle as a crucial piece. Older guy. Rich guy. He was the last one she called. Too coincidental? I'd find out soon enough.

"You know anything about the Sagamore Resort on Lake George?" I asked since we were on the topic of snuggling down in the lap of luxury.

"Heard of it. That's about it. Why?"

"Just lookin' for answers. It may or may not mean something to the specifics of what I'm looking into." I had to keep up the generic facade, although I knew that the damn thing was about to crumble all around me, especially when I started talking to heavy hitters such as Carl Hendrix and Rachel's landlord, Curtis Granby. But, the way things looked, opening up this baby like a freshly caught rainbow trout with a well-honed filet knife seemed about the most logical way to proceed. Mick would have to understand. He wanted me to do a job, and whatever means it took, then so be it. I'd stick with the subtle approach for as long as possible, but that well was soon to run dry. Real soon. And real dry. I wanted to straight out ask Amy if she thought Rachel had any reason to light her eternal flame, but that would not fall under subtle in any dictionary. I also couldn't ask if she thought anybody would want to whack her. What next? Maybe take my soaked shirt, my tennis racket and my sorry ass and go bass fishing at my favorite farm pond until I thought of what to ask next. Could be awhile. I decided to be a little more direct. What the hell. The rain was going to start falling soon anyway.

"Here's a crazy question for you," I mused. "Think Rachel would take off on a whim with Daddy Warbucks? Fly to gay Paree? Do some body surfing and bikini waxing in Hawaii?" I didn't think it was the case, but I had to ask. Amy might know more than she was telling me.

"Christ, I don't know. Maybe." She caught on and gave me a look that let me know. "Is she missing?"

"No," I lied.

"Then what's this all about? Really?"

I thought about the black Caddy. I also thought about the guy driving the Caddy. Amy didn't need some ape like that busting her door down and rattling her cage at three in the morning. The less she knew the better. And right now, I figured she knew nothing. I decided to keep it that way.

"Like I said, personal stuff with Mick and Rachel."

"Come on, Holden. She's my best friend."

"Nothin's goin' on." I had trouble looking at her. My Fed buddy once told me that one of the keys to knowing if someone's lying to you is that they look down and left when they prevaricate. So, if I didn't look at Amy, I couldn't look down and left. At least that she could see. "There's really nothing I can tell you." That at least was honest, because I knew nothing about Rachel's whereabouts.

"Jesus Christ," she said as she rolled her eyes in disgust. She bounced up from the bench, still with an abundance of energy, angry energy, I was sure, and started packing up her stuff. "Now you decide to play Mr. Private Dick. Tell you what. If I hear from her, I'll be sure to mention you're lookin' for her." Her sarcasm was not lost on me.

I stood up. "Amy. Listen. Right now, all I want to do is talk to Rachel. That's it. And I can't find her. Mick hasn't heard from her in a coupla days. She hasn't returned your call. If I knew where the hell she was, I'd be there and not here wasting your time. This is what I do. I ask questions and hope the hell I get intelligent answers once in awhile like yours. If I thought something was really wrong with Rachel, don't you think I'd be inclined to spend less time playing tennis and more time kicking down doors? Amy, do me a favor and cut me a break, would ya?" I softened my tone on the last line and gave her that big Holden grin that the coeds said they loved. Just then the sky decided to spit on us. So much for grilling.

"Oh, all right. But if something is wrong..."

"I promise, I will let you know. You deserve that much."

I had a pretty good idea that when Amy wanted to throw a real tantrum, the earth would shake and the sky would open up wide. Something I could go without witnessing. The cool rain felt good on my bare chest and back and would soon feel too cold, so it was time to go. I told Amy that if she heard from Rachel or thought of anything that might be pertinent to call me. I was in the book. She then reminded me that I had her number and that I shouldn't be shy about calling with any news or if I wanted to talk more or knock the balls around some more. I assured her that I'd see her again. In what capacity, I told myself, I didn't have a clue. Some detective. We bid a wet farewell and sprinted toward our vehicles in opposite directions as the rain intensified. While I parked near the basketball courts, Amy had parked on the other side nearer the volleyball courts. Just a matter of taste, I guess. As I reached my Jeep, I noticed that I was the last vehicle parked in the area. The smart ones sniffed out the rain as I was sniffing out empty clues and wisely beat a hasty retreat. I was thankful to get out of the rain.

As soon as I closed myself in, the windows did their best impression of an English morning in the countryside and fogged up fast. I started it up and cranked the defroster and sat and thought while it worked its disappearing act. The clock read 4:03. I thought about how tired I felt. Not just from the physical activity, but from thinking about Rachel. A diversion tonight seemed like a great answer to both forms of weariness. I powered up my cell phone and dialed Maggie's number as the hills of clear windshield grew into mountains through the fog. Just as her answering machine kicked on with one of her silly messages, the driver's side window exploded and something moving like a catapulted boulder slammed into my left temple and rendered me unconscious.

## *Chapter 10*

I woke up at four thirty, covered in broken window glass and rain water, my head throbbing like the world's worst hangover and pissed off. A nap might have been nice, but not prescribed by someone else. The driving rain was now accompanied by slashes of nearby lightning and booming thunder. I found my cell phone on the passenger side floor. The connection was still open to Maggie's machine. I hung up and reached around for my dry shirt and felt a railroad spike being driven through my skull. Or at least what I imagined it would feel like. All my belongings were still in the Jeep, so it wasn't a robbery. The Cadillac Man. I'd bet my wine collection on it. Warning me to back off Rachel Allen's whereabouts. But who the hell was he, and how did he know I was poking my nose around? I had only spoken with three people since yesterday, and I didn't spot the Caddy until after I talked with Gary Howard. It led back to Rex Steinman or someone at the condo who traded information for who knows what.

I pulled my shirt on with great effort and sat for a minute in an effort to clear the cobwebs a little more. I instinctively scanned the park for movement, knowing full well that my attacker was long gone, sitting in front of a big screen TV watching professional wrestling with a bag of peanuts and a bunch of bananas. I needed to get home and down a handful of aspirin, call Maggie again and take a long hot shower. I also had to call my buddy Wade Reynolds to see if he'd trace the Caddy's plate for me. Things had certainly turned.

I was about to leave when I realized that whoever sent me into that not so long goodnight had been watching Amy and me talk. I found her number and punched it in my cell phone. Three rings and an answer. It was her voice, she sounded fine, so I just hung up. The sound in the phone hurt my head anyway. Luckily, I parked with the passenger side facing west, so the rain rattled against that side of my Jeep. I only took on residual water on the east side. I still had bits of busted glass in my lap, but I ignored them. I recalled how my father had kept a few classic English Fords in our yard when I was quite young. Somehow, a couple of windshields were shattered, and the fragments littered the inside of the cars. I would pick up the pieces and pretend they were diamonds, reflecting in the sunlight, and I had enough to be a millionaire. Now I squirmed as the remnants from my window weaseled their way under my bare thighs. Oh, how reality mutates the reverie of youth.

Five minutes later, I was home and my headache was worse. The weather stayed nasty as the thunderstorms cycled around the area. This was prime weather for some twister action. I always felt sorry for people who lived in trailer parks when Mother Nature acted this way. For some reason, trailer parks were tornado magnets. Come and get me. I'm helpless. I'm not rooted into a foundation, so blow me the hell all over the county. It's only my home. I wheeled into my garage and instantly reached into my glove box for my Glock. From this point on, my baby was going with me wherever I went. The shitter. The shower. The golf course. The tennis court. The bedroom. The grocery store. Normally, I felt secure when I returned to my home. Nice, quiet neighborhood. Country road for the most part, flanked mostly by a farm to the west and modest, older homes to the east. Now, I took nothing for granted. I had carefully looked for the black Caddy on my short drive home, just to be sure.

I entered through the back door as usual, wary of oddities in the familiar surroundings. Everything seemed fine upon my entrance, but I had to check the entire house before I could relax. I searched each room and found nothing. Thankfully. At least my home hadn't been violated like my face, which had swelled up nicely on the left side. I wasn't sure I wanted to look at myself in the mirror.

I returned to the kitchen, grabbed a beer and dumped a tray full of ice into a towel and stuck it on my face, then went to the bathroom for the pain reliever. Not that it would actually relieve the pain. More like dull it. But, anything that would help was welcome. I stripped off my clothes and hopped into the shower, my gun on the toilet tank, only a quick reach away. As I let the hot water beat on my body, I continued to hold the ice to my face and sipped my beer. Christ, what a sight I must have been. At least my aching head superseded the muscle pains from trying to keep up with a twenty-something on the tennis court. The steam filled my small bathroom, an eerie reminder of the fogged windows that preceded my assault. I stood under the spray for nearly half an hour, finished my beer and milked the last of the ice out of the towel before it melted into oblivion. I felt better. Not like the dashing guy I was, but better.

I toweled off, rubbed my hair for luck, threw on a pair of SU Brine lacrosse shorts and went to call Maggie. I got her damn machine again. Good thing that I won some cash in golf earlier, because this day was steadily declining.

"Hi, you've just reached the number you just dialed. We have better things to do right now because we have lives. Feel free to leave a message. We may return in a week and get back to you. Otherwise, call again sometime soon. Beep."

Maggie always said "we" on her incoming message to give the illusion of a man living there.

"Hey, Mags, it's H. Thought I'd..."

She picked up. "Hey, H. Hang on." I knew she was punching her pound button to cut off the machine.

"Screening calls again, huh? Too many male suitors harassing you?"

"More than you know."

"Must be after your money."

"Right." She laughed. "Just like you."

"I'd like to think that I was an exception. I appreciate your aesthetic qualities."

"There you go, using those big words again. Doesn't that hurt?"

If every other woman was a White Zinfandel, Maggie was a '61 Petrus. Of course, at the time, I was digging in my freezer

97

*Daniel Surdam*

for more ice.  That damn intuition that I didn't have and could have used in my line of work.  I had hunches, theories and wild guesses while blindfolded in the blackest of black, but intuition wasn't my bag.  Like this most recent event in my Jeep.  It was a hunch, not intuition, because I had seen the guy tailing me earlier.

"Only when I think real hard.  Which, fortunately, isn't too often."

"That's because you usually don't have to..."

"Well, thank you."  I reapplied the ice to my face and grabbed another beer from the refrigerator.  The storms had retreated for the moment, either plotting their next assault or deciding to take the rest of the night off.

"I meant that you're so incredibly intelligent that thinking comes easy to you."  There was a distinct playfulness in her voice.  A playfulness that came so naturally to her. But the attitudes ran the entire gamut, from silly to serious, sexy to steadfast, carefree to resolute and everything in between, around, near or whatever preposition one could dangle.

"You do flatter so.  You must want something."

"Hey, buddy, you called me, remember?"

"So I did."

I slipped on a pair of unlaced black Nike high tops and stepped out onto my back deck.  The rain water beaded up to my satisfaction.  I looked to the west and the break in the clouds hinted at clearing.  The smell of the fresh showers was strong in the air, conjuring memories of childhood and the agony felt while waiting for the storms to clear so I could run back outside and play again.  Now the agony came after the playing was through.  "Any plans for tonight?"  I crossed my fingers.

"Depends on the offer."

"The simple fact of being in my company would send ninety-nine percent of the female population swooning," I said.

"Perhaps I'm part of the one percent."

"I'll cook for you."

"Hmm.  What's on the menu?"

I absent-mindedly fiddled with the grill cover as I spoke. "T-bones, grilled to a perfect medium rare. Linguine tossed lightly in olive oil and garlic and steamed baby carrots."

"Tempting, but I need more. Good beef can only go so far." If I was capable, her tone would have made me giggle. She made any conversation an artform when she chose.

"Well, we can watch the Yankee game together." For most women, that would have been a strike against me, but not with Maggie. She loved baseball. She felt the game had calming qualities, when read between the lines, and the spitting, and the crotch grabbing, and the cursing at the umpires, and the beanballs, and the styling after a big fly, and the outrageous salaries. She did, however, appreciate the tight uniforms.

"There's still something missing," she offered.

"How about the opportunity to exchange a valuable commodity, wherein pleasure becomes the goal and ultimate sacrifice for one to the other? Huh? How's that?" I asked, hoping that when she saw my face she wouldn't allow her mothering mode to kick in.

"I'll bring the wine."

Her final response came quickly. Games always ended. And then started again at a later time.

She asked, "Would you prefer a fine Cabernet or a fashionable Merlot?"

"Mags, if you're bringin' the wine, it could be Mad Dog."

"Great. I happen to have a jug right here. See you in an hour or so?"

"Perfect."

After I hung up, I realized that I left my gun on the toilet. That boded well. If Mr. Cadillac came knocking, I'd have to ask him to excuse me while I visited the facility. He'd think it was to clean my soiled shorts upon the sight of him, but not quite. I instantly fetched it and set it on my kitchen counter where it was quickly and easily accessible. I grew tired of a wet towel pressing against my face, so I dumped the ice and tossed the towel in the washer. I wanted to call Wade Reynolds but decided that it could wait. I promised Maggie those t-bones, so I prepared them by rubbing minced garlic and black pepper into the nicely marbled meat and set them aside to briefly age before I introduced them to my grill. After reading about the carcinogens in the blackened parts of grilled meat, I had to adapt my grilling style to eliminate as much of the dark browning as possible. It really was a damn shame when you had to worry about how much you seared your meat when you cooked. I was certain that at some point, we'd all have to either become organic vegetarians or boil all meat if we chose to remain carnivores or say the hell with it, our forefathers cooked over open fires, so I'm going to do the same and take my chances with my burnt on the outside, yet medium rare on the inside steak. Seemed like the world wanted to focus on the negativity. Misery and their company and all that pernicious crap. I saw it. I felt it earlier today. Well, I say, "Deal with it and get over it."

I went back outside and uncovered my grill and positioned it for its cooking mode. The sun had actually made a return and sparked life into the countless drops of rain clinging to the blades of grass in my lawn. That reminded me that I'd have to cut it tomorrow, a chore that I actually found appealing. Few things beat the look and smell of a freshly cut lawn and the satisfaction that accompanied tending the grass that grew from the soil you could claim as your own. It was your piece of the earth, your stake to claim, as insignificant as it may seem in the grand scheme of things. In the tree tops beyond my back yard, the black birds were gathering, before they swooped down on the unsuspecting critters in the grass, presumably safe in their world. But you can't avoid the cycle of nature. The strong feed on the weak and hope like hell something or someone else doesn't come along stronger than they are, and if that's the case, they just hire someone until the feeding frenzy gets out of control. It was supposed to be about checks and balances, not about the balance in the checkbook. Hell, what did I know? In my little corner of the round world for the evening, I foresaw steaks, a fine red wine, baseball and the best company a man could ask for. The pain in my head and face had pretty much scrammed. A lot of it, I felt, was a state of mind. Goes along with the "get over it" philosophy. Too many people felt they were the victims or embellished their suffering to educe sympathy when they needed to stand on their own two feet, accept responsibility for their actions and make the best out of their lives. Admittedly, there were monsters out there who made a practice out of preying on others. That goes back to the strong and stronger deal. If they felt it necessary to act like parasitic power mongrels, then they were scared shitless of where they stood on the cosmic food chain. And that goes back to the standing on your own two feet business and accepting the onus for your own actions. Like everything in life, even my cranial meanderings swirled about in a vicious circle, not unlike a funnel cloud.

I could feel the heat making a hard charge like Tiger Woods on Sunday's back nine of a major. The intense storms that moved through cooled things for awhile, but that seemed a temporary solution to the high temperatures. It was fine with me, because I had one of my brilliant hunches that sleep would cradle me swiftly tonight. I didn't have any air conditioning in my house. Only a few well-intentioned fans that soothed me more by the calming sound of their steady whoosh of air than the breeze they created. Hazy, gray skies that looked more like a watercolor than reality dominated the western horizon. More storms were on the way.

I didn't have to worry about preparing any other parts of the meal since the baby carrots were purchased in the ready condition and boiling linguine wasn't rocket science, so I decided to plug in and jam on my Gibson Les Paul Custom for twenty minutes or so. Enough to loosen the fingers and purge some of the anger I knew was roiling from the sucker punch I took earlier. Maggie didn't deserve to catch any wind of that. The guy who decked me did. I set my Fender Bullet amp on the kitchen counter, took my Les Paul out of its custom hardshell case and powered up. I cranked the gain and drive on the amp that produced a metal shred sound that I found hid a lot of

101

mistakes when playing. It was a cool sound and forgiving. I jumped right into a Holden Grace original entitled "Ode to a Postal Worker" that consisted of crunchy fifth chords and, I supposed, some disturbing lyrics. The volume was loud. I knew the neighborhood could hear. The sweat beaded lightly on my bare skin. And with each chord, I felt better. I moved onto another dark original, "Ownership," about a sexually frustrated arson who kills some bums sleeping in the buildings he torches and eventually takes ownership for their lives. I always believed it was much easier to write dark songs than uplifting ones, although I had some of both in my repertoire. When I played, I felt separate from every other part of me -- the hard-assed private detective, the athlete, the painter, the homeowner, the neighbor, the friend -- I was a musician playing for the sake of me. Each chord, each note, each line, each word was a catharsis not unlike attacking the heavybag, yet so different. I had read a book once called *Zen Guitar* by Philip Toshio Sudo, a man of Japanese descent who honed his craft in New York City and applied the philosophies of Zen with playing the axe in a text that taught one to achieve harmony when picking up his or her guitar. The read was interesting. The points relevant. Whenever I picked up one of my guitars, I had a purpose, whether it was as simple as playing the perfect sounding chord or running through a song and feeling good about it. Purpose was key, and as a self-taught player, it meant a lot.

I had totally lost track of time and was belting out a Bush song when I turned and saw Maggie standing in the doorway holding a brown paper bag in one hand an overnight bag in the other and wearing the most genuine and captivating smile ever to grace my presence. She wore a pair of khaki shorts that covered too much of her tanned and firm thighs, at least in my opinion; a sleeveless white top that buttoned down the middle and a pair of sandals. Her tanned face was etched with smile lines. Maggie stood about five-seven and probably tipped the scales around one thirty. I never asked. Had no reason. She wasn't beautiful in the classic sense of breathtaking looks, but she resonated a pure beauty she could claim as her own. She never wore make-up and didn't have to. Her long brown, extremely curly dark chestnut hair was pulled back into a ponytail, a popular style in the summer heat. Her deep brown eyes nearly matched her hair. Her teeth were straight and white and very prominent when she smiled. She had a small nose and a small mouth and small ears. Everything about her had symmetry. A near perfectness that had to break dozens of hearts, and probably mine some day. I stopped mid-chorus and cocked my head.

"So, how long have you been there?" I asked.

"Not long enough," she said. She beamed. "I love watching you play. You're like... a different person. And you're good."

I set the guitar down and noticed that the perspiration had coated my body. Not a nasty, smelly sweat, but a clean, heat-induced lather that made my body glisten.

"Oh, you don't have to stop," she said.

"Sure I do. I want to leave you wanting more."

She set the bag with the wine in it on the counter nearest the door, dropped her bag, popped off her sandals and came to greet me with a vigorous hug. She didn't seem to mind my moisture. I hugged her back hard. I knew she had noticed my face when she got close, but she stayed silent. The strength of her embrace supported my suspicions. I broke the bond and saw the look of concern in her eyes.

"Jesus, Holden, what happened?" She brushed a delicate hand to my bruised face.

"Tough tennis match."

Her stare burrowed into me. She could be so intense. It was an aura she had and projected when needed. I believed that every person possessed an aura that helped define who they were, and that amorphous quality could be read through bullshit emotional or false facade fronts. Some of the meekest people I've met have frightened me with their crackling bad-ass auras that I was sure they never suspected they had. Maggie exuded a strong I've-had-to-battle-through-life-to-get-where-I-am-so-don't-fuck-with-me aura. She was a person to be taken seriously. My aura simply said, "Don't fuck with me." My aura believed in simplification.

"Don't bullshit me," she said.

"Rough golf game?"

She put her hands on her perfect hips and shifted her weight in a pose that was meant to show disdain for my answers, but all it did was elicit a stare of lust from me. The way her thigh pulled taut against the fabric of her shorts. The intensity in her face. She recognized the look.

"Listen, Mister, you'd better start talking or it's strictly dinner and a ballgame tonight. Now, what the hell happened to you?"

"Well, you know I've never met a fist I didn't like. This fist felt the same way about my face."

I stepped past Maggie and into the kitchen and pulled the bottles of wine out of the bag. A '96 Duckpond Merlot and a '95 Sterling Cabernet Sauvignon. Both worthy choices without shelling out too much cash.

"Nice choices," I told her.

"Don't change gears on me, Holden." Her tone softened.

I looked at her. "Okay. It has to do with a case I'm working on. This really is no big deal." I pointed to my face. "What's worse is that Mick Allen's sister's vanished. I'm in the process of looking for her."

"Jesus, poor Mick."

"And poor Rachel. Something stinks about it, and I've only been poking around a couple of days."

Maggie approached and slid her arms around me and rested her head against my chest.

"Tell you what," I said. "Let me get the steaks goin'. We'll grab a beer, sit down on the deck and I'll bounce all this shit off you. Sound like a plan?"

She looked at me and smiled the smile. "You're eloquence has won me over. But you should put ice on that handsome face of yours."

"It's beyond the swell mode now. Besides, I think it makes me look very distinguished."

I tilted my chin skyward in a mock pose. Maggie swatted me on the ass and backed away.

"Let me see your beef, big boy," she demanded as she headed toward the refrigerator and not the bedroom.

I pulled out two Rolling Rocks, popped the caps and hauled them, myself, the steaks and cooking utensil out to the back deck with Maggie. I set the t-bones down on the wooden rack of the grill and fired it up, then sat down in a low beach chair next to Maggie and stared out at the gently swaying tree tops in the distance where the black birds remained, their bellies full and singing their awful screeching arias.

"So what about this case?" Maggie finally asked after a minute or so of listening to the caw of the wild.

I told her about Mick's appearance at my office Friday morning and his insistence that Rachel had killed herself. I filled her in on the lunch, the condo experience, the golf game with Gary Howard, the incident with the Cadillac Man after golf, the tennis match, the sudden trip to unconsciousness that I took not long after the tennis match and my hunch that the Cadillac Man was the guy who put me out.

"But why would this guy attack you?"

"He's involved. Somehow. Some way. It's like he's warning me. He didn't show until Saturday after golf. Then he follows me home, cruises by real slow and a few hours later, I'm laid out in my Jeep with one helluva a strong punch. I know big money's involved here. Rachel had a thing with an older, rich guy. Carl Hendrix, who made an offer for the sporting goods store that Rachel had a stake in, was the last guy she called before she disappeared. He's older. Rich. He's someone I need to talk with. Cadillac Man's nothing but someone's hired goon. And he seems to have a thing about throwing his punches when his victims aren't expecting them. I got the plate number, and I'm gonna call Wade to see if he can trace it."

The flames were leaping high under the grill cover, feeding on the residue of grease like someone was squirting gas on the blaze. I got up, lifted the cover and scraped more of the charred ghosts of past barbecues off the metal racks, holding my breath as the smoke swirled about my head. The lava rocks were catching their ready-to-cook glow. I cranked the burner switch down to low, closed the cover and sat back down.

"I've only talked with Mick, Rex Steinman, Gary Howard and Amy Simpson about Rachel, and I've done my damnest to avoid telling the truth to the last three without them thinking I was lying through my teeth. Obviously, someone knows I'm on this. Someone's not happy I'm on this."

"So you'll keep pushing?"

"Like an outside in swing."

"God, you and your golf references."

"Hey, you understood what I meant."

"Only because you taught me by example."

An outside in swing in golf means you pull the clubhead to the outside on the swing path with your takeaway, and when you strike back through the ball, you cut back inside, giving a spin to the ball that sends it bending to the right after trajectory. That's a push. It's not a beneficial swing.

"So, what're you going to do next? This Cadillac Man friend of yours seems like some trouble," Rachel said.

"I'm not even gonna worry about him. He's a strong arm chump, well down on the list of significant people in this one. If he shows again, I'll handle it."

"Like today?" There was a look of concern on Maggie's face.

"I'll give him the first lucky one, but beyond that, he'll wish he was shakin' down geriatrics for protection money in Boca Raton."

"Hey, my mom lives there."

"And a lovely woman she is." The lava rocks were ready to receive their sacrifice, so I got up and dropped the steaks on the grill. The sizzle was loud. I turned back to Maggie, the tongs still in my left hand as the smoke curled up around me. "Okay. Seriously. I have to pay a visit to a Dr. Amanda Russell, an OB/GYN in Syracuse. It seems that Rachel had an appointment with her a couple of weeks ago. It might've been one of your routine annual visits that I know how much you dread, but right now, it's too coincidental. I also have to have a chat with Carl Hendrix, like I said. And Curtis Granby, who owns the condo where Rachel lives. I might stop in and see Bennie at Morris's to see if he knows anything..."

"Who the hell is Bennie?"

I drained the remainder of my beer. Maggie still had half a bottle left.

"Bennie? He's the local dope dealer, and everyone knows it. But, he's left intact, because he keeps all the noveau riche blue bloods knee deep in nose candy. He pokes his nose in all the dirt that's happening. Mostly because he deals with the scum that's involved. He just might know a thing or two, if he's coherent enough. Besides that, I don't have much else. I might make a trip to Burlington if nothing else pans out."

I turned the steaks and closed the grill lid.

"There was also a weekend Rachel spent at the Sagamore on Lake George. She had that highlighted in her appointment book. My money says she spent it with her Daddy Warbucks. Ya know, I gotta start writing this stuff down."

"Might be a good idea. You can only hold so much in that head of yours," Maggie said.

"I'll have to make a trip up there. Flash Rachel's picture around."

"So, what do you think? About all of this?"

"I find Daddy Warbucks, I find Rachel. She didn't kill herself. I'm just hoping that she didn't get in over her head with something or someone. She liked the good life, and it costs money. I hope it didn't cost her her life." A short silence fell between us. "Okay, enough shop talk. I'd better get the linguine and carrots goin'. Ready for another?" I held up my empty bottle of Rolling Rock.

"I'm all set."

I headed toward the back door. "How can you do that?"

"Do what?" She kept staring out toward the trees as she spoke.

"Nurse what was once an icy cold beer until it becomes as warm as your heart."

Maggie turned to me and said matter-of-factly, "That's why."

When the steaks were perfect, I moved them from the lower cooking rack to the warming rack and turned off the grill and finished preparing the rest of the meal. I opened the bottle of Merlot, took a whiff of the cork and set it aside to breathe for awhile. I pulled two plates out of one cupboard and two red wine glasses that read "Uncork New York" on them from another and set them on the counter. I dug out two steak knives and two forks from the silverware drawer and set them on the plates. It was time to eat.

We sat at my oak dining table, making quick work of the meal and the first bottle of wine. Before we had gone through the Merlot, I uncorked the Cabernet so it would be ready when we were. Maggie and I were both quick eaters. She came from a large family and learned that if you wanted seconds, you'd better gulp down your first serving as fast as possible. For me, I just liked to eat fast. I enjoyed a good meal. I enjoyed food in general. I just didn't like taking too much time in enjoying it. I had thrown on a shirt before we sat down for our meal in an attempt to discourage Maggie from jumping my bones instead of the one on her plate. She reassured me that I was safe. The dark clouds had slowly rolled in while we ate, but no lightning flashes or booms of thunder accompanied them, yet. The night was still young. We avoiding talking about the case, although I was sure that Maggie still had a multitude of questions, ones that might even help give me some insight, but she kept them to herself for now. She would find the right time and the right place to bring them up. I didn't mind. I appreciated her objective view and where it could lead me. We cleaned our plates, gnawed our bones and drained the last of the wine and sat in silence for a short time. We did that often, just let the silence linger between us. There was no reason to constantly bombard each other with conversation for the mere sake of filling the empty spaces that make most others as uncomfortable as hell. It was a little after eight, and the Yankees game had started, so Maggie flicked on the television as I cleared the dishes, rinsed them and stashed them in the dishwasher. I grabbed two beers from the refrigerator and joined her on the sofa. A commercial for a money lending institution was on.

"Any score?" I asked as I handed Maggie her beer and sat down next to her, nearer the TV.

"Thanks," she said as she took the beer. "Mets 2, Yanks 1. Goin' to the bottom of the third."

The commercials ended and the game came back on. The Yankees had the top of their lineup coming up. Their was a slight drizzle coming down at the stadium and the crowd wasn't capacity, which was a damn shame when a city of eight million people couldn't fill one of the greatest stadiums in the world, especially when the team was fighting for first place and playing their cross town National League brethren the Mets. As I settled in, the day caught up with me. I tried to concentrate on the game, but found myself staring at the back of my eyelids more than the action. I made it through the sixth inning with the Yankees up 4-3, but that was it. Sleep swept me away and any romantic notions I held earlier.

## *Chapter 11*

I was dreaming about being chased by giant cars that slammed into each other as they narrowly missed squashing me when the phone rang. Initially, I was disoriented and concentrated on where the hell I was. The last thing I knew, I was watching the Yankees game on the sofa, and that's where I still was, with a blanket over me. Outside, the lightning cracked repeatedly, joined by bone-jarring rumbles of thunder. The phone rang on.

Maggie's voice called down from the back bedroom, "Holden, should I get that?"

I was slowly coming to, a difficult task since I was so deeply buried in sleep.

"No, I got it. Go back to sleep."

I stood up and snatched the phone off the end table in the living room. The storm outside was right on top of us. I thought of how I was always told as a youngster to avoid talking on the telephone during an electrical storm. I actually listened, because I never liked the idea of toying with one of Mother Nature's mean streaks. Lightning worried me a lot more than someone like the Cadillac Man.

"Hello?"

There was a brief silence on the other end of the line that encouraged me to hang up and join Maggie in the bedroom where I belonged, but before I could end the connection, a raspy voice reached out to me.

"H, I need some help, buddy."

The voice was strained but recognizable. It was Mick. Damn it.

"Mick, what happened?"

Maggie had gotten up, wearing nothing but her panties and a flimsy light blue thin-strapped t-shirt with a little bow in the middle of the neckline. One of my favorite outfits on any other occasion. She heard the concern in my voice immediately and came up close to me. She turned on the halogen lamp near the end table until just a soft glow filled the room.

"I got my ass kicked, buddy."

"Where the hell are you?"

"Home, man. They busted in. Three of 'em. Worked me over good, too. Said I wasn't as pretty as my sister. If I wasn't then, I'm sure not now." He tried to laugh but failed.

It sounded as if every word he spoke hurt like hell.

"Son of a bitch." I was reprimanding myself for not thinking the Cadillac Man would go after Mick next. Maggie held onto my arm. "Mick, just hang on. I'll be there in ten minutes. I'll call you from the car."

I hung up the phone without waiting for his response. I looked at the clock on the VCR, and it read two-thirty five. They must have been patient bastards to wait that late into the night before making their move. Mick lived in a new house on the outskirts of Camillus, one of the many suburbs of Syracuse, and it was about a fifteen-minute drive on any normal occasion. I'd easily make it in ten tonight.

I didn't need to worry about throwing on any clothes since I crashed in my shorts and t-shirt, so I could head out right away. The only accessory I needed was my Glock, loaded, with one in the chamber.

As I broke Maggie's light grip and headed to the kitchen to grab my keys and my gun, which I had tucked in a drawer earlier, she asked, "Holden, what's wrong? What's happened?"

"Mick's been beaten up by three guys. He's at home."

"Jesus Christ. Holden, this is getting scary."

"I know."

She grabbed onto my arm again. This time with more authority. "I want to go with you."

I turned and faced her. "Mags. This is the nasty part of the business you don't need to see. I don't know where the hell these three goons are. They might be waiting for me to show, using Mick as bait. Waiting to teach me another lesson."

"Or they might be waiting for you to leave here. I don't want to be alone. They seem to know a helluva lot about where you go and what you do. I'm going. I'll be ready in two minutes."

I couldn't argue with her. There was no way I'd leave her alone or send her to drive home alone, possibly easy pickings for a tail and an attack. Outside, the storm raged on. The brilliant flashes of energy easily penetrated the closed miniblinds like a strobe light gone haywire. Rumbles of thunder shook the air.

"Okay. But Mick's not gonna look good. I guarantee we'll have to get him to a hospital. If he had three guys workin' him over, he's probably in bad shape. Depends how much damage they wanted to do. But I'll have to talk to him first."

As Maggie went back to the bedroom to change, I pulled a container of flour out of the cupboard and dug up some wooden matches from a drawer. If we were going to be gone for awhile, I wanted to make sure that I marked my territory, in case these animals wanted to lie in wait when we came back or had plans of looking for me since we would leave the Jeep behind, and they might try to put two and two together without smoke steaming from their ears and assume if the Jeep was in the garage, I was home. Even though I knew they wouldn't be so stupid to attempt a break-in through the front door, which was only about thirty feet from the road and was going to be well lit by an outside light, as well as pretty well illuminated by a nearby streetlight, I tucked one of the wooden matches, broken off halfway down below the head, underneath the lowest hinge on the inside. I made sure I placed it directly under the hinge, in case they were professional enough to look for the little warning sign and attempt to stick it back in the door. I flipped on the outside light and went to the back door and waited for Maggie.

She returned from the bedroom in her shorts and my Sorrentino's Gym sweatshirt that was one of my favorites. She seemed incredibly under control for the circumstances. She knew I was dealing with some badass people. She knew that Mick would look like he was dragged behind a car on his face for a few blocks on chewed-up asphalt. She knew the attackers might be hanging out looking for me. She knew she wanted to be there. Confidence. No mulling over a situation, wavering from one decision to the next, weighing out every minute detail. In times of crises, an individual has to act on his or her instincts and trust them. I did it every day, or at least every day I had a client. Maggie didn't face so much of this dilemma as a member of a small, yet very successful, public relations company in nearby Auburn. Her gig was all about planning. Making sure that everything is just so for the uptight clients who feel that they are the top rung of the ladder, no matter how many rungs there are. Yet, she still had the mental acuity to handle a given situation that rears its ugly head from the standards of convention and demands to take on a destructive life of its own for those unprepared. Life is about dancing with the unexpected and you being the lead.

She saw me holding the flour and asked, "What's that for?"

"I'm going to set a little trap, in case these assholes want to sneak in here while we're gone. I'll spread a thin layer of flour on the floor as we leave. If they get in, they'll step in the flour and leave tracks."

It meant some cleanup duty for me later, but well worth the effort if it could save me from catching a slug in the chest. Yeah, a small trade off.

"What if they come in the front?" she asked, ever the thinker.

"Taken care of with one of these fine crime fighting devices." I held up a wooden match. "Besides, too risky for them."

"But what if they see they've stepped in the flour, then just smooth it back out?"

"Well, number one, I'm taking the flour with us. Number two, when I pour it down, it'll fall naturally. Nice and soft. If they try to cover their tracks, it'll be obvious. And number three, more of these as a backup." I held up more matches.

"I love how you think," she said.

I left the outside light near the back door off and scattered the flour carefully as we exited.  I also pinched one broken match below the lowest hinge on the outside of the interior door and another just below the upper hinge of the full-view screen door.  Not quite as good as a high-tech security system, but effective nonetheless.

I grabbed my cell phone out of the Jeep, and we jumped in Maggie's Honda Accord.  I determined that it would be better to take her car since she had a driver's side window and the rain was still coming down substantially.  I drove.  Maggie called Mick on the cell phone to keep him alert as we drove.  I drove too fast down the dangerous Route 321 as we headed east toward Camillus, but the Accord handled better than my Grand Cherokee would have.  I hoped that no State Boys were sitting on a tractor path with their radar guns aimed at me.  Fortunately, there was no other traffic and the raging storms quickly cleared out, which made visibility much better.  I hung a right onto Route 5 East and put the peddle down.  I could hear Maggie talking with Mick, keeping him from that gray area of unconsciousness that I spent some time in earlier.  It's not a fun place to be.  I kept my speed around seventy as I slammed the Accord into fifth gear and sped toward downtown Camillus, which wasn't much but a few bars, the famous Camillus Cutlery plant, a post office and a decent restaurant.  As I headed down the hill into the heart of the village, I had to downshift quickly and ride the brakes considerably.  It was a steep hill.  A real bitch in the winter.  I cruised through downtown, caught green at the only red, yellow and green traffic light then hung a right at the flashing yellow light where Milton Avenue split with West Genesee Street.  Another quick right as the road bent to the left and I was on Munro Road that led to Mick's housing development.  All the houses were new, built within the last few years.  The lots were all the same size and most of the houses looked the same, the kind of cookie-cutter neighborhood I could never deal with from day to day.  Great for kids growing up with all the professional families and their two and a half kids to play with, but a little too patterned for my taste. Reminded me of the *Stepford Wives.* It's not that it wasn't a nice neighborhood, because it was, with one hundred fifty thousand dollar, three- or four-bedroom homes with two and a half baths, two-car garages, paved driveways, enough room for a pool in the back and a chicken in every pot. Upper middle-class suburbia. Away from the city. Away from the violence. But it never completely works that way. The quiet cul-de-sacs invited crime just as much as the low-rent urban housing. Sometimes it just took the crooks longer to find them.

I turned right onto Whispering Pines Way, one of the neighborhood's cul-de-sacs that Mick lived on. I looked around. I didn't see too many pines. Mick's house was the third on the left, a two-story colonial with white vinyl siding and maroon shutters. He bought the place new three years ago, and I had helped him move in. He had the standard neighborhood landscaping out front with various bushes, shrubs, flowers and small trees surrounded by cedar chips. His lawn was well tended, and a brick walkway led to a side door into the garage to the left and the front door. The fancy brass lamp outside the front door was lit up, as well as most of the downstairs lights, from what I could figure. As I turned into his driveway, Maggie told him that we were there, and I saw him poke his face out around the blinds in his living room. I looked at the clock in the car. Two-fifty. I wasn't tired now at all. The adrenaline that was pumping from the drive received an extra jolt when I thought of how busted up Mick must have been and the possibility that the lowlifes who did the damage could still be lurking around somewhere, maybe hiding in some whispering pines, commenting on what a lovely neighborhood this was as they compared notes on which part of Mick's body that they dented.

Maggie hung up the phone and we hurried to the front door. I had my gun out and surveyed the bushes, neighbors' yards and the street as we moved, just waiting for the slightest incongruity with the natural surroundings to tip me off. I didn't want to have a firefight right outside Mick's house at three in the morning, especially with Maggie in the line of fire, so I was relieved that all was well. Or as least appeared to be for the moment. As soon as we reached the maroon front door that tastefully matched the shutters, Mick opened up and I slid past Maggie, so I could get a look at him first. I kept my gun poised as a precaution.

Once inside the door, the house opened up to the right into what Mick used as a study complete with oak desk, matching oak bookcases, a home computer and a couple of expensive arm chairs; straight with a short hall that ran to the kitchen in the back of the house; and to the left into the living room that ran the depth of the house. Just to the left of the front door, a staircase ran up to the three bedrooms and full bath upstairs. I had noticed that the front door lacked a forced entry. My guess was they either came through the back door near the kitchen or the garage. In a neighborhood like Mick's, you didn't anticipate that violence would come calling, and if it did, you'd never think that you'd be the one singled out. Unfortunately for Mick, it wasn't a random roll of the dice; he was the target, and he wasn't prepared. Wait until the Neighborhood Watch heard about this one. They'd be electing new officers and demanding around the clock surveillance by police cruisers instead of safe guarding their homes better.

Mick led us into the living room. Wall to wall beige carpeting. Television and VCR in an entertainment center. Sofa. Coffee table with a bottle of Courvoisier and half full brandy snifter that joined the usual magazines. Recliner. End table with framed photos of his late parents, Rachel and a few of me and him, along with other shots. Contemporary art and photos on the walls. He was a mess. His face was swollen, and it had begun to bruise already, disguising his usual handsome looks. He could barely open his eyes. His nose, thankfully, didn't look broken, but did have dried, crusted blood trailing from both nostrils. Both lips were split and twice the size as normal. I hoped he kept all his teeth and that his jaw wasn't broken. I wondered how he was able to down the brandy. His hair was matted with his own blood. I could tell that he had cleaned up numerous cuts around his eyes, but that didn't completely stop all the bleeding. He was hunched over, like a man twice his age, holding his ribs gingerly. Odds were he could count on a few busted ones, cracked at the least. His hands were also bloodied, probably from fighting back as much as possible and from absorbing the blows from six fists and six feet. His arms were certain to bruise, along with his legs and pretty much his whole body. When three guys set out to mess you up, and they know what they're doing, which by the look of Mick, they did, then there's not a spot on your body they missed. He was wearing a terrycloth robe, belted at the waist. He tried to smile, but I knew it hurt too much. Behind me, I heard Maggie gasp.

"Thanks for comin', buddy."

The words were more from the result of forced air than actual speaking. Christ, even his windpipe had to hurt. He retreated to his expensive cream-colored sofa and lowered himself down with great effort and reached for his glass of brandy.

"You don't mind if I sit, do you?" he asked.

Always the good host. He hoisted the liquid to his mouth and winced as he gulped down about an ounce, then set the snifter back on its coaster.

"Oh my God, Mick," Maggie said as she walked up to him and gently took one of his banged up hands.

"Oh, it's not that bad. Still have all my teeth. They might be loose, but they're there."

Maggie looked hard at me. "Holden, we've got to get him to a hospital."

"I know, but I gotta talk to him first." I finally lowered my gun.

She let go of Mick's hand. "Can't you do that on the way? Look at him, Holden. He needs a doctor. Now."

"Listen, Maggie. I warned you about this. About how Mick would look. And I also said I needed to talk to him. Trust me on this, okay?"

Maggie turned to Mick with one of her most impressive looks of self-defiance and simply said his name. "Mick?"

With that one word, she was imploring Mick to agree to go to the hospital immediately and not listen to a single word that I had to say. This was one of the few times that look would lose.

"Tell ya the truth, Maggie, I'd rather not even go. I'll heal." Stubborn, like me. We could be brothers.

"You could have internal injuries. Maybe a concussion. You need to be stitched up at the least," she urged. She turned back to me, and I gave the famous guy shrug of the shoulder move. "Jesus Christ. Sometimes I just don't get it." She was not happy.

I said, "Sometimes, Mags, you're not supposed to."

She sat down next to Mick and took a sip of his brandy, then said, "Well, go ahead and talk, so we can get him taken care of."

I nudged the blinds back a bit to scan the front. Nothing. No thugs clad in black storming the house. Just a lot of wet grass and asphalt and dark houses with mom, dad and the kids snug in their beds dreaming of a Sunday breakfast of pancakes and the New York Times. I wished I was curled up with Maggie right now, naked with the sheets kicked off and dreaming about something a hell of a lot more pleasant than the reality in front of me. Well, alas, poor Mick, I knew him Holden, and all that heaven and earth, to be or not to be, perchance to dream symbolic rhetoric. When I was convinced the scarce pines had nothing to whisper about sweet Ophelia, I turned back to Mick and Maggie.

"Tell me about it, buddy." No sugar coating. No kiss on the forehead. Just the facts.

"I was home all night. Worked a little. Watched the tube for awhile. Went to bed around one or so." He took his time speaking. I didn't mind. "Next thing I know, three guys are standing over me in black masks. I knew I was fucked."

119

"What made you wake up?"

"One of the guys was sayin' 'Hey, asshole' in my ear. Swear to God. Thought I was dreamin'."

He knocked back some more brandy and filled the glass.

"Then what?" I asked. I walked over to the recliner and sat down on the edge of the chair.

"They said they had a message for me. So, I pop the guy leaning over me in the face and tried to roll away from the other two. Guess I didn't roll fast enough. They grabbed me and threw me up against the wall. Pinned me there and waited for the guy I hit to come over. He stepped close and said 'You may be pretty, but not as pretty as your sister, Rachel.'"

"He used her name? You're sure?" I asked.

"Oh yeah. I'll never forget that moment. His breath stunk. He had cold, blue eyes and the thickest goddamn neck I ever saw. Wide upper body. Six-feet, two-thirty-five, maybe. So, I'm standin' there in my boxers, my mind overloading, and he starts poundin' me. I noticed they all wore gloves. Didn't want to hurt their knuckles when my chin kept gettin' in the way, I guess. After the one guy worked on me for awhile, he let the other two get their licks. They took their turns goin' from my head to my body. A few times, I was ready to pass out, but old Blue Eyes wouldn't let it happen. He wanted me conscious for as long as possible. Said I'd get the message better that way. I finally slumped to the floor and they kicked me a few times. I tried to block them, but that didn't stop shit."

Maggie sat in silence. A serious look on her face as Mick recounted the incident. That type of behavior first hand probably shocked her some. Violence waits in every life, but not often does it rear its gruesome head so vividly and ugly.

"What about the other two? It sounds like they were following Blue Eyes' lead."

"Yeah. They didn't make a move without his approval. One of the guys was big, too. Bigger than Blue Eyes, but not as solid, ya know? And the other was built like me."

"After you fell to the floor, what happened?"

"Like I said, they kicked me a few times, then just left."

"You see them leave?"

"Na. I could barely move. I was lucky to stay conscious. I didn't even hear a car start."

"They probably parked in a neighbor's driveway, then walked over and busted in."

I got up and checked the rear sliding glass door. Sure enough, that was their point of entry. There was still duct tape on the glass where they used it to muffle the sound when they busted it.

"I thought you were getting a security system." I said as I inspected the floor around the break-in.

"I was gonna, but look at this neighborhood, H. Didn't think I'd need it. Thought I could take care of myself. Besides, I have my gun."

"Probably just as well you didn't get your hands on it tonight."

Maggie finally spoke up. "Does everybody carry a weapon these days?"

I answered her. "Unfortunately, it's the sign of the times." The intruders didn't leave a damn shred of evidence at the door, so I returned to the living room. "They take anything, did they?"

"Just my dignity and peace of mind."

"Mick, there were three of them. They surprised you in your sleep," Maggie said, very aware of the fragile male ego.

"Still..."

"Still nothin', buddy. These guys were good. Not amateurs," I said.

"You mean professional thugs? Sent to my house in the middle of the night to deliver a message that has to do with Rachel? What the fuck is goin' on, H?"

Maggie looked over at me. Mick worked on more brandy. It looked as if his face was turning a darker shade of bruise as we sat there. I wasn't happy. First, the cowardly sneak attack on me. That pissed me off. But this? For three guys to jump Mick in his quiet Beaver Cleaver neighborhood, in his own house, in

121

his own goddamn bedroom as visions of sugarplums danced in his head, really flipped my switch. And then say some smartass comment about his sister. Cowardice. Hiding behind something. Doing someone else's dirty work. Making a tidy sum of greenbacks from some weasel who could afford to pay for goons like this. Someone with a licorice stick for a backbone whose idea of a confrontation was facing his recreant image in the mirror every morning. Mick deserved to hear the truth, or at least the suspicions I had concerning what the truth may actually be, about Rachel's disappearance. It was evident they wanted him to tell me to back off the case. They wouldn't go after me yet. They didn't want a full-scale encounter with someone who could play their games. They were hopeful that this exercise in knuckle dragging and knuckle cracking would suffice. Big mistake. And I knew that Mick would insist that I push on until I dug up the answers, whether we liked them or not.

I said, "Tell ya what, I'll tell you in the car. Let's get you stitched up. We'll take your MB and Maggie will follow in her car."

I heard a sigh heave ever so slightly from Maggie, then she asked, "Where we taking him?"

"Community."

I helped Mick get into some clothes, and it was going on four in the morning when I loaded him into the passenger side of his Mercedes. The storms had cleared out entirely, and the sky was mesmerizing, filled with blinking stars until infinity or whatever lay out there beyond any understanding. When I tried to put the universe into a concrete perspective, my brain literally overloaded and wanted to shut down. It was one helluva phenomenon. Almost scary. Community General Hospital was about ten minutes away, on the southwest outskirts of Syracuse, in Onondaga Hill, overlooking the city and the valley south of the city. We headed north on Munro until it intersected with Howlett Hill Road, where Tuscarora Golf Club was located, of which Mick was a member and where I had played a few times as his guest. Right now, it was just a quiet stretch of green. I turned left on Howlett Hill, checking the rear view mirror to make sure Maggie was still behind us and no one else. All was okay. Howlett Hill Road runs into Route 173, which in turn intersects with Route 175 East in the heart of Onondaga Hill. From there, the hospital was less than a minute away. As I drove, I told Mick everything. He seemed surprised that so much occurred in the short span of thirty-six hours and slightly upset that I hadn't returned his call to fill him in and possibly warn him. I told him that I honestly didn't think he was in any danger. We were nearly to the hospital.

"So, what's next?" Mick asked.

He was hanging in there pretty well considering he was recently three guys' punching bag and had knocked back a good amount of brandy. The pain helped him stay awake. His desire to know more kept him alert.

"Well, I think Old Blue Eyes is definitely the Cadillac Man. I'm gonna track him down. Start from there. He can obviously lead me to the money man and hopefully Rachel. I still need to talk with Hendrix and Dr. Russell and find out who the hell tipped my hand."

Mick looked at me. His eyes, through the swelling, held a combination of fire and sorrow. "Think she's dead, H?"

"I honestly don't know, buddy. Remember, it seems she left her condo alone. No body's turned up. I keep digging, and we keep hoping. It's not a lot, I know, but this thing is coming together."

"She didn't kill herself."

"No. No way."

I wheeled up to the emergency room entrance with Maggie right on my tail. We parked and guided Mick inside. I always hated hospitals. I think most people do. They're a reminder of sickness and death more than a hope for recovery and wellness. This particular emergency room was quiet. It didn't look like a television show with action in every corner. Just an ordinary, if not unpleasant, place to be. We walked with Mick to the nurse behind the check-in desk, a black woman in her early forties who

looked a little like a younger Della Reese, decked out in the traditional looking white uniform. She looked like she swallowed a bad clam when she saw Mick's face. Her tag read "JUDITH LECLAIR."

"I bet you need some help," she said, surprisingly friendly.

Mick said, "I seem to've had an allergic reaction to somebody else's fists." Amazing that he could still have a sense of humor.

"Well, we'll see if we can't remedy that for you." She handed him a clipboard with a standard ER form. "I'll have a doctor out here in no time. Don't you worry." And she winked at him.

As she was reaching for the phone, I said, "Excuse me, Judith?"

"Yes?"

"When you wake the doctor from his nap, tell him God called earlier about his golf game and he missed it."

She grinned. "You are a devilish one, aren't you?"

"And I hide my horns well."

"I bet you do."

She picked up the phone and paged a doctor. Maggie was busy helping Mick with the form. I liked Judith LeClair, so I decided to honor her with more of my well-honed conversational skills.

"So, where's your Canadian accent, eh? With a name like LeClair, you should be a hockey coach."

"It's like this. On my way down from the Great White North, I passed through Queens, and hallelujah, I lost the accent. I think some boys from the hood stole it, but I couldn't press charges. They were just babies. Hockey coach. You are somethin'."

"I like to think so."

"So, what's your name, Mr. Funnyman?"

"Now, don't laugh."

"Try me."

"Holden Grace."

124

"Sounds like a preacher's name to me. Come to save my soul at four-fifteen in the morning. Just don't ask me for a donation. I'm all tapped out. Besides, from the look of it, your friend there could use the savin'. What happened to him, anyway?"

"Didn't pay his neighborhood Home Association dues. They get kinda rough. So they made him an example for all the others. In case they were lookin' to stiff. Those angry sit-on-their-ass professionals can get pretty violent when it comes to money."

"You don't have a straight answer for anything, do you, Holdin' onto Grace?"

"Makes things too serious, even in serious times."

She just shook her head in amusement. Maggie brought back the clipboard and handed it to Nurse LeClair just as a young doctor made his way into the emergency room. Fresh faced and doing a residency I would have bet. He instantly went over to Mick, who stood on his own and walked away with the young physician. I sat down next to Maggie and picked up a *Field & Stream* magazine, only three months old, and flipped through it casually. I didn't spend a lot of time reading the informative stories and tips. It acted more as a distraction, especially because I knew I could slip into a nice sound sleep very quickly even propped up in an uncomfortable emergency room chair. I looked over at Maggie. Despite the ignominious circumstances for Mick that led us to this point deep into a Saturday night or early into a Sunday morning, she looked great. Tired, but great. She smiled at me, took my hand and simply held it. She knew I hurt about Mick. She knew I wished like hell I could have prevented it. She also knew that I would take care of business. It was one of the aspects about my life that pushed her away from me at times. I very rarely had encountered the prospect of physical harm from my job, but Maggie knew I wanted more from it. More excitement. More intensity that I felt would bring more meaning to my life. The Feds didn't want me, at least for what I wanted them for as a

125

career, so if circumstances dictated danger, I relished it. Back in the seventies, people would have called it "machismo," but now, they just call it self-destructive. Fine with me. But not always fine with Maggie. We sat in silence for awhile until Nurse LeClair offered us some coffee. We both declined and sat in silence some more. The good nurse stayed preoccupied behind her desk, waiting for another graveyard shift to end so she could get the hell off of her feet and into a soft bed. Or so I thought. Hell, for all I knew, she'd go home, reserve a tee time at Lafayette Country Club and get in eighteen holes while the greens were still soft and very forgiving. I've learned, or I've tried to, not to slap a label on people, especially the ones I didn't know too well.

Mick finally exited one of the sacred rooms of medicine, looking much better and walking a bit more steadily. It was nearly five o'clock. I needed some sleep. It looked like Sunday would be a washout for accomplishing too much. That depended on how I felt after a few hours in the sack. The newly sewn in stitches were evident over both of Mick's eyes. Just a couple, but enough to make it a pain in the ass for him. He held a slip of paper in his right hand. Most likely a pain killer prescription.

Nurse LeClair spoke first. "Well, handsome, you're lookin' better. I would say a sight for sore eyes, but I figure you wouldn't appreciate that one." She gave him a sly grin.

"Well, Ms. Canuck By Way of Queens, I'd like to say 'See you soon,' but my instincts tell me that wouldn't be good for me," Mick countered.

"Ain't that the truth, sweetheart. Now get out of here, and don't let Mr. Funnyman Preacherman Holden Grace get you in anymore trouble," she said.

Maggie said goodnight and good morning to her as we left. I just smiled at her and shot her with my left forefinger. She loved that one.

As we walked outside, I asked Mick, "So, what's the damage?"

126

"Twelve stitches over the eyes. A couple inside the lips. Jaw is fine. Just sore. Nose is fine. No broken ribs, but three cracked ones. The Doc said it was a damn good thing I was in such good shape. Could've been a lot worse. He asked me what happened."

"What you tell him?" I asked.

"Got in a barroom brawl with some guys I didn't know. You and Maggie were a couple who just helped me out. He wanted to know about the cops. I told him it wouldn't come to that. He didn't say another thing. Probably used to late-night appearances by guys in my condition."

We reached the cars. "What do you say we get you home for some sleep?" I said.

Maggie looked at me. Then Mick did. He made a face. A pained one. Not from physical pain, but from a thought running through his head. And that had to be more difficult than taking the beating he did tonight, because I thought I knew what the look was about. Maggie's look had the same theme, one that projected "Don't bring Mick back to the same house where he was just accosted and doesn't feel too safe sleeping in right now." I could read that. From just one look. Too bad I couldn't read other more simple looks on other occasions.

I caught on and recovered. "But, ya know, it's only about twenty minutes back to my place, and I'm tired as hell. We'll just head there and sleep like fans at a Boston Red Sox game." I thought about the crude traps I had set and hoped like hell that they were still in tact when we got there.

"That sounds good. What do you think, Mick?" Maggie asked.

"Works for me."

We headed west on Route 175 through Onondaga Hill into Marcellus, a small village with a great new golf course called The Links at Sunset Ridge of which I was a member. Straight through the village, 175 became Old Seneca Turnpike all the way into the town of Skaneateles. A right hand turn onto Mottville Road, through the stop sign over Route 321, then

127

through the stop sign across Jordan Road and over the bridge where the road became Crow Hill Road, followed by a quick left onto Mill Road and home. About twenty minutes. A very long twenty minutes when I fought sleep so hard and the Mercedes purred along like a content kitten as Mick snored next to me. The radio helped keep me aware. Thankfully, Maggie was on course behind us. Seemed like I never doubted her in anything she did. I wondered if she felt the same about me. Unlikely. But I couldn't blame her.

We parked in the driveway, I woke Mick up, and the three of us headed to the back door with me leading the way. I carefully checked the doors and the matchsticks were still in place. Mick asked me what the hell I was doing, and I explained as I probed. When I opened the inside door, the flour on the floor was just what it should have been -- flour. No footprints. Just a mess to be cleaned up. Once inside, I investigated the status of the front door. All seemed well. I still pulled my gun, which was chafing my side from being tucked in my waistband for so long, told Maggie and Mick to hang in the kitchen and gave the house a quick once over. Empty and ready to welcome three tired people into the rapture of sleep. I dug out some sheets and tossed them to Mick who was going to sleep on the sectional sofa. One small hitch in my house was the single bathroom. It wasn't accustomed to accommodating three individuals. We took our turns, and it was time to catch a few hours of sleep. Maggie was back in her t-shirt, and I was in my favorite boxers that featured dozens of leaping largemouth bass. We settled into bed, but suddenly, sleep was the furthest thought from my mind. I kissed Maggie passionately, and she returned it.

When we broke the kiss, she said, "But Mick's out there."

"He is so out right now, that even your wild screams of passion won't wake him."

"We'll just see about that," she said as I pulled that wonderful t-shirt over her head and tossed it across the room.

## *Chapter 12*

The smell of coffee woke me up. I reached my hand across the bed to the right and felt emptiness, then rolled over to check the time. Eleven-seventeen. At least it was still Sunday morning. My head only hurt when I touched it, so I just had to remember to keep my hands off. I was naked and looked around the room for my boxers. I found them on the floor near the dresser. I wasn't a coffee drinker except for an occasional hit or two of some hazelnut, but Maggie didn't start a morning without a few cups of caffeine to give her system a jolt, so I always kept some beans on hand in the refrigerator. I heard the shower running, and I didn't know if it was Maggie or Mick. My guess was Mick, because Maggie always got up early, and she was most likely showered, dressed and reading the Sunday paper.

I tugged on my boxers and headed down the hall to the living room and kitchen. I was right. Mick was in the shower, and Maggie was seated at the counter working on *The New York Times* crossword puzzle with a mug of coffee steaming before her. She didn't look like she only had a few hours of sleep. She was wearing black and white shorts, a blue tank top and her million dollar smile.

When she saw me, she said, "Hey, Bass Boy. Finally decide to get up?"

"Not my fault someone drained me in the wee hours of the morning. So, did you leave me any of the puzzle?"

"Enough to make you think you really helped."

"You're always thinkin' of others, aren't you?"

"Someone has to. Half the times, you guys can't think for yourselves."

"Hey, I resemble that remark." I stepped up to her and she kissed me on the cheek. "So, how's Mick doin'?"

"Seems okay. He looks better but worse, you know?"

"Yeah, I do," I said as I pulled up a stool next to her and eyed over the puzzle. She smelled like lilacs, clean and fresh.

Her hair hung loose, and I could still see the wet ringlets where the hair dryer failed to reach. Her tanned face was fresh looking and, as usual, free from makeup. Her appearance reminded me of how I must have looked the beast next to her beauty. I never woke up an attractive person. Made me wonder how the hell I managed so much morning sex through the years. Guess I had to thank the Sandman for that one. The puzzle was about half finished, the letters neatly filled in with ink, not pencil.

"Forty-three across is Bela Bartock," I said as I pointed at the puzzle. Maggie shot me a questioning look. "Composer Bartock. Bela. Write it in." I got up and mixed my protein and skim milk drink and slugged it down immediately just like the directions on the container told me. Made me wonder what the hell would happen to the stuff if I let it sit for a few minutes. Coagulate into a pre-digested protein mass that would take on a life of its own? I put the dirty dishes in the dishwasher and that reminded me of the mess of flour on the floor that needed to be cleaned up. I looked over at the base of the back door, and the floor was clean.

"Mags, thanks for cleaning up the mess..."

"Don't thank me," she said. "Thank Mick."

"Now, that's one helluva guest. Someday, he'll make a fine wife." Maggie rolled her eyes at me as I poked my head in the refrigerator and rummaged to see what could be turned into a quick meal. I was hungry, and I was sure Maggie and Mick could use some sustenance.

"You guys eat anything yet?" I asked as I located some boneless breast of chicken leftovers from late in the week.

"No. We were waiting for our host to feed us," Maggie answered.

"I see. And just what did you have in mind?" My head was still buried in the refrigerator.

"Surprise us."

I removed the chicken, some lettuce, extra sharp cheddar cheese, red hot sauce and a package of burrito shells and set everything on the counter near the microwave just to the right of

Maggie and her puzzle. I got out a sharp carving knife and a cutting board and sliced the chicken into very small pieces. I grated a pile of cheese and set it aside. I pulled off some of the lettuce and set that aside also. As I was warming up some of the burrito shells in the microwave to make them more pliable and easier to work with, Mick entered down the hall from the bathroom wearing a pair of my shorts and a Hospice volleyball tournament t-shirt. He did look better but worse. He sat down next to Maggie.

"How ya feelin'?" I asked.

"A lot better than last night. And hungry. Whatcha got workin' over there?"

"Chicken burritos."

"What a host," he said. "Need a hand?"

"Na. Takin' care of. Just don't you dare finish that puzzle."

I whipped the burritos together, and we took turns eating the creations while the next batch was heating in the microwave. There's nothing better to have around than burrito shells for throwing together a quick meal or snack. You could stuff anything into a burrito shell. After lunch, I stashed the dishes in the dishwasher and started it. The three of us relaxed and worked on the puzzle together, sharing some time between three friends without the outside influence of the volatile world and the out-of-control people who made it that way. We didn't discuss the case. We didn't mention what happened to Mick. We didn't express concerns about Maggie's safety should she return home alone. We didn't allow that ruinous influence to seep into our sunny early Sunday afternoon where we found safety in numbers. I knew that I had business to take care of, but all I could do today was call Wade Reynolds and have him trace the Cadillac plate for me. The day was for enjoyment, relaxation and recuperation. We'd address Mick's and Maggie's living arrangements later. Monday would prove to be an eventful day, since I planned on visiting a few people who could shed a serious amount of light on the whereabouts of Rachel Allen.

131

We spent the day drinking beer and relishing the eighty-degree temperature, which was a result of the cold front that finally blew away the heat wave that overstayed its welcome. The humidity was low. The skies were blue. And the company was impeccable. I called Wade and left him a message to get back to me. I was going to have to feed three people that night, so I made a quick trip up to the only supermarket in the village and picked up a case of cold beer and some turkey Polish sausage for the grill. A little high in sodium, but when marinated with my beer, Italian dressing, garlic and dijon mustard mixture, it was a culinary delight hot off the grill. On the way home, I stopped at a local farm stand and selected some good looking potatoes and fresh cucumbers and tomatoes. When I pulled into my driveway around six-thirty, Maggie and Mick were still out on the back deck, stretched out in the beach chairs. They both looked like they were napping. They were. A very tempting prospect, but as the host, I couldn't enjoy that luxury. The sound of my Jeep door closing stirred them both from their afternoon siestas, and they got up and walked over to see what I had brought to feed their bellies. Maggie was Queen of the Naps, and she normally took a quick one every day and immediately made a beeline to food upon awaking. It wasn't the smartest habit, especially when she told me she started munching on whole coffee beans one time. When she poked her tanned nose into the bags, I directed her inside to some cocktail peanuts in the cupboard. Mick looked better and moved better.

"Wade called. Said you could reach him at home. He'd be in pretty much all night."

"How ya feelin'," I asked. He was going to get tired of hearing that. Better than no one caring, though.

"Good. Good." He wasn't enthusiastic.

He took the plastic grocery bag and the brown paper bag from the farm stand from my left hand. I held the case of beer in my right. We went inside. Maggie had the peanuts out and was eating them one at a time and going over the crossword puzzle, wearing a look of concentration that furrowed her brow and pursed her lips. Mick set the bags on the counter nearest the refrigerator, opened a fresh beer, dug out a handful of peanuts from the can next to Maggie and headed back outside to enjoy the rest of the sunny evening, even though the back deck was now in shadows and the front deck would be the place to soak up the soothing August rays. I removed the potatoes, tomatoes and cucumbers from the bag and set them on the counter in anticipation of their sacrifice for dinner and put the sausage and beer in the refrigerator. I took out one of the few remaining cold brews and stashed the empty cardboard case in my coat closet just to the left of the outside door. I walked over to Maggie, who was silent the entire time, focusing on the puzzle, and picked up the cordless phone that was sitting next to her to call Wade. I dialed, and he answered.

"Hey, Wade. It's Holden."

"Hey, Holden. What's up?"

"I need a favor. A quiet favor."

"Sure."

"I'm onto something. I need a plate ID'd. I think the guy's responsible for a coupla inappropriate activities, if you can understand."

"Sure, buddy. How many stitches you get?" Wade was busting my chops.

"Not me. Mick."

"Shit. Sounds like you might need a little law enforcement on your side."

"Not just yet. You know I'll turn to you first, though."

"That's a comfort. What's the tag number?" he asked.

I gave it to him and he said that he'd check it out first thing Monday morning and get back to me. He also told me to watch my ass. I hung up the phone and set it back on the counter near Maggie.

"I'm gonna step outside and talk with Mick," I told her.

She rubbed my right shoulder with her left hand and said, "Take your time. I'll be here." Her calm amazed me.

I stepped back outside and briefly soaked in the beauty of the late summer day. It was outstanding days such as this that made the nearly unbearable winters worthwhile in Central New York. Days such as this offered contrast to zero degree January days with a wind chill of thirty below. Days such as this were the ying to the yang, completed the other half of the weather polemic, represented Mr. Heat Meiser as opposition to Mr. Cold Meiser. Days such as this symbolized the ultimate summer day, just as a fifty degree, slightly breezy day with puffy clouds lolling in the October sky typified the poet's view of autumn; or a day with gently falling large flakes over an already snow covered landscape when the temperature comfortably held at thirty degrees embodied a perfect winter day; or a bright, sunny, yet cool day that highlighted the burgeoning greenery that promised a new cycle of life exemplified spring. It was the seasons that kept people here. It made one appreciate each perfect day more than the perfect day that wasn't quite as good as the next one. It was why I wore shorts year round. Not necessarily outdoors, but if the thermometer decided to get its ire up to forty during the winter, I wouldn't hesitate to bare my legs in public. Of course, with legs like mine, it was a no-brainer. Mick was back in a beach chair, staring out at the trees.

"Hey, Mick, what d'ya say we hang out front where the sun is?"

He kept his gaze locked on the ethereal treetops.

"This is kinda nice," he said. He sipped his beer.

"C'mon, buddy. Let's hang in the sun." I walked up next to him. "Come on." I dragged both words out. He shrugged. "Tell ya what. I'll break out both acoustics, and we can jam." I piqued his interest. He looked up at me. "It's been awhile," I said.

"Okay. You're on. But one favor," he said.

"Yeah?"

"You don't sing."

"Ya know, jealousy has broken up a lot of bands."

"And so has bad talent."

134

"So, is that why we've never been an act?" I asked.

"Probably. You can't sing, and I can't play."

"Sounds like half the bands making millions these days. So what d'ya say we torture my neighbors and anyone foolish enough to pass by on a bike or with their windows down?"

"Aw, what the hell."

He labored out of the beach chair, picked up his beer and walked around the side of the house to the small front deck.

I yelled to him as he turned the corner around the house, "Meet you on the deck with our instruments of torture." Too old to rock and roll, but too young to die.

I grabbed my Ovation Collector's Series and my Fender twelve-string and as I moved back through the house, Maggie stayed focused on the last of the answers to the puzzle. That, or she was just pretending to, so I felt I had a clear shot at talking with Mick about what happened to him, Rachel, and even me, and what was going to possibly happen next. Possibilities seemed the most guaranteed events right now. Maggie caught my eye as I headed toward the front door. She understood that Mick and I needed to talk alone. I offered up what I hoped was a reciprocal look and stepped through the front door onto the deck. I handed Mick the Fender, set the Ovation down carefully and opened a new beer. Mick began to strum a few chords.

"This thing in tune?" he asked, his face slightly contorted from listening to each string as he played the chord.

"Like it matters when you play."

I picked up the Ovation and started into a Hootie and the Blowfish song. Mick joined in. We didn't sound half bad. Of course, that only means we sounded half good. But at least no dogs howled or neighbors screamed for us to knock off the racket. We played a couple of more songs, sounding more synchronized with each one, using the session as a release for what occurred over the weekend. We finished up Pearl Jam's "Alive" and took a break. We sat back, sipping our beers and stared out at the farm fields in their apparent tranquillity. I thought about how the soil was ripped open by man's hand, turned inside out year after year in order to bring forth life and fill our stomachs. It was an interesting phenomenon if you wanted to take the time to break it down and sort it out.

"Hey, you ever go out looking for nightcrawlers in a freshly plowed field as a kid?"

Mick looked at me and said casually, "I didn't spend a lot of time around farms as a youth."

"You missed out, buddy. It was like a treasure hunt. Those poor worms were turned inside out. One minute all cozy under the earth, the next uprooted, cut in half with the sun bearing down on 'em. And the lucky ones that came up whole. Well, they were ripe for the pickin' by a bunch of rugrats who wanted to go fishing."

"Sounds like a ball. What is it with you and your worms, anyway?"

One of the guys who lived across the road steered his white Taurus into his driveway. He got out, popped the trunk and unloaded his golf bag. He shot us a wave as he stashed the clubs in his garage and went inside the house.

"I don't know. It's a good memory. Ya know? Unspoiled. I can pick a night when everything's quiet except the crickets. Grab a coffee can and a flashlight and go out into my yard, focus and fill the can with a mass of squirming worms. No one's around to tell me that one's too small. That one's mating. That one's got a wife in kids. That one's on the endangered list. That one's gay, so don't touch it. That one's into child pornography. That one's a hired goon. I know it sounds really insignificant, Mick, but it's a piece of the past when innocence wasn't necessarily a bad thing. When we worried if the new girl next door thought we were cute. When we spent every hour outside, skinning our knees, picking worms, catching snakes and salamanders and not planted in front of a computer screen or watching mindless drivel on the tube. It's a connection I never want to lose. Too many of us lose too much every day -- our honor, dignity, peace of mind, freedom... the list goes on and on,

Mick. And I know you lost a big chunk of your existence this weekend, buddy..."

"I wouldn't necessarily say 'big chunk.' But, yeah, it disturbs me." He picked up the Fender and aimlessly strummed chord progressions. "Those bastards probably fucked with my head more than my body. The pain'll go away. The memory won't."

"That's why I hold onto a lot of memories from my childhood. They can't be fucked with. I've heard the philosophical pyschobabble about how there's no past or future, only right now. Sure, maybe as far as the reality of the moment, but life and existence stretches far beyond the boundaries of this instant. Hell, Mick, I just want to make sure you're gonna be all right, ya know?"

He stopped playing and looked at me. "Yeah. I know."

"So, what're feeling?"

"Honestly?"

"Yeah."

Cars passed by intermittently. A little faster than the speed limit. Windows down. Stereos blaring. For a rural back road, it took on its share of traffic.

Mick still held the guitar. He looked back out across the road at the fields of what I wasn't sure. I knew they weren't corn.

"I'm angry. I want revenge. I'm concerned about going back home. And that makes me feel like a failure. That I'm afraid to return to the scene of the crime, as it were. I couldn't defend myself in my own home." He paused a moment. "The word 'violated' comes to mind. The word 'wimp' comes to mind, too."

He drained the rest of his beer. I wondered how many he'd had today, and if he was taking his painkillers. He seemed coherent though, and knowing Mick, he didn't take the meds.

"Mick, you're not the only guy to get his ass kicked. It took three of them sneaking into your house at two in the morning to do it."

"Doesn't matter. You know. It could've been ten guys. It's the feeling of helplessness. It's a humiliation that leaves a sick lump in your stomach."

"It passes. Believe me. I've been there. We all wanna be tougher than the next guy. Well, guess what? It doesn't work that way, 'cause if I'm holding my Glock at some asshole's head, what's tough gonna get him? Dead. It's all a matter or circumstance and perspective. Yeah, you feel bad about yourself. You'll be fine. You just can't dwell on it and let it sink you. It's up to you, and only you, to deal with it. You've got me and Maggie to lean on, but we can't turn the screws inside your head. You're responsible."

"Yeah."

"And don't forget about Rachel."

"Never. I'll never forget what Blue Eyes said. You gotta promise me something, Holden." I looked at him. "If Blue Eyes is the tough guy with the Glock aimed at him, don't hesitate to pull the trigger."

"I promise you this, Mick. Blue Eyes will get his. And anyone else who deserves it."

I went back inside and to grab two more beers. Maggie was still at the counter, and I gave her a thumbs up gesture as I passed her.

She almost whispered, "I know. I heard most of it."

"You mean you listened?"

"The windows are open, Brainiac."

"Oh. Yeah. Not that you couldn't have listened anyway. So, did you pick up some insight into the male mystique?"

"Only that men use the strangest analogies when trying to make a point. Worms?"

I shrugged my shoulders. "Seemed relevant."

I rinsed out the empties and set them back into the case and took two more out of the refrigerator.

I asked Maggie, "You wouldn't want to get the sausage marinating, would ya?"

"Sure you can trust me? My version of your marinade might not be up to you standards."

"Come on, Mags. You've seen me do it enough." I put my arm around her. "Besides, it's not an exact science. A little beer, Italian dressing, Red Hot sauce, dijon mustard, garlic and various spices of your choosing. When you're done, you can come out and be mine and Mick's appreciative audience."

"Well, since you put it that way, how can a girl refuse? But here's the deal. You handle the rest of dinner. Fair?"

"Since you put it that way, I think I have no choice."

"Good. No go out and entertain me while I slave here in the kitchen." She swatted me on the backside as I pulled away and headed for the front door.

Mick and I strapped the guitars back on and played to an unseen audience. After ten minutes, Maggie joined us on the front deck. We played, sang and laugh. It was one of those moments to remember. Not particularly outstanding in any way, but more Norman Rockwellesque. As the sun decided to call it quits for the day, we packed up and went back inside. It was time to get dinner going. Mick dragged the grill out and fired it up while I peeled the cucumbers and sliced them up with the tomatoes, then doused them with a red wine vinegar and olive oil mixture punctuated with a fine blend of spices. I put the potatoes on to boil with enough salt to make them a toned down version of salt potatoes. When the lava rocks were glowing like a volcano ready to spew, I introduced the marinated sausage to the grill grate. The sizzle was a comfort. I turned the sausage repeatedly, basting it with the remaining marinade. I also kept a close eye on the potatoes, since that was part of the deal with Maggie. It wasn't a problem. I was comfortable with having many irons in the fire, so to speak.

By the time we sat down to eat, it was nearly nine o'clock. We had knocked back quite a few beverages throughout the day, and I was feeling a little tired, especially since I wasn't able to catch a nap like Maggie and Mick. I think we were all pushing exhaustion, because the conversation was sparse, and the focus was on eating quickly. There were no leftovers. We worked together to clean up the mess. I put the grill away, and it was nine-thirty. We still had to discuss sleeping arrangements. I wouldn't make anyone drive home after the number of beers we had consumed. Besides, it was late and I knew I'd be drooling on my pillow and snoring like my father within the hour, so I expected the same from my guests. I didn't want Maggie going home alone anyway. In fact, I didn't want her alone again until the case was put to bed. We sat down on the sectional in my small living room with ESPN's Sunday Night Baseball game on the television with the sound very low. It was the Arizona Diamondbacks visiting the Florida Marlins. Mick agreed to sleep on the sofa for one more night before returning home. That was the easier of the two arrangements. Maggie's situation needed to be broached, and she and I waited to discuss the topic until we all turned in for the night.

I was already stretched out on the bed with my nearby fan blowing on me when Maggie came in from the bathroom wearing a Renaissance Festival t-shirt that we had picked up a couple of years back at the annual shindig in the small town of Sterling, New York, in the northern reaches of Cayuga County near the southern shore of Lake Ontario. For a couple of months every summer, a troop of Elizabethan performers took up residence in a hamlet in the woods and performed various routines for the masses, from comedy shows to jousting competitions. It was a worthwhile all-day excursion once, especially to check out the incredible array of individuals who visited, but beyond that, it was like seeing the same play by the same performers again. That, and you could shell out a fine roll of cash for food and beverages while crowds kicked up a lot of dust that left an Elizabethan film over you and your clothes.

Maggie settled into the right side of the bed and flipped off the table lamp on the small table near her.

"Long day, huh?" I mentioned, attempting not to sound cliched. I wanted to start the conversation.

"Yeah. But it was nice. I've missed you and Mick playing together."

She rolled to her left off her back to face me. I turned to the right so that our faces were inches apart.

"I'm glad that he's ready to go home," she said.

"Yeah. It's a big deal, even though it may not seem like it. But, he'll be okay. He knows it's gonna be tough for awhile. Every noise'll wake him up, and he'll probably sleep with his piece, but those guys won't be back."

"What makes you so sure? If you stay on the case, won't they go after him again?"

Being so close to Maggie would normally distract me beyond all normal speech capabilities, allowing me to only unleash a guttural growl of lust from deep within, but the subject was serious.

"No. Not Mick. They'd increase the stakes." There was a moment of silence between us as what I said registered with Maggie.

"You don't mean me, do you?" she asked very softly and very calmly.

"Maybe. They might just go for me, but I don't know if they have the balls. If they thought you were an easier target with more influence over my decisions... I don't know."

"I want to know who the hell 'they' are." A firmness worked its way into her quiet voice, making it sound slightly raspy, almost like Kathleen Turner.

"That makes three of us. And I'll find out tomorrow. Hopefully. And when I do, I'll do something about it. But, until I find Rachel and why she disappeared, I don't want you staying at your place."

I saw the look in her eyes.

"No, Mags. That's not an invitation to stay here. We both know that won't work."

The look quickly changed to one of relief.

"You have someone you could stay with?" I asked. "A friend? What about Katie at work? She's single, right?"

141

"But what if they follow me to work? Then follow me to Katie's? What then?"

"They won't make it more complicated than it has to be. With the two of you, they're spreading things too thin. They'd have to tail you to work, then wait all day and tail you to Katie's. It's not economical. Believe me."

"Not economical?"

The stress showed in her voice. She turned on her back and folded her arms across her chest. No wild screams of passion tonight.

"Listen, Mags. They went after Mick 'cause he was a guy. They knew they could work on him. They knew they could deliver their message without putting him in the hospital. There was a line they knew they could cross. With a woman, they don't know. Hell, they can't even be sure that I'd care about you more than Mick."

"Well, thank you."

"Oh, Christ. Maggie. You'll be safe with Katie."

I wanted this conversation to end. We both were tired. We didn't need to spoil the day by acting like a disgruntled couple, which we weren't. A couple or disgruntled.

"I'm worried, Holden. Is that okay? I know you expect the chin up, deal with it, tough guy attitude all the time, but this is my safety we're talking about. I saw Mick, remember? I'm worried for me and for you." She turned back to face me.

I put my arms around her, my right arm underneath her back and my left arm over her chest. "I know. I know. I will take care of this. I promise." I held her like that for awhile.

She seemed like she was drifting off when she suddenly asked, "Did you set the alarm?"

I whispered, "Yes." Then I set the alarm as quietly as possible. Details.

## *Chapter 13*

At six on the nose, a disc jockey's voice suddenly cut through the silence of a Monday morning like fingernails across a blackboard. Before I could even turn the alarm off, Maggie was out of bed. I didn't know if she planned on going straight to her apartment to get ready for work or hanging around for a bit while she had her morning coffee. As I stretched out on the bed, I heard the coffee start to brew. The day's first answer without working for it. Hopefully a portent of things to come. I knew Mick would be getting up now. He would definitely go right home, and I wanted to see him off, so I dragged myself out of the rack and into the bathroom. When I finished my business, Mick was patiently waiting outside the door for his turn. Take a number, please.

I said, "Hey, buddy, how'd ya sleep?"

"Solid. Right through the night."

"That's good."

We both knew what I meant. I slapped him on the shoulder and walked out to the kitchen. Maggie had gone out and gotten the morning paper and was reading it at the counter, steam dancing from her coffee that she drank from a very old Bethany College mug of mine. I took the milk out of the refrigerator, dug out my protein mix and my Cornell Football Association mug and mixed a quick four-scoop breakfast. I needed to get a workout in this morning before chasing down a handful of people, most of whom wouldn't want to spend a lot of quality time with me, so I needed a solid dose of those whey peptides.

"Good morning, Sunshine," Maggie said as she turned a page of the paper. I never knew of anyone who was so together so quickly so early in the morning like Maggie. I admittedly wasn't a barrel of laughs, but I had improved through the years. Maybe she rubbed off on me.

"Hi there, Cupcake. I thought you'd be on your way home by now. Hard to pull yourself away, huh?"

"Yeah, that and I'm out of coffee at my place."

"You have such a way of makin' a guy feel good."

"Don't you know it."

Mick came down the hall wearing his clothes from Saturday night, which was actually Sunday morning. He walked up to Maggie, she jumped off her stool and he gave her a hug.

"It's been great to see you, Maggie. Wish the circumstances coulda been different."

"Me too. But you know Holden will get to the bottom of this."

"Yeah. Yeah I do. H, you're the best, man." He stepped around the counter into the kitchen and gave me a tentative hug. A surprising show of male emotional bonding in front of the female species. Normally, it's a high five and a grunt, but Mick was my bud and he'd been through a lot to this point, so it was okay by me. "Thanks for everything this weekend. You'll let me know if you find out anything?"

"Yeah. I will. I'll piece this together. Don't worry."

"All right. I'll see you guys later." Then he walked out the back door, got in his Mercedes and drove away.

I turned to Maggie. "So, what about you?"

"I'll see if I can stay with Katie."

"Good. Now, about how you can make a guy feel good. Care to demonstrate in the back bedroom?"

"A wonderful idea, but, unfortunately, the game clock's expired. I gotta go. I'll have to pack some extra things to bring to work. It was your idea, remember?" There was a tone in her voice that grabbed me in a very delicate spot and made me thankful that I planned to workout when Maggie left.

She finished the paper, her coffee, put the mug in the dishwasher, then went to collect her things, which were few, especially since she never had to bring much for an overnight stay. She had put her dirty clothes in a plastic bag before stuffing them in her overnight bag. She was wise not to trust me to run them through the wash with my stuff. I had discovered through the years that most females preferred their laundry done a specific way, whether it was the amount of clothes in the load, the water temperature, water level, amount of detergent, fabric softener method, drying method, folding method or rhythm method. I guess they view their clothes like I hold my golf clubs so sacred. When I did laundry, I knew enough to separate darks and lights, and I used cold water mostly to save on the gas bill, and I did my best to not overdry. I used fabric softener at the proper time in the rinse cycle. I even poured in a color safe bleach on occasion. But my folding did leave something to be desired at times. I could live with a few wrinkles, and if I needed to look really spiffy, I'd break out the iron and do my best. Clothes do not make the man.

I was reading an article about the Syracuse University football team and their major bowl chances for the upcoming season in the Sports section when Maggie came down the hall with her bag over her shoulder. She was wearing denim shorts and a blue sweatshirt with "Notre Dame" stitched in gold letters on the left breast. Her hair was loose and a little on the wild side. I took the bag from her so she could put her shoes on near the back door and walked out with her to her car. I handed her the bag, she got in and rolled the window down.

"Thanks for the good time, Handsome. The check's in the mail," she said with a smile.

"Anytime. I'll call you at work later, just to make sure everything's okay."

"You don't have to do that. I'll be fine. Really. If I need anything, I'll call you."

It was my turn to offer a look. It was one of perplexity.

"Just find Rachel, okay?" was her response to my furrowed brow. "I'll talk to ya."

I leaned down, and she kissed me. She turned the key, put the car in reverse and backed out the driveway. I waited outside until she pulled away and shot me a wave. With my guests having departed, it was time to get to work. I went back into the house and put on a pair of blue mesh shorts and an old

Sorrentino's t-shirt. I grabbed my gun, a couple of Springsteen CD's and my cordless phone and headed for the garage.

I slipped *Darkness on the Edge of Town* in my boom box and started with ten two-minute rounds on the heavy bag with a one-minute rest period in between each round. I started the session by throwing mostly left jabs. Quick and precise, that made loud snapping noises as leather connected with leather. I concentrated on footwork, moving around the bag as I worked. To help keep my focus, I left about eighteen inches of loose chain hanging at the top of the bag, so when I sent the bag dancing, the chain would whip out toward me in no specific pattern. Very rarely did I allow that chain to connect, but when it did, it hurt a lot. By the time I got into the tenth round, I was bombing heavy combinations and bobbing away from the spinning chain much more frequently. I could feel the sweat trickle down my head and down my back, soaking into the shirt. I finished round ten with a thunderous right and sat down to cool off. Bruce was singing "Streets of Fire," lamenting, "I walk with angels that have no place. Streets of fire." I liked a lot of the modern rock that was being turned out today, although there certainly was a lot of crap, but there's nothing like some old Bruce, singing about work and cars and girls and the swamps of New Jersey. A retrospective on America in the seventies. Not self-absorbed discourses, but songs for everyman.

The phone rang.

"Yeah?" I answered.

"Hey, Holden. It's Wade. Got that information you wanted. The tag belongs to William Hanley, 100 Willow Circle, Apartment 7, Camillus. I checked him out. And Billy has been a bad boy in the past. Mostly assault. Did some time at Jamesville. Got out not long ago. He lives with his younger brother, Ricky. Another tough guy. Wants to be like Billy when he grows up." I could hear the sarcasm in Wade's voice.

"Nothin' like settin' your sights high, huh?"

"Christ, yeah. Listen, Holden. Be careful with these assholes. They don't seem to know right from wrong."

146

"Or right from left, I'd bet."

I thanked him, told him I owed him a beer and hung up the phone. Blue Eyes and the Cadillac Man finally had a name to go with the bad behavior. Billy Hanley, tough guy. Odds were that brother Ricky was in on the slugfest of Mick. They sure didn't live far away from him. Not even eight o'clock and the day was shaping up. I had a feeling this was going to be a busy day, if not completely productive. I put on *Born to Run* and started in on the weights, using mostly forty-pound dumbbells, along with a triceps bar loaded up to seventy pounds and a long bar for bench presses and squats. Since it was Monday, I didn't want to get carried away, so I kept the workout around an hour in length, but I didn't skimp on the intensity. When I finished, I felt damn good. The blood was flowing. The heart rate was up. I was amazed at why more people didn't workout. If you thought about it, it wasn't a big chocolate chunk of your life. At three hours a week minimum, that's less than two percent of your time. Christ, you spend more time on the shitter during a week. And the benefits. Not only physically good, but a good workout did a hell of a lot for the mental state of mind. I don't know. I could never understand how people could live day to day when something like lacing up their shoes could leave them out of breath. It was just too easy I supposed. Too easy not to exercise. Too easy not to care. Too easy to sit on your ass and watch reruns of *She's the Sheriff*. I returned to the kitchen and had a couple of bagels for breakfast, then shaved, showered and dressed for my big day. I needed to present two distinct looks for my journey -- one of an upstanding Private Detective when I graced Dr. Amanda Russell with my presence, and one of a dirtbag fresh from doing a little time for my friend Billy Hanley. The key was how I accessorized. I also learned that from the ladies through the years. A pair of jeans worked for both instances. I chose a tasteful shortsleeve almost turquoise green Dockers shirt and my Nike Air Max Triax cross trainers to go with a pair of Levi's 550's for the good doctor. For Billy Blue Eyes, I selected an old Finlandia Vodka tank top with sand stains from hours of beach volleyball, a ratty Bomber Lures ball cap and my Timberland boots. I planned on changing in the Jeep. I snatched up my Glock and my cell phone, and I was ready to roll. It was nine-thirty. I'd be at Dr. Russell's office on Genesee Street around ten o'clock.

The sun shone brightly as I cruised east toward Syracuse, a route I had taken many times to my lonely office. But the drive was different today. I had a definitive purpose. I needed some questions answered, by Dr. Russell and Billy Boy. I hoped I could crack the doctor and patient confidentiality conundrum of Dr. Russell, but I had no idea what to expect if I actually met up with Billy. He'd recognize me. He'd be indifferent. Hostile. Uncooperative. I might need to do a little convincing. Or not. I was still thinking about how to play that scenario, whether to attempt low key for now or just say "What the hell?" I still had others to speak to. Press too hard and someone might spook before I could close in. I looked at too many uncertainties, which I wasn't too fond of at the time.

I played the lane change games with the last of the late commuters as I neared downtown and off-ramped Route 690 to Interstate 81 South and immediately exited at the Harrison Street ramp, drove underneath the elevated highway through two traffic lights and hung a left onto Adams Street that led past University Hospital and up to the Syracuse University campus. The front way. I was accustomed to slipping into most places the back way, which included the SU campus. A left off of the one-way Adams onto Irving Avenue just past the hospital, which actually connected to another, Crouse Irving, and I was heading toward the medical complex where Dr. Russell plied, or should I say, pried, her trade. I found a tight parking spot on the street and wedged my driver side windowless Jeep into the space between an old green Buick Century and a Volvo station wagon. I dropped a couple of quarters into the meter, made sure that I left nothing too tempting to would-be thieves in the vehicle and went to start my detecting day. My ratty tank top and old Timberlands would have to take their chances. My shirt was untucked, and it hid the Glock which was tucked in a familiar place. Odds were I wouldn't need it to make the Doc talk, but who knew what kind of hormones I'd be facing in the waiting room when I demanded to see her. The thought made me tap the gun to remind me of its presence. An old, trusted friend. Like a good dog. An old putter.

The building was unimpressive. Four stories of concrete and glass against the skyline, connected to a parking garage that I was more than happy to avoid. Too expensive and too easy to be ambushed. The complex obviously lacked the aesthetic qualities of the modern women care facilities springing up on the west and east sides of the city. No ad agency designed sign. No free parking. No fancy landscaping. No layout that looked like it belonged in *House Beautiful*. Just a functional place close to the heart of the city and the SU campus. Hey, if we all lived in Eden, who'd need Sodom and Gomorra? I entered a door at the southwest corner of the building that deposited a visitor in a stairwell with the option of an elevator. No front lobby with carefully planned plant placement, nice carpeting, a welcoming front desk with a warm-hearted command center director with great legs and a better smile awaited to guide you through the structural maze. Just to the point. Get in the building. Find your designated area. Get on with your business. I could see why women would want to make this their gynecological stomping grounds. Hell, who needed compassion when so many bodies needed to be moved in and out the doors every day? Either the healthcare was top notch or there was some reason for the external sterility that I didn't get. My money was on the care provided. Of course, I didn't get a lot of things. Dr. Amanda Russell's office was on the third floor. I opted for the stairs.

I pushed open the door to the third floor and it led me into a neutral-colored carpeted corridor that branched off at a right angle. A directory in between the door and the elevator pointed me toward Dr. Russell's office. As I strolled down the corridor, a young couple passed me looking very somber. They never noticed me. They were wrapped in their own world with their own concerns about how to make it through each day. They couldn't have been more than twenty-five, but their auras made them seem much older. The wear and tear of life. Maybe bad news about having a family. Or maybe just going through the process. It was easy to find Dr. Russell's office. A few women were seated in the corridor on uncomfortable looking chairs, flipping through magazines and keeping a reign on their young children. Inside, it was wall-to-wall patients. Full house. The office itself was tasteful. Nice art on the soft green walls. A few real plants scattered about to suck up all the carbon dioxide being exhaled by the nervous patients and the occasional boyfriend or husband. To the left, four padded chairs rested against the wall. All occupied. A coffee table filled with an assortment of reading material sat in front of the chairs. Straight ahead was a closed door that must have led back to the exam rooms. Just to the left of the door a couple of more taken chairs sat. To the right of the closed door was the reception counter with sliding glass windows. Two women in dress whites did their thing behind the glass. Rows and rows of charts were visible. Even with the skyrocketing progress of computers, hard files were necessary. To the right of the reception desk were more occupied chairs. I felt the eyes on me as I strolled in and headed alone to the looking glass. I turned on one of my best smiles.

One of the two women behind the glass looked up at me. Very dark eyes. Stunningly piercing. She was probably in her late twenties. Short dark hair. High cheek bones. Full lips. Slightly prominent nose with a small bump in the middle. Little makeup. Her eyes made her attractive. She offered a smile. Slightly crooked.

"Can I help you?" she asked.

"I'm here to see Dr. Russell."

"Uh... do you have an appointment?" She looked at a clipboard.

"No, but the morning sickness is getting worse. And I feel so bloated. I rushed right in." I cocked my head to line up with her still-holding smile.

"I'm sorry, but... really... I. It's just that..." She stopped searching for a response and went to a stock response. "Why do you need to see Dr. Russell?"

I pulled my credentials out and flashed them at her. "I have a few questions for the good doctor about a case I'm working on."

She studied the ID through the glass.

"Well, Mr. Grace, Dr. Russell's with a patient right now, and as you can see, we're a little busy right now. Could this wait? I mean, could you find a time later when she could put some time aside?" She worked the eyes on me. The smile remained.

"I wish I had the luxury, but I need answers now." I remained pleasant, something I had been working on more lately.

"Really, Mr. Grace, I'm sorry, but we're so busy."

Behind Dark Eyes, the other keeper-of-the-files took notice of our exchange and sidled up to the window. She was short and rotund, with red hair pulled back tightly. Her green eyes were squinty. She chewed gum. Nice touch. She had to be the elder stateswoman of the two. More years in the trenches fending off irate husbands and frustrated women or frustrated husbands and irate women. I'm sure it works both ways.

"You need help here, Tracie?" She looked at me as she asked the question. I just smiled and winked at her.

"Mr. Grace is a Private Detective, and he says he needs to ask Amanda some questions."

"Tell him to make an appointment like the rest." Her gaze stayed on me. Unwavering. Didn't want to give an inch. Her pants probably felt the same way.

"Listen," I directed my point toward Big Red. "I will see the doctor today. In fact, I will see the doctor after she's done with her current patient."

Big Red scowled at me like I was a box of empty donuts. I wondered if we were going to duke it out right there.

"You need to make an appointment," she said between clenched teeth. Her face became flushed. It nearly matched her tight red locks.

"You know, you shouldn't do that," I said amiably.

She just stared and turned a brighter shade of red.

"Let your blood pressure skyrocket like that. Not good for you. You need to relax. Let your hair down."

"Listen, Mister. I don't care who you are..."

"Patty, it's okay. Really," Tracie interjected. "I'm sure we can work something out. It's not worth getting upset over."

The closed door opened, and a women who looked like she was very late in her third trimester came through it and headed for the reception desk. I stepped aside so she could take care of business with Tracie. Patty had to let her systolic abate some, so she moved back to deal with more paperwork, but she kept a sideways eye on me. I would have bet that she was the type of kid to pull the wings off of flies. And eat chalk. As Tracie dealt with the patient, a woman in her mid-forties dressed in tan pants and a blue shirt with a white medical coat entered the waiting room. Her brown hair was straight and medium-lengthed with bangs and a few streaks of noticeable gray. She was around five-five, medium build and wore one hell of a large diamond engagement ring that practically hid her wedding band. The light show coming off that thing would have made Pink Floyd proud. Had to be Dr. Amanda Russell. I made my move before Big Red could vault herself through the glass and lay me out with a flying body block.

"Dr. Russell?"

She turned toward me. "Yes?"

I walked up to her. I caught Big Red moving quickly out of the corner of my eye.

I stuck out my hand and she took it.

"Holden Grace, Private Detective. I have a few questions for you."

She looked confused. Just then, Big Red came through the door huffing and puffing. For a portly gal, she moved fast. I'd love to see her go to work at a crowded Ponderosa buffet. She insinuated herself between me and the doctor, facing me. Her bold move broke our handshake. If Dr. Russell was slightly confused before, now she was completely addle-minded.

"Patty, what is the matter?" she asked Big Red.

"I told him he couldn't come busting in here like Bruce Willis thinkin' he could do what he wanted. I told him we were too busy and that he needed to make an appointment. Your time was too valuable. Obviously, he ignored me." She gave me her stare. This time I felt like a batch of ground beef with ecoli.

"Mr. Grace?"

"Yeah, Red here jumped to Tracie's rescue, fearful that I'd beat her into submission with my charm. She instructed me, in her oh so charming way, that you wouldn't have time to see me today. That my investigation into the disappearance of a young woman doesn't mean squat unless I conform to the standards of an appointment book that means nothing anyway when patients get backed up for more than an hour." I backed away from Patty for a little breathing room. "I decided I didn't like her attitude. I decided that when I saw you, I'd simply ask you to speak with me. It's not like I want you to strap me onto a table and and grill me about my sexual history. A few quick questions and I'm done."

By now, the waiting room had grown quiet and all eyes were focused on the strange trio stacked like a vertical toasted cheese sandwich arguing about matters that didn't mean a damn thing to them. They just wanted to get on with their appointments and get the hell out of there and get on with their lives. I could appreciate the way they felt. They had their gynecological demons to deal with, I had my gynecological Gestapo fraulein to face. Dr. Russell took a step back from Patty's human shield and cocked her head at me. Her hair fell over her face a bit. She looked pensive. Then she checked her watch, tapped her upper front teeth with a pen she was holding and stepped toward the patient door.

"Patty, Mr. Grace and I will only be a few minutes. Isn't that right, Mr. Grace?"

Suddenly, the one set of burrowing eyes that belonged to Big Red multiplied by twenty as every patient and the few significant others who thought about being anywhere but at an OB/GYN office locked their gazes on me. I'd been there. Not the same surroundings, but the same scenario. Waiting to be served at a restaurant, for example, and some asshole loudmouth gets the attention even though he walked in twenty minutes after I did. Now I felt the pressure and expected the numerous under-the-breath nasty comments when I slid through that magic door with Dr. Russell.

"Absolutely. In and out. Trust me."

Patty finally turned away unhappily and exited through the magic door. Maybe she'd be lucky and Willy Wonka would have an Everlasting Gobstopper waiting for her on the other side, because it was clear that she wouldn't sell out.

"Trust me? Sounds like what a lot of my patients hear," Dr. Russell commented as we both walked through the door behind Patty.

"Can I rephrase that?" I asked.

"Too late." Her tone was light.

We walked down a very short corridor, hung a right and passed a few examining rooms until we came to Dr. Russell's office at the end of the corridor. The door was open, she showed me through and closed it behind her.

"Have a seat," she said and motioned with her right hand.

I sat in one of two comfortable chairs that fronted her large desk -- it looked like maple -- and she went in behind it and sat down also. She folded her manicured-looking hands in front of her. The office, which I was sure was a reflection of Dr. Russell, had large, nicely framed black and white pictures on the walls of Dr. Russell with whom I presumed to be her husband and children, certainly snapped by a professional photographer. The scenes depicted were straight out of a *Country Living* spread about the happy American family and how they played together to stay together. Mother and Father romped in the snow with their young son and daughter with a rustic barn in the background; Mother and Father cheerfully strolled through a field bursting with what looked like a million dandelions each with a child hoisted up on their shoulders; the four giggled at a farm pond as a bluegill dangled from the hook of the daughter; and leaves were scattered everywhere as all four looked up from large piles of raked maple leaves. A picture for all seasons. Posed or real? Maybe a little of both. Dr. Russell's diplomas held the standard niche on the wall directly behind the desk. They weren't nearly as large as the family snapshots. Also behind the desk and behind me were bookshelves occupied by tomes ranging from child psychology to Dr. Seuss books, camping to anatomy books, and the expected women's health books. All neatly arranged. Her desk was also neat, with a few more family pictures, an appointment book spread before her, a couple of folders and a very curious set of teeth that looked like they were sculpted out of beige clay. I knew they were a form from a dentist or orthodontist.

"Yours?" I asked as I pointed to the set of very straight choppers.

She couldn't help but smile. If she chose to put a set of teeth on her desk, she had to be ready to answer a multitude of questions about them. I thought mine was quite simple.

"Actually, my husband's."

"Really? And do you give them back at the end of the day so he can eat dinner?"

"Only if he asks nicely, which is very difficult when you're missing your teeth."

"Almost like a catch twenty-two, huh?"

"Oh, I suppose you could say that."

"Ever notice how a lot of things in life work that way? Kinda like playing the lottery. You can't win the big bucks if you don't lay out your dollar to play, but you know that dollar would be much more wisely spent on a half gallon of milk for the family. But if your numbers came up, and it doesn't even have to be all of them to win back the buck and a little extra, you'd have made a wise investment. But odds are, you just flushed that dollar down the toilet. There's always a catch. There's always something that makes you think twice before saying it or doing it. But you gotta ask yourself what ultimately is the best thing to do." I paused. "And it can be tough."

"Very insightful, Mr. Grace. All that from a set of teeth?"

She rested her folded hands under her still-tight-for-her-age chin and focused her gaze on me. She wasn't so foolish as to be easily duped by my rhetoric. She knew there was an angle to it. I had to start somewhere.

"Na. Just one of my many observations on life. And death."

I stood up and stepped behind the chairs, looking at the photos on the walls. Obviously, family was important to Dr. Russell. I was hoping to tap into that resource when I brought up Rachel, because I knew that the doctor was going to hit me with the doctor-patient confidentiality issue, and if I could make her see the importance of releasing what could either be a trivial piece of information or possibly another piece of the Rachel puzzle as a gesture toward preserving what was left of Rachel's family, in this case, Mick, then that was my goal. I was going to make Dr. Russell choose. And I was betting that her priorities lay with the family. I faced Dr. Russell.

"And that has led me to you," I said.

"I see." She leaned back in her ergonomic chair and folded her arms across her chest. "So, what exactly do your observations have to do with me and the disappearance of the woman you mentioned earlier?"

She suddenly seemed a little more guarded. I needed to work on the charm some more. I sat back down. But this time I chose the other chair.

"The woman, Rachel Allen, was a patient of yours," I answered. "Just last week, a promising young businessperson in the very chic village of Skaneateles, but as of last Friday, gone.

156

Missing. Disappeared with no trace. Her brother, who, by the way, is her only relative that I know of, is worried. His baby sister's vanished. After their parents died, he vowed to take care of her. Think how he feels now. So, it's up to me to find her. That has led you to me, because I know that she was your patient. Maybe it's nothing. Standard maintenance stuff. But four weeks ago to the day, Rachel Allen had a four o'clock appointment with you. I need to know why."

"I don't think I can answer that."

"Yeah, yeah, yeah, I know, the doctor-patient bullshit. But this isn't shrink material. It's not about AIDS testing. It's about a young woman who hastily scribbled a note in her appointment book when everything else in her life was pretty much in order. Or so it seemed to the rest of us. She was anxious about seeing you. If it has any bearing on this case, I need to know. Her brother deserves to know. Her last family."

She leaned her elbows on her desk. "I understand your dilemma, but you need to understand mine. If I release information to you, then where do I stand with myself and my principles? Where do I draw the line?"

"How about around the dead body when they find it?" I was assuming a little bit to make a point.

"You can't assume that. You just mentioned that she was only missing."

"The "she" has a name, Rachel Allen. And if she's not dead at this point, maybe you can do something to help me prevent it. That's my job, and I need your help." I stood up again. This time I leaned in over Dr. Russell's desk and gave her the eye to eye. "Your job is what? To make sure women are healthy? To make sure they deliver healthy babies? To make sure life is protected? What the hell good is the goddamn doctor-patient confidentiality crock of shit if you may be only harming your patient? You have a full house out there." I cocked my thumb in the general direction of the overflowing waiting room. "How would you feel if one of them was your sister, and she suddenly disappeared? Huh? Let's say she was sitting out there, reading

157

*Bon Appetit*, the next patient to step on up, and when you came out to call her in, she was gone. No reasons. No clues. Just gone. And you had some information. Maybe not earthshaking, but something that could help. Would you hold it back because of your pompous rule? Or would you open your heart and her file?"

I stood for a moment, my hands resting on the edge of her desk. She ran her hands through her hair and placed them behind her head. There was a slight twitch in the left side of her jaw. She closed her eyes.

I continued. "Dr. Russell, this woman was a close friend of mine. Her brother has been beaten like an egg at a fireman's pancake breakfast. What you know about Rachel, as little or as much as it is, can only help. And if I don't succeed in my investigation, it will be turned over to the cops, and I will make it known that Rachel was a patient of yours and that could bear some significance on the case. I'd rather not go that route. I'd prefer to handle it now. The way that Rachel and her brother Mick wants me to. Don't impede my investigation Dr. Russell. Help it."

She had opened her eyes and fixed them on the one window in her office overlooking Irving Avenue and brought her hands palms down on her desk. After a few seconds, which seemed like an eternity, she turned her gaze back to me, cocked her head to the right and finally offered a response.

"Rachel Allen, you say?"

"Rachel Allen. Four weeks ago."

"I'll pull her chart."

She picked up her phone, punched in an interoffice code that I presumed hooked her into the front station manned by Patty and womanned by Tracie, and asked for Rachel's file. I sat back down. I felt it was the best thing to do if Big Red burst into the office with the file, ready to rumble. The silence was strange. I glanced out the window and watched the cars weave up and down Irving Avenue. Dr. Russell sat very composed, occasionally glancing at her watch knowing that her patients were backing up even further as she sat there with a private detective who didn't comprehend the severity of her medical endeavors. Tough shit. If she didn't overbook, she wouldn't have the problem. I had a hunch that she remembered Rachel. Even though most doctors see hundreds of patients, they do their best to remember the faces and the names that went with them. Helps to have that personal touch when you're applying a very personal touch.

A soft knock broke our silence. It wasn't Big Red.

"Come in," Dr. Russell said.

The door opened and Tracie walked in holding a very slim folder. She offered what seemed to be an almost apologetic look to me with those dark eyes, presumably for her co-worker's actions, and walked straight to the front of Dr. Russell's desk and handed over the medical dossier on Rachel.

She started to turn away, then stopped and faced Dr. Russell.

She said, "I just want to say I'm sorry for the scene earlier. I mean, with Mr. Grace and Patty...and you. I know it upset some of the patients. I tried to handle it, but..."

"Don't worry, Tracie. There's no blame here. You had a job to do. Patty had a job to do. And Mr. Grace had a job to do. It's fine. Really."

"I just wanted to make sure, because Mr. Grace was very pleasant to me. And I...I didn't want to give the wrong impression. Like he was rude to me."

"Thank you for your honesty." Dr. Russell moved her gaze to me. "I'm sure Mr. Grace was a complete gentleman."

I shrugged my shoulders like it should have been assumed by everyone involved. Tracie, feeling a bit better about approaching the boss and clearing the air just a bit, spun on her flats, flashed me a slight smile and locked me up with a gaze that lasted barely an instant but burned an everlasting archetype into my soul. Carl Jung, you had some solid ideas, pal. She glided from the room and closed the door behind her. Dr. Russell was busy sifting through the minimal information in Rachel's file as I stared absent-mindedly at the closed door. It never has to be much. A movement. Simple body language. Attitude. A toss of the head. A few words. The cut of a dress. A look that bores into you. An aura. I had no idea if women saw it in men, but I knew a mystique enveloped certain women. Not perfection or the idea of it. Just something that conjures appreciation for their existence. And yours. Few women I knew embodied the simplicity, yet complexity, of it. Tracie was one. And Maggie. In my life, she was still tops at it, but, of course, I never told her that.

"Mr. Grace?"

The voice seemed distant, like through an AM radio. I finally snapped to and reverted my attention to Dr. Russell.

"So, what can you tell me?" I asked, jumping back into the flow of the situation like the pro I was.

Dr. Russell looked at her desk pensively. She was struggling with a decision. On the one hand, she knew the best thing for the patient was to tell me why she came in to see her, but on the other hand, she knew the patient was counting on the confidentiality that existed.

"Why did Rachel Allen come to see you, doctor?"

She looked up at me.

"Why was she here?" I asked again.

"Rachel was pregnant. About six weeks along."

Damn. There it was. I put my hands behind my head and stood up. Rachel was knocked up by someone. Odds were her rich, older boyfriend. Jesus Christ. How could she let that happen? She had aspirations for the future, but maybe this was one of them. I had to remind myself that I didn't know her as well as I thought. Mick was going to blow a gasket.

"How'd she take the news? Being a single professional with high expectations."

"She was very excited. She radiated."

I looked out the window. The traffic didn't stop at the news. Their lives went on. Rachel was pregnant. Six weeks along four weeks ago. That meant the blessed event occured after she moved back. At first, I suspected the excursion at The Sagamore as the jumping off point, or, actually the jumping on point, but that was too early. I didn't know why The Sagamore bothered me so much right now, but it just seemed to be either an incongruity or a vital link. The Sagamore took a back seat right now to the new piece of information. Amy Simpson had mentioned that Rachel stopped partying with her. The pregnancy was why. Perhaps her curious behavior as of late was directly related, and not just with the fact of her ready to become a mother, but with her situation and the father of the child. One hell of a bomb to drop on a guy old enough to be a grandfather. Or so I assumed. Maybe the gray hair would have been all jacked up about being a father at his age, however old he was, even if the procreation took place out of wedlock. No. I doubted that. Chances were that the proud poppa caught a punch he never saw coming on this one. That is, if he was even told. All I knew was that Rachel was pregnant, and she seemed pleased by the blessed event. She suddenly disappeared. The two were connected. Period.

I fished for one of my simple cards and stepped up to the front of Dr. Russell's desk and handed it to her.

"I'm sorry for the intrusion," I said. "If you think of anything else, or if you hear from Rachel, please, call me. I appreciate your help."

She stood up and shook my hand firmly.

"I hope you find her. And I hope you find her well. If you could have seen her face..."

"Perhaps I will. Thank you again, Dr. Russell."

With the final exchange, I exited her office, walked slowly down the corridor hoping that I could avoid a confrontation with Big Red, because I didn't have the patience to do the two step with her.

*Daniel Surdam*

# *Chapter 14*

I stepped outside, glad for the late morning sunshine and prepared to tackle my next task. I wasn't quite sure what the hell I was going to say to or do with Billy Hanley, but I wanted to get in his face and let him know that he had an adversary who was smart enough to figure out who he was and tough enough to step up to his bulging pecs without feeling physically intimidated. One of my few hunches told me that I didn't have to worry at all about the attempts of mental intimidation. I changed into my grubby tank top and Timberlands and made the fifteen-minute drive out to Camillus with a lot of thoughts swirling in my head like lyrics to a song I couldn't remember the title of. Rachel disappeared pregnant. Who knew? Somebody had to besides Dr. Russell. Billy "Blue Eyes" sure knew something.

I pulled into the standard brick building apartment complex and weaved through a few "Lanes," "Courts" and "Ways" until I found 100 Willow Circle. An empty playground was at the far end of the circle. The place reminded me of a scene from one of those nuclear holocaust movies. A Toyota Tercel and an old Plymouth Fury were the only two vehicles parked in the alloted spaces that fronted the building. Billy wasn't home. Maybe Ricky was. It was a nice day to sit inside, watch talk shows and soap operas, soaking in the brilliant rhetoric and knocking back a six-pack of Old Milwaukee tall boys. It would be considered studying for Ricky while his heroic brother was out stomping on computer nerds to help amass the family fortune. I parked at the far right end of the building and headed inside after I pulled on my Bomber cap and tucked my gun in my pants and hid it with my tank top. I figured that I could bluff Ricky into telling me where Billy was, if Ricky was even home. Maybe it was Take Your Little Punk Criminal Brother to Work Day, and I didn't know. A row of stainless steel mailboxes rested against the left wall inside of the door. Billy's name was taped onto one of the designated boxes. The carpet was not particularly clean and the walls were a rather benign and ugly shade of yellow. Quite a contrast from Rex Steinman's place of residence. Another guy I needed to pay a visit to. The stairs were to the right and split the building in two with two apartments on either side for the three floors. Apartment seven was at the top of the stairs to the front left. I heard *Four Walls of Raiford* by Lynyrd Skynyrd from their *Legends* release coming from inside.

There wasn't a doorbell, so I banged on the door with the side of my fist so Ricky could at least hear it. I waited thirty seconds, filling the time by counting the debris piled up in the corners of the landing, and banged again. The door finally cracked open, the chain securely in place. I assumed it wasn't Ricky peeking out at me, because I saw a somewhat attractive, sweaty face with a little too much makeup looking back at me. Her dark hair was messy and fell around her face. I made another clever assumption. Ricky and the young lass were engaged in a little extracurricular activity. It helped that I could see that she was still naked, and she possessed a fine body from my slim vantage point. Maybe Ricky was an aspiring painter, and his current subject was nudes. Then again, sometimes my optimism gets the best of me. But I had to think, if they were in the throes of sexual bliss, why the hell would Ricky send her to open the door? Had to be that this was big brother's place. And listening to Lynyrd Skynyrd?

"Yes?" Her expression displayed her annoyance.

Before I could utter a word, a voice from beyond shouted out, "Well, who the fuck is it, Tracie?" A double Tracie morning. This one didn't quite have it, though.

She turned away from me and said back to Ricky, defiantly, "I don't fucking know. I just opened the goddamn door. Looks like one of your brother's buddies. Jesus Christ."

She reverted her attention to me. I didn't waste a Holden Grace killer smile on her. It wouldn't have worked; I interrupted a vital ritual. No dose of my high wattage teeth would have helped, so I decided to play the role of Billy's pal -- a role for which I wisely dressed.

"What you want?" I could see why Ricky might want something spiritual with this Tracie. To the point. Ready to get back to the action.

"I'm lookin' for Billy."

"He ain't here."

"Who the fuck is it, Tracie?" Ricky again piped up from somewhere inside the apartment.

Tracie turned away again. I hoped her neck didn't get sore from the workout.

"Someone lookin' for Billy."

"Who?" He wasn't happy. Big surprise.

"Lemme ask, okay? Jesus." Back to me. "Who's askin'?"

"An old buddy from the Pen. He told me to look him up when I got out. Surprise. I got out."

I offered up a cheeseball, wiseguy laugh. Or at least what I thought one would sound like. The seat of my pants had just cleared for takeoff.

Tracie updated Ricky. "It's an old friend of Billy's"

"Christ. Hang on. I'm comin'."

"Fine, Romeo. You take care of it."

Tracie took her fine package and left me to stare at a slice of living room. I saw part of an entertainment center and some green carpeting. The view I just had was far superior.

"I'm makin' myself a drink," Tracie continued. A statement muttered more to herself than anyone.

I heard some basic profanities easily slide from Ricky's mouth as he positioned himself in front of the door. The chain remained. Ricky didn't have the stunning blue eyes of his brother. They were green. His greased light brown hair was spiked on his head.

Short around the ears, with long, thin sideburns that didn't quite work their way down to the goutee he sported. He was still a good-looking kid. Had to work on his personality, though.

"So, you lookin' for Billy."

It was a statement.

165

"Yeah. We spent some time together at J.P." J.P. stood for Jamesville Penitentiary.

"You pen pals then, huh?"

Hey, clever kid. I could detect the suspicion. I couldn't blame him.

"All I know is, Billy told me to look him up here, 100 Willow Circle, apartment seven, when I got out. Said I might help him with some stuff. You wanna give me shit, that's cool. Don't blame ya. But don't piss me off, 'cause if you do, it'll piss Billy off too, believe me. You know, as much as I do, that behind those blue eyes is a mean son of a bitch. Christ. You know. Am I right?"

"Yeah. Billy's bad." He seemed less defensive.

"It's obvious he ain't here," I said. "'Cause I damn sure interrupted something good goin' on between you and Tracie. Hey, my bad on that." I pushed it and called out through the door crack, "Hey, Tracie, sorry, okay? My bad."

All I heard was a disinterested, "Whatever."

That lit Billy's fire a bit. "You got some balls..."

"Hey, just wanna atone, Ricky. And I wanna do what's right, ya know."

I could tell that he was looking me over. He saw the way I filled out the tank top. I looked like I could have been the real deal. He was in that catch twenty-two now, if he could count that high. Blow me off, I'm legit, and Billy kicks his ass from Camillus to Calcutta. Send me to Billy, and I'm not who I said I was, and Billy would have to kick my ass. Wait a second. This was no conundrum for Ricky. Even if I was a bullshitter and Ricky sent me Billy's way, Billy would kick the crap out of me. Ricky would tell me where Billy was, if he had any common sense at all.

"I could just hang around and wait for him," I offered.

Ricky turned away, most certainly to offer a look at Tracie and her finely shaped form, probably sipping on a Mai Tai or some other exotic drink. He was weighing the options. I knew

Tracie would win. That and he knew that Billy could handle me. Or so youthful thinking goes.

"No need to do that, dude."

I was getting tired of this whole scenario, especially carrying on conversations with half-faces through a six-inch crack between door frame and door. I was getting to the point where I was ready to kick the door off its hinges just to make a point.

I asked, "Know where I can find him?"

Ricky had committed. "Yeah. Sure. He's workin' at the Jungle Gym."

Ricky gladly gave me the address so that I would get the hell out of there and he could finish doing his body work on the lovely Miss Tracie. I could swear that I heard moans and groans before he even slammed the door in my face. I guess Tracie's earlier indifference met a sudden death through the almighty bottle. That can only do so much for you, I suppose.

I was on my way back to Syracuse, this time downtown. The morning had aged into early afternoon, and I could feel my stomach begin to protest. I needed to sooth the savage beast with words of culinary comfort.

"Relax," I began. "Have I ever neglected you? Just think Mexican." An offering guaranteed to make any tasteful stomach happy.

The Jungle Gym was actually not very far from my office, so I had no problem finding it. I knew the place had a reputation for recruiting the most intense muscleheads in the city for workouts, those who bulked up naturally and those who relied on a regular dose of unnatural supplements to build layers of unnatural muscle. This visit was sure to be interesting. I still had no idea what I was going to say to Billy. He'd know me right away. My appearance in his world would most likely give him a jump start. He'd need to display his badness in order not to lose face to his brethren as they tossed stacks of metal like I tossed linguine. I nosed into a parking space on Montgomery Street, stuffed some change in the beat up meter and prepared to meet the animals in the Jungle Gym, more conscious than ever of the metal weight of my Glock pressing against my stomach. I left my trusty fishing cap behind this time.

The Jungle Gym was a one-eighty from the recent establishment of the user-friendly fitness centers. As soon as I stepped through the old scarred, wooden door, the odor slapped me in the face with a serious one-two combo. No chrome. No mirrors. No wall-to-wall carpeting. No fancy equipment. No gorgeous "personal trainers" to get the best out of you. No plump middle-aged men looking to lose a couple of pounds so the women in their office might offer them a second glance. No one out of shape. No women. A lot of Olympic barbells. A lot of clanging metal. A lot of perspiration. And a lot of huge individuals who dwarfed me. But did they have my quickness? I doubted it. A few eyes turned my way when I entered, but most everyone continued intensely with their workouts.

I found him quickly. Billy Hanley was spotting a monster doing bench presses with so much weight I was surprised the floor could hold up. Billy was in the guy's face, urging, no, screaming for him to hoist the metal equivalent of a steer five more times. He called him unfriendly names. He questioned his manhood. He drove him to press the bar six more times, one more than the ultimate goal. When the behemoth dropped the bar on the rack, Billy high-fived him and praised his efforts like a parent offering words of encouragement to a favorite child. Maybe I needed Maggie's presence when I lifted to bring out the beast in me. No, I'd leave that for the bedroom. Billy's protege unfolded himself from the bench, wiped his sweaty head with a yellowish towel that was white once in its lifetime and drained some liquid from a bottle before moving over to an area where squats were the exercise of the moment.

I strolled right up to Billy and stopped a few feet in front of him. He did recognize me, and my presence brought a sneer to his face. He seemed much larger up close. And his eyes were an amazing blue, kind of like Alec Baldwin's, I guessed. He was wearing a miniscule "Jungle Gym" tank top that was cut wide to show off as much muscle as possible. His forearms put Mark

McGwire's to shame. His biceps were simply "pipes." His neck was a tree trunk. His body had a consistent theme. He was tan and handsome, if you liked the psycho-looking type. I was a solid guy, but Billy "Blue Eyes" Hanley was a wall. I shot him a smile.

"Hey, Billy. Nice to see that laying a sneak-attack, pussy-ass beating on one guy by three didn't disrupt your employment. Thought maybe your knuckles would be bruised. Force you to take a coupla days off. Rest up for when you and your buddies went after a nun or something."

Billy stepped closer. The sneer remained. As natural to him as googly eyes to Marty Feldman. He cocked his head in dramatic fashion and looked at the left side of my face where his sucker punch had landed.

"Listen, puke, we don't let rodents in the Jungle Gym, and you got a mouse on your face."

He smiled. Nice teeth. Funny guy. His bulked-up client noticed the exchange and decided he might need to move in a little closer to hear the discussion better, probably so he could improve his vocabulary along with his triceps through the wisdom of Billy. So, he passed up the squat area for now and bent an ear toward our discussion.

"How long you been workin' on that joke? Since you blind-sided me? 'Cause that was pretty good. Mouse on my face. You must've done a lot of stand up at J.P., huh? Well, that and a lot of bending over."

His smile vanished. I had a way of doing that to people.

"Listen, asshole," he growled mean and low, "don't think I won't squash you like the piece of shit you are."

"Sure, you put on a nice show with your pump buddies all around. Especially when you're probably all juiced up. But I'm not an unsuspecting guy sleeping in his bed. I'm not a pregnant woman who had a hell of a lot of living left to be done." I was searching with that one. "You may have planted a nice one on me Saturday, but you needed to do it like a coward. You know

169

what's going on. You know what you've done, and I just want you to know I'll find out. Sooner or later."

Billy had inched closer. His jaw muscles tightened noticeably. I could smell the adrenalin oozing from his pores. That and a mix of cheap cologne and sweat. Not pleasant. Worse than my bathroom after a lunch of Mexican. The rythmic din of banging metal abated as the patrons of the Jungle Gym became aware of the confrontation. Slowly. A few hard core and dedicated lifters ignored our discourse and continued breaking down their muscle tissue only to build it up again bigger and better. Billy's mind was churning, trying to calculate a course of action. Being subjected to complicated situations wasn't one of Billy's regular habits. His blue eyes shot right through me. Oh hell, I knew he wanted to lay me out like a sack of fetid laundry. Right there. In front of his cronies.

"Sure would hate to see you mess up parole in the heat of the moment, Blue Eyes," I baited him.

He finally decided to speak. Slowly, like it was an effort. Like it was a transference of his pent up desire to have me join the many dead and trampled bugs on the floor below. He kept his voice low. A gift for me only.

"I ain't got a clue 'bout what you're talking about. I'm just a guy doin' his job, and you're in here hasslin' me. I'd hate to see my buddies feel like they had to defend me and stomp your sorry ass right here. Right in front of my smilin' face."

He was surprisingly holding his composure. Interesting.

"That's only 'cause they know you need the backup. Kinda like your brother Ricky needed earlier." I winked. That was the ticket.

"You fuckin' worm, Grace." He knew my name. I expected that. "If you laid one monkey paw on my brother, I swear, man..."

Billy must've liked the animal kingdom.

"You'll what, Billy Blue Eyes?" I returned the low voice. What the hell, I could be dramatic, too.

170

He had his fists balled up. The muscles in his forearms bulged like pythons straining to burst through the skin. The veins protruded from his neck. He pointed a finger at me that looked like he did curls with.

"You don't know who you're fucking with. Period," he growled. "So far, you been a very lucky man. Too lucky. But keep pushin' it, and it's goodnight Gracie. Now, get the fuck outta my gym before I turn loose the hounds."

Christ, this guy must have grown up on a farm or next to a zoo. I surveyed the gym. I had a lot of mean eyes staring at me. I had made my point and extracted a bit of information from Billy, so I figured that now was as good a time as any to make my exit. Hell, considering I had no plan when I waltzed through the door, I assumed the adventure to be rather productive. I turned to leave, not concerned about watching my back. I could hear plenty of under-the-breath comments from the clientele, none of it friendly, but that would be the extent of it.

As I reached the door, I turned back to Billy, who was still staring me down, and reassured him, "By the way, Ricky's fine, unless, of course, sweet Tracie overpleasured him. See ya around."

And with that I was again back in the August sunshine and damn happy about it. I took a deep breath of the small city air and enjoyed it. I really needed some lunch.

## *Chapter 15*

I was in my Jeep, heading back to Skaneateles, my stomach pleasantly filled with chicken burritos, refried beans and Mexican rice from a Mexican restaurant in Syracuse. I had thought of stopping by my office, but when I went to count the reasons on my fingers, I couldn't get to one. I could call Carl Hendrix from home, and since he lived in Skaneateles, well, there you go, one plus one makes two. Simple stuff. The drive was uneventful except for what transpired in my head. Billy had let out more information than I'm sure his boss would like, whomever that boss may be. He appeared, if Billy was to be believed, to wield some serious influence. Right now, it appeared that Rachel disappeared at the hands of her rich, powerful, older boyfriend. While with child. Billy Hanley was hired muscle. Whether he had anything to do with the disappearance or whether he was just taking the boss's orders now still remained to be discovered. The boyfriend showed no patience for anyone poking around about Rachel's whereabouts. Smelled bad to me. Worse than the Jungle Gym. Grim reality convinced me not to be too optimistic about Rachel's well being. A thought I wasn't about to share with Mick just yet. Damn, if Carl Hendrix wasn't looking pretty good right about now.

I pulled into my driveway around two o'clock. The day was still beautiful, weather-wise, anyway. No messages on my machine. Good news, I supposed. I had hoped for a call from Maggie, but she was so self-sufficient that she would purposely not call me to prove it. I dialed the Hendrix's number. I wasn't expecting Carl to be around, but I'd rather call now than wait around three or four hours. The same female voice that answered when I called from Rachel's apartment greeted me after three rings.

"Hello?"

"Is Carl around by any chance?" I asked.

"No, Carlton won't be home for... oh, two, three, maybe six hours." There was sarcasm on the edge of her voice. Not thick, but evident in the way she said his name and rattled off the number of hours. I knew I was in the right line of work with such sharp senses. "Can I take a message?" she continued.

"Sure, that'd be great. Is this Mrs. Hendrix?"

"Perhaps. Who wants to know?" Definite flirtation.

No point in avoiding who I was and why I wanted to speak with Carl. The cat was out of the bag as far as I was concerned once they, whoever "they" specifically were, tenderized Mick.

"Holden Grace."

"Nice name." I could picture her tongue flicking at the mouthpiece when she said it.

"Thanks. You can call me Holden. Can I call you Stephanie, or would you like to stick with the formalities and Mrs. Hendrix?"

She snorted. Literally. "Please."

She made it a two syllable word. More sarcasm? Oh, I think so.

"You can call me Steph. Now, Holden, what is the message you would like to leave for Mr. Hendrix?" she continued.

"I'm a private detective, and I'd like to stop by to ask Carl, uh, Mr. Hendrix a few questions about a case I'm working on."

"A real, live detective? Must be exciting work."

"In all honesty, Steph, pretty boring most of the time."

"I'm sure you underestimate your position."

Stephanie Hendrix was very good at the art of flirtation.

"You're very kind."

"Perhaps..."

"Yes?"

She was toying with me a bit. Not a problem, if I accomplished something.

She continued, "Perhaps I could shed some light on this investigation of yours. You could come by, ask me what you need. Maybe by the time we were finished, Carl would be home, and you could put the screws to him. Isn't that what private detectives do to those they're questioning? Put the screws to them?"

Now she was out of control.

"I'm not sure, but that sounds like something a carpenter would do."

She snorted again. Easy to please, I guessed.

"So, what about my offer?" she asked.

I swirled it in my mind like a mouthful of Cabernet. How did this taste? Like one hell of a setup by the not-too-subtle Stephanie Hendrix. Either she was looking for some side action while hubby was at work or romping with someone else, or she just enjoyed busting balls. While option A was flattering, depending on how she looked, and she didn't have a clue as to what I looked like, option B was preferred at this point. So, if I could get some information, I felt that duty called.

"I could be there in ten minutes, but only if you promise me one thing."

"Yes?" she cooed.

"Tell me where I'm going."

She laughed. "You're the detective. You can't find the way?"

"Maybe I'm not a very good one."

"Sure."

Steph told me the address on the west side of Skaneateles Lake, a couple of miles down where the new money erected beautiful lakeside homes on huge parcels that once were farm fields. I changed into something a little more presentable for Stephanie Hendrix -- a pair of gray Haggar slacks and a white golf shirt with the letters CNN embroidered in dark blue on the left breast. I wheeled my Jeep down a winding driveway through a small stand of old, stately trees before entering a clearing where an impressive southern-style brick colonial house sprawled behind a circular-paved drive with the shimmering lake in the background.

The lawn was a perfect green. No weeds were visible to my human eye, eradicated, I was sure, by a weekly assault of the best pesticides money could buy. The landscaping was impeccable. A lot of flowers, shrubs and small trees I could never identify. Some I did know, and I felt a small sense of accomplishment for that fact. The asphalt turned to well-laid brick where the driveway led to the decorative front door recessed behind four twenty-foot columns. The main part of the home was two stories with five windows on the second floor and four, two on each side of the front door, on the first floor. The main section had single-story wings on each side. The place had to be at least five thousand square feet, and that was most likely a conservative number coming from a guy whose house fell short of one thousand square feet. The place was gorgeous, and that wasn't even factoring in the location. A spread like this had to be well over one million. Someday, Holden. Someday.

Despite my earlier promise to myself, I locked my piece in the glove compartment -- I was getting irritated, mentally and physically, from it being in my pants, and I didn't think I'd need it to beat back Steph -- walked up and rang the front doorbell, almost expecting a maid in the obligatory outfit to usher me in and seat me in the library while she fetched Mrs. Hendrix. Thankfully, that wasn't the case. An attractive woman in her late thirties or early forties, wearing a pair of dark blue Umbro soccer shorts over a one-piece bathing suit that was also dark blue, answered the door. She was around five-eight, in nice shape, with a healthy chest, an admirable waist and nicely proportioned hips. Not perfect, but a head turner in public. Made you wonder why her husband, especially an older guy, would look elsewhere to clean out his pipes. It sure wasn't from any physical shortcomings. Strangely enough, she resembled Rachel. Her dark hair framed her tan face quite nicely, seemingly softening the age and sun lines that were visible upon closer inspection. She must have had one hell of a stylist to pull off a trick like that.

"Mr. Grace, I presume?" More great teeth. I'd seen a lot of those today.

"There we go with the formalities. I thought we settled on Holden."

"Let's start over. Holden, I presume?"

"Your presumption is accurate."

"Won't you come in?" she quite nicely offered.

"Absolutely."

I stepped into the two-story gray ceramic-tiled foyer complete with chandelier, exotic-looking potted plants, appealing artwork, an antique-looking table and an expensive-looking Oriental carpet. I was quite sure that everything I saw was authentic and not just "looking." A wide, open staircase led up the left side of the foyer and took a right turn up to a second-floor landing. There were two sets of French doors, one on each side, and Steph led us through the doors on the right that led into the formal dining room. A large dark-wood table sat in the center of the space surrounded by what was more than nicely crafted-looking chairs. I was going out on a limb on that one. The hardwood floor gleamed. I noticed the crown molding, which always added an aesthetic touch to a room. Beyond the dining room was the spacious kitchen with oak cabinets as far as the eye could see.

"This is a very lovely home," I offered.

"Thank you, Holden. It has its high points."

We walked through the kitchen into a sun room that was bright in the mid-afternoon sun and filled with plants, all of them healthy and thriving. Through a set of sliding glass doors, and we finally arrived at our destination. I'd need a map to find my way back if I left alone. We stepped out onto an outdoor deck, stained a pleasing cedar, that wrapped around an amazing kidney-shaped in-ground swimming pool with a cabana. But that wasn't the highlight. The view of the lake. Spectacular. Sailboats drifted lazily along the top of the water, as if an intergral part of the whole equation. The lush back lawn sloped gently down to the lake's shore, a boathouse, larger than my home, perched at the edge with a long dock extending well into the water. A brick retaining wall had been built at the water's edge.

"Would this, perhaps, be one of the high points?" I asked when I could find my voice.

"You are a private detective, aren't you?" she answered with a question.

We sat down at a patio table near the pool, which was large enough to drown half of my house. Steph put on a pair of sunglasses that were on the table. She also hoisted up a glass that contained a Bloody Mary. The ice had melted dramatically. The condensation rolled down the glass as she drank. It just seemed appropriate for her.

"Would you care for a drink, Holden?" she asked as she set the glass down.

All the ingredients lay before us on the table, including a bottle of V8 and not tomato juice, which for me was a key to a better Bloody Mary. Steph had out the Stoly vodka, some necessary hot sauce, worcestershire sauce, celery salt, celery stalks and a bucket of ice.

"If a Bloody Mary doesn't suit you, I could get something else," she added.

I liked Bloody Marys. Especially spicy ones.

"No," I said. "The house drink will do just fine. Extra spicy, though. Please."

Steph mixed it like an expert, of which she probably was. She finished the job and handed over the drink. I sipped, rolled it in my mouth like everything I drank when I wasn't drinking to quench my thirst.

"Tastes great, and all of those wonderful vitamins," I said.

"Glad you approve."

"Hard not to," I said. "This is all very impressive, from the drink on up to the top-of-the-line view."

A wooden boat, maybe a Chris Craft, cruised by leisurely. The group aboard waved even though they were hundreds of yards away and couldn't tell if we were Stephanie Hendrix and

Holden Grace or Jimi Hendrix and Princess Grace. Steph shot back a wave out of habit, or so it seemed.

"Yes, living the good life on the shores of Skaneateles Lake is rather glamorous. Or so most of us think so. But, take a look. Where exactly are we? This isn't the Riviera. It's Central New York. The real New York is five and a half hours away."

"Forty minutes by plane," I interjected.

"Right."

She reduced her Bloody Mary to a Bloody Stump with a long pull.

"You can wear a gold Piaget on your semaphore wrist. You can dance the old adage with a new dapper twist," I offered.

"Excuse me?"

She still held the glass in her right hand, the hand that extended from the wrist that sported the Rolex.

"Jethro Tull lyrics. *Crazed Institution*. Thought they fit. I like to be clever sometimes."

She set her glass down. I raised mine and took a healthy swallow.

"I suppose we're all entitled," she said.

Stephanie Hendrix was turning out to be an interesting piece of work. From flirtatious to bitter to sullen. I needed to work her back in the other direction. Maybe flashing some leg would help. Or refilling her drink. Ah, there's the ticket. I took her glass and began the ceremonial mixing. Ice cubes, vodka, the hot sauce, worcestershire, V8 juice, the celery and the stir. Steph just sat back and watched, hopefully pleased that I was taking the initiative for her. I finished the process and set the glass before her. She cocked her head to the side, smiled a nice smile, picked up the glass like a superheroine scooping up a defeated villain and sampled my offering.

She said, "Not bad. A bit on the spicy side, but that works. Better than being too damn dull."

"I concur."

We clinked glasses and sipped and looked out over the lake.

"You gotta admit, Steph, it's a pretty damn impressive little spread you got here. Hell, if megastars like Paul Newman are looking to buy property here, it's gotta offer something. Am I right?"

"I'm not gonna deny that. This is beautiful." She stressed the word "is."

"Is there supposed to be a "but" to follow?"

"No." She shook her head. "I couldn't ask for more."

She stood up, peeled off her shorts and dove into the crystal-clear waters of the pool. Her backside held up as well as the rest of her. She swam effortlessly to the far end, disappeared for a moment, flipped and made the return swim to the end nearer me, which was the shallower end. She stood near the side of the pool, slicked her hair back and just looked at me. In silence for what seemed like too long. Hell, I had nothing to say in reply to a silent stare like that. I knew better. Too much experience.

"So what do you say we discuss this case of yours?" she finally asked.

She rested her arms over the side of the pool. She had herself under control. She steered the direction of the conversation now. That was fine with me. I sipped my Bloody Mary and thought about where to start. After all, I suspected her husband in the disappearance of Rachel Allen. I suspected her husband of having an affair with a much younger woman, knocking her up and then snatching her up for some reason, most likely tied to the fact that he was still married and had this Camelot to tend to along with a seemingly bored, yet very attractive, wife. It suddenly occured to me that Stephanie Hendrix never showed concern about her husband being linked to a case led by a private investigator. Either she didn't give a damn or she had no reason to be upset.

"Where to begin," I mused.

"How about anywhere."

A statement, not a question.

I stood up, walked around the table toward the pool where Steph was positioned so naturally and comfortably and stared out

180

toward the lake. She was obviously accustomed to living this life, her father being Curtis Granby, the real estate mogul, who, I believed, owned an old-money estate on the east side of the lake. I stuck my hands in my pockets, a reflective gesture I imagine. A few boats were making wakes in the water. I turned and stared at the house. I again marvelled at the estate, and I felt at ease thinking of the Hendrix compound as an estate. I didn't think it cracked the top ten in property value on the lake like Granby's surely must have, but it held its own, undoubtably. I could have pictured myself living there. Maybe it was a very faint picture, but I saw it.

"How long you and Carl been married?" I asked while still facing the house, my hands still buried in my pockets.

"Fifteen years in July."

I turned back to face her. I folded my arms across my chest. Ah yes, Holden. That's it. Look reflective.

"You must've been pretty young," I said.

"I don't know if that's a compliment or simply stating a fact."

"Would you settle with both?"

"Sure. And, yes, I was rather young."

"And Mr. Hendrix must have been slightly older." I tweaked the work "slightly."

"Carl is fifteen years older than I am." She emphasized "is."

Steph climbed out of the pool. I saw a towel on the back of one of the chairs, grabbed it and handed it to her. She carefully rubbed her hair, dried her shoulders, and worked her way down her tanned body. She took her time, which was perfectly fine with me. I didn't mind the show at all. Hell, it was only PG anyway. She eventually wrapped the towel around her waist and retrieved her drink, of which she drained much. We faced each other.

"So, how's married life?" I asked like a buddy would ask another how the fishing was. It was an attempt at levity. The tone was not serious, but the question was actually meant to be.

181

"Married life? Fix me another one of these," she held up her nearly empty glass, "and maybe I'll enlighten you."

"Less spicy this time?"

"Doesn't matter."

I took her glass. She sat down. I mixed up a fresh Bloody Mary for her. I was losing count of them. I handed it to her, and she instantly made an acquaintance. Her smile expressed her approval. At this rate, I'd be as much of an expert as she was at mixing them up. I sat down also. I couldn't help but to scan the surroundings for the sheer beauty.

"You're not married, are you?" she asked, still rather sober sounding.

"No, no, no."

"Emphatic answer."

"Don't see it happening to me too soon."

"Wise choice. Let me tell you, all those goddamn ideals and dreams and hopes and wishes that are part of the formula that you imagine as the perfect... the perfect wedding package are bullshit. It all starts out like it should. Great sex every night. Joy in being with each other after being apart. Little things still mean alot. Thoughtfulness is still there. No petty crap that starts terribly ugly fights. But then, it slowly breaks down, like an eroding sea wall." She pointed out to the brick wall near the edge of the lake. "And then, it all comes to a head. One night. One mistake, and you can kiss the good times good-bye. You can remember when each other mattered the most, but memories can't heal the wounds. Not even close. A terrible mistake becomes the final wedge driven between two people who so once cared for each other. And from there, you can just forget about it."

She raised her glass to me and then syphoned half the contents, expertly draining the liquid around the cumbersome ice cubes.

"It's not that Carl hasn't provided for me." She spread her hands dramatically, the glass still in her right hand. "As you can plainly see. But..." She chewed her lower lip and paused. "But, how much does all this material shit mean if you don't have someone to either share it with or give it to?"

I wisely assumed that it was a rhetorical question. Chalk one up for me.

"When you commit to someone for life," she continued freely, "you plan for a family. You want children, then grandchildren. You want them to visit Mom and Dad, Grandma and Grandpa. You want to spoil them. You want to provide for them. And you look at other couples who have children who don't even deserve them. Who curse their burden, when their ignorance can't comprehend that there are people out there who cry every night because they can't have children. That they would cherish caring for a crying infant, a mischeivous toddler, a snotty teenager. But, guess what? I can't. This big fucking house is empty. And it didn't have to be."

I squirmed in my chair. This was important information, and I was certain that more was to come, but I wasn't comfortable. I saw a speed boat rip up the surface of the calm water, spraying a rooster tail out behind it. The boat didn't seem to fit on the lake, but... Steph finished her drink and prepared another with no hesitation. My first one wasn't quite finished. Sure, V8 was good for you, but the stuff packed enough sodium to shrivel up a family reunion of snails. If this was Steph's standard operational procedure, her blood pressure had to be skyrocketing.

"It's not that Carl and I didn't want children. They were part of our plans for the future. And a few years ago, after years of surgery and infertility treatments, surprise, we were gonna to be parents. We were both ecstatic. One of the reasons we built this house was to raise children."

I ignored my drink. Steph didn't ignore hers.

"But as the pregnancy progressed, things became more difficult for Carl at work. Bad deals. Canceled deals. Bad employees. Bad fucking timing. We also needed to be really careful about the pregnancy because of my medical history. When we found out I was pregnent, I used a home test. So, I called my doctor, and he naturally wanted me to come in for an official test. So, Carl went with me, and sure enough, they all congratulated us. It was amazing. Just amazing. The thought of a life inside of me. But we still had to be extra cautious. I needed to have a sonogram right away. They were concerned about my history, with all the surgeries. But everything was fine. It was fantastic, but the ups and the downs. Why couldn't it just be simple? Ya know?"

It looked as if tears started to well in Steph's eyes, but she quickly put the brakes on.

She went on, "With Carl's struggles at work and the worries about me, the tension became unbearable. It was too uncomfortable. On the cliched pins and needles, where chills run up your spine when the other approaches because you're worried about the consequences. Frankly, it sucked, and it shouldn't have been that way. It wasn't good for me or the baby or the marriage. So, one night, we decided to go out to dinner, the two of us, actually, the three of us, and just relax."

The boats had seemed like they decided to stop churning along this part of the lake, leaving the stage completely to Steph, which, from the degree of the story, she deserved.

She went on without hesitation, "It was a nice dinner, at first. But Carl kept knocking back drinks. He opened with two Stoly vodka tonics, then went through a bottle of Cabernet Sauvignon with dinner. In fact, a 1985 Diamond Creek Volcanic Hill. After dinner, a couple Remy Martins. Booze was his tonic. It should have been the prospect of our child. I wasn't happy with his, ah, consumption, and on the ride home, I expressed so much. The exchange became heated. He diverted his attention from the road and toward me, and I still remember what he said -- 'Right now, if you had a job instead of a kid, I'd be drinking a lot less.' He should have been watching the fucking road, not like it mattered in his state. We swerved off the shoulder, flipped over a culvert and sheered off a telephone pole. Carl broke an arm. I lost a baby and the prospect of ever having another."

Steph looked away, out over the lake.

"Jesus Christ," I thought, "this was some really heavy stuff."

Steph belted more of her drink. How come she wasn't getting numb yet? Maybe because she was so numb in her life that the booze didn't matter much. She looked back at me. The tears were there. I had to summon up my tough guy image to hold my composure. I knew she had more to say. I had nothing to say.

"We recovered. Physically. Then, we chose to ignore the most important healing of all -- the emotional healing. Instead, we chose to act like the loss never happened. Pull yourself up by your fucking bootstraps and move on with life. Be tough. Handle it. Ignore it. That's resulted in a worse pain than the physical loss. I've lost a husband. I've now chosen to really lose me."

She tipped her glass to punctuate her comment. "It's not an excuse. Just a reality. I suggested therapy, but Carl was proud. He protested it. Said it was all bullshit that anyone couldn't handle on their own. He didn't realize how much I resented him for the loss. Maybe he did, and this was his way of punishing himself. We just never talked about it. We never grieved. We never suffered emotionally. We never cried together and held each other and screamed at each other and just released. And now, we go through the motions. Does he love me? Maybe, in his distant way. Do I love him? I haven't been sober enough in years to even consider that, which, I would assume, means I'm avoiding the question, and, therefore, answers it by default."

I simply sat in the sunshine, looking into eyes that were far from simple. I searched for a diversion and drained the mostly water remains of my drink. At this point, I could use another, mostly for the process of giving me a break from the intense listening I had unwittingly committed to. I still had questions, though. And I needed to ask them. I poured and mixed a very weak Bloody Mary. Steph remained silent, rather composed after her catharsis.

I decided to venture into shark-infested waters.

I asked, "What about adoption?"

"I'm too selfish."

185

No hesitation. An honest answer.

"Why?" I asked.

"This may sound egotistical or elitist, and, frankly, I don't care, but I didn't want to take a chance on a child that wasn't from my gene pool. May sound sick to you, but those are my honest feelings."

"How'd Carl feel about that?"

"Not happy. But not unhappy enough to push it, so it was swept under the carpet along with everything else."

This was one damaged relationship.

"Then why the hell stay together?" I questioned.

"Comfort. Convenience. I don't dare say the sanctity of marriage. That would bring a bolt of lightning from the sky."

She toasted the heavens with her empty glass, finally showing signs of the alcohol's influence. Surprisingly, it still hadn't affected her speech to the point of slurring. Give us this day our daily booze, I suppose.

"I guess we just reached an unspoken understanding. For Carl, that meant seeking comfort in the beds of other, and younger, women. For me, that meant seeking the comfort of a good stiff drink. And my right hand when the occasion arose."

Oh, shit, too much information, except for the younger women mention. She saw me blush. Tough not to, even for a tough guy like me. She enjoyed it.

"You see, I just didn't have the need to seek out another man. The one I truly loved already fucked me up and fucked me over and elected to leave it at that. Not man enough to face it down. Instead, he took it elsewhere, and the crazy thing is, I still feel he is, deep down, a good man. He just fell into an abyss and couldn't or wouldn't climb out. I believe convoluted describes the situation."

"May I be so bold as to ask how your father, the extremely wealthy Curtis Granby, feels about this, ah, arrangement, for lack of a better word?"

"Funny, you should bring that up. I thought maybe you didn't know of the gene pool of which I earlier spoke."

"Remember, trained detective."

"But, of course. Daddy was heartbroken about the loss. I'm his only daughter. He's not a big fan of Carl, never was, and the accident helped enhance those feelings. But he has stayed out of it, for the most part. Plus, he had his own broken marriage to worry about. He just finished up a messy divorce with my mother. It was really sad to see. But, I suppose that's the kettle calling the pot black, huh? I guess I should applaud them both for seeking closure, no matter how nasty it got, and no matter how they used me in the process."

"So, here you sit, dealing with your life on your terms."

"So, here I sit, dealing with life with an empty glass in hand, and now ready to speak with you about your case. Sorry it took so long."

"I don't know whether to praise or condemn you," I said.

"Nice way to get me to help you."

"I'm just being honest. But, Christ, it's all very confusing, isn't it?"

"I'll drink to that. No, no I won't. Be a dear and fix me another?"

She handed me her glass. The sun was beginning to take its mid-August arc toward the western horizon beyond the roof line, casting shadows that were soon to spread their cool fingers on our warm flesh. Once August passed the midpoint, it was all downhill as far as weather was concerned in Central New York, at least for those of us who cherished the summer and despised autumn. For me, it was just a bad time of year with bad memories. Thank goodness there was college football, professional football, pennant races and the World Series and the start of hockey season. They helped make the onslaught of fall more bearable. Sure, we had just experienced a perspiration-inducing August heat wave, but there was a certain smell in the air that clued me into the fact that the recent hot stretch was merely an anamoly. The trees were going to be stripped like fresh meat at a maximum security prison. Thick, ominous gray clouds would roll in like bullies, kicking out the clear skies for

Daniel Surdam

the pure enjoyment of the act. Cold winds would swirl the dead leaves about, pleased with the disruption and the dishevelment. Winter in Central New York may be a predictable nuisance, but fall was a fickle, taunting enemy who knew how to push all the right buttons.

I performed the drink-mixing ceremony for Steph and handed her the glass. Again, she immediately sampled and expressed her approval with a smile. I surmised that it was time to bring up Rachel Allen. I stood up and stepped to the edge of the crystal-clear pool. I thought of how I saw none of the flirtatious behavior that I sensed over the phone. I thought of how Steph easily unloaded on me and wondered if it was the vodka loosening her tongue or if I was just a great listener. I thought about the damage to the Hendrix's lives. The losses all around. Now I had to pry about Rachel Allen and possible involvement with Carl Hendrix. Yeah, I could feel fall coming on fast. I faced back to Steph.

"Have you ever heard the name Rachel Allen?" I asked.

Steph stopped in mid-sip, lowered her glass and offered a wry smile.

"Beautiful girl. Carl thought so, too," she replied.

"One of the younger women with whom he sought comfort, I presume?"

"Can't put one by you. She was one of his most recent, shall I say, accomplishments."

"How did you find out?"

"Word travels fast in a small town. Plus, he didn't do a hell of a lot to conceal it. Never did."

"Any idea if he's still seeing her?"

"Probably. I know that he was supposedly 'talking business' with her about her store."

"Is there anything there?"

Steph shot me an exasperated look.

I continued. "I mean, as in an actual relationship?"

"Holden, you really aren't that naive, are you? Carl simply sought to conquer these women. They were flattered because of

188

his wealth and power. Is Rachel Allen any different? Highly unlikely."

It was time to drop the big question.

"Did you know that Rachel Allen disappeared last Friday?"

She set her glass down. Calmly.

"No, no I didn't."

"And did you also know that your number was the last one she called from her apartment?"

"No... are you looking to make a connection between Rachel Allen's disappearance and Carl?"

The question was not put forth defensively.

"I don't have to try. It's already been established."

"Well, I'm sure she just took off on a little jaunt..."

"Rachel Allen is also pregnant," I interrupted.

"Oh my God. You don't think?"

"Seems like a good fit to me right now."

It looked as if Steph didn't know whether to laugh about the news from the sheer irony or to break down in tears by the ultimate insult to her as a woman and the man's wife. I honestly couldn't tell. It could've been the booze weaving its usual magic. I took this as an opportunity to wrap things up. I asked Steph to have Carl call me when he got home. I left it up to her as to how much she wanted to tell him. Very little, if anything at all, I would bet.

## *Chapter 16*

The rest of Monday passed uneventfully, actually a refreshing change from the constant action that unfolded since last Friday. Maggie still didn't call. Neither did Carl Hendrix. In fact, no one called, not even a telemarketer. That actually allowed me to bring my Jeep to a friend so that he could fix my window. Nice how sometimes things work out. It was Tuesday morning, and I was driving through the Adirondacks on my way to Burlington, Vermont, and then a backtrack to Lake George and a stop at the Sagamore. I knew I should have stuck around Skaneateles and waited for Carl Hendrix to call. I knew I shouldn't have left without at least leaving a message for Maggie, but she was a big girl, and I needed a road trip. A one-day road trip. Long, but necessary. I figured six hours to Burlington. A couple of hours poking around. I didn't expect to dig up very much, since everything pointed to occurences in the lovely village of Skaneateles, but I had to at least give it a shot. A couple hours to Lake George. Sniff around for an hour or so, and back home in four hours or so.

I was on the road by five a.m., the sun not yet up, traffic at a minimum. Driving very early in the morning was probably the best time if you had a long run to make. The weather had decided to act like late October, cold, cloudy with an ever present threat of some kind of precipitation. I grumbled about it, but there was no one to listen. I had taken the New York State Thruway east to Utica and headed north on Route 8, which eventually wound its way east into Route 9N that would lead the way to Burlington. The drive through the Adirondacks was a relaxing one. You saw a lot of forest, lakes and not a lot of civilization. Sometimes, that was the only way to go.

I crossed the Champlain Canal at Chimney Point State Park, then headed north on Route 7 into downtown Burlington. The skies had leaked a few times, like a dog shaking off after a swim in a pond, but there were no deluges. The Green Mountains were to the east and Lake Champlain was to my west as I made the drive. Burlington was not a thriving metropolis, forty thousand people or thereabouts, but they had three colleges that I knew of and an international airport, not just a municipal or an aerodrome, which was what Skaneateles had for air traffic. This was kind of a hip place to be, so I had heard. I took a left on Flynn Avenue, then a right onto Pine Street. Rachel had lived on Pine Street. I found the address, located at a restored brick factory on the lake side of the street. Looked like some pretty sweet digs. The brick had been blasted to bring out the original rusty orange color. Modern, tall and narrow windows were installed. The landscaping was nice, not quite up to par with the Hendrix's, but nice nonetheless. I parked around back in the private lot and headed for the front entrance. One perk about the cooler weather was being able to throw on a shoulder holster for my good friend Mr. Glock and covering it up with a jacket, in this instance, a fine piece of workmanship directly from the Bronx -- my New York Yankees jacket. Potted plants, carefully arranged on tiered levels, lined each side of the brick steps that led to the solid wood double-front doors. I entered a foyer that went from floor to a very high ceiling. More potted plants adorned this space. Hardwood floor, looking as if it were just buffed, gleamed. There were no stairs, just four doors, two on each side of the foyer, numbered one through four. Brilliant. Rachel's old apartment was number three, which was the back apartment on my left. I came to the assumption that each place was actually two stories. Even out-of-state, my mind worked wonders. So, what to do? Knock on number three, just before noon on a Tuesday morning, expecting the tenant to be home and not at work? Then ask, "Hey, you know anything about the former tenant? Yeah, the one who lived here before you, who you probably didn't even know. Well, mind if I come in anyway and look around?" Jesus Christ. Sometimes I really could be a major idiot. I started thinking that the main reason I made this road trip was to put this small part of the investigation behind me as soon as possible. If I could just close out this whole

Burlington and Sagamore part of Rachel's life, then I could concentrate on what happened back home in Skaneateles. And with whom. I also had to remind myself that this sort of investigating was not standard operational procedure for me. I was still learning the ropes, and I was sure that I was making mistakes. Being here, right now, was most likely one of those. Especially since I didn't grab a picture of Carl Hendrix from Stephanie to flash around. Damn good thing that Mick wasn't shelling out any dough for my services.

For the hell of it, I tried all four apartments, hoping to score with a neighbor who knew Rachel before she moved out. It wasn't like she left years ago. It was only months. No life. No luck. No doubt that I was hungry. I was ready to leave, find a Taco Bell and then head to the store that Rachel once managed, when the front door opened, and a business-type looking woman in her early thirties entered. Her auburn hair was pulled back. Her eyes were green. Her face was attractive without being pretty. Her makeup was applied carefully, at least it looked that way, but what woman applied makeup sloppily? She was about five-three, a little on the plump side, but not fat. She wore a pinstriped suit that screamed of no nonsense and sported what was left of a cigarette still burning in her right hand. A black leather purse was slung over her right shoulder. My hand was on the doorknob, and I held the door as she strutted in. She exhaled a plume of blue-gray smoke that floated inside the building like a cloud of poison gas. Such a nice touch. She must've been on lunch. A small place like Burlington would afford the luxury of going home for that purpose, especially if it was one of those executive one-hour lunches.

Lunch Lady looked at me briefly and curiously and offered a "thank you."

I said, "You're welcome," and hovered around the door, waiting to see which apartment she chose.

I felt a bit like Monty Hall on *Let's Make a Deal*. The excitement was almost overwhelming. I thought about offering her one hundred bucks for each condom she had in her purse but realized I didn't have that kind of money on me and wisely kept my wise-ass mouth closed for the time being. Chances were that she wasn't accustomed to seeing too many strange guys in the building, especially since there were only four apartments. I needed to take a cautious, charming approach. Right up my alley. Never mind the fact that the alley usually left me with a seven-ten split. She flipped her butt into one of the potted plants and walked confidently to door number four directly across the foyer from Rachel's old digs. I walked out the door as a pretense of leaving.

I looked up at the gray sky for a few seconds, allowing for the Lunch Lady to slip comfortably inside her apartment, maybe pull out her leftovers and pop them into the microwave. What was being served today down in "Lunch Lady Land?" Sloppy Joes, perhaps? Man, I did miss the antics of Chris Farley. And Phil Hartman. And John Belushi. And John Candy, for that matter. I thought about the Farley and Patrick Swayze routine on *Saturday Night Live* when they were two competing dancers for one spot with the Chippendales. Hilarious stuff. One of the best of *SNL*. It reminded me that sometimes you can't take everything for granted. Who says that an overweight guy can't have the best moves on the dance floor and maybe there'd be some ladies out there who'd appreciate those gyrations. Chances were slim, but, hey, don't always look for the obvious. A subtle reminder to me regarding this case.

I decided that I had lingered or loitered outside long enough, so I headed back inside, checked to make sure the plant didn't ignite from Lunch Lady's butt and knocked politely on her door. It opened. About six inches. The chain still in place. The obscured view I was getting all too accustomed to.

"Yes?" Lunch Lady stared at me. Her green eyes were penetrating. Her nostrils flared slightly.

"Excuse me, Miss, or, ah, Ms., but I'm with the Potted Plant Protection Program, and I noticed a blatant violation upon your entering the building, and I'm afraid I have to give you a citation." Charm. Oozing like sap out of a maple.

Lunch Lady's face scrunched up.

"You what? Who the hell are you?"

I think I had won her over. I saw the smoke of another burning cigarette swirling up around her face.

"You know. That's a terrible habit. Stains your teeth. Makes your clothes smell. To say nothing about your lungs. And, of course, the potted plants when you use them for an ashtray."

If she started to disrobe right then and there I wouldn't have been surprised in the least. I was so smooth. Really making her feel special. I prepared for her to slam the door in my face by sliding my left foot near the opening.

"How 'bout I use your asshole as an ashtray? Get lost, creep," she eloquently responded.

The door made its move, but my well-placed Nike hiking boot interrupted the intention.

"Sorry, can't let you go so easily," I said.

She scowled. It was a good, practiced scowl, one I had seen often in my youth in bars from uninterested and downright unsociable ladies who weren't about to give the time of night, a second glance or the benefit of a second of awkward conversation to some punk who had no tact with the opposite sex. I thought I had come a long way, but then again, life could be a vicious cycle.

I pulled out my creds and flashed them.

I said, "Actually, I'm a private detective. Surprise. The name's Holden Grace."

"Jesus Christ," she muttered. "I thought you were some goddamn creep. Not that you're not..."

"Well, thank you."

"Well, what the hell kind of approach is Potted Plant Protector or whatever?"

"Just being charming?"

"Keep working on it. Hard."

"Promise. Here's a start. Could I come in and ask you a few questions, please?"

195

"About what?"

She took a drag from her smoke. The ash looked Pinocchio's nose. She exhaled through the door. Nice.

"Rachel Allen. So that would be a whom, not a what." Oops. Not very charming, Holden.

It seemed to have bypassed her synapses.

"Good old Rachel," was her comment.

The sarcasm surpassed her brashness, which seemed like a tough thing to do.

"Ah," I said, "I've struck a familiar, if not pleasant, chord."

I stared her down. She stared back, now half uninterested, but half wanting to tell me how much she hated Rachel and why. The urge to vent proved victorious.

"All right," she finally said. "Move your foot so I can close the door and get the chain."

"Now, you're not just gonna pretend to let me in and slam the door on me, are you?"

"Alway that chance."

She took another drag. The ashes somehow stayed connected to the butt as if a magic trick by David Copperfield, or more like Penn and Teller. Another blow of smoke through the door.

"I'll take my chances. Otherwise I could get lung cancer from second-hand smoke."

I removed my foot. The door closed. I heard the chain unfasten, and, a bit to my surprise, the door reopened.

I said, "Thank you," as I stepped across the threshold.

"Don't think it had anything to do with your charm, pal," she reminded me.

The apartment was spacious, immaculate, tastefully decorated and commanding of some good coin. I entered the great room as I stepped in. The room ran the length of the wall to my left with three floor to ceiling windows that looked out over Lake Champlain. The windows had expensive-looking window treatments, no simple white mini-blinds like at my house. The interior walls were brick with exposed wooden

196

support beams between the windows. The ceiling was nicely finished open joists. Lunch Lady's furniture was earthy looking, overstuffed a bit and arranged carefully around a rather extraordinary Oriental carpet that hid too much of the beautiful hardwood floor. But that was my opinion. She had a sofa, a matching loveseat and a straightback chair that looked more braggadocio than functional. A bookcase rested against the far wall. Artsy prints were hung on the walls along with many photographs. In fact, I saw a lot of photographs, but I didn't see one of Lunch Lady with Rachel. The television was set in one of those oversized entertainment centers, surrounded by photos, a Bose stereo and more frogs than a farmer's pond could hold. Interesting. As I looked around, I saw more frogs. Maybe she was still in search of her prince.

The dining area was to my right, large enough to hold a table with seating for six, a china cabinet, two straight back wooden chairs, a wine rack, all with plenty of room to push back the chair after a fine meal, let out a belch and undo your pants in ample comfort. Beyond the dining room was a set of open metal stairs that obviously led up to the second floor of the apartment and at least two bedrooms and one and a half baths. Pure conjecture on my part. The kitchen was on the other side of the stairs and had enough room for a small table, which currently had a salad sitting on a green woven placemat. Keen eyes and keen insight allowed me to home in on that. Plus, I knew I was interrupting Lunch Lady's lunch. At least it wasn't a once steaming bowl of chili or split pea soup that was cooling quicker than most of my dates. The appliances were modern. Surprise, they were white, not a fine bullfrog green. The cabinets were ample and white. The key to people who rented out space like this was to make everything top of the line, with loads of space. That way, tenants wouldn't want to move out and buy a house that might not have been as large or fashionable. Hey, it was a good strategy if you thought for a second that most people wouldn't trade larger, beautiful rental space for smaller, needs-some-work ownership. It all depended on your business optimism.

Lunch Lady rushed to find an ashtray in the kitchen as I stood and surveyed the place. I stepped to get a closer look at some of the photographs on the bookshelf. Many were of Lunch Lady with an older man or Lunch Lady and the man with other young women, who I assumed were her sisters (that's me doing my great detective work again, especially since there was a distinct family resemblance). She returned with her salad bowl in her left hand and a fork in the right. Lunch Lady was no nonsense. I liked that. She dug in.

"So, what do you want to know about Rachel Allen Wrench?" she asked around bites of what looked like leftover chicken Caesar salad. It looked good, too.

"Allen Wrench?"

"Sure. She loved to turn the screws to you."

That had a faint ring of familiarity.

"How so?" I asked, rather surprised about a development concerning Rachel where someone loathed her. I didn't. I liked her much. At least the Rachel I seemed to know. But, then again, I didn't think that she would willingly and knowingly engage in a relationship with a married man, even if the marriage looked like it was deader than a sun-baked worm on an asphalt basketball court. And then jeopardize a future of the businesswoman she wanted so badly to be by getting pregnant. Apparently by this married man. Or maybe by that married man. Or maybe by some young stud. I didn't know.

"Oh, she loved to brag about how much money she had. About the car she drove. Her nice clothes. Her jewelry. Said she only fucked rich guys. That one day she'd wipe the dust of Burlington off her ass..."

"She said she only... uh... had sex with rich guys?" I asked. I stressed the word "guys."

"Yeah, guys, as in more than one," she replied rather bored. She fed some more greens into the human hopper.

I watched her chew for a moment and realized, the astute P.I. that I was, that I didn't even know Lunch Lady's name. Christ. She knew mine. Maybe I had better start thinking less about being clever and more about being thorough.

"By the way, I don't even know your name," I said.

"Makes you one hell of a private dick then, doesn't it?"

"In more ways than you know or could ever dream of knowing."

"Yeah, right. You weren't doing the mattress mambo with ole Rachel now, were ya?" she asked with a raised right eyebrow.

"Not my type," I countered. "Apparently I wasn't rich enough."

"Lucky for you."

"Must be my week. Now, how about a name?"

"Sure. I got nothing to hide. Especially from you. Brooke Kamiskey."

She set her fork in the bowl and stuck out her hand. I shook it. Firm grip. No surprise there.

"You want to sit down?" she asked. "I stand all day at work."

"Sure."

We stepped into the kitchen and sat. Brooke went back to her lunch. She was a loud chewer. Her noisy mastication brought back thoughts of my father, and how us kids always thought that he could make a marshmallow go "crunch." Now, following in his footsteps, I'm told that I chew loudly.

"So, why you askin' about Rachel?" she asked around bites.

"She's missing."

"Probably on some money-spending, sex-filled getaway with one of her many sugar daddies."

She said it so matter-of-factly, like Rachel was a leg-spreading golddigger who played Russian roulette with wealthy men who were happy to lay out a few bucks to have a gorgeous, young brunette at their sides and hopefully in their beds. It seemed more and more like I missed the boat on Rachel somewhere.

"A regular practice of hers?" I asked.

"From the way she talked."

"But you guys were hardly considered friends, right? Why would she bother sharing that kind of info?"

I received another one of her looks. This one bordered on "what the hell kind of idiot are you, anyway?"

She enlightened me. "Someone like that, if you're anywhere in earshot, will make it a point to clue you in. We lived across from each other, Smart Guy, so it wasn't like we were total strangers. She wanted me to know. Get it?"

"Got it. So you guys were never close?"

"We were friendly at first. Then the true Rachel came shining through."

"How so?" I asked.

"It started with comments. About my clothes. My job. My car. My men. Or I should say, my choice in men. She just really came on strong. When we first met, she told me how her parents died when she was young and how she felt deprived of that. So, she decided to strive for wealth and power. My guess, to replace her parents. Of course, that's just my guess. Not like I'm qualified to analyze."

She had finished eating and pushed the dish aside, a few pieces of romaine drowning in the Caesar dressing at the bottom.

"She talked about her older brother and how he had to take care of her. How she thought he sort of resented her for that. But she also praised him for driving an MB, living well. Then, she'd turn around and blast him for not wanting more. I just don't think she's too healthy." She held her hand up. "Again, just my opinion."

She started to chew on her lower lip in thought, looking like she wanted to share something else with me. I mulled over Brooke's latest words. The woman seemed wise.

"It's like she lost out in the battle of good versus evil within herself. See, I believe that everyone fights with those choices every day. Some choose to do what's right. They push back the urges and lead constructive lives. Others give in. They destroy. Simple example. As a man, you probably enjoy looking at attractive women." I nodded. "Even young, attractive women. Say, seventeen, eighteen." I shrugged my shoulders in a "you caught me" gesture. "It's hard not to, the way they show themselves off these days. Nothing wrong with appreciating the beauty. So, let's say, you stop there. You get your eyeful. You go on with life. But others. They see that young, beautiful woman, and they feel they have to have her. Have to touch her. That is losing out to the evil within. I don't know if there's something in their lives that triggers it, like Rachel losing her parents, but it is inherent in all of us. Some win the battle. Some lose. That's my take."

"Wow. You've put some thought into that."

It was her turn to shrug.

"So, what do you do?" I decided to ask.

"Why?"

"Curious. You seem to do well for yourself."

I looked around her apartment to emphasize my point.

"And," I continued, "I guess I'd like to know what Rachel thought was the kind of job that deserved negative criticism in comparison to hers."

"Art Director for an ad agency."

"Works for me."

"Me too."

"So, why would Rachel think your gig didn't hold a candle to hers? I don't get that. Was this sporting good store of hers so kick ass? I know being a manager is great and all, but unless you're going to own the business..."

"That was it. She said she'd own a franchise some day and that I was just a puppet for someone else in the advertising biz."

"Well, she did, I mean, does own a sporting goods store back home. That's why she came back. For that chance. I guess that was another step for her."

"Or another one-night stand."

201

She gave me another look. Her eyes said it all. We sat in silence for a moment. She picked up a limp piece of romaine from her bowl, held it so as much dressing leaked off as possible, started to put it in her mouth, but changed her mind and dropped it back into the Caesar sea below. Then she stared me down. Seriously.

"This is all I truly know about Rachel Allen. She showed up here a while ago. Got that apartment across the hall. Somehow. It wasn't even empty a day when she nabbed it. Believe it or not, this place is a hot commodity. So, she slides right in. We get all girly girly for a bit, then she starts to lose it. She goes off. She turns out to be a pretty much ruthless individual. Looking out for herself. She manages some sporting goods store that I guess does all right, but it's not like big shit. But, for some reason, she thinks it is. She comes and goes. Brags about her men and her money, which, by the way, I'd like to know the jackass who would pay her so well to run that store. Anyway, she does her thing. I do mine. A few months ago, she packs up and leaves. Good for me. Good for this building. Then, you show up. She's missing. Oh well."

"Okay. Fair enough. Know who owns this building?"

I was getting tired of sitting, so I stood up and paced a bit.

"No. I rented it through a real estate agent."

"Got a name and number? And an address?"

"Sure. I gotta find it."

I waited as she gathered the information and wrote it down on a small notepad for me.

"Here," she said as she handed me the slip of paper.

I looked. Green Mountain Realty. Another stop for me to find out who owned the building. Maybe it was nothing, but it was quite interesting that Rachel was able to land her apartment in Burlington just as easily as the one in Skaneateles. Could be coincidence. Could be important. Brooke remained standing.

"Rachel ever talk about any specific men? Or specific ways of attaining her franchise?"

"That was the funny thing. She'd brag about the guys, but I'd never see one or knew one by name. Like it was all a big secret. Unless, of course, she was always banging married guys. Like I said. That's probably where she is now."

I decided to drop the big one on Brooke.

"Rachel's pregnant," I said.

"Now there's a big surprise. Guess that's your specific way of snagging your fortune. Have one of your Sugar Daddies knock you up and take your pick. 'Sweetheart, I know you're sixty, but you're gonna be a daddy... again. You'll take care of Junior, right?'"

This Brooke Kamiskey sure made a lot of sense for being such a smart ass. I supposed that's why I liked her. But from the way Brooke spoke, it seemed to put Carl Hendrix out of Rachel's league. At least for the taking care of Junior part. But, he could have sufficed just fine for step one.

"Listen, Magnum P.I.," she chimed in, "I've enjoyed our little chat, but I gotta get back to the office."

I asked her a few more questions that secured me no pertinent information, thanked her for her time, handed her one of my cards and left her to clean up her lunch dishes.

## *Chapter 17*

I left Lunch Lady behind and headed for the sporting goods store that Rachel managed when she lived in Burlington. The drive wasn't long. It gave me just enough time to kick around Brooke's comments about her mortal enemy Rachel. I liked Rachel. I liked Brooke. They seemed to hate each other. So, who was genuine? I liked to think that I had a certain sense when it came to meeting people for the first time. I felt that I could gauge them as good or evil individuals almost immediately. It was funny, or ironic, how Brooke made it a point to share with me her thoughts on that subject. And I felt it was a brief summation. I had only met Rachel after knowing her brother. He spoke highly of her, raved about her. Could that have been an influence? I knew of Rachel's loss when I met her, and I walked on eggshells a bit to make her feel comfortable and welcome. Was it a matter of subliminal signals from Mick that assisted in my opening my arms to her? But there was no denying that she was charming and beautiful and perhaps fucked up. Man, I needed a taco. I wasn't even certain that I'd find anyone at the sporting goods store who could or would help me out. They probably turned over summer help since Rachel had been there and now had a completely new staff. But it was worth a shot.

The store, Varsity Sports, was in a strip mall off of Pearl Street in the vicinity of the University of Vermont. The mostly-glass fronted building was joined by a small liquor store -- Varsity Liquors; a national-chain drugstore; a laundromat -- yes, Varsity Suds; and China Wok, obviously a Chinese restaurant. The businesses were like aging Siamese quintuplets who had once captured the public's fancy, but through the years had faded away into anonimity while malls and outlet stores popped up, wooing customers away with bright lights, mega-stores and massive food courts. Actually, it was kind of sad. Each storefront offered signs designed to lure in potential customers.

The liquor store featured neon signs for Jack Daniels, Absolut vodka and Black Velvet, along with handmade signs that boasted of recent specials such as five-liter wine casks for $9.99 and cheap vodka for $6.99 a liter. Varsity Suds claimed to be the cleanest laundromat in Burlington. The China Wok advertised Miller Lite in neon, as well as take-out available. The drugstore let me know that they had one-hour photo service and a closeout on many summer items.

Then there was Varsity Sports. They also had a summer clearance going on with prices slashed up to fifty percent off the regular. Window displays featured bathing suits, golf and tennis outfits and watersport gear. Wasn't it about time to set up for fall sports and the incoming college kids? Varsity Sports most likely had a high percentage of college-type clientele during the fall and spring and maybe some tourists and locals during the summer. Right now was a transition period. Or so I assumed, which is usually a mistake. I thought about Felix Unger again. Ah, the *Odd Couple*. Great movie. Great series.

I had no problem finding a parking space in the oversized, patched pothole-filled asphalt parking lot with tall mercury vapor lights strategically placed around the empty spaces to illuminate the way for the anticipated shoppers. A few scattered vehicles occupied random spaces, looking very lonely. I didn't see any Beemers, MB's, Lexuses or Volvos. The weather hadn't improved any while I had my chat with Brooke Kamiskey, but for some reason, my outlook on gaining some ground had.

I locked up my Jeep, patted my Glock inside my jacket out of habit and stepped inside Varsity Sports. A young, good-looking black man with a neatly shaved head wearing a long-sleeve, multi-colored Izod polo shirt and dark blue slacks and Adidas cross trainers was adjusting a soccer display when I entered. He gave me a glance and continued his work as I casually looked around. I was the only other person in the store; there was no need for him to jump all over me. No sense in seeming overeager, even if I may have been his only prospective sale for the day. It made me think of how Rachel thought that this was such a big deal, being the manager of this store, and why she would abase Brooke for being an Art Director, seemingly a successful one at that. Varsity Sports certainly was no Dick's. The place maybe took up one thousand square feet. There was no fishing gear. No weightlifting equipment. No boxing. No bowling. It seemed mostly a niche store with a lot of sportswear, footwear and some gear to get by. I lingered around the cross trainers briefly, then decided to approach the dedicated employee.

"Excuse me," I opened amiably.

"Yes?" Mr. Izod responded as he turned away from his display to face me.

He stood about six-two and was lean. He smiled.

"I was wondering if you could help me out."

"Sure. What do you need?"

The smile remained. He either liked me or held the expression out of practice.

"Actually, I have a few questions about the woman who used to manage this place. Rachel Allen."

So much for the smile. It was like someone reached into his nicely pressed pants and yanked his briefs into a Windsor knot. Mr. Izod was not a comfortable man. I stuck out my right hand and fished for my credentials with my left. Confused, he shook my hand.

"Holden Grace. Private detective. I'm looking into Ms. Allen's disappearance."

No sense beating around the bush with this guy.

"Uh, how can I help you?"

"You can start with who you are."

"Sorry." He finally took his hand away. "Dwayne Reese. I manage the store now."

"I assume you knew Ms. Allen."

"Yeah."

"You work for her?"

"Yeah."

"You like it?"

207

"Like what?"

"Working for Ms. Allen?"

"Truthfully?"

"Nothing but."

"Heck no."

"Why not?"

"Let's just say she wasn't a nice person."

"In what way?"

"Condescending. Like she was it. Like she was the only one who knew anything about this store. She blew in here, took over, gave her orders and would take off whenever she felt like it."

"How'd the store do? Under her management?"

"You know, that's something I don't quite get. Store did great. Not sure quite how, or when, but merchandise moved."

"What do you mean?"

I sat down on the edge of the soccer display.

"It didn't seem like we had the customers when I was here, but we always had new inventory coming in. I guess someone would place large orders or something. I was never clued in."

"So, merchandise moved, but store traffic didn't increase?"

"Yeah."

"And Rachel was a success as manager?"

"Apparently. Mr Granby loved her."

I stood up. Holy shit. Hold it right there. Take a TO, baby. Mr. Granby? As in Curtis Granby? If so, there was no way this was a coincidence. Jesus Christ. Recently divorced Curtis Granby. Messy divorce Curtis Granby. Rich, rich, rich Curtis Granby. The same guy who owned the condos in Skaneateles where Rachel lived. Before I dropped a happy load in my pants, I had to verify my incredibly insightful hunch.

"Mr. Granby, as in Curtis Granby?" I asked, containing my excitement.

"Yeah. How'd you know?"

"It's a small world after all."

"What?"

"Nevermind. So, Curtis Granby still owns this place?"

"No, a new owner took over after Rachel left."

"When Rachel would take off, did she ever say where and with whom?"

"Are you kidding? I was lucky she let me know. It was always on weekends, and even if I was off, I'd have to run the store last minute."

"Curtis Granby ever show up?"

"Yeah. Once in a while."

"How did he and Rachel act?"

"Professional. She called him Mr. Granby, and he called her Ms. Allen."

Made sense. If you were involved in full blown warfare in a divorce, and you were shagging a beautiful younger woman, you'd be damn careful. But, you can never be careful enough when you're nailing someone on the sly and want to keep it quiet. You cannot do it. Something falls through the cracks.

"You know of any guys Rachel spent time with?" I asked.

"No. It's funny, too. Rachel was a looker, but I never saw her with a guy. You don't think... you know?"

"Trust me, Dwayne, Rachel likes men. Maybe too much."

"I'm just glad she's out of here."

"Seems to be the popular opinion."

Just then, the door opened and a group of young guys piled into the store. They eyeballed me closely before giving Dwayne the high sign as they moved to the shoe display. I really had nothing else to ask, and I was sure that Dwayne had nothing else to offer, so I handed him a business card, wished him luck and left Varsity Sports, the store formally owned by Curtis Granby and operated by Rachel Allen.

As I sat in my Jeep in the nearly empty strip mall parking lot with the rain now beating a steady and heavy beat upon the sheet metal, I collected my thoughts and fought off the deja vu. I would bet Mick's MB that Granby once owned the apartments in Burlington where Rachel once lived. It only made sense. To me. It wasn't logical, but that seemed like the pattern. Granby was handing everything to Rachel. He set her up away from Skaneateles as he went through the divorce. It was only after the divorce was settled, I'd bet, that Granby brought her back home, so to speak. And even though he had enough wealth to take care of Rachel forever, he knew she was an ambitious young woman, so he ensured that she gained possession of the sporting goods store in Skaneateles, even if Mick was in on the deal somehow. The weekend jaunt at the Sagamore that Rachel had marked in her planner was with Curtis Granby. Discreet. Quiet. Out of town. That's why Brooke never knew any names or met any of the guys that Rachel bragged about. Rachel probably mentioned so many lovers as a smoke screen. But what about the pregnancy? Whose kid was it? Carl Hendrix's? Granby's? Did Rachel get knocked up on purpose for a little insurance with Granby? But Dr. Russell said that Rachel beamed when she got the news. For the child, though, or the leverage of being with child? And what about Billy Hanley? Where did he fit? Granby's hired muscle? And the biggest question remained. Where the hell was Rachel Allen?

## *Chapter 18*

I didn't need to stop by the Sagamore now or even bother checking out Green Mountain Realty. Curtis was the link. Funny sometimes how well laid plans can change. Getting back to Skaneateles was the first order of business. Actually the second. I needed some Taco Bell, which I found on my way out of Burlington. As I drove, the rain cleared up and the mid-afternoon sun managed to poke its head out between some protective and surly gray clouds. I had quite a few people to have words with, and I was sure that most of them would not receive me too warmly. My estimated time of arrival back home was somewhere between and seven-thirty and eight. That would leave me enough time to make some calls and pay a visit to Bennie at Morris's Grill and maybe see what my old pal, Rex Steinman, was up to.

The drive was uneventful accept for what went on inside of my head, which was probably more dangerous than driving in bad weather. I cruised a steady seventy miles per hour and still watched as most people zipped by me like I held the reins to a horse and buggy. I rolled into my driveway at ten to eight just as the sun began its nightly descent behind the farm hills to the west. Mr. Sandman wanted to pay me a visit, but I had plans, so I shook off the weariness that comes from driving twelve hours in one day and thinking too much. The Taco Bell carbo fix had worn off somewhere between Utica and Syracuse, but food had to take a backseat on this occasion -- time didn't warrant a meal. Later, I promised myself.

I grabbed my mail, happy to see a check from a previous client, went inside and checked the answering machine. Two messages. The first was from Mick. Just checking in, he said. The second was from a nervous sounding Carl Hendrix. He said he'd be home all night tonight if I wanted to call him back. Yeah, I did. No call from Maggie. Hmm. I passed on calling Mick back. I wanted something more before I enlightened him about the Curtis Granby connection. I punched in Carl Hendrix's number on my cordless phone, hoping that the intriquing and almost frightening Stephanie Hendrix would not answer. I got my wish. I got their machine.

"You've reached the Hendrix residence. We're unable to take your call right now. Leave a message, and we'll return your call at our earliest convenience."

It was Stephanie's voice. Very proper and sober sounding. She must've recorded it in the morning before the straight V8 became diluted with certain spirits. I waited for the beep.

"Yeah, this is Holden Grace returning Carl's call. It's a little after eight..."

There was a loud beep and the clumsy sound of a phone being picked up and dropped. I was quickly becoming a screen star, but unfortunately not the Hollywood-type.

"Hello?"

The voice was shaky.

"Carl Hendrix, please."

"Who may I ask is calling?"

I knew it was him. Same voice as the message on my machine. Damn, I was on a hot detecting streak today. I wondered briefly when it would end.

"Holden Grace. I'm returning Mr. Hendrix's call."

"This is he. Sorry about the machine, but, well, sometimes there are just certain people whom I choose not to speak with."

"Nice to know I'm on the A list."

"Well, it's...you wanted to speak with me?"

Hell, I hadn't even threatened this guy with physical harm yet, and he seemed scared to death of me. What could have dear Steph told him?

"Yeah. You know who I am and why I want to talk?"

"Steph said you were a private detective looking into a woman's disappearance and that I may have some information."

"Bingo. You got some time tonight?" I asked, but it was more of a statement.

"Uh... yeah... sure."

"The Bluewater Grill in fifteen minutes. I'll be wearing an FBI hat in one of the back booths."

"All right. I'll be there."

He didn't sound very convincing, but it would have been an ill-advised decision to blow me off. I was sure that he understood that, no matter what kind of guilt he may have been carrying around. If Steph was right about his philandering, his mind must have been spinning with the possibilities. Hey, you mess up the bed that someone else has made, you've got to face the dry cleaner. Or something like that.

A shower would have fit the bill nicely, but I had to settle with what I called the Marilyn Monroe bathing experience -- just swipe on a little deodorant, brush my teeth and grab my hat. I threw my Yankees jacket back on, had my keys in my hand and was heading out the door when the phone rang. I hesitated, thought about answering it, but I assumed it to be an annoying telemarketer and left. I was on a hot streak today, so I followed my hunch. Plus, I needed to beat Carl Hendrix to the Bluewater.

I had no trouble finding a parking space on Genesee Street near the Bluewater, which was conveniently located right across the street from Morris's, my next stop after the engaging conversation I had planned with Hendrix. The restaurant/bar was pretty well thinned out. It used to be a pizza place until a couple of smart guys realized the potential as a restaurant and bar, in fact, the only one right on the water in the village of Skaneateles. The menu featured dishes that were just a little bit different, good stuff such as pulled pork barbeque sandwiches, pesto and turkey club wraps, steamed mussels and pasta, southwestern-inspired entrees and other piled-high platefuls of creative and delicious food. A nice looking hardwood floor greeted your first steps. The walls were painted a subtle shade of green, not blue as I'm sure everyone expected, and they were covered with photographs snapped by a renowned local Finger Lakes photographer. Four large windows, all connected, covered the right wall and offered a view into the outlet of the lake and the park beyond. Tables filled the space along the wall.

Across from these tables was the line, where the chefs performed their magic. Straight to the back of the establishment were double French doors that led to the multi-tiered outdoor deck, always a favorite of diners in the summer. There, the tourists would sit sipping their Anchor Steam or margueritas and rave about their time spent in the village that once had a president and his family as guests. If a patron took a left before he or she reached the French doors, he or she would see a couple of high gentlemen's tables to the left followed by a few booths. Across from the booths was the small bar, which seated maybe ten people. The Bluewater Grill was intimate and busy as hell throughout the height of summer, when diners expected to wait forty-five minutes for a table. The place was a gold mine. The fact that it was rather personal influenced my decision to meet Hendrix there, so as not to intimidate him.

The two televisions propped up in opposite corners behind the bar had ballgames on -- one was the Yankees and the other was the Mets. A few regulars sat at the bar, deep in animated conversation about which cartoon character was the hottest. They didn't know who the hell I was, which worked for me. The bartender, Dale, who did know me, gave me a quick and slight nod as I passed by on my way to the most distant booth, which had its advantages, mainly that it was closest to the bathroom. You can't be too careful when considering urinal proximity. At least in a bar. I took a seat facing the "L" at the main section of the restaurant so that I'd see Hendrix approaching. I didn't know what he looked like, but I pictured the look -- well dressed, stylish long hair for a guy in his forties, out of shape but not totally gone, tan, good looking and worried. As I waited, I wanted to at least stay apprised of the Yankees game, but the TV facing me had the Mets game on. That wouldn't work. I stepped up to the bar.

"Hey, Dale, do me a favor?" I asked.

He leaned in.

"What do ya need, Holden?"

"The Yankees game on that TV right there," I said as I pointed.

I noticed the three huddled regulars had made it a point to take an intellectual break from their intensely analytical and meaningful dialogue and settled their attention on me and my request. Before Dale could answer, a fat guy with red hair and a red beard and an even ruddier face felt it appropriate to make a comment. He was wearing cut off jean shorts and a red short sleeve polo shirt that was two sizes too small. He looked like a wannabe Santa Claus in training.

"Sorry, bud, but we're watchin' that."

"Excuse me?" I asked rather amused.

"We're watchin' the game there. You can just move your ass so you can see the other TV."

"What's the score?"

"Huh?"

"The score. Of the game. The one you're watching as you're discussing who's hotter, Wilma or Betty."

"Don't matter. We're still watchin' the game. You can move."

He turned back to his buddies and said under his breath, "Asshole."

There was a collective giggle, then they emptied their pint glasses.

Young Santa motioned to Dale for refills all around. I guess Mr. Claus felt rather good, impressing his buddies and all. Dale did his duty, pouring the three Labatt Blue Light drafts, which elicited a chuckle from me as I watched them grease up their fingers in a heaping pile of fat-filled Texas nachos. The oxymoron made me think of those people who ordered a shitload of fast food and then ordered a diet Coke or Pepsi for their beverage.

Young Santa said too loudly, "Put it on the tab, Dale."

I felt honored. He was trying to impress me. Dale nodded, marked off the drinks and came back down to where I was standing.

"Now, Dale, about the game..."

"Hey, didn't I say you were shit out of luck?" Young Santa asked.

Dale gave me a pained look. One I had seen from every bartender in the village.

I reassured him quietly, "I'll do my best to control the situation. I'm meeting someone in about five minutes anyway. It wouldn't make a good first impression if he walked in and saw me tossing these bozos through the windows and into the outlet. Besides, I wouldn't want to poison the fish."

At least Dale smiled.

I faced Santa Claus-to-be.

"Here's the deal, Kris Kringle. Dale'll switch the games on the TV's, you can get back to your cartoon fantasy world, and I won't break your fucking nose. Sound good?"

"Fuck you, shit-for-brains."

"About the response I expected."

"You think you can take the three of us?"

Santa made a grand gesture toward his two pals, who looked like they were more interested in whether Marge Simpson would look better as a blonde than getting into a free-for-all on a Tuesday night with a guy in an FBI cap.

"I won't need to. Just you."

"Who the fuck you think you are?"

"Just a guy who wants to watch the Yankee game on that TV," I said as I pointed up and took a step toward him.

Santa Claus looked at his buddies, but they wouldn't meet his gaze. Then, he looked at Dale who gave him a slow, serious shake of the head. It meant, "Don't push it, dumbass."

"Fuck it. Go ahead and watch your pansy ass game."

"Thanks. By the way," I added, "I'm not a huge fan of redheads, so I'd go with Betty Rubble."

Dale switched the televisions. I sat down. A cute, tired and tanned wait wearing khaki shorts and a green Bluewater Grill polo shirt gave me the standard spiel. I told her I was meeting someone and that a glass of sparkling water would be just fine.

216

She flashed me a worn out, but I hoped genuine, smile and vanished. The Yanks were losing badly to the Blue Jays at the Skydome. Conversation at the bar had turned to the hottest sitcom actresses. At least they narrowed it to a genre. As the wait returned and set down my water, Carl Hendrix walked around the corner of the bar. I knew it was him. The three amigos at the bar lifted their eyes long enough to realize he wasn't some hot babe and instantly returned to their world of fantasy.

Hendrix was wearing a blue suit coat over a white button down shirt, gray slacks and loafers with no socks. He carried a blue umbrella in his right hand even though the rain stopped hours ago. He wore small, oval glasses. His brown hair was brushed back and slightly long over the back of his collar. He was maybe five-foot nine and didn't look broad shouldered. I was proud of myself for nailing his appearance pretty well. He looked at the three at the bar before settling his eyes on me. He hurried over and sidled into the booth across from me. His face was tan. Another point for me.

"Mr. Grace?" Hendrix asked.

"You presume."

"Excuse me?"

"Nevermind."

So much for being clever, again.

"You are Holden Grace?"

"Yeah. And you're Carl Hendrix."

"Right."

We shook hands.

"Something to drink?" I asked.

"Sure. Sure. Scotch and soda. No. No. Just a beer. Murphy's would be fine."

The wait approached and took Hendrix's order after I gave him my approval. He damn sure seemed nervous. We sat in silence, me watching the game and Hendrix watching his manicured fingernails, until his dark brown draft arrived. The wait looked at me, I shook my head and she left. Hendrix lit into

217

his beer. It did look good. I think he was waiting for me to get the conversation rolling. Fair enough.

"Mr. Hendrix..."

"Carl, please."

"Sure. Carl, you nervous about something?"

"A little uneasy. It's not every day a private detective wants to question me about a woman's disappearance."

"True, but if you don't know anything, then what's to sweat?"

"I don't even know whom we're speaking about."

Good grammar. Must've had fine schooling.

"Well, my sources tell me that it could be a number of young ladies of which you are quite, ah, esoterically familiar with."

"And your source, undoubtably is Stephanie. She has a habit of creating dispersions that help her get through each day."

"I see. So the story of her losing the baby is just that, a story?"

I thought I'd get tough fast. Hendrix looked down at his hands again.

"No, that's true."

He kept his voice low, although he was struggling with it.

He continued, "And there has been a lot of distance between us since. And I have heard the stories. A small town. A lot of talk. One indiscretion multiplies in the eyes of those who need to feed on such nonsense. Mr. Grace, I'm not absolved of sin, but I am not the playboy, if that's even the correct word, that Stephanie makes me out to be. For God's sake, I'm a high profile businessman in this community. I will not jeopardize that for the sake of multiple trysts with any good looking, young and eager woman to come along. I've done nothing malicious."

Well, now I had two sides of the story, without even asking for it. But he did seem particularly edgy without my looking to push any buttons.

"So, if you could do us both a favor and just ask me what you need, I'd be happy to cooperate," he finished.

"Okay. I'm not going to blow any smoke. Rachel Allen is missing. She is also pregnant. Your wife said that you were intimate with her. Very recently. I know that you were looking to buy her store. I know that your home was the last place that she called from her apartment before she disappeared. I know that certain other individuals place her in the company of an older, wealthy man. I know that Rachel's brother and I have both met a tough guy named Billy Hanley who claims that if I don't back off the investigation, there is some serious firepower behind him to stop me. So, straight up, William, were you sleeping with Rachel Allen?"

I conveniently omitted any mention of Curtis Granby and his connection with Rachel. No sense is giving out more information than was necessary. It fell under the "need to know" rule. In this instance, Hendrix didn't.

Again, the finger inspection. Maybe he needed a new manicurist. He looked up and into my eyes. There was fear there.

"No. Almost. But no. We became close. Or so I thought. She showed the first interest. We talked about business and money a lot. And dreams. Hers were grandiose. Almost twisted. She wanted money, power, status. She said she craved it. Needed it like a drug. She was out of my league. So, no we never slept together. Never."

"Who approached whom about the sale of the store?"

"I approached her. I thought it a fine investment, but she wanted too much."

"But she was willing to sell?"

"So it appeared."

"Did you know her brother, Mick, was a partner?"

"No. She mentioned a silent partner, but said she was the majority owner and had the final say on any sale."

"Mick told me that you made one hell of an attractive offer, but that Rachel was hedging on the sale. He was for it. They were supposed to meet about it, but never had the chance."

"It was a very fair offer."

"Think maybe she was playing you?"

"What do you mean?"

"You said she spoke of her champagne dreams and caviar wishes. Maybe she was feeling you out. See what kind of coin you really had. Maybe you were non-bachelor number one. Who knows?"

I kind of felt strange speaking of Rachel in this manner, but from all signals, she was a couple of wedges short of a fourteen-club bag. Even Mick admitted that she was money hungry, that she wanted to far surpass his financial success. There was no sense in trying to protect what I thought was a solid reputation at this point. The main thing was to find her, hopefully alive, and then from there work on her neuroses or whatever they may have been.

"Come on... You don't think... Jesus, that's slightly deranged, don't you think?"

"Can't say. But you fit the bill. And now, she's gone."

"She's just off somewhere, I'm sure. I don't know anything. Really."

He didn't reassure me.

"So that's the story I've gotten from everyone. She's just off somewhere. Like she would simply disappear. Not telling her brother. Her employees. Just pack and go for no goddamn reason."

I could feel the anger rising. Not particularly at Hendrix, but it was like one of those body-gripping moments when you knew it was safer to be away from individuals. You needed to strike out. Memories of when I was a hormone-charged teenager flashed into my tired mind. Moments of punching the sheet rock to dust in my bedroom... of cranking the stereo too loudly. And for foolish reasons. Frightening times. But I could have done worse. Through the years, I've learned that wise people channeled the impulse into constructive directions. I required practice at being constructive.

"Frankly, Carl," I continued with a little more degree of control, "I don't buy your complete lack of knowledge bit for some reason. Care to enlighten me as to why I feel this way?"

He looked around, at nothing in particular. It was just a nervous act.

"I've told you all I know."

"I doubt that. Why do you and your wife stay together? Why does your wife make those claims about you? Why does your wife sit out by the pool all day knocking back Bloody Marys like some kind of nectar? Why does Curtis Granby allow you to screw around on his daughter?"

Hendrix stared right at me. Hard.

"I told you. It was one indiscretion. Stephanie and I stay together because I believe that when you get married, it's for keeps. Even if it is a sham."

"Plus, let's not forget that you stand to get your hands on some substantial assets once your father-in-law goes to that great big shopping mall in the sky."

"Sure, that's true, but I do just fine."

"I see. What about the other stuff?"

"Such as?"

"Such as the other questions I just asked?"

"Why does Stephanie spread her infidelity gospel? It must make her hollow world just that much more interesting. And as far as her relationship with the vodka, she chooses to escape that way. I wish she wouldn't, but it is her choice."

"And Curt's take on all this?"

"He has his own problems to worry about."

"His divorce, you mean?"

"Yeah. That. Not a pretty picture, I guess. Now, like I have said, I know nothing of the whereabouts of Rachel Allen. I have nothing to do with that."

Now, that was a curious statement to make.

"What's that mean?" I asked.

"What?"

221

*Daniel Surdam*

"You had nothing to do with that? I didn't accuse you of anything. I just said I was having a hard time believing you."

Again, Hendrix scanned the room, like he was waiting for someone or something to morph out of the woodworks and rip his head off.

"It meant nothing," he said without looking at me.

"What do you know?"

"Nothing."

"You're a lousy liar. You tell me with true conviction that you don't play the field. That I believe. But when you say 'nothing' to me now, you're full of it."

He leaned back in the booth and studied his hands some more. His left thumb twitched rhythmically. I waited. Toronto had the bases juiced with no outs and Carlos Delgado at the plate. Long night for the Bronx Bombers. My three pals had moved onto movie stars. They were loud, but that was fine. Their boisterous voices provided enough background noise to help wash out my conversation with Hendrix. Dale was busy cleaning glasses. Delgado crushed a lazy slider off the right-centerfield wall, clearing the bases with a stand-up double. Hendrix leaned over the table. He cupped his left hand over his right and leaned his forehead on them and closed his eyes. He spoke softly, like an ashamed child.

"I have been threatened."

He opened his eyes, but he wouldn't look at me. His gaze locked on the table between his chest and his arms.

"About what?" I asked.

"That's it. I don't know. I really don't."

"You were threatened, and you don't know why?"

He nodded.

"Tell me about it," I said.

He finally looked up. There was the fear. So, it wasn't me or the possibility of what I brought to the table that spooked him. Someone beat me to it.

"It was a phone call. Tonight... about six-thirty. That's why I screened your call. Anyway, it was a man with a deep voice.

222

He told me that he knew what I had done. That he had proof. And that if I didn't come clean, he'd kill me."

"That's it?"

"Isn't that enough?"

"No, not really. The caller didn't want any money? He wasn't blackmailing you? He just wanted you to confess to something you have no clue about?"

"Yes."

"That's all he said?"

"Yes."

"Don't you think the coincidence would be a bit too strong? The fact that Rachel Allen disappears and you get a threatening phone call a few days later?"

"But I swear, I don't know anything."

"Any idea who it could be?"

"None."

"So why the hell would someone threaten you? You clean in your business dealings?"

"Yes. I mean, there are always a few under the table instances, but nothing of a serious nature. Not serious enough to warrant my death."

Now that the cat was out of the bag, Hendrix almost seemed to enjoy the drama of the threat. Maybe it made him feel just a little more self-important.

I asked, "You ever do business with papa-in-law?"

"Yeah. We've gone in on projects together, but I keep my nose clean. I don't ask questions, and he let's me handle what I need to."

"You think old Curt is on the up and up?"

"I refuse to pass judgment."

"I'll take that as a 'no.' And by your not asking questions, you're just as guilty as he is."

"The projects that we are involved with are legit -- a string of exercise clubs, a health center. They are profitable and reputable businesses, and I can guarantee you that I have nothing to hide regarding those business practices."

A fine short speech said with conviction. My guess was he was convincing himself more then me.

"But nonetheless, you're in bed with Curtis Granby," I said.

"But why threaten me? I wouldn't know anything?"

"The exercise clubs, wouldn't be the Jungle Gym, would it?"

"No, they're high-end health clubs."

Kiss that hunch good-bye.

"But it's funny you mention it," Hendrix continued.

"Why?"

"The Jungle Gym is actually a venture of Carla Granby."

"Mom-in-law?" I asked curiously.

"Yes. It seems that Carla has a fondness for large, sweaty men."

Okay, one hunch gone, but an even better connection to replace it. We fell into a thoughtful silence. I wasn't surprised that there was a business connection between Hendrix and Granby, but the more I thought about the situation, the messier it got.

"Ever hear of a guy named Billy Hanley?" I finally asked.

"No. The name's not familiar."

"Okay. Let's say you're being honest about Rachel. Let's say you're being honest about any shady business deals that might be worth a round between the eyes. What're you going to do?"

"I... I don't know. What can I do?"

"Nothing," I offered very matter-of-factly.

"But what if he makes good on his word?"

"Why?"

"Because he said he would."

The reality of a thirty-eight slug into his brain nudged him not too gently from his world of importance. He reverted to his earlier nervous state, like a child worried about punishment from a parent, but not quite sure what for, only realizing he probably deserved it.

"No one is going to risk a murder rap unless they have a real good reason. From what you say, there's nothing to worry about. So, do nothing," I reassured him.

"How do you know? What makes you so goddamn sure?"

"Call it an experienced hunch."

Of course, that line was a heaping load of shit, because I had never been placed in this predicament before, but that didn't mean I didn't have a sense about the scenario. Come on, this was Skaneateles, village of the beautiful. What moron would stick his neck so far out on the chopping block when news about someone's most recent nose job spread faster than pate on Carr's cracker in the fashionable Skaneateles circles? Oh wait, check that. Maybe the person or persons responsible for Rachel's disappearance. Damn, I didn't have all the answers. Carl Hendrix would have to take his chances. He obviously wasn't the biggest fish in all of this. Hell, he was like the small male bass protecting the spawning bed of the large female. As in Stephanie Granby Hendrix. Wrapped in her little distilled world. Daddy on one side. Unfaithful Carl on the other. Money from Daddy when he croaked. Money from Carl for now. A nice arrangement. And a little shallow. Maggie and I knew of a few couples who had lost children, some of whom would never bear children, and that did not completely destroy there lives. They battled. They fought. They fucked up in some ways. But they ultimately chose to continue with life. Stephanie and Carl gave up easily. Or so I thought.

"Listen," I said, "I don't think you have anything to worry about. Seriously. No one's going to cap you."

"Easy for you to say."

"Yeah. Yeah, it is. I'm not the one who's fucked his life up. You may think that you've got it good, with your nice house and mutual funds and stocks out the ass and a nice insurance policy with old man Granby, but you might just as well have performed a self-lobotomy when you wrecked that car that killed your kid and your marriage. And you don't give a damn about fixing the damage. You simply look ahead, with unemotional tunnel

225

vision. Making the almighty buck. Occasionally nailing some babe. Or one by your count. It could've all been very different. Ever hear of the Chaos Theory?"

Hendrix only shook his head. I think he was rather shocked by my diatribe, but, damn it, I'd had enough of the self-indulgent, I'm-not-to-blame-for-anything attitude, so I was going to continue until I said my piece.

"The Chaos Theory. If a butterfly flaps its wings in China, the disturbance of air eventually effects the weather, say, in Skaneateles, New York. Simplified, and I think you'll understand this, if you change one little thing you do in a day, in a week, in your life, it will change the outcome. Maybe not drastically, but, then again, who knows. So, yeah, it is easy for me."

The three locals at the bar slid off their bar chairs, taking great effort to look tough and not introduce their inebriated faces to the floor. Santa flashed me a hard look before the triumvirate disappeared around the corner. The few diners that remained didn't seem to pay much attention to my speech, as they had enough to handle in their own worlds. Hendrix wasn't too thrilled with me at the moment, but I could care less. Of course, I didn't want someone to whack him, if that person was actually serious, and I already had a hunch as to whom that person was. He had very blue eyes.

Now that my speech was finished, I decided to back off a little. I didn't want Hendrix to bolt, either.

I told him, "Listen, if you need to call me for any reason, here's my card. I just need to know that you're being on the level with me."

"Completely."

He took my card and put it in an inside pocket of his jacket. Then he reached for his wallet.

"Forget it," I said. "I got it. But one more question."

"Sure."

"Where were you last Wednesday night?"

"Away on business. I came back early Thursday."

"And you have witnesses?"

"Absolutely."

He shook my hand and left, most likely feeling no better, chances were worse, than when he arrived. I sat and enjoyed the silence briefly, contemplating the Chaos Theory and how it may have been relevant with this seemingly dysfunctional group I was involved with in the case.

*Daniel Surdam*

## *Chapter 19*

I stepped out of the Bluewater Grill after saying hello to one of the owners and promptly encountered my three friends from earlier, who apparently decided to loiter around on the sidewalk and wait for my exit. My patience had escaped me, like the air from a slow leak in a tire, and I didn't feel like waiting for the macho ritual of hurling obscenities and posturing, so I beelined for Mr. Claus and offered one of my best headbutts to the bridge of his nose. He dropped without knowing what really hit him. His buddies had a split-second decision to make -- go for me or help their drunken and unconscious friend. They chose wisely.

I stepped around the three and jaywalked across the street to Morris's, a place self-proclaimed as being world famous. The bar was a one-eighty from the Bluewater, but it had been the longest standing drinking establishment in Skaneateles. The bar was in a three-story brick building that stretched east on Genesee Street toward the main intersection of downtown, where it continued north on Jordan Street. It was an old building and housed apartments on the upper floors and many of the small shops that made a killing every summer and during the December holiday season on the first floor. Morris's had developed a reputation a few years back as a rough and tumble place, especially on weekends, but that was mostly hype drummed up by the regulars to scare away the trendy tourists. The place was dark with a scarred center bar, old-fashioned red padded barstools and a few tables with mismatched chairs. It was all part of the charm of the place. At least they got rid of the old cable spools they once used as tables. A separate room straight back from the main door and up a few steps was home to the pool table and where you could order food. The steps were a nice touch, especially for the heavy drinkers who shot stick and had to negotiate them with increased difficulty as they made more frequent trips to the men's room. Standard bar games stood unoccupied at the moment. Tonight's crowd was sparse, but my query was right where I expected, perched on his favorite tattered stool with a half-empty draft beer and empty and full bags of beer nuts in front of him. His long, straight white hair was pulled back into a ponytail. His Fu Manchu moustache was wild and drastically needed a trim. He wore a blue denim shirt, denim pants and well-worn cowboy boots. The bartender, a tall and lanky guy with curly blond hair, shot me with his finger from the far end of the bar. I settled down on a stool to the right of Bennie. He didn't look at me.

"S'up HG? Need a drink?" he asked.

"Nah, I'm good."

"Suit yourself. I was buyin'."

"Must be a good summer for you."

"Always are."

"Yeah."

He took a long pull from his Pabst draft and popped a couple of peanuts in his mouth.

He was still chewing when he said, "Now, I know it ain't no case of sheer coincidence that you're sittin' on the stool next to me on a Tuesday night."

"Mighty perceptive, Bennie."

"Keeps me in biz, know what I mean?"

"That and some heavyweight investors, so to speak."

"We all gotta make a buck."

Bennie polished off his beer, and the bartender had a new one set before him before the liquid could settle in his stomach.

He held up his beer, looked at it lovingly and continued, "Beer is just 'bout perfect, know what I mean? It's beautiful. Tastes great. Got no fat in it. And it gives you a nice little buzz. A legal one at that." He laughed.

"Yeah, Bennie, beer is good stuff."

When I needed info from Bennie, I had to play this game with him -- listen to his musings about life, liberty and his pursuit of happiness. He shook the last few nuts out a bag, popped them in his mouth and tore open another bag.

"Now, peanuts are good, too. Not as well-rounded as beer, though. But they sure the hell go great together, know what I mean? But it's gotta be beer nuts. Why the hell else call 'em that? Couldn't imagine eatin' 'em with a Coke." Again the laugh.

He finally faced me. His skin was pale and pockmarked. A scar ran down the left side of his face from the outside of his eye to the corner of his mouth. His nose was large. His eyes were set deep and dark. His teeth were perfect, though. And white. Too white. I had always thought that they were false. I didn't know why I never asked him. Maybe tonight was the night.

"Small crowd tonight," he said.

"Lousy weather. Tuesday night. You're here."

"Ouch. HG, not too kind."

He turned back to his beer.

"Just an honest observation," I offered.

"S'pose it is. I got one for you. Ever wonder why people would give up a lot of shit and stuff for money?"

"What kind of shit?"

"Family, I guess. Happiness, if you could believe that."

Bennie was playing again. He knew what I wanted. He knew I was looking for Rachel. There was no way I could keep it from scum like Bennie. It was his business to know the malevolent side of life in Skaneateles.

"Geez, Bennie," I began sarcastically, "you're not decribing yourself are you? And now you want to unload on me? Damn, I must be someone you truly look up to."

"Oh, sure, sure, HG. If that's what you wanna think, I'm down with that. And now maybe I got nothin' else to say."

He dramatically lifted his beer glass and tipped it to his lips in such a slow, theatrical gesture that some of the liquid spilled out around the edges of his mouth and soaked his moustache. Nice touch. He wiped his face with his shirt sleeve without missing a beat and casually set the glass down exactly on the same wet ring where he lifted it from. As I watched his cutesy

231

one-man dog and pony show with minimal amusement, the village fire siren belted out its song of lament.

"Damn, I sure hope no one's hurt," Bennie sarcastically managed to get out between belches.

"Yeah, be a shame if one of your best customers got some bad stuff and croaked on their beautiful Italian marble tile."

"Come on, HG. You're gettin' a little personal in this wide open location. Know what I mean?"

I was finally making him uncomfortable. The last thing he needed was a conversation about his dealing that could fall on the wrong ears, although from the look of the scattered clientele, they were well-versed in Bennie's occupation already. A blue village police sedan sped by heading east on Genesee Street, the full package of lights and siren opened by the cop behind the wheel. I wondered if it was Wade. Moments later, more sirens filled the usually quiet evening air as a rescue truck swung around the corner from Jordan Street to Genesee. Excitement in the village. Maybe someone's BMW got keyed and the owner was suffering chest pains. The sound of the sirens stopped before they went too far, so whatever emergency it was that needed the cavalry had to be close by. But right now, Bennie had other worries. Or worry. Me. As we sat in silence, most of the patrons in the bar ran out the doors hoping to sneak a peek at some death and destruction. Nothing brings a crowd of strangers together like good old suffering. Call it morbid curiousity. Call it some kind of survival instinct. Or maybe it was something deeper. Maybe it was a reminder that served as a connection to mortality. We've all done it. The first time I saw actual photographs of a murder victim, I was truly intrigued. I thought about her family and the suffering she went through before the bastard pulled the trigger that sent the slug through her forehead. I thought of how I know she had to have smiled and laughed the same day her life tragically and unexpectedly ended. When I saw the close-up picture, I thought about the frozen grimace that transformed a once beautiful face into a visage of terror and torture. And it happened all over again when I saw my first dead body in person, actually, first two dead bodies. They were what was once Mick's and Rachel's parents, but the car wreck that claimed their lives much too early twisted and bent and bruised and battered their bodies into something else besides two caring human beings. It took me a long time to forget that image. I was sure it would take eternity for Mick and Rachel to forget.

"All right, Bennie. Enough foreplay."

The bartender was still at his post, knowing that the rubberneckers outside would fill him in on the gory details, if there were any.

"Hey, Andy, what's Bennie's tab at?" I asked him.

He checked a piece of paper, pulled out another one, wrote the figure on it and handed it to me. I peeled two twenties out of my wallet and tossed them on the bar. Andy promptly gathered them up, rang Bennie's bill into the cash register, deposited the twenties in the drawer and pocketed the change and proceeded to rip up Bennie's tab. Andy keeping the change was part of our deal, because he occasionally had some helpful information for me.

"Okay, Bennie. Let's take this to a more private location," I said as I pointed to the pool room, which had been empty since I arrived.

"Sure, HG. Whatever you say."

Bennie scooped up his beer in his right hand and his bag of beer nuts in his left and swiveled off the stool. His cowboy boots clacked or clicked or whatever cowboy boots do on the floor as we walked to the pool room. He set his goodies down on a beat up table and fished around in his tight pockets for some quarters. He looked at me.

"Do you mind?" he asked.

"Go ahead."

He deposited his dope-selling change, racked up the balls, settled on a cue stick after testing about ten and finally broke. The balls careened around the table like brightly colored cockroaches scurrying away from a sudden burst of light. A few fortunate ones found escape into the pockets below. Bennie pondered his next shot, leaning his cue across the corner of the table.

"So, you know I'm looking for Rachel Allen, right?" I began.

"Yeah, word's out."

"Know anything about it?"

"Nope."

He lined his shot up and cleanly drilled the seven ball into the far right corner pocket.

"Nothing?"

"Not about this Rachel Allen chick."

Bennie walked around the table and surveyed the situation.

"How about a goon named Billy Hanley? Big guy. Lifts. Drives a Caddy."

"Maybe."

"He says he's well backed."

"Rumor has it he's hired muscle. One badass dude, I guess."

Bennie knocked the five ball into the side pocket with a nice cut shot. The cue ball settled nicely for a straight shot on the three.

"Any idea who he's connected with?" I asked.

"A name comes to mind."

"Curtis Granby."

"That's a name."

Bennie leaned over the table and slammed home the three ball with a lot of back spin that sent the cue ball racing backwards, not unlike one of my incredible wedge shots to the green. The cue danced back too far and left him stimied.

"But remember," he continued after his shot, "the key name just might be Granby and not Curtis."

He offered an all-knowing smile and missed on the two ball. He handed me the cue.

"You got the big ones," he said, referring to the balls on the table.

"You can bet on that, Bennie."

I surveyed the table, but my mind concentrated on what Bennie had just said. Billy Hanley was under the employ of a Granby but maybe not Curt. What about Mrs. Granby? Or Stephanie? I sized up the thirteen ball.

"So, Hanley recently gets out of the Pen, and he's scooped up by a Granby, but, and I'm speculating here, not Curtis," I said.

"Could be. But, what if Billy Boy was muscle for ole Curt before he went to the little big house and was recruited by, let's just say, like a friendly rival, know what I mean?"

"Old lady Granby."

"Now that sounds entirely possible. You gonna shoot?"

I ignored the pool table and pressed Bennie.

"A messy divorce. A guy who used to work for Curt. A tough guy with shit for morals. A guy who'd do anything for the right price. Billy switched teams, didn't he?"

"Hey, he was a free agent. We all gotta look for the best deal."

It was only appropriate that Bennie put the scenario in those words. So, the financial and powerful backup for Billy Hanley was Mrs. Granby, a woman I had never met, and I woman of whom I didn't even know her first name. Goddamn it, I thought, why did this have to get more complicated? Why couldn't it be nice and clean, with Curtis Granby being the bad guy and Billy his weight? Now, another player had anted up. I really needed to speak with Curt. My guess now was that Carl Hendrix was just some sucker caught up in his reputation and truly fucked-up in-laws. Made me think of that saying about being able to choose your neighbors but not your family. Guess it counted for in-laws, too.

"Come on, HG, take a shot here already," Bennie pleaded.

I bricked the thirteen worse than missing a two-foot putt. The table was Bennie's, and he had nice openings to drain his final two balls before dunking the eight ball, but a lousy loss to Bennie at pool hardly registered to me. I still needed some more goods from him. He took the cue stick and wasted no time in dropping the two ball into a corner pocket. The cue ball settled right where he planned. Bennie spent many hours shooting stick. Morris's was his office, and during idle times, which was often, thankfully for the image of Skaneateles, he worked the pool table like a masseur. He purposely lingered over the table as the one ball waited to be planted into the side pocket like the summer sun eager to set after a long, hard day. Before he took aim, I spoke up.

"What about Carl Hendrix?"

"Ah, yes, Carlton. From the way people talk, he's got a twelve-inch dick and sticks it into any hole he sees."

"And?"

"Shit, it's a buncha bullshit. So, the guy crashes his Volvo, kills his baby and fucks up his wife in the head. He bangs one broad while his old lady is sortin' through her emotional problems, and now he's a fuckin' skirt chaser. Gimme a fuckin' break."

"What about him and Rachel Allen?"

"You kiddin'? I had a better shot with her than that rich preppie ass."

"So, he wasn't nailing every young lady that he laid eyes on?"

"Puh-lease."

Bennie took a tour around the table once for effect. He knew he had the game, but he enjoyed being able to put the screws to me in that small window of his world. I watched as he postured. Bennie's world was supported by the expendable income of the habitual user in Skaneateles, the men and women who owned the lakefront homes or the old money village estates. After a hard day's work or a tortuous dinner with a spouse, Bennie's clients could count on a little nose candy or crack or reefer mixed with the scotch of the day to bring them out of the stink known as life. Or the stink known to them that would be regarded as a pretty damn good existence to the common folk that lingered on the periphery of the village's white collar image. Bennie finally decided on his course of action for the one ball. He sank it casually as the cue ball crept into position on the eight ball. It made me wonder how many people thought of eight ball as a racist game. Seriously. The ultimate goal is for the white cue ball to drill the black eight ball into some pocket where it disappears from sight. Maybe I thought too much. Maybe not. Bennie called corner pocket, and that's precisely where the eight ball made its home. Game to Bennie.

"Guess you owe me a beer, HG," Bennie said.

"Just put it on your tab. I'm sure I'll take care of it."

"Right. We done here?"

"Yeah. Enough said. Stay the fuck away from the kids."

"Not my thing, HG. Know what I mean?"

"Yeah, and you'd better really mean it."

I left the darkness and emptiness of Morris's, thankful to put distance between me and Bennie "the Vermin" Berman, a guy who thrived on the free-drug enterprise. I was always torn about dealing with a scumbag like Bennie, wondering if the payback was worth it. Wade and I had discussed Bennie's entrenchment in the community and how we both were disgusted by it. Especially Wade. He hated the idea of a known dealer able to peddle his rotten candy while wrapped in a heavyweight financial cocoon that kept him on the wrong side of the vertical metal bars. I had less of a moral dilemma, but I still struggled with the concept. While Bennie was good to have as an occasional informant, I always left his presence with a lousy taste in my mouth and the feel of evil fingers running up and down my spine. I was certain that he was always happy when I parted company with him for a few reasons -- his bar tab was paid up, the threat of having his nose busted just disappeared and he could stop worrying about being seen with me. It was not a fair trade off. Next time I'd either not pay his tab or break his nose. Choices. And, damn it, I forgot to ask about his teeth. Okay, so maybe next time we participated in the unpleasant discourse of suffering, I'd pop a few of those pearly whites out of his grinning face and onto the squalor of Morris's floor.

## *Chapter 20*

Out on the street, I could see the stroboscopic illumination of the emergency vehicles in front of the condos where Rachel and Rex Steinman lived. The multitude of rotating lights bounced off the buildings on each side of Genesee Street, making for a sort of low budget and ghoulish laser light show. I didn't see any smoke or a tanker truck, so I ruled out a fire. More super detecting on my part. People were beginning to collect on the sidewalk around the rescue vehicles, pointing as gawkers do, offering theories to one another. It had been a long day, and I thought about heading home, but the coincidence of this emergency's location easily made me reconsider. So, why not make the day longer?

I crossed Jordan Street at the light, feeling the coolness of the August night eat through my jacket and settle into my bones. You could always count on weather variety in Central New York. From sweating buckets to freezing your ass off in a matter of days. Purely unpredictable. I didn't give a damn what the so-called well-informed local meteorologists had to say, even with their hi-tech Doppler radar, crystal balls and tea leaves. They were lucky to get their forecasts accurate half the time, and when they did, the event was cause for celebration. Too bad their paychecks weren't based on how well they predicted the weather. Might make it more interesting.

After crossing the street, I turned left at the big bank building, which wasn't a bank anymore, but another one of the quaint village shops, and walked purposefully past shop row toward the condos. I went by jewelry stores, clothing stores, health food stores, curio shops, junk stores, hair salons, gourmet stores, all with their dressed up windows, now dark since clientele would be scarce this time of night. Before I reached the condos, the ambulance pulled out from the street and down behind the building where the entrance to the apartments was located. It took its time. No lights. No siren. No good news for somebody. After the ambulance wheeled down the small alley toward the lake, a local cop returned to his post in front of it, instructed to keep out nosy civilians. It wasn't Wade, but I knew the guy. He was a young cop, mid-twenties, been on the force a couple of years. Nice guy. Unassuming. Chad Houston. About five-ten, rock solid, and cleanly shaven -- both his face and head. His jaw was square, his eyes dark and his appearance no-nonsense. What made his role on the Skaneateles police force interesting was that he was a young, black male. To say that he was in the minority in Skaneateles was an understatement of epic proportions. Kind of like finding a piece of brown rice co-mingling in a big old bowl of white rice. Unfortunate, but true. That was part of the village's, well, certainly not charm, but more like image. But Chad was cool about it. He was well-educated, intelligent and handled himself well. His superior, on the other hand, was a fat jerk and a bigot and a smalltime symbol of authority who planned on retiring from the Skaneateles force and living comfortably on the kickbacks he probably received from Bennie and his wealthy customers and other blueblood donators to the cause of selective justice or injustice. Clearly, he was not one of my favorite people and the feeling was mutual. I had to hand it to Chad for keeping his composure. But he had bigger plans, and he knew that keeping his nose clean now would pay dividends later. And I had no doubts that he would fulfill his ambitions. Some people, you just knew they met their goals. I elbowed my way past a group of gawking kids and approached Chad.

"Evening, Agent Houston."

"Hey, Holden, what're you doing here?"

"In the neighborhood when my detective alarm went off."

"You and half the village. People sure do jump on mayhem around here."

"Perks up their otherwise boring, tedious lives."

"Money'll do that to you."

"Don't I know."

"About what? The boring life or the money?"

"Is that sarcasm I hear coming from a future Secret Service Agent of the United States of America? Because if it is, I don't know if I can be a good reference for you."

"Can't be zipped up all the time... sir."

The "sir" was emphasized and added as a joke.

"Good. Otherwise, I'd be damned worried about you," I said.

"I appreciate the concern."

"So, what's up?"

"Can't say, Holden. Vic, I mean Chief DiFranco, is inside running the show."

"This might pertain to a case I'm working on, Chad."

"Come on, Holden."

"And, a good friend of mine lives here. Rachel Allen."

I decided to toss that out in case this service call was somehow for her.

"Uh huh," was Chad's response.

"And I know Rex, uh, Steinman. In fact, I spoke with him last Friday concerning my case."

"You spoke with Steinman?"

"Last Friday. About my case."

"Shit. Hope you got what you needed, buddy."

"Rex?" I asked, already sure of the answer.

"Someone croaked him."

I turned away from Chad. Shit. Shit. Shit. Not good. Why did Rex have to buy it? For talking with me? He sure the hell didn't offer up anything that pointed a finger in any direction. Except that Curtis Granby owned the condos. And he was the only one who could've informed the bad guys that I was snooping around. I mean, I wanted to rattle his cage a little, but I didn't want to see him stiffer than an unwashed oil-paint brush. Christ, who the hell was going to tell his fiancee that her wedding had been terminated? What about that feeling I first had that someone was staring at me? Could someone really have been in that other apartment spying? This was getting out of control. I needed to make some serious headway before another person ended up missing or dead. Like me. I surveyed the street, looking for anyone suspicious, hoping to get a glimpse of his or her handywork. Hell, Professor Plum could deduce that Hanley was involved in this. But what'd he use? A lead pipe? The rope? And where did it happen? The billiard room? The study? Guess what, Holden. You still need a clue, pal. A couple of village police cruisers were dramatically angled in toward the sidewalk. The crowd continued to grow, lured by the spiraling lights. Traffic that headed east or west on Genesee Street slowed to a crawl as rubberneckers strained for a peek at someone's misfortune. An Onondaga County Sheriff's car pulled up with its lights flashing and no siren. I wondered how long it would be before the state boys arrived. The Sheriff hopped out of his car and walked our way. Another acquaintance. Doug Egan. Twenty years as a Sheriff with ten to go according to his calculations. Egan was a local boy who initially wanted to be an engineer, but somewhere along the way, the plan changed and law enforcement became his life. Egan was mid-forties, short brown hair, about five-ten, one-ninety, well-tanned with a big smile and a hard-working attitude so lacking today with America's youth.

"Fellas," he said.

I greeted him with, "Hey, Doug."

Chad responded professionally. "Sheriff Egan."

"This isn't a case of yours, is it, Grace?" Egan asked.

"Hey, you never know."

"Hope it ain't a client."

"Me too," I said.

I left Doug and Chad to tend to the doomsday crowd and headed down the alley. The lake was choppy and ugly in the darkness. Amazing how beautiful it could be during the day when a clear blue sky reflected onto the mirror-like surface. Yeah, well, just like anything else, you have to watch out for appearances and look under the surface. We all have two sides. Some of us hide it better than others, like the lake right now. It waited until after sundown today to reveal its nasty side.

I knew that Vic DiFranco was going to be nothing less than an uncooperative pain in the ass. If they taught the strategy as a course in the world of academia, DiFranco would surely have written the curriculum. We first met years ago when he was a young, tough-guy cop on the Skaneateles force and I was a young smart mouth punk who didn't quite fit in with the upper crust around town. Back then, I thought I'd wipe the dust of the place off my ass and never return. So, plans change. A small group of us outsiders hung pretty tight in those days. It's not like I was considered some kind of pariah by the cool and heavily financed elite, because I did have some crossover friends who must have realized that I was okay. That or they knew I could always do well with the cheerleaders and wanted to be around to cash in on the action.

That particular Friday night, three of us -- Jeff Miller, Dan O'Shea and I, the core of the outsider cadre -- were out cruising, smoking Robert Burns Black Watch cigars and knocking back seven-ounce Michelobs like they were prescribed medication for erectile dysfunction. We usually avoided the village limits and kept our adolescent fun and games to the outskirts where farm fields dominated the landscape, roadside signs were easy targets for empty beer bottles and urinating our names on backroads was safer than squeezing it off in a public restroom. But we ran out of beer, and it was early. There wasn't much of a discussion. O'Shea was behind the wheel, and he headed for a small store in the village, pushing his old green Chevy Caprice hard, as if we were late for dates with a bunch of horny soriority girls. The windows were rolled down. We had Rush's *A Farewell to Kings* album cranked up on a portable cassette player. To that point, it was a great night, like one of those teenage angst flicks where the buddies talk about sports, chicks, older women and bust each other's balls and not worry about any consequences of drinking and driving. Thank God most of us learn lessons that carry on later in life.

We rolled into the parking lot of the store the same time as a Volvo station wagon packed with snob-nosed prima donnas. A few boys. A few girls. They were the cream that rose to the top, or so they believed. We all knew each other. Miller, O'Shea and I had no amicable ties with the guys, but I was on good terms with one of the girls in the car. She even flashed me a small smile and wave as everyone piled out of the vehicles. The fireworks quickly ensued, provoked by a few comments hurled by the Volvo Boys, which were immediately addressed by us, the Outsiders. The first fist thrown belonged to some cream puff who must have thought assets translated into fighting prowess. He was also trying to impress the young lady who acknowledged me. I happened to have been the recipient of the sloppy and weak right hand toss, which I blocked. Without hesitation, I countered with a short and strong right hand that connected solidly with a soft chin topped off with a mop of blond hair that flopped wildly as it rocked back and eventually met the pavement and split like a melon dropped from a third-story balcony onto a private back yard tennis court. He looked really hurt, and before anyone could decide whether we should stop throwing haymakers and take care of the kid, the distinctive flash of a patrol car's lights lit up the scene. Enter Vic DiFranco. Already tied in with the wealthy and about to demonstrate.

Fed by less-than-accurate facts from the Volvo Boys, DiFranco slapped the bracelets on me and introduced me to the back of a patrol car for the first time. As I sat and contemplated my chances of kicking out a window, DiFranco radioed for an ambulance for Blond Boy Soft Skull. He let O'Shea and Miller slide. I was the one who laid out the pretty boy and offered up the best anti-law attitude toward Vic the Gut. Remember, I expected to leave and never return. I didn't give a damn about how I treated some flash-in-the-pan lawman who had a penis thing working with his night stick and service revolver. I never forgot the degrading way he spoke to me that night on the way to the holding cell...

"You fucking punk. You fucking lowlife. What the fuck makes you think you can come into my village from wherever it is you come from and start a fucking fight with the local boys?

Huh? Smart ass? You ain't shit. Understand? You and your pals oughta stick with fucking chickens and sheep, know what I mean? I don't need crap like you stinking up my town. Hope you enjoy a night in the stir..."

DiFranco thought he scared the shit out of me, that I'd quiver at the thought of spitting on the sidewalk in "his" village or take off running at the sight of his patrol car. His mistake. Sure, I did leave for a while, but I came back, and we've continued our hate-hate relationship. Now, I had the bad fortune of having to deal with him at a murder scene, one in which I'm sure he was going to utilize his upper-curriculum tactics of how to act like a fat, racist asshole. Big surprise.

Rachel's car still sat in the same spot, almost like a memorial to her. Sooner or later, someone would notice that it hadn't moved in a while and would do their civic duty and call the police. But that didn't matter now. With Steinman snuffed, the lid was going to blow. Another village cop, Ray Stinnett, late thirties, short, dark hair, glasses, one long eyebrow and the kind of five o'clock shadow that needed a razor's attention a couple of times a day was stationed in front of the entrance to the condos. The guy kind of reminded me of Burt Young with specs. He offered a wave as I flashed my creds on the way through. I didn't have to unlock the back door tonight, because it was propped open for the comings and goings of the civil servants. I took the stairs two at a time, deja vu prodding me not too gently, and stopped on Rachel's floor to take a quick look around, to find what, I wasn't sure, but the idea struck me as valid. I tried the door opposite of Rachel's, and it was locked. I knocked but no one answered. Same as last Friday. An important key to this whole deal was hidden behind that door. I was ready to take the next flight up to Steinman's place but stopped to straighten out one of the landscape paintings that helped to spruce up the space. I was surprised that it was even just a little out of skew. I recalled how immaculate the place was during my last visit. I needed to find the person who did the cleaning. He or she had to know everybody and everything that went on in the building, or so I hoped. And the who the hell was going to point me in the right direction? Rachel. Not likely. Rex Steinman. Not now. Door number two, the mystery door across from Rachel? No. Not there. But I still wondered what was behind that door. My best shot was another neighbor, but only if I was extremely lucky and they didn't sic their maniacal French poodles on me. Maybe I wouldn't find out who cleaned the joint afterall. Maybe I should just get my butt upstairs. Finally, a solid idea.

Satisfied with my leveling job, I headed upstairs. The door to Steinman's place was wide open. Wade was inside and so was DiFranco, his big ass turned toward me. I didn't see Rex's body. The apartment looked pretty much the same as before. No broken lamps. Nothing tossed about. But it didn't smell the same. It smelled of decay, fowl and putrid. Thank God for an empty stomach. Wade nodded at me silently as I stepped over the threshold of death. DiFranco, the superior law enforcement officer that he thought he was, sensed the presence and spun around quickly, defying the great heft he laboriously carried. I expected to see a bologna sandwich and a beer in his hands. DiFranco wasn't just fat. He was big. Six-two and somewhere in the range of three hundred pounds. But his fat wasn't the typical lazy, couch potato fat that drooped in folds, except for his multiple chins. His graying hair had thinned out to the comb-over stage, of which he practiced. His eyes and mouth seemed too small for his head and his nose had a pronounced hook at the end. Vic DiFranco was not a picture of health.

"DiFranco," I said, "should you be on your feet like this? So close to the due date?"

I thought I heard Wade snicker softly. Busting DiFranco's hump worked as a diversion from the reality of the situation. I intended no disrespect toward Rex Steinman.

"Shut up, Grace. And what the fuck're you doin' here, anyway? Case you can't figure it out, this is a crime scene, doucebag."

"You always had a way of making me feel special, you know that DiFranco? Glib is the word for you."

"Yeah, well here's another, say 'Good night, Gracie.' Take a walk."

He dramatically pointed the large thumb of his right hand toward the door. I thought it made him look like an overreager hitchhiker.

"Nothing I'd like better, Chief, but this might pertain to a case I'm working."

DiFranco walked toward me.

"You? A real case? Right," he said.

"Go figure, huh? And don't get too close with that thing," I said pointing at his gut. "It might go off."

My sarcasm was not lost on him.

"You think you're a real comic. Lenny fucking Bruce. Well, here's what I'm thinking," DiFranco mused out loud. "I think you're a possible suspect. And you come to check out your handy work. Make sure the donut puncher is really on ice."

"Oh, that's good stuff."

"More realistic scenario than you working a case involving this hump."

"Hate to break your heart, but it's true."

"What the fuck would you need from this guy? You working some fag thing or something?"

DiFranco's breath had that nasty coffee smell.

"You never cease to impress me with your objective thinking. You know that? I questioned Rex Steinman for some background information. Standard stuff."

"Well, I hope he answered all your questions."

"Actually, he raised some more."

"Yeah, I bet he raised something all right. That's what I think."

"DiFranco, you think too goddam much."

"How 'bout this? Now I know a crime took place here, no matter if the guy was a fudge packer..."

"His name was Rex," I interrupted.

247

"Whatever. So anyway, the queer's dead and someone's gotta pay for that, but the way I see it, whoever whacked him did him a favor."

"This I gotta hear."

"Sure, saved him from a life of suffering with that AIDS shit."

"Jesus Christ, DiFranco, the guy was getting married. Just because he's different from you and me doesn't mean he's gay," I offered.

"Yeah, smart guy? You ain't seen the crime scene, now have you? Reynolds, I'm goin' out for some fresh air, wait for the coroner and the state boys to show up and act all big shit. Don't let this asshole touch anything."

And with that, DiFranco lumbered from the late Rex Steinman's apartment to fill his lungs with Skaneateles lakeside air. I stood frozen for a moment, staring at the open doorway through which DiFranco had just passed. I knew I needed to check out the crime scene, which I presumed was in the main bedroom. But I was hesitant. This wasn't the norm in my detective career, studying a corpse, a corpse that I knew and, from DiFranco's words, not an ordinary corpse, if there was such a thing. Wade remained silent with his head bowed. He waited for me to steer the conversation. I stepped into the hallway for a brief respite from the rotting flesh redolence, deducing that the body must have been festering for a few days to stink like this, especially with the air conditioning still cranked up like it was Friday night when I spoke with Rex. I tried to draw a good, deep breath but failed. Seeing death was one thing, but having it fill your nose as a flesh and blood reminder was another. Decay. Waste. Deterioration. If Rex Steinman's body remained where it was, untouched, it would eventually decompose to a pile of bones. A glimpse at our own mortality. I stepped back inside, ready to talk with Wade.

"So, who called this in?" I asked.

"Anonymous female. Reported a terrible smell," Wade answered in his matter-of-fact police tone. He wasn't about to engage in our customary banter.

"How the hell anonymous can someone be if they're around to catch a whiff of this? Had to be a neighbor, right?"

"Probably the old crone across the hall. Or whoever cleans the place."

"But why anonymous?"

"Come one H," he said, "this is Skaneateles. Keep your nose out of crap. It's okay to blow someone in, as long as you stay out of it."

"So, I'm gonna assume that DiFranco checked the neighbors."

"Correction. I checked."

"Anything?"

"Nothing but unanswered knocks. Even Rachel, downstairs. I see her car is here."

Wade knew Rachel through me.

"Probably away somewhere." I only hoped I sounded sincere.

"Suppose. You want to take a look?"

I hesitated. Wade looked at me and nodded his head in the direction of the back bedroom.

"Yeah," I finally responded.

Wade led the way through the pieces of art that defined Rex Steinman's life, once a living memorial to his passion and now a mausoleum built by his own hands. As we moved closer to the source of the stench, I pulled my jacket up over my nose. Tough can only take you so far. I kept my head down in concentration. Wade held up pretty well, considering he had few occasions to inhale the scent of a ripe body, if any. The final steps stirred thoughts of dreams when you couldn't move your legs no matter how hard you tried, only in this instance I wasn't try to run from something. The bedroom door was open. We stepped inside.

An instinct inside of me instantly forced me to raise my head to look at the literal death bed. Rex Steinman lay naked on his stomach on his king size bed, his wrists and ankles lashed to the bed posts with leather straps and a necktie wrapped around his thin, white neck. His head was strangely twisted to the left. His right eye was still wide open. His face was bloated and discolored. I needed to block out the ugliness before me and survey the scene. What I presumed to be Rex's clothes were strewn across the floor, like someone was in a hurry to get them off. The bed covers were also tossed about on the hardwood floor. Besides those dishevelments, the room seemed in order. There were no bruises on the body that I could see. No signs of struggle. But, how the hell are you going to struggle when you're lashed down like a pioneer on an anthill? Only in this case, this pioneer seemed to prefer being lashed down. So, was this a crime of passion? Where a lover become overexcited during that magical moment? And he freaked with fear and bolted? How the hell do I know? DiFranco may have actually been onto something. But, damn it, Rex was getting married. He told me. I was in the apartment when it happened. He was higher than if he was sniffing paint thinner. Why this? My head hurt. I was tired and hungry and confused and worried and ready to leave. And then I saw it. I think Wade started to say something to me, but I didn't hear a word. I only stared in recognition. Silent recognition. The odor of shuffling off the mortal coil disappeared. My stomach gnarled up for another reason. It twisted and turned, a wringing sponge spewing acid up my esophagus. Why was there a portrait of this person hanging on Rex's bedroom wall?

# *Chapter 21*

One of my best friends stared back at me. An eerie stare, distant and abstract, expressing a look I had never noticed before, influenced by the brushwork of the artist, Rex Steinman. I continued to study the face of Mick Allen. Mick's head was turned to the right, but his eyes looked back to the left, at me and past me. The painting revealed Mick from his bare shoulders up, with a dark, cloud-filled sky surrounding a yellow glow in the background that reminded me of Raphael's *Vision of Ezekial*. Mick looked reverant. Or maybe he looked frightened. The steady stream of silence that escaped my lips prompted Wade to share in my art appreciation.

"Jesus Christ," he managed.

"Yeah."

"That's too wierd."

"Out of left field."

"Think it means anything?" Wade asked carefully, not wanting to flat out ask if I thought Mick was involved with Rex in an intimate way.

"I have no fucking clue," I answered, basically summing up my knowledge of anything at that moment.

I knew that I didn't need to stick around for the formal State Police proceedings. The sooner I escaped from there, the better. I craved a good night of sleep, but I suspected that my chances were slim in that department. Too much swirling in my head. Like after a night of competition when I recounted every play, every shot. Physically, my body was ready, but mentally I wouldn't allow the Sandman to whisk me away to some obscure lands ruled by irrational thought in which I lacked the control I had while competing. I knew that Wade would fill me in on any details I needed, so I said goodnight and headed for some fresh air with anticipation of breathing the deepest breath I had ever managed. I quickly descended the steps in no mood to trade insults with DiFranco, who, fortunately, was busy with the fresh arrival of a couple tall, strapping New York State Police. Good for me. I slipped back up the alley past Chad and Egan and the legion of ghouls and walked swiftly back down Genesee Street eager to sit my ass down in the front seat of my Jeep. I crossed back in front of the bank building, enjoying the solitude, and pulled out my keys when I caught sight of my ride parked like a chariot waiting to whisk me home. I was spinning the key ring around my right pointer finger when a stereotypical black Lincoln Town Car pulled up to the curb facing me. Two big lugs with no necks and nice suits squeezed out of the sedan with great alacrity, conjuring thoughts of those coiled up snakes released from joke cans when the top is popped off by an unsuspecting target. In this instance, I was the one removing the top. And the whole scene seemed like a joke. This wasn't Queens. This wasn't Chi-town. This was little piss-ass Skaneateles, where the most protection anybody ever needed was a good rubber. The two no-necks approached me unmenacingly but with purpose. The guy who sprang from the passenger side was the first to reach me. He was six-five, two-sixty, short blond hair, spiked with enough mousse to keep a building erect and good looking in a menacing sort of way. Despite the quickness of his movements, he walked with a limp. Ex-football player, probably. Stuck his toe in the artificial turf wrong one day and good-bye ACL and MCL and a career of legally hurting people. He calmly stepped in front of me without physical contact and waited while the driver joined the party, which wasn't long. The driver stood six-three or four and carried more heft than Spike, but that extra girth didn't seem to affect his ability to track down his query. He didn't quite have the Hollywood looks of his partner. He was older, his brown hair cleanly zipped off in a crew cut, with plain features except for a large mole on his upper left cheek. Spike did the talking.

"Mr. Grace," he said.

I was so tired that I was getting punchy. The day was turning out to be almost surreal, and this episode only fueled the effect, so I acted accordingly. Sure, I risked getting turned inside out right on the main drag of peaceful Skaneateles, but if that happened, maybe they'd knock me unconscious and I could get some rest before ending up in a hospital bed.

"Perhaps," I offered. "Hey, you wouldn't be that washed up football player slash actor Brian Bosworth would you? 'Cause if you are, I really liked your work in... in... oh, hell, I don't know."

"*Stone Cold*," Driver said.

"Yeah, that's one," I quipped. "Very convincing stuff."

Spike failed to see the humor. "Curtis Granby would like to speak with you," he dutifully relayed.

"Tell him to call me sometime. I'm in the book."

Driver shook his head.

"Wait a second. Hold on here," I said to Driver. "You're Robert DeNiro, aren't you? Prepping for a new role. Damn, you gained a lot of weight." I faced Spike. "Now that, Boz, is character acting at its best."

Spike spoke up. "Final chance, Mr. Grace. Are you coming?"

He didn't smile as he said the words slowly and clearly. Neither did Driver. Play time had ended. Time to weigh my limited options. One, try to pull my piece and get both of them to back down before either could pull his. Two, tell them to go screw and look forward to visiting the same sidewalk that Mr. Claus did earlier in the evening. Three, scream for help like a blueblood would if he dropped his Beamer keys on a dirty parking lot. Four, join my new friends on a trip to Curtis Granby's estate. I deduced that option four made the most sense, especially if Bennie was on target about Billy Hanley's recent affiliation with the newly divorced and certainly filthy rich Mrs. Granby.

"Boys, what say we go for a little drive. One condition. No country music," I said.

Spike proceeded to frisk me. He found my Glock, removed it from my person and deposited it in a suit coat pocket.

"You'll get it back when business is done," he told me.

I felt like a child whose mother stuck her fingers in his mouth and pried out a piece of well-chewed bubblegum and informed him that he'd get it back after the visit with grandma in the home. In either instance, I had no choice but to take the deal. It was that or a whack on the side of the head. Spike opened the back passenger side door, and I stepped into the lushness reserved for those who could shell out the kind of dough for a classy ride such as this. The leather seat was quite comfortable. Hell, I could've stretched out and crashed on the spot, but I didn't want to be rude to my pals. Spike and Driver got into the car more casually than they exited it. With a couple of slammed doors, we were on our way to the great Granby residence, down Genesee Street straight past the murder scene, of which I refused to bend a neck to peek, and right onto East Lake Road. There was no music. There was no conversation. So, I sat and pondered. How the hell did Granby know where I'd be at this particular time? Coincidence was as likely as Mick being on Rex Steinman's bedroom wall by, well, coincidence. Mick obviously knew Rex Steinman, and from the subject matter of the portrait, Mick knew him very well. Was the association purely a random act, a shooting star on a hot summer night? Unlikely. Unless Rex had an obsession. But why? He was getting married. But how old was the portrait? Mick. Mick. Mick. You seemed overdramatic in my office, now that I think about it, even if you were soused. Mick, I hardly knew you. We needed words. Okay, onto my host awaiting my arrival. He and Rachel were an item. Straight up. Or should I amend that to say "are an item?" Oh, Christ, Holden, give it up. Rachel was as dead as Rex. Open your eyes. Clearly, somebody wanted her to take that big bus ride. Not Curtis Granby. Maybe not. Not Carl Hendrix. Unless he was Daddy and lying through his nervous teeth. Who was left? Stephanie Hendrix? She acted like Rachel's pregnancy was a complete shock. So what? She might have been filling me full of shit about her husband's multiple trysts. And the mysterious Mrs. Granby? What was her deal? If she did employ Billy Hanley, she was number one on the list.

But why? Would she allow jealousy to spoil her megabuck existence? Doubtful. And stupid. Maybe Billy Blue Eyes was freelancing on this one. He had a thing for Rachel and he couldn't deal with the rejection when she opted for divorcee number one. But man, if it was him solo, he wasn't too bright about it. Truth was, he wasn't bright at all. So, what did I have? More questions than before. No problems. After I chewed the fat, probably pate-based, with Curtis Granby and confronted Mick, answers would come out faster than from Regis Philbin's contestants on one hundred dollar questions on his big money game show. That is, if I ever left Granby's drawing breath.

The drive down East Lake Road was not a long one on this chilly August night. As we headed beyond the village limits, the side-by-side houses with little to speak of for front yards disappeared, replaced by farmland and a smattering of homes on the left and a multitide of sprawling lakeside homes on the right, many not visible from the street. The fire lanes were labeled alphabetically on the east side, as opposed to numerically on the west side. I wondered if that led to a letter and digit rivalry at the club. "Say, Randolph, I'm on the A team in this year's championship." "Big muffins, Kendall, I'm simply number one." Then they'd start slapping each other with their Foot Joy golf gloves until someone's face turned redder than their fake suntan, and the war would be over. Sounded like fun to me. Or maybe the sides of the lake were split into certain factions -- creative types on the east (you know, for using the written word) and numbers people on the west. Of course, Curtis Granby was a big numbers guy, and he resided down the east side. But he could have been an aspiring poet for all I knew...

"There once was a woman named Rachel,
who turned out to be so ungrateful.
She wanted much more
than I could afford,
so I killed her because she was hateful."

"Hey, " I said, "you guys like poetry?"

I needed to say something to stop my mind from becoming gray matter compost. Driver glanced into the rearview mirror at me, but that was the extent of the response. I stuck a sock in the conversation attempts. We had traveled a few miles, past streets named Pork and Coon Hill, reminders that we were out in the sticks, far away from the trappings of big village life. Before we reached the bustling town of Borodino, a humble berg landmarked by a flashing yellow light at the only intersection and a golf course that did present a damn good view of the lake, Driver hung a smooth right onto a private road. I had lost all concept of time. I knew it was night, but that was strictly my detecting talent. After weaving down what I presumed was Granby's driveway, apparently designed by a drunk behind the wheel, we pulled up to an impressive estate, complete with an illuminated in-ground swimming pool and tennis court, resting quite comfortably on the edge of the lake. Hell, the two-story boathouse seemed larger than his daughter and son-in-law's house. Old money defined the spread. The white, clapboard Greek Revival mansion, which must have been more than a century old, stood three stories high with what I conjectured to be a stunning view of the lake. I wasn't sure if we had parked at the front or rear of the home, but my guess was the back, because I was certain that ample porches or decks sprawled toward the lake like luxury box seats at Yankee Stadium reached out to the field. But who the hell cared when you owned a chunk of real estate like this.

Spike got out and opened the back door of the Town Car for me. Such a gentleman. I stepped out, feeling underdressed in my Yankees jacket, non-pressed casual trousers and without my piece. A breeze borne of frigid origins slid up from the dark water and greeted me with a bear hug. I fought back the urge to shiver. Wouldn't look tough. Driver waited until Spike and I were clear of the vehicle, then he pulled it into a multi-car garage that held a Mercedes SUV, a Lexus sedan and a classic MG convertible. The door slid closed, and Spike and I were alone.

"Kind of romantic, don't you think?" I asked.

"Excuse me?"

"You. Me. The lake."

Spike ignored me and started walking toward the house.

He said, still completely poised, "Follow me, Mr. Grace."

He didn't turn around to make sure I fell behind him in stride. He knew I'd accompany him. Besides, who could resist getting out of the wind? We stepped up to a burgundy door that had an alarm system glowing beside it, which Spike manipulated with learned precision. Red turned green, and we were a go. We walked into a large and softly lit two-story foyer. The floor had to have been marble, covered by a fine looking, predominantly dark-blue Oriental carpet. What I gathered to be original Impressionist paintings carefully covered beige wall space, individually lit by small lamps. Antique furniture was laid out just so, some of it supporting smaller pieces of art such as vases and what could have been some Cornell boxes. Two bronze statues, naked and busty women, stood six-feet tall in opposite corners, begging for closer inspection. A large glass trophy case against the wall to my right held an array of shiny kudos for all to see. This was no mere curio cabinet. Heavy double doors were to my right and left, leading somewhere into the depths of the mansion. Straight ahead, the walls angled in to create a hallway that ended with another door. A door, which I guessed to be a closet, was in the right side of that angled-in wall. There was no staircase. I guessed it was actually on the other side of the foyer. Kind of different. So, which door would it be, I wondered? More deja vu. As I studied my surroundings, Spike rearmed the alarm system, and Driver re-joined us from the double doors to my right.

"Didn't get lost, did ya?"

Driver just scowled at me.

"Mr. Granby will see you in the library," Spike offered.

"Good. I like to read. Think he's got the Kama Sutra in there?"

No response.  As expected.  We headed straight, went through the door at the end of the hallway into what could have been another foyer.  The wide staircase was to my right.  We passed through a set of double doors straight ahead, took a left at some abstract sculpture made out of metal and wood and stepped through a set of detailed sliding wooden doors into the library, which was a colorful and richly appointed space.  Granby relaxed in a green wingback chair, his right ankle propped up on his left knee, *The New York Times* resting over his right thigh.  Composed personified.  He had the goods, though, to pull it off.  His hair was thick and gray with a resonance of brown, well-styled and parted high on the left side.  He was tan, of course, clean shaven and apparently in good shape for a guy his age.  He didn't have a lot of that extra skin hanging around the jowls like unwanted baggage.  His face was square.  His chin was strong, not unlike Carey Grant's when he was younger.  His nose seemed straight and perfect.  His eyes were dark, but they hinted of incompleteness.  He wore black slacks, argyle socks and black loafers with the fancy tassles.  A diamond-patterned gray, black and red sleeveless sweater covered the majority of a garnet, long-sleeved button-down dress shirt.  Curtis Granby was styling.

And so was his library.  The room must have been twenty feet by twenty feet, with a turret-style bay window splitting the opposite wall from the doorway.  Green was the predominate color, in different shades on paint trim and the furnishings.  The floor was hardwood and gleamed, with area rugs selectively placed around the furniture, which included two wingback chairs, a green leather sofa, what looked to be cherry end tables, a small mahogany table and four straight-back chairs.  Standing lamps were well placed and recessed lighting in the wooden-planked ceiling offered a high-angle glow to the place.  The walls to the left and the right and opposite the doorway to the bay window were floor to ceiling bookshelves, filled to capacity with hundreds, no, probably thousands, of volumes. This room was truly a library, not someone's haughty thought of what a library should be like.

Granby lifted a finely-etched crystal beer glass half-filled with a deep-amber liquid with his right hand, took a careful sip and placed it back down on a coaster on one of the end tables. He crossed his arms in his lap. He did not appear too jocular. The eyes. Something about the eyes.

"Mr. Grace," he said in a smooth voice worthy of being on the radio. "Please, have a seat. Would you care for a drink?"

I shook my head.

He motioned to the other wingback adjacent to the one he sat in with his right hand. Smooth. Everything about Curtis Granby seemed smooth. I sat. Spike and Driver remained standing, quite erect, their arms crossed in front of them. They could have been statues. I looked around the room some more as the silence picked at my brain. Silence wasn't always golden.

Granby finally said, "I apologize for the fashion in which I brought you here tonight."

I nodded in acceptance.

"I trust that Jeffrey and David were civil."

Again, the nod. Then Granby looked over at Jeffrey and David, motioned his head toward the door, and they dutifully left, Spike sliding the door into place behind him. I guessed that Spike was Jeffrey.

"It was essential that I speak with you," he continued.

More silence. I looked around at the bookshelves. I saw a lot of the classics from Hemingway, Faulkner, Dickens, Poe, Tolstoy, Vonnegut, Bradbury, the Bronte sisters, Dickinson -- Granby ran the gamut with his collection. There were also many educational tomes, non-fiction volumes and pictorial collections. As I scanned the shelves, Granby absently studied *The Times*.

"About Rachel Allen," he finally added as he looked over at me.

Suddenly the books weren't so interesting. I looked at Granby, but I decided to stay with the strong, silent approach.

"She's missing. I know you know. I also know that you've been investigating the matter. I have certain connections," he said.

DiFranco. When he stepped out for that breath of air, he exhaled into a cell phone to Granby that I was poking around. DiFranco was in Granby's pocket. It only made sense. That's how Jeffrey and David knew where to grab me up.

"I need Rachel found, Mr. Grace."

Was that the incompleteness that I saw earlier in his eyes? His actually missing Rachel? Or was his showmanship as rich as his environment? I had to keep both options open.

"Take a number," I finally offered.

"I suppose that's only fair. But know this, I will pay you well for your efforts."

"I don't doubt that."

"So, what would you doubt?"

"Possibly your motive for me finding her."

"Which would be?" Granby asked coolly.

"To ensure that I can't."

"Interesting logic. But seriously flawed. As I am sure you have discovered in your investigation, Rachel and I are romantically involved. We have been for quite some time. But I had a calamitous divorce to settle before we could cease our efforts of discretion. Thankfully, the divorce was finalized just recently, and while my avaricious ex-wife walked away with more than she deserved, I was pleased for the closure, as they say. Mr. Grace, I am a man in his early sixties, with absolutely no financial concerns whatsoever. I offered Rachel Allen so many of the dreams she wished to attain. Initially, I accepted that she may have been simply using me for her financial gains, but as we spent more time together, I realized our relationship went far beyond that. She told me of her parents' unfortunate accident, and, not one to live life with blinders on, I understood part of my role in Rachel's life was as a father figure. I am also her mentor. I helped her out in her business ventures, to give her a taste of success. To whet her appetite for accomplishing great things. She doesn't know how much I helped, because I wanted her to succeed independently of me. And I know she wanted the same. Rachel is an ambitious woman, and she would not have been satisfied being just my lap girl, so to speak. That would have eventually bored her, unlike many other women I could think of. And it goes even deeper."

He finally paused, looking misty-eyed, and turned his head away to face the far wall. He knew. He knew that Rachel was pregnant, and the child was his. But was he going overboard? Perhaps emoting worse than a soap opera actor?

"She was carrying your child," I said.

He nodded. A different sense of silence settled in for a short stay. I wished I had a drink to focus on. Granby collected himself and turned back to me.

"So, you see why your logic is flawed? That I don't want her found? She was pregnant with our child."

"Excuse me for being crass, but I have no choice. Who says you wanted a kid? Like you said, you're in your sixties. Like you needed the burden of a baby in your life, whether on the up and up with Rachel in your life or in the shadows as a syphon of this majestic estate. I know you say you don't have any money concerns, but after the divorce, and now a surprise baby possibly cutting in on the action. Maybe it was too much. Maybe you were tired of people taking from you," I said, hopeful that he didn't call Jeffrey and David back in to make me retract everything.

"I accept your rationale. It's important that you study all sides to a situation," he said. Then he leaned forward with his forearms on his knees for effect. "But, in this instance, wildly grasping at straws."

"Convince me," I said as I leaned toward him.

Hey, an eye for an eye, a lean for a lean.

He sat back casually, scooped up his beverage and drained just enough to fill his mouth with the flavor of what I presumed was a high-priced stout in the glass. He set the glass down, again perfectly on the coaster, and adopted a pensive

261

deportment. For Curtis Granby, is wasn't merely demeanor, but deportment. So, where was he now? A moment ago, he looked like the NYSE dropped five hundred points while he was chopping shallots. Now, he appeared like a game show contestant mulling over the one million dollar question. I was getting a headache. Lack of food. Need of sleep. Talk to me Curtis.

"When my marriage took the final leap from joke to travesty a while back, I happened to have met Rachel at the Syracuse Business Showcase. She asked me a great deal of questions. I didn't want to stand around and answer them. I was actually on my way out after checking in our booths, seeing how everything looked. But she was adamant. She knew who I was. So, I asked if she wanted to take the conversation to dinner. Afterall, she was a beautiful young woman. She accepted my invitation. We spent some time together until I disclosed that I was a married man -- unhappy and dangling on the end of my marital rope, but that didn't matter. She would have nothing to do with me after that. Not while I was still married to Carla, with no prospects of change."

"So, Rachel broke it off?"

"Yes, she did."

"And your reaction?"

"Disappointment. But respect for her."

"So, who ended up the driving force behind the divorce proceedings? You or Mrs. Granby?" I asked.

"Carla."

"Why?"

"We hated each other. And she had pictures."

"Of you?"

"Yes."

"Obviously incriminating."

"Not in the throes of sexual passion."

"But incriminating, nonetheless?" I pointed out.

"With Rachel. But nothing more than hand holding and embraces."

"So, you and Rachel were never intimate before the filing?"

"Never."

"But that changed once the whole shebang was set in motion, didn't it?"

"It was quite a time later. I had forgotten about... no, not the right words... I had dismissed any prospects of being with Rachel, but we met again after Carla filed the papers. When I informed her of the situation, she took it in stride, and I knew her interest had rekindled. Eventually, we ended up being with each other. But it was dangerous."

"Is that when you sent her to Burlington?"

"I didn't send her anywhere. Yes, it was a convenient opportunity, but Rachel was very willing to be the manager of that store."

"Until the divorce came through. And it was time for her to come back."

"I won't deny that. Believe it or not, Mr. Grace, we care for each other. Beyond the fiscal implications."

"So, Rachel came back to lovely Skaneateles. You set her up in business with her brother and the condo in the building you own. You were an item. Still discreet for the most part..."

"It was still a short time after the divorce," Granby said.

"You wanted to keep your image solid, or something like that. Then, a lapse in judgment, or maybe not, and Rachel is pregnant. So what happened?" I questioned.

Granby drained the last of his beer, putting it out of its misery after suffering in the warmth of the library for too long. He finally removed the dead newspaper from his thigh and placed it carefully on the end table next to the empty crystal.

"I mean, careful as you thought you were with your external appearances, you screwed up, and she got pregnant? Or was it a screw up? I don't get this part," I continued. "I don't get how her getting knocked up could be such a surprise."

"Have I, at any one moment, expressed to you that Rachel's pregnancy was a surprise, Mr. Grace?" Granby asked slowly, choosing each word as if a gambler at the track picking the trifecta with his last ten bucks to burn.

But Granby wasn't a gambler. He was a man who usually got what he wanted. Witness the surroundings.

"Are you saying it was planned?" I asked.

"Let's just say not purposely avoided. Both of us understood that."

"So, the pregnancy wasn't a surprise?"

"You're catching on."

"I'm trying."

I stood up to work some of the weariness out of my body with a few laps around the library.

"Okay. You admit to being in a relationship with Rachel," I said as I walked. "You admit to helping her career along. You admit to being the father of her unborn child. Are you saying that the two of you were planning a future togther? Even though you're thirty-something years older? Recently divorced? And now, you're brokenhearted, because she's gone? Let me ask you, what do you think happened to her?"

"I don't know. That's what I want you to find out."

"I'm asking what you think," I said. "Did she run off with a younger, richer, better looking guy? Did she snatch up tens of thousands and make a beeline for Vegas? As her significant other, what do you think happened?"

"I simply suspect foul play."

Granby was even smooth when delivering a cliche.

"Do tell," I said as I sat back down.

"Last Wednesday evening, around eight or eight-thirty, Rachel came to see me. My daughter, Stephanie, who unfortunately does not hold Rachel as dearly as I do, was visiting. We were together in the downstairs study when Jeffrey showed Rachel in. She seemed nervous. Not negatively so, but excited nervous..."

"Like when you know a stock's going to skyrocket," I interjected.

"If the analogy helps, so be it. Rachel had news for me, but she wanted to tell me in privacy. I was slightly torn. I did not want to simply kick my daughter out, but Rachel made the decision untenable. She determined that Stephanie should also hear what she had to say. I believe it was a way for Rachel to try to include Stephanie, to make an attempt to pacify any hostilities."

"Fortunate for you that you weren't forced to choose between young daughter and younger girlfriend."

"Shall I continue, or should I wait for more clever quips from you?" Granby questioned in a condescending tone.

"Consider the quips clipped," I answered. I didn't need him clamming up now.

"Thank you, Mr. Grace. So, Rachel proceeds to inform Stephanie and me that she is indeed pregnant."

"And how did Stephanie react? Considering her loss not long ago?"

"Her drink seemed to disappear rather quickly."

"Bloody Mary?"

"You've done your homework."

"Besides the quick drink drain, anything else?" I asked.

"She said she was happy for the both of us. That she thought we should be alone to share the moment. And she left."

"Awkward moment?"

"I won't deny that."

"How did Rachel feel about the moment?"

"Unfazed. But that was Rachel."

"Okay, what next?"

"We toasted the occasion. Champagne for me, sparkling water for Rachel. At that moment she swore off the booze. And, believe me, Rachel did have quite a knack for celebrating."

"So her best friend informed me. How long did Rachel stay that night?"

"She left reasonable early. A little after ten. She had a business meeting in the morning with her brother and Carl Hendrix."

Steinman said that Rachel didn't come home until around three in the morning. It sure the hell took her a long time to get home. And how much did Rachel tell Granby about the meeting? Did he know it was about selling the store?

"What did you know about that meeting?" I questioned.

"That it concerned selling the store. But Rachel was against it. The store was important to her. I believe Mick drove the proceedings."

"Ever hear the rumors about Hendrix and Rachel? Your son-in-law and your girlfriend being friendly?"

"This, as I'm sure you're well aware, is a small town. Rumors abound. Such as the wife swapping ritual amongst a close circle of well-to-do couples."

That one was news to me. And it was hard to comprehend, especially when the women seemed all so uptight with their matching bleach-blonde bob hairdos and tight faces and the men were mostly doughboys who got off being rude to old ladies, women and children.

"So, you don't believe the rumors?" I asked.

"Absolutely not."

"Any idea who might be spreading them?"

"My first guess would be Stephanie. Second, Carla."

"Interesting family dynamics you got working here, Curtis."

"I will not sit here and claim that this family is free from their psychoses and neuroses. Stephanie suffered a tragic loss. It scarred her. Affected her deeply. It also had its repercussions on her mother. She also lost a child. Carla is an only child. Stephanie is an only child. Their paths are too similar."

"Are you aware of the arrangement that your daughter and her husband have?"

"I do not pry into their personal lives."

"Let's just say that Stephanie and Carl have a love-hate relationship, with it being about ninety-ten on the side of hate. Stephanie claims that Carl is a philanderer. Carl admits to one liaison. Conflicting opinions, to say the least."

"Unfortunate circumstances."

"That's putting it mildly."

"The whole glass houses thing, Mr. Grace."

Granby enjoyed using my name often. Maybe he thought it brought a personal touch to our gathering.

"So, you stand behind Carl Hendrix? Even though he may be a suspect in the disappearance of Rachel? Like you said, you suspect foul play. He's a candidate."

"He doesn't have the brevity to be involved in something as sinister as this. Carl is a good businessman. Despite my guarded feelings toward him, he's been a decent husband to my daughter," he said.

"Despite the drunken crash that killed their kid?"

"Yes. Despite that episode."

"Despite the fact that your daughter is probably an alcoholic with no respect for her husband? Despite the fact that she makes the accusations she does? Despite the fact that the last number Rachel dialed was the home of your daughter and son-in-law?"

"I'm sure that call was related to the meeting."

"Okay," I said. "Let me ask you something else. Are you in partnership with Carl Hendrix in a string of health clubs?"

"Yes."

"High end stuff. Fancy, juice bar places?"

"Yes."

"What kind of partner are you?"

"What do you mean?"

"Who's the name on the bank loan or whatever? Who calls the shots? Do you? Or does Carl?"

"I let my son-in-law handle that venture."

"Kind of you."

"It's not about kind. It's about business."

"I'm going to presume that you know about your ex-wife's involvement with a musclehead place called the Jungle Gym?"

"Yes."

"Curious business for a women in her sixties to be involved with, don't you think?

"Carla is a curious woman."

"I've been informed of her passion, shall I say, for beefy guys. And you say she got the goods on you with seemingly harmless pictures of you and Rachel. You had nothing on her?"

"Nothing to substantiate."

"Odd. You mean you didn't go after her with your own PI once the shit hit the fan, looking for anything to turn the tables?"

"Of course I did. But she was careful, I suppose. My guess, to the point of paranoia. I heard things but had no evidence. And when my lawyers told me it was better to try to just get the damn settlement over instead of stirring up more dirt, I paid heed."

"Fair enough. So, you know a guy named Billy Hanley?"

A sudden pause in the conversation. Granby instinctively looked around the room. He chewed on his lower lip.

"And now where is this conversation leading?" he asked.

"Mr. Granby, there are too many close-knit coincidences in this whole wretched ordeal that make my head spin. Billy Hanley used to work for you. He either got to excited in his duties or off duty or whatever and bashed one too many heads. He ended up in the pen. He recently got out, no longer an employee of yours, of which I don't blame you. But Billy, he has a j-o-b at the Jungle Gym in Syracuse, a joint owned by dear old Carla. Now, Billy, he's a psycho. We've met. He's involved. You suspect foul play? What's Hanley's connection in this? You blow him in? He got it in for you? Rachel left here after ten. Did you know she wasn't seen returning home until around three? Long time to get home from here. Guess who the witness was? Rex Steinman. The guy just croaked in your building. Of which I know you are well aware. Okay, Curtis, you want me to find Rachel? Are you ready to accept that your family is responsible for her being missing, with a solid assist from Billy Hanley?"

"What about her own brother?" he suddenly asked.

"What? Mick?"

"Rachel told me of his affinity toward the same sex. His relationship with Rex Steinman. And his reluctance to set the record straight, pardon the pun."

*Daniel Surdam*

## *Chapter 22*

Despite Granby's words validating what I now suspected about my buddy Mick's sexual preferences, it was still a jagged pill to swallow when coming from a rich, pompous man such as Curtis Granby, a man who had probably dabbled in the homoerotic arena at some point in his life. And he wielded that silkiness again by turning the attention away from his family and toward another suspect, one of which I sincerely doubted was a concrete lead. Come on, Rachel's own brother? What would he have to gain from her demise? Maybe her share of the store so he could sell it to Hendrix? But that store was peanuts in relation to his other financial ventures in real estate and whatever else he did to drive a Mercedes and not be stuck in an office forty to fifty hours a week. I had to press Granby on this notion.

"What the hell do you even know about Mick Allen?" I asked and not too politely.

"I learned of his being gay from Rachel the night she disappeared. And she had spoken of him in the past. In fact, it was Mick's inability to come out of the closet that prompted Rachel to visit me last Wednesday. Apparently, the two had just had a heated argument at her condo. Mick's affair with Rex had been quelled by Rex, because he chose to travel the straight and narrow path. He had been seeing a woman named Danielle in New York, and he determined that his experiment with men should end. I don't think Mick took it too well. Rachel and Mick fought about his failure to accept who he was. That he hid behind a manly veil. That he should accept being gay and come clean. Then she said she made a deal with him, or, I should say offered a deal. She told Mick that she'd confess to a secret to someone important in her life, and if she would do that, would he come out of the closet, to use a trite saying. Mick wanted to know the secret she was to reveal, but she refused to enlighten him due to the fact that she needed to tell it to someone else first."

"And that someone was you. And the secret was her pregnancy."

"Correct on both counts."

"And this tiff they had leads you to believe that Mick would take out his own sister? I don't see the theory holding much water, Curt."

"Oh, not just because of this particular disagreement. Mick was possessive of Rachel, being the role model and the parent and the sibling in her life after they lost their parents."

"Did he know about you and Rachel?"

"No. Rachel had kept our relationship a secret. But I believe that Rachel told her brother what she told me after she left here last Wednesday. I believe it was a crime of passion. He allowed his emotions to rule his mind, and he acted on them. "

"But you have no proof of this."

"None whatsoever. Simply my theory."

"Well, here's something for you," I said as I got up to stretch my legs again. "Last Saturday, your suspect, Mick Allen, was beaten pretty badly by three guys who broke into his house. One of them, I'm certain, was Billy Hanley. He even had the balls to mention Rachel's name. Kind of throws a wrench into your theory, don't ya think?"

I had walked over to the windows and stared out at the night.

"Mr. Grace, please do not tell me that you would be so gullible as to think that simply because Mick Allen received some rough treatment precludes him from being a suspect. Do you not recall a *Dirty Harry* movie in which the suspect hired a man to beat him to an inch of his life in an attempt to frame Detective Callahan? Could Mick Allen not do the same?"

I turned to face Granby.

"That's psychotic. I know Mick, and I know that's not in the cards."

"Did you know he was gay?"

Mr. Smooth got me with that one. I answered by keeping my mouth shut. Funny how suddenly Granby got a loose tongue about Rachel's disappearance. When I first asked him his

272

thoughts, he said that he didn't know and that he suspected foul play. Then he maps out a brother/sister scenario, one that I felt had too many holes. Of course, it seemed like everything else I thought about did also. I needed to tie Steinman in with Carla Granby or Stephanie or Hanley. I looked around the room. Granby certainly was enamored with art. Wait a moment. Art. Go ahead, Holden, what do you have to lose? Give it a shot. After all, Rex was an artist.

"I see you like art, Mr. Granby," I noted, returning to a more formal tone.

"Only good art."

"You mean like those styrofoam boxes and Bongo balls out there?"

"Those are very expensive and highly-regarded Cornell boxes, Mr. Grace."

"I know a Cornell box when I see one. Personally, I don't consider that art, but hey, what do I know?"

"Very little, I'm sure."

"You collect any of Rex Steinman's stuff? He was supposed to be quite popular among some of the Big Apple jet set."

"I did. A few early pieces. It was rough, but it had feeling. Carla was much more taken with it than I. In fact, she has all of the pieces now. And, chances are, she's collected more."

What do you know. Some easy and useful information, and all I had to do was ask. Who needed to take jaunts to Vermont for information?

"Interesting."

"And why would that be?"

"Well, I've been trying to figure out who Rex ratted me out to when I first came to see him last Friday."

"Why would he do that, rat you out?"

"Good question. But he did, because the very next morning I had a tail. A blue-eyed and muscular tail in a Cadillac. Care to guess who it was? Right. Billy Hanley. So, why would I suddenly have a tail? Because I was asking Rex Steinman about Rachel Allen, and he ratted me out." I sat down again. "So, who did he call? You? He lives in your condo. You collected his art. Could be..."

"Mr. Grace," Granby interrupted in a stern tone.

I held up my hand and said, "Now, now, Mr. Granby, allow me this train of thought. I don't think it was you. Not completely convinced, but..."

I left it dangling out there, a juicy morsel for Granby to chew on.

"Where is this leading?" he questioned.

"Hopefully in the right direction. Did Rex call Hanley directly? I don't see a connection there. But then again, you have heard of *Beauty and the Beast*? So, then there's Mick Allen, for the sake of argument. Rex calls Mick and tells him I'm snooping. Guess what? Mick knows I'm snooping. So, why have me tailed on Saturday and then hire the guy to bash your face in? Can't see the logic. What about your daughter Stephanie? Hmm. I'm quite sure that she had made the acquaintance of Billy Hanley."

"That is ludicrous."

"One man's ludicrous is another man's solid idea. Of course, there still is dear old Carla. A woman I have not had the pleasure to have met. A woman who divorced you. A woman who knew Billy Hanley while he was in your employ, I'm certain, and now employs him at her gym." I didn't want to share the information I gleaned from Bennie that also linked Carla with Hanley just yet. "And a woman who knew Rex Steinman. Well now. Let's do a process of elimination. I'll count you out. I'll eliminate Mick. And Hanley. Leaves me Stephanie and Carla. One of them is pulling the strings behind this whole disaster, Curt, and you can stop trying to convince yourself otherwise. I just need to find out what happened and why. And I think I have an idea."

"Which is?" Granby asked, not knowing whether to feel excited about the prospects of a solution or dread if his daughter was involved.

"Uh uh. Too early to say a word. Remember, I don't work for you."

"But you can."

"Only if Mick fires me."

"I can make that happen."

"But you won't."

"And why not?"

"Because it would hinder my progress. And we don't want that."

"No, I suppose not."

"But," I said, "you may be of assistance in another capacity besides financially, but I'm not sure exactly how yet."

"At this point, Mr. Grace, whatever it takes."

Granby looked weary then, his true age clawing through the tanned and proper exterior, forcing its way to the surface as a reminder of mortality. No doubt few people refused his offers, and although the concept of being paid well for my work was tempting, I couldn't screw Mick over. I could, however, have serious words with him about his lack of information provided to me, and tomorrow, that would be the case.

I stood up as a signal to leave, and Granby joined me.

"I'll have Jeffrey and David return you to your vehicle," he said. "They will also return your firearm."

"I'd like to say I enjoyed this, but I'd be lying. If you let me do my job and follow through on what I'm thinking, you'll have your answer about Rachel. You may not like it..."

"But I'll accept it," he interrupted, "if it is indeed the truth."

"I'm sure that we'll be talking soon."

Granby intercommed Spike and Driver. They led me back out of the house, to the Town Car and drove me to my Jeep on a now deserted Genesee Street in downtown Skaneateles. We didn't share any clever comments. No dialogue on how I liked the house. No opinions about the books in the library. Silence. Which was fine with me. Once inside my Jeep, Spike handed me back my Glock.

"Stay out of trouble," he said.

275

"I'll do my best. See ya around."

Then I thankfully drove home with a singular goal -- straight to bed. Any messages could wait. Food could wait. Sleep could not. And that's how I ended one very long day.

## *Chapter 23*

No dreams haunted me. No repressed demons of the subconscious came out to play while I snored and drooled and shut out the world for a handful of precious hours. When the trill of the neighborhood birds woke me, I was in the same position as when I wearily dropped my tired bones onto the bed. The clock read seven-fifteen, and I could see the morning sunshine peeking in on me through the blinds, which was an intrusion I didn't mind, considering the cold, gray day that I had just packed away. I surmised that I needed to return to some semblance of a routine in order to set me on a focused and guided path for the day, so I decided that a workout was in good order, followed by a journey to my dusty office for some phone calls, including one to Mick so he could stop by for a chat, and some much needed reflection. If my theory had any merit, I needed to concoct a scheme to nail the guilty parties, because I still had no proof about Rachel's disappearance, which I might as well have classified as a death, and due to the big money behind the scenes, I wasn't expecting to find any.

The first order of business, after dragging my still-groggy self out of the rack, was to retrieve the morning newspaper and catch up on meaningful events outside of the pseudo-Eden called Skaneateles. The walk down to the paper box and back was refreshing in the early-morning August sunlight. Sometimes you forget to appreciate the really important things. I pulled the paper out of the box, unfolded it and saw the front-page headline that didn't surprise me in the least -- "Body Found in Skaneateles Condo." There were no specifics on the case mentioned in the story. Thankfully DiFranco and the State Police did their job in keeping Rex's identity unknown until a family member could be notified. The story did mention that it was a male and that an investigation was pending. If Mick read this, which I knew he would, he would deduce that the corpse was Rex. Damn, it was going to be a tough conversation with

*Daniel Surdam*

him today.  I tossed the paper on the kitchen counter and checked the messages on my machine.  I didn't expect many and hoped for fewer.  To my surprise, the little red indicator light flashed eight times repeatedly.  I wasn't gone that long.  Was I that popular, or was the machine on the blink again?  I found a PGA Tour Partners Club pad of paper, grabbed a pen and prepared to scribble some fast notes.  I hit play.  The first message, which I presumed to be the call that I ignored when I headed out to meet Hendrix last night, was nothing more than silence followed by a laugh in the background, which sounded feminine, and then the hang up.  Call number two mirrored number one, and I determined that a pattern had been established.  A master sleuth has that kind of ability.  Calls three through five were more of the same with variations that included a man joining the woman in the laughing department, shorter silences and louder hang ups.  Number six on the hit list came from Mick, who was anxious to speak with me.  That made two of us, Mick, old pal.  Call number seven came from my anonymous friends again, who were not that unknown in my opinion, and featured a sinister laugh by the man that hinted of condescension and joy, if that were possible.  At this point, a concern began to gnaw at my insides.  When I first saw the multiple flashes, I expected at least one of the calls to be from Maggie.  Not that we were locked into each other, but we each acted as a presence in the other's life.  I knew that we would both be fine if, for some reason, we were no longer destined to spend time together, and that we would get on with our lives, but we had a certain connection, which I hated to label as "special." It also would have been nice to know that she was okay.  My emotional infirmity was soothed, as the eighth message resonated Maggie's voice.  She said she wanted to check in and see how I was doing and that she was off to work with a client in New Mexico for a few days.  If I wanted to call her next week, that would be great, if I had the time, especially in lieu of my current investigation.  Maggie was special, but we had different lives and lifestyles.  It worked well that we both enjoyed our

278

independence. I was glad to hear her voice. I was glad that she was going to be far away when I hopefully flushed out the bastards who iced Rachel. I looked down at the pad, and the only thing I had written was "ha ha ha." So, the joke's on me Billy Blue Eyes? Not yet. No proof. No problems. You're a scumbag. A cocky, stupid motherfucker scumbag backed by the money of Carla, who you were probably laying your lumber to, if you had any penis left to speak of after your steroid diet. Laugh now, asshole. You too, Carla, you old, rich bitch. I'm coming at you both. I wasn't sure how. I was sure that I needed to meet the ex-Mrs. Granby, if only to get a read on her. I would never expect to gather any useful information, but sometimes information is not the most useful goods you take away from a face-to-face meeting. I'd have to count on that.

I sat down to a protein drink, scrambled egg white and twelve-grain toast breakfast and read the rest of the paper, concentrating on the sports section, and knocked off the daily crossword puzzle. When I had finished, I cleaned up the dishes and went into the bedroom to make the bed. They weren't chores of necessity, but I did them for me. As a youth, I never made my bed, and every night I climbed into an unkempt bed with blankets that seemed to purposely twist me up in knots in rebellion to my neglect. Maybe I was lazy. Maybe I thought I had more important things to do. No excuses cut it as an adult. You are responsible. There is no question about what is right or wrong. The question is whether you have the morals to make the right choices. In today's case for me so far, I made myself proud, and it would only continue with my workout. I debated on whether I should shower before I hit the weights and the heavy bag, which may seem ridiculous, but being freshly scrubbed always makes me feel better, and I could take that with me to the workout. I often showered before a late-night ballgame I had, even though I knew I'd be soaping down again after the game. I thought that the French were wrong when they implied that we bathed too much. I recalled the cleanliness being next to Godliness thing. This time, however, I passed on the shower, mostly due to the eagerness I felt toward getting at the weights. I headed out to the garage and got right to it with Pearl Jam as my musical training partner.

I had finished showering by ten o'clock and had a knew attitude strapped on along with my trusty Glock. I dressed casual in Levi jeans and an Izod polo shirt, untucked, of course, to cover the bulge on my pants. It felt like I hadn't been to my office in weeks, and it smelled that way when I stepped over the threshold for the first time since last Friday. I instantly pried open a window to air the place out. I had no messages on my machine, and wasn't that a sad testament to my detecting prowess? Not that I expected to be suddenly bombarded by calls demanding my services on high-profile cases just because I was poking my nose into Rachel's case, but one call would be good. An insurance fraud. A workman's comp fraud. A telemarketer. Okay, not that desperate. Since the phone only appeared to be working one way, I thought it best to utilize that opportunity, so I tried Mick at his office. A nasally voice greeted me on the other end. It was Mick's office manager or administrator or whatever was the proper word these days, and while the voice stirred visions of a hooked-nose, narrow-faced, tight-bunned (hair, I mean) wallflower, that wasn't the case whatsoever. Nancy was major eye candy. She was actually one of those lookers that could pull off wearing the stockings with the line that ran up the back. Honestly. Tall, blonde with every curve essing just as God must have planned, and a serious face that could make a guy run with fear or drop to his knees in reverence. Nancy also had smarts and a lawyer husband who could have graced the cover of *GQ*. Thank God Nancy had that irritating voice, otherwise her perfection would annoy me. Same with her husband, Robert. Fortunately, he possessed a lousy golf game, couldn't hit the outside jumper and couldn't hit for power on the softball field. That made him so much more likeable, even if he was a likeable guy to begin with. I now had a new understanding or at least a comprehension of why Mick hired Nancy, besides her great office skills. My guess was that he wanted to surround himself with beautiful women to help with his charade of being heterosexual. Then again, I could be as wrong as the time I picked Andy Pettitte to win the Cy Young, only to have Pat Hentgen of the Toronto Blue Jays steal it away from him. And, as I've discovered a little more lately, I can be damn good at being wrong. Nancy informed me that Mick hadn't been in the office yet and that I might want to try his cell number. I thanked her and hung up. Late morning and Mick hadn't been to the office. Not a good business acumen, my friend. But that was like the wedge calling the five iron a shanker, or something like that, since this was my first foray into my office since last Friday. I knew Mick's cell number by heart, so I dialed it up, and he answered on the second ring.

"Hey, Mick, it's Holden."

"Hey, what's up, bud? Sorry about all the calls, but...but, I don't know, this whole thing with Rachel has me messed up."

I could hear the tension in his voice and not just from the worry about his sister. It ran much deeper into his conscience. He knew he misled me and left out vital information about himself and Rachel that could have helped my progress, and I knew he saw the article.

"Understandable. You got time to come to my office and talk? I know you're anxious to, but this time, you bring the bottle of Jack."

Mick snorted.

"No Jack this time, buddy. Maybe tequila."

"Just so you know, Mick, we got a lot to talk about."

"Yeah. I figured. I'll see you in about ten or fifteen."

Then he hung up. He almost sounded like he was to the breaking point, where one more setback would either send him shrieking from my office a total lunatic or drive him to hop on the next plane to Barbados with a one-way ticket. I always knew Mick to be a strong person. After all, he took care of Rachel after the loss of their parents. He succeeded in business. He was outwardly confident. But maybe he forgot to take care of himself emotionally, especially when you're carrying baggage like his that he checked with an absent-minded skycap in hopes that it would get lost somewhere between reality and denial. The thing was, I had no choice but to tell him about Rex Steinman and the crime scene. I'd rather he heard it from me than later on a local television broadcast where the anchors and reporters made it seem like Jack the Ripper had reincarnated in Skaneateles or in tomorrow's paper once they got the goods they needed to print more details. I only wanted one thing from Mick when we spoke -- the truth. After that, we could work on other issues together.

I had some time to kill before Mick dropped by, so I thought I'd try to push Carla Granby's buttons just a little. First, I called Curtis Granby's home. One of his servants gave me his direct office line once I identified myself. A sharp stick like Granby would have that covered. I phoned my new friend Curtis and caught him at a good time, somewhere between a nap and an administrative assistant I imagined. He willingly supplied me with Carla's home number. He told me that she would be there, unless she had jetted off to Europe or some other exotic locale, but Stephanie would have been sure to have told him if that happened. Carla enjoyed using Stephanie as her pipeline of information. We hung up, and I punched in Carla's number. Two rings and a man answered.

"Granby residence."

"Carla Granby, please."

"Ms. Granby is busy at the moment. May I take a message, sir?"

"No, but you can give her a message, right now."

"But sir..."

"Tell her Holden Grace is on the phone and that I'm dying to spend some quality time with her."

"But Mr. Grace," he pleaded.

"Tell her. She'll take the call."

"Yes sir."

I sat listening to silence for a minute or two, looking around my office for more silverfish. I put my gun on the desk in front of me. I rifled through my drawers for a Yankees schedule but never found one, because the voice of the enigma known as Carla Granby greeted me.

"Holden Grace. Do I know you? Should I know you? I hope this call is indeed important, because you, sir, have interrupted a tanning session."

"You know, too much sun prematurely ages you. We don't want you looking seventy or eighty before your time, do we?"

Why be pleasant? She was not a pleasant woman.

"I did not take this call to be insulted. Now what is your business, Mr. Grace?"

"I just thought that we could get together, have a few laughs, talk about weightlifting, art, relationships, you know, that kind of stuff. I've heard so many things about you."

"I'm hanging up now," she teased, not really serious, because I knew she wanted to know my motive for calling.

"That would be too bad. We could have tanned so well together."

"Oh really?"

"Sure."

"And what makes you think that could happen?"

"Listen to this," I said. "Hear that?"

"I heard nothing, Mr. Grace."

"That was the sound of me flexing my bulging biceps. What do you say we get together and tan?"

"You are an amusing man, but I must go now."

Time for the direct approach.

"Ms. Granby, I'd really like to ask you some questions about Rachel Allen..."

"I'm afraid I don't know her, either."

She pronounced "either" as "eye-ther."

"Rachel Allen is a young woman who has recently disappeared, and, by coincidence, she was known to have spent time with your ex-husband. That makes you an individual whom I really need to speak with, considering your divorce is rather

283

recent, and I'm to understand the parting was not entirely amicable."

Of course, she knew everything I was telling her.

"Well, if you insist. Just be sure to bring your, how did you phrase it, oh yes, bulging biceps. Does this afternoon work for you?"

"I can make it work."

"Fine then. Say three o'clock. Steven will give you the directions. Now I must go back and age some more in the sun, Mr. Grace. Ciao."

The charming Carla exited stage left or right, and Steven came onto the line and instructed me as how to get to the residence. No question I could be stepping into a hornet's nest, and I was familiar with those and how they operated. They often took you by surprise, and the results were painful and put you in a panic. Years ago, every time I cut the lawn at my parents', I would always get attacked and stung by a swarm of ornery hornets as I ran through the yard waving my hands like a third base coach on speed. And the siege always happened in the same area, but I couldn't find the nest. Then, one day, as I was hitting golf balls on a hot and dry summer afternoon, I discovered their secret. One of my shots shanked a bit and landed near a shed in the back. Next to the shed was an old garden tiller that had been sitting, what I thought harmlessly, for a couple of months outside. My ball had rolled under the tines of the tiller, and as I reached down to grab the dimpled stray, I saw "it" in all of its mud-spun glory -- the cause to my suffering and the secret location of those nasty bastards. They had constructed a massive nest inside the shoot and around the tines of the tiller, and every time I cut the grass, I moved the tiller to cut the space it occupied. So, every time I moved that tiller, I moved the nest, and that pissed those bees off, and they proceeded to attack me for disturbing them. That night, I laid waste to the thing while the hornets weren't prepared. Yeah, that worked as a decent analogy for what I could encounter at Carla Granby's house that afternoon, but I actually had a few thoughts on how to watch my backside when I went. Well, one thought. And it may have been reaching a little.

I searched out my basketball and starting firing up shots from around my office. My touch had not deserted me. Even on a toy rim with a string net, fewer things sounded more beautiful than a sweet swish that makes the net jump back up, almost as a cheer out of respect for the stroke. A swish; the wind through the trees and crickets and peepers on a summer night; the gentle, pleased sounds of a woman in the midst of passion; a golf club clipping the top of the grass on a perfect practice swing; a big bass blowing up on a topwater lure; tires on gravel -- these were a few of my favorite sounding things... I cleared Julie Andrews out of my head and went back to shooting the rock. I must have been one hell of a professional looking private dick at that moment. I thought about what I needed to do in order to wrap this case up and save my ass at the same time. If two people had already been eliminated, there was always the chance to add a third member to the group. You do one, you might as well do a whole bunch. Or at least that's the way I thought creeps like serial murderers thought, not that this was the case here. Focus, Holden. I knew who was involved. I needed to flush them out. I needed to let them know that despite the coin that they thought protected them, it would only help to pay for high-octane lawyers who could sing and dance all they wanted, if they had clients to represent. Maybe violence would beget violence, and the eye for an eye adage would ring true. That wouldn't be my first choice, but when dealing with psychos and meglomaniacs, who knew? Okay, talk with Mick. Make a phone call or two. Have some lunch. Meet Carla. Have a beer. Yeah, shooting hoops definitely helped one plan an itinerary.

Mick walked into my office around eleven-thirty, much more calmly than the last time he visited, although the circumstances were really no better. He looked tired, and he was dressed more casually than I would have expected for a business day in wrinkled gray slacks and a burgundy long-sleeve dress shirt with the sleeves rolled up and no tie. And he hadn't shaved.  Beware the breaking point, Holden.  He held a brown paper bag and tossed it to me upon entering.  Thankfully I caught it, because it was a bottle of Jack Daniels.

"That's for last time," he said.

"Not necessary, but thanks."

I stashed it in a desk drawer.  Out of sight, out of being cracked open as a placebo for mental medicinal purposes.

"You're looking tired, Mick," I said.

"Feel okay, I guess."

He sat down in one of my armchairs and instinctively looked around the room before turning back to face me.

"No, really," I said, "how you doing?"

"The truth?"

"That would be refreshing."

He offered a wry smile.

"Suppose it would.  I feel like I'm swimming and I've got cement shoes.  I feel like shit."

"Now we're making progress."

"Yeah."

"I'm gonna go out on a fat limb and assume you know about Rex," I said.

Mick looked away.

"I read the paper," he managed.  "I figured it was him, being the same condos as Rachel's and all."

"Mick.  Mick, look at me."

He did, and when he did, I almost wanted to tell him to turn back away.  Man, he was fucked up by this whole ordeal.  The loss of his sister, the beating, and now the loss of an ex-lover.  Lesser men...

"Mick, you don't have to hide it anymore.  I know about you and Rex.  I know you're gay."

Wow.  Strange words coming out of my mouth to my best buddy.  He damn sure had me snowed.

"I suppose it had to come out," he said.  "Once you started looking into things.  I thought that maybe if... who am I kidding,

I didn't know what to think. Holden, I am gay. I'm sorry I could never tell you."

I'd bet that was the first time he actually said it to anyone, even Rachel.

"It's all right."

"No, it's not. Because not only have I misled everyone I know about this, I've conveniently left out important information about Rachel's disappearance."

"I know about the argument. I know about the painting in Rex's apartment. I know about the deal that Rachel wanted to make with you, and I know what her end of the deal meant."

"How could you know that? You haven't found her, have you?" he asked.

His eyes widened, and he leaned toward me.

"No, not yet. But, I do have a few things to tell you. The first being that Rachel was pregnant."

I expected stunned silence, but I was about to be the one left momentarily speechless.

"I know," Mick replied.

I could only stare at him. Every time I thought I had a grasp on things, they'd slip away like a greasy putt.

"And I know who the father is. And I know he's responsible for her disappearance. Fact is, I think he killed her."

"Okay. Go on," I finally managed.

"I got a phone call the other night. From an anonymous friend of Rachel's. She said she had news for me. That I could use. She said that Carl Hendrix had gotte Rachel pregnant, and that Rachel wanted to keep the baby, but Hendrix would have nothing to do with it. He was married. He was a businessman in the community. He killed her to protect himself. The fucking bastard."

"Mick..."

"There's more. So, I called him up. Disguised my voice and threatened to kill him if he didn't confess."

"It was you, not Billy Hanley."

"You know about the call?"

"Hendrix told me. That the caller was real mysterious about what he had done. And he was scared shitless."

"You met with Hendrix?"

"Yeah."

"And you let him go?"

"Mick, he didn't do it. Someone wanted you to think he did, maybe take justice into your own hands."

"I'm not that far gone, yet. But, Jesus Christ, H, what's going on?"

So, I filled him in about everything, including the less than rave reviews about Rachel as a person and even the details of Rex Steinman's murder scene, which caused Mick to turn slightly green. I really thought he was going to puke right there, but he held it back. He also didn't react very kindly to Curtis Granby's accusations about him, but I convinced Mick that Granby could actually be an ally in the situation, if everything he had told me was truthful. Maybe the whole damn thing was a massive conspiracy. Maybe Rachel's baby was induced by some strange government experiment backed by Granby's funding, and when the feds involved wanted to take the fetus out of Rachel, she ran for her and her baby's lives. And then maybe UFOs came down and gave me a sake enema while we discussed Soren Kierkegaard's *Fear and Trembling*. It was either time to take care of business or time to look for a new career. I told Mick I had a plan, which was only slightly stretching the truth, because I did -- to nail the guilty parties, but I didn't have the details hammered out yet. Based on the comment Granby had made to me earlier about Stephanie being the town crier to her mother, I figured that I was going after a three-headed monster or creature with three bodies, kind of like Hercules looking to slay the Hydra or Geryon. Anyway I sliced it, the fun was soon to begin, initiated by my rendezvous with Carla Granby and who knew what other evils that may have lurked.

I offered to take Mick out to lunch to any one of the hot lunch spots in Syracuse, but he declined on the premise that he really needed to get some work done. He left me with a slap on the shoulder and a reassurance that he would stay strong and wished me success. I assured him that I'd put it all together shortly. When the door closed behind him, I asked myself how I could, for even one moment, consider him to be a suspect in his own sister's demise. I pretty much knew everything up to ten o'clock last Wednesday night. Then there was that five hour window that ended at three in the morning. And after that, no trace of a human being. So, what happened between ten and three? And then what happened after three when Rachel seemingly walked away from her condo? I had an idea, and it would've helped if someone came right out and told me. But is life ever that convenient?

I narrowed lunch to two places, flipped a quarter, and Phoebe's Garden Cafe won when it came up tails. Before I headed out, I placed another call to Curtis Granby and asked him for a favor, which he generously granted. That made the prospect of lunch more appealing, knowing that pieces were falling into place. It was like a crossword puzzle, where each word set up all the others, and if one letter was wrong, the whole thing was ruined. And in this case, I didn't have an eraser as a backup. I tucked my gun back into my waistband and locked up the office around one and went to have some lunch.

Phoebe's Garden Cafe labeled itself as an American bistro close to all of the arts and attractions in Syracuse, with lots of greenery and a casual atmosphere. I guessed it was a safe assumption to make, since Syracuse Stage was directly across Irving Avenue and Syracuse University and the famous Carrier Dome were a few blocks up Irving Avenue. Plus, the medical center where I met Dr. Amanda Russell was just up the street. The place wasn't terribly busy when the hostess, a little thin and sporting too much makeup, showed me to a small table. She was polite as she told me that my wait would be there shortly. I flashed a smile. She returned it. Yeah, a bit too skinny I confirmed while watching her sashay away. But certainly no charity case. I looked around the dining room or atrium or eating arboretum and saw that I was the only patron lunching alone. Some people get embarrassed if eating alone in a restaurant. They feel it makes a statement about their standing in society or lack thereof. As if other diners, not going stag, would say what pariahs or lunchtime lepers individuals without a lunch date were. Personally, I could care less if I ate alone. Came with the territory. And if someone wanted to give me a hard time about it, I'd just bust their nose. I wasn't in the mood to loiter too long, so when a young, plump wait with freckles and bowl-cut hairdo approached, I rattled off my order before he had a chance to ask me if I wanted a beverage.

The food was okay, but it was usually difficult to impress me. I dropped some cash on the table and was on my way out the door when I bumped into a familiar face. She recognized me too.

"Hello, Dr. Russell," I said.

"Mr. Grace, isn't it?"

"Very good."

"I need to be."

"Ah, yes. So many patients, so little time."

She looked professional in a navy blue pant suit. We were standing in the foyer of the restaurant and blocked the path of a couple trying to get in. We shuffled to the side and let them pass.

"So, how goes the investigation?" she asked.

"Lot of cloak and dagger. Danger and mystery. The usual."

She smiled slightly.

"But, seriously," I continued, "I am making progress, but it's not pretty, I'm afraid."

"That's too bad."

"Yes it is. Well, I'll let you get to lunch. I see that you're not intimidated by eating alone, either."

"With my schedule, I'm happy to even eat. Nice to see you again, Mr. Grace."

"The pleasure was mine. And be sure to tell Tracie I said 'Hello.' One fine assistant."

"Yes she is, and I'll be sure to tell her."

I considered it a portent of good luck running into Dr. Russell. I liked her, and I liked her style. Of course, the same could have been said for Tracie. I walked out of Phoebe's not much past one-thirty. I still had time to head back to my office and think about my tactics with Carla before making my three o'clock appointment with her.

## *Chapter 24*

Carla Granby owned a home on Cazenovia Lake, which was southeast of Syracuse and about thirty miles due east from Skaneateles. I surmised that she wanted her own lake to lord over away from the tyrant to the west. As I drove along Route 92 that eventually intersected with West Lake Road in Cazenovia, my destination, I rehashed some pertinent numbers that I had worked on after lunch at my office that calculated into the troublesome five-hour window, which was the key to the whole damn thing. They worked out. Every time. The drive from Cazenovia to Skaneateles would take about forty-five minutes, and if someone pushed the pedal harder than most, knock off five minutes. Another piece locked into place. From downtown Skaneateles to the Hendrix residence was a mere five-minute drive. And then back around to the east side to, say, Curtis Granby's estate took maybe fifteen minutes, depending on the speed attained by the driver. So, if a call went out to Cazenovia from the west side of Skaneateles Lake around eight forty-five p.m., and the person or persons on the Cazenovia end made a trip to the source of the call, they'd arrive around nine thirty, give or take a few minutes. Then, if this group hit the road again and the east side was their destination, add another fifteen minutes. Makes nine forty-five. More pieces fitting in. Rachel left Granby's around ten, and she had an escort waiting for her, courtesy of the Stephanie pipeline. Sure, they took a chance that their quarry would still be available, but they had news from a pretty good source, Stephanie, that Curtis and Rachel would be spending some quality time together cuddling and giggling and toasting a new fucking baby that others weren't able to bear.

I drove past the Syracuse suburbs of DeWitt and Manlius, the adrenalin hopping me up more and more the closer I got to Caz, the familiar term for Cazenovia. I was a bit amazed that I was about to set a plan into motion so quickly. But it all felt right once I looked past the peripheral bullshit like a woman's personality, people's sexual preferences, threatening phone calls, business deals, big money, fat cops and dope dealers. Passion was the key, and passion could be borne of love or hate. I hung a left onto West Lake Road, noticing a Lincoln Town Car parked on the side of the road, and drove up less than a mile to a narrow fire lane on the right, framed on both sides with tall trees. I made the turn and followed the road that led me to Carla's castle. The mid-afternoon sunlight flashed like a disco ball as the rays danced through the leaves on the trees. I had to maintain a speed under twenty miles per hour, which compelled me to think about how easy it would have been for an ambush. But it didn't matter. Forget about it, Holden. If Carla wants to take the chance and have you whacked, she'll do it, whether here on the road or in her compound. Drive, you son of a bitch. Drive, and then get into her head. Walk out. Drive away. Nail her later.

I cleared the trees, and the bounties of a major divorce settlement grabbed my attention. Par for the course, I supposed. First, the nice digs of the Hendrix's. Then, the serious old-money estate of Curtis Granby. Now, the new-money spread of Carla Granby. The sprawling white colonial with three-car garage overlooked the water majestically. An in-ground swimming pool, large enough to hold a pod of whales, with attached Jacuzzi glimmered between the house and the lake. The pool changing room was the size of a small house. To the right of the pool were two bright green tennis courts, unoccupied at the time. A spectacular boathouse with a multi-tiered deck perched at the water's edge. The landscaping was impeccable. Not a weed in sight. Carla Granby, you've done well for yourself, or, more accurately, Curtis Granby has done well for you. I half expected an armed sentry to greet me when I parked behind one of the closed garage doors, but to my surprise, an older, tanned and attractive woman in pretty damn good shape wearing an over-sized gardener's hat and purple and gray work gloves walked around the side of the house. Her smile was already firmly in place. Let the games begin. She removed her gloves and thrust out her right hand with confidence. I gave her a firm shake.

"Mr. Grace?" she asked, already certain of the answer.

"Ms. Granby. Or is it Miss Granby. Surely not Mrs. Granby."

"How about Carla?"

"Makes it easy. Holden works for me."

"I do so like that name."

"I'm rather partial to it myself."

"Shall we walk?" she asked as she put her left arm through my right and led me down toward the swimming pool.

She was wearing a white, short-sleeve button-up shirt, untucked over a pair of khaki shorts, light-brown socks and a pair of Hi-Tech hiking boots. I could see her age making a better appearance once she was close up, but she was doing an admirable job of keeping it at bay. I imagined that her plastic surgeon had a hand in the process. She enjoyed the physical contact. Her son-in-law was right about her preferences for muscular guys, not that I was soon to to vie for Mr. Olympia, but I had the goods and she took notice.

"Nice place you got here," I offered.

Flatter her, Holden. What woman doesn't like to have her spread noticed?

"Thank you," she replied. "It serves me well."

"So, then, I'm going to guess that you're a tennis player and a swimmer and a gardener?"

"Right on all counts. Shall we sit by the pool?"

Like mother, like daughter. Except Carla had a pitcher of iced tea on the table, not the goods for a slew of Bloody Marys. We sat on heavy, white wrought-iron chairs with thick cushions around a white, wrought-iron table with a glass top and an umbrella jutting up out of the middle. I felt like an ingredient in a tropical drink. Carla poured a tall glass of tea and handed it to me.

"I'm not much of an iced tea fan," I said as I took the glass.

"Would you care for something else, then?" she asked with a glint in her eyes.

"No, this is fine. Thanks."

She carefully poured a glass for herself and sat back to look at me.

She finally said, "You work out, don't you?"

"On occasion."

"It shows."

"I could say the same for you. Hard to believe you're a day over..."

"Be careful, Holden."

"Forty-five?"

"I'll accept that."

"I can see where your daughter gets her looks."

"You've met Stephanie?"

She knew I had. Play the game.

"Oh yes. Delightful woman."

"That's a new one."

I sipped the tea and fought back making a face only a circus sideshow operator could love.

"She has a fresh approach on life, let's say."

"Another new one. Are you this flattering about every woman you meet?"

"If they deserve it."

"Do I?" she asked, again with the glint.

"It's early yet."

"So, I have time?"

"There's always that."

She took a careful pull from her drink. The condensation on the glass beaded up and trickled down the side, and she wiped the tears away with her right index finger in slow up and down movements. It wasn't a come on. It was the game. We weren't going to have sex. I mean, we never would've anyway, believe me, but we knew we were feeling each other out. Kind of like the first few rounds of a heavyweight bout. It was a process we had to go through. I knew she was in on Rachel's disappearance and death. She knew I knew. So, we would dance until my feet got tired and I'd leave. And not alone, I conjectured.

I looked out at the lake, which was smooth and had little boat traffic. Cazenovia Lake didn't quite make it as one of the Finger Lakes. The glaciers chose to slide to the west to create their masterpieces -- long, narrow and deep lakes that the Native Americans of the area claimed were created by the hand of the Great Spirit, Manitou, who wanted to reward the Iroquois Confederacy by bringing part of the happy hunting ground down from the heavens. And of all the Finger Lakes, Skaneateles was actually the bluest, and Native American legend says that the sky spirits would lean from their homes and admire themselves in the mirror of the lake. The lake spirits apparently fell in love with the narcissistic sky spirits and absorbed the color of their robes into the water. There were many fascinating stories and legends about the Finger Lakes Region, but chances were that this caper would never qualify.

I turned back to Carla, who sat patiently.

"Mind if we talk about Rachel Allen?" I asked.

"Ah yes, the little tart who shamelessly pursued my husband, I mean ex-husband."

"Okay. That Rachel Allen."

"And what would you like to know, Holden?"

"It seems she's disappeared without a trace."

"Oh, I do hope Curtis is taking it well."

"He's holding his own," I said.

"It is rather ironic, though."

"What is?"

"That Rachel actually helped me attain a lot of what you see here, and I never thanked her."

"You mean, you never invited her over for some iced tea, some tennis and a friendly chat between girls, trading stories about the same man?"

Carla graced me with a condescending chuckle. Then she became serious.

"No," was her answer.

"Now you'll probably never get the chance."

"Tough break, Rachel."

The real Carla Granby was beginning to shine. All of her pleasantries and iced tea simply proved to be window dressing.

"That's true. You are a gracious host," I said.

"Depends on the company."

"Sure. So, Carla, know anything about Rachel's whereabouts?"

"Off on a shopping spree, would be my guess."

"I think your daughter said the same thing. Is that all you women care about is shopping?"

"When you're loaded, baby, no sense saving it all."

"You ever meet Rachel?"

"Never had the pleasure."

"You don't think something sinister happened to her, do you?" I asked.

"Now, why would I think that?"

"I don't know. Maybe Curt caught her with the gardener? Maybe your son-in-law had a thing with her and needed to shut her up. Maybe..." I trailed off and shrugged my shoulders.

I chose not to go too far, even though I knew I had Carla on the edge of her seat waiting to pounce if I accused her or Stephanie. Sorry, Carla. Not this time.

"And maybe you're just blowing a lot of smoke 'cause you're spinning in circles. I appreciate the fact that you need to ask questions, but you're wasting your time if you think I've got anything useful for you. Curtis and I were unhappy for years. The arrival of golddigging Rachel allowed me to take the initiative and put an end to our marital suffering. It wasn't pretty by any means. I wanted to make sure I was taken care of. I got used to being financially comfortable, and I wasn't about to kiss that good-bye for the sake of escaping a lousy marriage. Does that make me an evil person? Hell no, Holden. Makes me a realist."

"Curtis got caught and you didn't. That makes you lucky."

"Or smart. You think what you want, but I'll tell you this, both Curtis and I are much happier apart. Hell, he still has more money than he knows what to do with," she said.

"And a nice home and nice art."

"Right."

"But you have the Steinman's."

"Excuse me?"

"Rex Steinman's works. One of your spoils from the divorce. And you still collect it. And, here's good news for you. It's gonna go up in value, because he's dead."

I assumed that she knew, since Hanley had to have been the one to send him to the great art loft in the sky. Of course, Hanley could've done that one solo. Maybe Hanley enjoyed playing patty-cake with the other boys in the pen and liked the cut of Rex's jib when he saw him dealing art with Carla, so he paid a visit, got rough and snuffed Rex. Good to know that I wasn't still concocting crazy suppositions.

"That really is too bad. Rex was a fine artist. I understood he was to be married."

Hold the phone. Rex didn't have Danielle's answer until last Friday when I was there. He was killed sometime over the weekend. Obviously, Carla and Rex had seen each other within that time frame.

"So, had you seen Rex recently?" I asked.

She hesitated for the first time. My thought was that she wasn't ready for the Rex Steinman line of questioning. You sneaky dog, Holden.

"Uh, no. I purchased a piece from him a short while back. That's when he told me about his plans," she answered.

Good recovery. But a load of shit. She looked back over her shoulder toward the house. It was the first time she did that. She had the itch to shove me off and wanted to let Hanley know, who had to be watching our exchange from somewhere in the mansion, that I was soon on my way.

Daniel Surdam

"It's nice that two business associates could discuss things about their personal lives," I said. "Gives me a warm, fuzzy feeling right here."

I put my right hand over my heart.

"Enjoy it, because those feelings are rare, my dear. Now, if you've had about enough of this useless line of questioning, I'd like to get on with my gardening."

"Carla, I'd hate to keep you from your snapdragons. Shall I show myself out?"

"That would be fine."

We both rose, I shook her hand again and walked back around the same side of the house without looking back. So much for the preliminaries. Time for the real confrontations to begin. I eased into my Jeep and took my time starting it up. I wanted to give Billy Boy a chance to put the weights down, find his keys and remember which door led him out of the house and into the garage where his ride was waiting. I slowly pulled away from Carla's estate, cruised casually back down the drive to West Lake Road and swung a left onto Route 92 on my way to Route 20, which would lead me west to Skaneateles through towns such as Pompey, LaFayette, Cardiff and Navarino -- the kind of small towns that make rural America so interesting, or boring depending on your point of view. My rearview mirror didn't indicate a tail as of yet, but I did see the Town Car still parked on the side of the road. It was a reassuring sight. I kept the radio off to better concentrate, if what I suspected would happen soon did transpire, so I was trapped alone in the silence of my thinking, which had its good points and bad points, like pretty much anything in life.

Just as I swung a right onto Route 20, I caught sight of a black Mustang barreling down 92. Company. The driver disregarded the red stop light and fishtailed through the intersection. No leisurely drive home for me. I punched the gas pedal, thankful I opted for the V-8 engine over the less powerful but more fuel-efficient V-6 when I bought the Jeep. I didn't plan to stay on Route 20 for very long, and, if the situation dictated,

300

I'd be more than happy to go four-wheeling through any of the abundant farm fields along the way, an option not too desirable or attainable by my buddies behind the wheel of the Mustang. As the needle on my speedometer pushed past twelve o'clock and headed for three, I noticed that the Town Car joined the parade. Ah, a plan actually unfolding as expected. Or so I hoped. I knew that it wasn't Popeye Doyle behind me, but then again, I was no Mel Gibson in *Road Warrior* in the seat, and this wasn't going to be some glamorous Southwestern desert chase scene with stunning vistas and lots of kicked up dust.

I now knew that Curt's boys, Jeffrey and David, had the back of my back covered in the Town Car, so I just needed to push the pedal down and go. If Billy Hanley and his partners in the Mustang were as illogical and unintelligent as I suspected, they'd never pay attention to the Town Car and focus on running me down and putting a bullet between my eyes to end my sniffing around for good. Hanley and Carla knew I was close. They couldn't afford to waste anymore time or nonsensical threats. They needed me iced, even if that meant a one hundred mile per hour chase in the middle of the afternoon. Part of what I couldn't figure, though, was that Hanley seemed like a liability to Carla. He was a hot head, an ex-con violating his parole with practically every breath he took and a flat out hammerhead. I supposed that she still needed his muscle and insanity to whack me, then she'd probably bury a slug in his brain at her place and say that he was a burglar. That would wrap it up nicely for her, if she could count on her daughter to keep her mouth shut. Hell, maybe she planned on taking Stephanie out also. Wouldn't surprise me. Carla's hubris would dictate such a twisted and bold move. I really needed to get to Stephanie again. She was the key to this now. She had to have been a coerced participant, an accessory and not the one who dealt Rachel's death blow. She had a chance if she turned on Carla and Hanley, and I planned on giving her the not-so-gentle nudge in that direction.

A unfamiliar sound jolted me out of my reverie. In the rearview mirror, I could see Hanley hanging out of the passenger side window with a gun aimed at me. He had opened fire. Fucking psycho. He didn't care that other vehicles were whizzing by in the eastbound lane. Now that spiraling lead had been introduced into the chase equation, the time had arrived to get the hell off of the highway and make tracks away from innocent bystanders and out to the backroads. That, and I needed to head south soon anyway, if what I had planned was going to come to fruition. The only problem was that if the Mustang was going to struggle in some of the locales I planned on driving through, so would the Town Car. But I had to either take my chances that way or gamble that I could outrun them enough on the open roads.

We were nearing Pompey when I whipped a screeching left turn off of Route 20 and onto Cemetery Road. Nice choice, Holden. The Mustang and the Town Car stayed with me. When this whole excursion formulated back in my office, I suspected that Hanley would be at Carla's. I also counted on Carla to send him and his boys after me to silence me. I hoped that she wouldn't go as far as to kill me right on her property. I called Granby and asked if I could borrow Jeffrey and David as back-up. My plan was to lead Hanley and his crew to a New York State Reforestation Area in the middle of nowhere, then with the assistance of Jeffrey and David, I'd either get them to surrender or shoot them. Simple plan. And hasty. And drastic. And the best way to clear Hanley out of the way. And I doubted that surrendering was an option.

Hanley's blond head still poked out from the Mustang, and the cold steel was still nuzzled in his right hand. I could see him screaming at the driver to get closer to me, spit flying from his mouth, veins and neck muscles bulging. He squeezed off a few more stray shots that could have ended up practically anywhere -- harmlessly in the trunk of a tree or tragically in someone's head sitting in their living room watching Maury Povich. I took a right onto Route 91 and then a quick left onto Chase Road. The Mustang gained and actually clipped my rear left bumper as I weaved to cut the car off. I could see Billy Hanley's blue eyes in all of their maniacal fury. He fired at the Jeep and hit the driver's side passenger window. The bullets ripped through the glass, whizzed too close to my head and exited out through the front passenger side window. An eerie sound, the path of a spinning slug cutting the air. I accelerated ahead of them as an old pickup truck came at us and hung another left, then a right. The Mustang was still with me. I didn't see the Town Car and only hoped Jeffrey and David had not decided that they didn't like the country. I knew I was nearing my destination. I blew through a stop sign and slid sideways as I turned left and wiped out someone's mailbox. The cedar splinters showered down on the well-manicured lawn. I intersected with Route 80, went left into downtown Apulia, if you could call it downtown, and met up with Route 91 again as I turned right. Honking horns, derisive shouts and hand gestures greeted my tour through Apulia. A left turn onto Jones Hill Road led me into the wooded area I seeked.

## *Chapter 25*

My palms were sticky on the steering wheel. I could feel beads of perspiration trickling and tickling down my back. Christ, what was I doing? In a matter of moments, I could be sprawled on a bed of pine needles, my mortality no longer a question with no victory in solving Rachel's death. There would be no more workouts, no more Mexican food, no more cold beers, no more playing guitar, no more sports, no more Maggie, no more any women. Prospects that I did not like at all. Maybe there was something wonderful and spiritual beyond a living existence, but I was not ready to find out. My breathing became shallow and rapid. It was damn hard being human. I drove up into the woods, past a couple of other parked vehicles, knowing full well that the Mustang would arrive at any moment. The deeper I could four-wheel into the trees and shrubs, the more space I could put between me and the Mustang, which would allow Jeffrey and David to stay with them, if the two were still in the chase. I started to contemplate whether my plan for back-up was actually a setup for me conjured by Curtis Granby. What if he was really actually pulling the strings, and that was why he was so easy to lend me his muscle? Instead of watching my back, they'd either drive away and leave me alone against Hanley and whoever else was in the Mustang or assist in turning out my lights. Maybe Granby was playing me all along, extracting information from me with a brilliant acting job, and I set this all up nicely for him. Guess what, Holden. Too goddamn late to worry about that. You committed yourself to this course of action; you follow through with it. Just be careful, smart and unforgiving. That would put me two out of three ahead of Hanley.

I had no idea what kind of arsenal Hanley had, but whatever he carried, I was certain that it outmatched my Glock. Hell, his fists for pistons nearly outmatched my firearm. I knew he'd be eager, perhaps a little cocky in tracking me down, assuming that he had me outnumbered. I needed stealth and luck. I had control over one. Fifty-fifty ain't so bad when your life's on the line. Then again, yeah, it is.

I wrestled with my Jeep through a walking path as far as possible before hanging up on a stand of small trees and rocks. I had one hand on my gun and the other on my cell phone after I stuffed my keys in my pocket and scrambled out the door and onto the path, looking back in time to see the Mustang buried about a hundred yards behind the Jeep. I saw no Town Car bringing up the rear. Luck may have been leaving the picture earlier than I would have liked. Stay positive. Stay focused. Stay unforgiving.

I hustled off the path into the thick woods. I could hear the excited voices rising behind me, like a pack of wild animals moving in for the kill. The near cackling struck me as eerie, as if I were removed from the equation and a bunch of guys were just whooping it up in anticipation of bagging a big buck. I was conditioned for the elements. Far better than my pursuers. My guess was that they'd split up, try to surround me and close in like a human net. I worked my way through the evergreens in search of higher ground. I questioned why I chose the location, since I had never been there before. I questioned a lot of things. Like why I selected this course of action. Like why I just didn't go to Wade with what I knew and... and what? Tell him my theories? I had shit for proof. I had no body. No real motive. I questioned the logic of visiting Carla at her estate. Sure, I wanted to rattle her cage, which in turn would set Billy in motion, but I think deep inside I believed that the wheels would fall off somewhere along the line. Harsh reality, Holden. You have to carry it through, even if it means snuffing out a life for the first time. You're a long way from rescuing cats from trees, huh, buddy?

I continued to run through the trees, the needles slapping and scratching me unmercifully. I concentrated on pacing my steps and my breathing. Staying alert for any sounds around me and the direction I had taken from the road. If I kept my bearings, I might be able to circle back to the vehicles. I knew that I had driven into the woods eastbound, and that, when I finally hung the Jeep up, I headed south from the walking path. I moved steadily in a solitary world, cloaked from the sun by the tall timber. I wasn't sure if the limbs stretching out were arms of protection or deceit. Thoughts of my youth filtered into my mind, delivered by the impending deja vu as I ran from Hanley's group. Many years ago, a neighborhood group of us kids would play a pursuit game throughout the woods near our homes. The chase itself offered an adrenalin rush for an adolescent who could easily conjure up life and death scenarios while ducking behind trees, crossing creeks and diving prone in fields, but we added an X-factor -- we all carried BB guns and would literally shoot at our prey. No one was ever seriously hurt, but when our parents caught wind of our game, they eliminated the guns, and that decision ultimately quelled the game. Those moments, years ago on summer nights when the chorus of cicadas and crickets brought a feeling of comfort and staring up at the stars in an infinite sky while controlling your excited breathing left you in amazement, were precious. Almost painfully so.

An echoing crack jolted me from my reverie. I knew the gunshot wasn't in my direction. It was distant. Somewhere else within the woods. Was it one of Billy's boys squeezing one off at an innocent hiker because he or she made a sudden movement? Oh, shit, Holden, score another one for your train of thought. Bring murdering scumbags with itchy trigger fingers to a public place so they could pop a couple of nature lovers. Christ, I needed a lot of work at this cloak and dagger crap. I reached down deep for a dose of optimism and hoped it was Jeffrey or David who had dropped one of the adversaries. The first shot was followed by a random burst of others. There were no screams. Eventually only silence. I stopped and listened hard, and I was rewarded. Slow, cautious footsteps revealed themselves to my left with the crack of small branches that were strewn on the forest floor. I huddled low to the ground and had my Glock at the ready, fully extended in my left hand supported by my right. I saw the movement about thirty feet ahead. My hands actually shook. Not violently, which may have been appropriate, but slightly, with enough motion to throw accuracy of a shot right out the window of opportunity. I aimed, paused and held my breath. Then, I quickly lowered the barrel. A hiker in his twenties, with long blond hair and an interest in everything nature-related around him walked past. He never noticed me. I wasn't part of his world. His large pack bounced with each purposeful step. I wanted to stand up and tell him to get the hell out of the woods as fast as he could, but that kind of warning and urgency would only lead to panic. I wondered what he thought about the sound of the gunfire. He didn't seem affected. Then, I saw the small headphones. There's the rub. Drown out the rest of the world.

I let the backpacker move on his way, and then I kept moving south for a while. I crossed a small creek that was clear and shallow and sounded perfect as the water rolled over rocks of various size. I should have added that to my earlier list of pleasurable sounds. Hanley must have realized that I'd turn back toward the road, and I was sure that he'd send someone that side of me. He'd also send someone to the east, if there were three of them, in case I ventured further into the woods. My guess was that Billy was the one who came straight at me, no messing around with diversionary tactics. The earlier trade of gunfire meant that someone might have been eliminated from the equation. So, where did that leave the odds? Who now had the number's advantage? No time to think that way. Only think of the greatest odds against you. Time to turn back, but not up toward the road. Deeper into the woods. The trickles of sweat had pooled their resources and started soaking through my shirt. Maybe I was onto a new weight loss program -- running through the woods with a murderous maniac chasing you. It might have had a chance in Hollywood, but I doubted that chic Skaneateles would adopt it anytime soon.

I wanted to locate higher ground, so I kept on moving, maintaining a steady pace and a rhythmic breathing pattern.

Bring it on, Hanley. I know you don't have the stamina. I was confident that I was putting distance between Hanley and me, which would allow me to take a break at some point to gather some extra oxygen back into my system. I eventually encountered a somewhat steep incline dotted with smaller trees that I scampered up. Once I reached the top, I stood in a small clearing, maybe fifteen feet in diameter. There were rocks gathered in a circle, with ashes, long since extinguished, piled in the middle like a black iris that no longer flickered with life. A large tree trunk, felled by age or wind or lightning, offered a temporary resting place. I gambled on time acting as an ally and sat. My breathing thankfully slowed. Beads of sweat dripped from my brow, and I flicked more off with the back of my right hand. If had been lifting weights, hitting my heavy bag or playing ball, it would have been what I classified as a "good" sweat, when the body almost cleanses itself through the physical effort, but this was more a combination of exertion and nervousness. I couldn't find too much good in it at the time. I took a moment to look around, almost surprised that the area wasn't littered with empty beer cans and other garbage. All around me, the trees, which I now determined as guardians, hovered majestically and drew my gaze to the blue sky framed by their gently swaying branches. That would have been one hell of a pallette to work with. Hard to believe that kind of tranquility existed a stone's throw away from the violence that pervaded the woods, violence that seemed like an impiety introduced by me.

As I sat, I began to feel soreness invading my body. Slowly. Almost imperceptibly. Like a slow-working drug introduced into my system. I stood up to keep from tightening up too much, and that's when I heard the rustling below the clearing. It was decision time. Did I wait in ambush for the person to reach the clearing and then mercilessly and cold-bloodedly pull the trigger before he even saw me, or did I allow him the chance to gain access and give him the opportunity to surrender? I stepped back behind the downed tree and squatted low with my gun aimed in the direction of the sound. Give the person a chance. Otherwise, it was murder. I worked hard on controlling my breathing and the slight shake in my hands again. Funny how easy it is to point and shoot at a deer or rabbit or duck. I had to remember, if it was Billy Hanley coming at me, he was just another animal. Period.

The approaching sound abated, then, to my left, a rustling and thud caught my attention briefly. It was a rock chucked by the person below the clearing attempting to draw my focus away from the direction he would come at me. Sure, that worked on *Gilligan's Island* when the cosmonauts needed to be distracted, so that Gilligan could scamper into their capsule to switch the bottle of vodka with water, but this was my life on the line, not a ratings war. I remained locked on the direction of the initial noises. And then he showed himself. The Cadillac Man. Billy Blue Eyes. Billy Hanley. He stayed low to the ground and behind whatever cover offered itself up, his impressive revolver poised in front of him. He may have been a moron in conversation and every day endeavors, but he was smart about moving up into the clearing. His ability to make it this far into the woods in such a quick time impressed me and reminded me to never underestimate him. Too bad I didn't have an extra clip with me for the Glock. Chalk up another mistake. I planned this excursion. I should have planned for more rounds. Maybe I trusted too much in the hope that Jeffrey and David would eliminate the need for excess shots. Maybe I was being overly optimistic and believed that Hanley and his boys would actually drop their weapons and say enough is enough. Oh, to get out of this alive would be really fine. Like a salmon slipping by a bear. Like an eland sneaking past a lion. Like a baby boar eluding a crocodile at water's edge.

Hanley paused for what seemed like an eternity. He almost blended into the scenery, forcing me to blink often and refocus my eyes, hopeful that the perspiration wouldn't run into them and further aggravate my vision. Finally, Hanley stepped cautiously into the clearing with his revolver leading him like a

310

dowser in search of water. I figured that he thought that enough time had elapsed since he chucked his diversionary rock that he'd be safe to step into the open. Lucky for him that I'm a stand-up guy. Anyone else would have squeezed off all their rounds when they saw his big head bobbing like a hot air balloon in the breeze. When he came up to the level ground, he dropped to a crouch and surveyed the area, and he immediately caught sight of the downed tree and the possible danger that awaited. He dropped to the ground and fired a shot into the rotting wood. Then another. And another. The scent of the spent gunpowder drifted my way. I once actually enjoyed the aroma as a youth. It was a unique odor that conjured thoughts of power, control and the ability to execute. At the moment, wildflowers would have smelled like heaven.

My mind locked up. Shoot while he was prone but in the open? Or tell him to give it up? Christ, no time to be a Boy Scout. He did open up on me, even if he may not have realized it. Shoot him. Shoot him. I eased my Glock over the trunk and took aim. I knew that I didn't have to worry about the sun glinting off the gun, because it was too late in the day and the trees blocked the sun's rays. I exhaled and squeezed. I missed. I saw the spray of dirt and pine needles to the right of Hanley's head. I must have shook. Damn it. I squeezed again, but Hanley was a slippery reptile and rolled to the edge of the clearing where the drop was. I pulled the trigger back again. Tree bark shredded. I saw a flash, heard the roar and ducked as Hanley's slug, probably a forty-four caliber, whistled over my head and ripped through the trees behind me. The duck wouldn't have mattered if the shot was accurate. I knew that I should have quelled my trigger finger, but I instinctively shot back. Once. Twice. A third time before I stopped myself. I hit nothing living. Hanley must have been laughing his ass off at what a imbecile I was, wasting valuable rounds when the odds of hitting him were miniscule. A rare silence developed. Eventually, Hanley razed it.

"Hey, Grace. How many rounds you got left over there, huh?" he yelled.

"All I need, Hanley."

"Ya think?" he said and offered a laugh reminiscent of Jim Carrey. "'Cause my money says that I got plenty over here to last us into night. And you got shit. Know why I think that?"

"Enlighten me."

"I think like a killer. You think a pantywaist. I got enough rounds to saw that tree in half you're hiding behind. Witness."

Two more shots lodged into the tree.

"Six more being loaded," he shouted. "What you got? Besides wet pants."

"I got enough balls to take you on."

"So fire away, Bambi."

Back to the animal kingdom.

"Tell you what, Hanley," I said. "Who needs guns to settle this? We could sit here until we both die of old age. Most likely you before me. How about we make this much more personal? Hand to hand? No weapons."

Hanley had guessed right about my ammo supply. I didn't doubt that he had enough rounds to bring down half the trees around me. I didn't have much choice. I knew I couldn't count on Jeffrey and David showing up to be my guardian angels. No way I wanted to lay out all night behind a tree knowing my few rounds left couldn't match Hanley's, unless he was bluffing, which I doubted.

"So, what, you wanna commit suicide or something?" Hanley replied.

"Just want to see of you can handle me as easily as Rachel Allen."

He snorted. I took it to be a sarcastic laugh.

"Give me a fucking break. That bitch could at least take a punch," he snarled.

"Then what's to lose?"

"Maybe I just want to shoot your ass to bits."

"You mean with your make believe dick, since your real one doesn't work anymore from all the juice?"

"Fuck you, Grace."

Driven by anger, he fired a couple of shots in my direction. They passed overhead into the trees behind me.

"You ever think about seeing someone about your repressed anger? You must have had one hell of a childhood, Billy."

"You might want to think about shutting up and start praying," he said.

"And why's that?"

"'Cause I'm gonna beat you to death and enjoy the look of pain on your busted up face. How's that sound?"

"Like a pipe dream, Billy boy. So, did you enjoy killing Rachel Allen and Rex Steinman as much as you think you'll enjoy taking me out? I mean, you kill a woman and a guy half your size. Must make you feel good. Give you something to brag about to your old roomies at the pen. Set a good example for your punk-in-training brother, Ricky."

"You don't know shit about fucking somebody up, do you? The rush. The power. The superiority. Even if it is a worthless skirt who refuses to have her baby cleaned out or a queer who wanted to raise his allowance for blowing you in and keeping his mouth shut about the things he did know. And the best part? That's doing it with your bare hands. Makes it a personal send off."

Neither one of us had moved from our positions of cover. I was happy to carry on the conversation for awhile. It gave me the chance to learn the truth.

"I appreciate you filling me in on your extracurricular activities," I said. "Maybe you can help clear a few things up."

"You mean the hot shit dick doesn't have it all figured out? It ain't that hard."

"I know you killed Rachel. When Stephanie found out that Rachel was pregnant with her father's kid, she went a little deeper off her usual deep vodka-induced end. She called Mommy. Enraged. Upset. How could this money-sponging bimbo have a kid when she couldn't? And by her father? And be in line to take away a substantial chunk of the Granby fortune? Carla assured Stephanie that everything would be all right. She'd take care of it. But she needed her help. You were around that night, because you were laying what shriveled piece of wood you have left to Carla. I'm sure, to work her money. And when she offered the scenario of beating someone into submission, you just couldn't turn it down. Keep Carla and her money happy. Feed your main passion -- violence. You drove out to Skaneateles, picked Stephanie up, who didn't have to worry about her husband, because he was out of town. You head back up the east side of the lake and wait for Rachel to leave Curt's place. And I guess you get lucky that she stayed long enough for you to get there in time. Or unlucky in Rachel's case. You cut her off, or whatever it took to get control of her. You take her and her Saab back to Caz. My guess is, thanks to your poignant comment earlier, that your job was to convince Rachel to have an abortion. Slap her around enough to get the point across. Send her back home knowing that she needed to do the job or you'd visit her again. But, you found out how obstinate Rachel was. She wouldn't give up the kid. But she didn't understand the gravity of the situation. You started feeling the rush. The power. The superiority. Even if she was a human being carrying another life in her womb. You smacked her too hard, too often. You killed her. And you probably loved it. My guess is, you dumped her weighed-down body in Cazenovia Lake somewhere, which ultimately would have been found. But you didn't think about that, because Stephanie was probably a basket case and Carla was pissed off. How am I doing so far?"

"Let's just say, close enough. And, yeah, I did like it. I did things to that hot chick you wouldn't believe. Yeah, the bitch was tough. And that just pushed me. Tough break. Especially for you, 'cause I think you had a thing for her. So, you gonna continue with storytime? Hey, after this one, could you tell me about Little Miss Muffet and the Three Bears?"

He snorted again. Pleased with, but not realizing, his literal mixed metaphor.

I continued, "Sure, then I'll share the story about Billy and the Dark Place. But that one's not suitable for children."

"Sounds like a real fairy tale. But I want to hear more about Rachel Allen."

I thought about what seemed to be an accurate understanding of what happened to Rachel on the night she disappeared. Now, I had to account for the return of Rachels' car and Rex's sighting of Rachel in the very early a.m. I took a stab.

"So, after you disposed of Rachel, you needed to cover your tracks. Or make a feeble attempt. You drove back to Rachel's condo, Stephanie behind the wheel of the Saab. And, since she's similar in appearance to Rachel, from a distance, you had her go into the condo. I don't even know if Rex actually saw her arrive that night or if you had him bribed to say he saw her. Stephanie goes into the condo. Still freaked out. She wasn't cut from the same psychotic cloth as you. She called her house, hoping that would somehow throw suspicion at her husband, who had a reputation, mostly conjured by Stephanie, for screwing around. You give her the gloves she most likely wore to not leave prints?"

The revelation about Stephanie returning to Rachel's apartment struck me as I spoke.

"Of course. Nice leather ones, too. Please, continue."

Well, wasn't Hanley just the most pleasant predator allowing his prey to speak his mind. No doubting that he was a lunatic.

"Stephanie walked away. You picked her up, dropped her off at home and went on your merry way. Then, when Rex Steinman tipped you off, or I should say Carla, the one really running the show, about me poking around, you decided to send me a message. Instead of leaving things alone, which would have been the better route to go, your need for the rush grabbed you like Carla's bony hands around your balls. You thought you'd send a stronger message by kicking Mick Allen around. Dumb. No, I'll go beyond dumb. Moronic. Like that would intimidate me? Bad move, Billy. It only pissed me off more. Now, the deal with Rex. That was more than moronic. Can I go as far as saying that was idiotic? Would that qualify? I know it's four syllables, but can you understand? You said he demanded more money for his silence. Wasn't it worth it to avoid a corpse to raise more suspicion? But, no. The trade-off wasn't worth it. Killing him was worth more than anything. Let me ask you. You rip off a piece? And if so, before or after you snuffed him? And to take that chance going in and out of the building. You are a dumb son of a bitch, Hanley."

"I'll give you credit, Grace, before I smash your skull in. You got it pretty good. But know this. I ain't no fucking pillow biter. Get that straight. And sure, Carla just wanted me to scare the Allen bitch into giving the kid the hanger. But her attitude burned my ass. She spit in my face. Questioned my manhood. Like she dared me to crack her head open. I ain't sorry. People die every day. She was one. Same with that artist fag. He flitted around Carla like some goddamn fairy Tinkerbell, 'cause she bought his art. I told her it was crap. But enough of this shit. Let's get down to it. Let's add another person to the death list. You ready, Grace?"

That was what I wanted, for Hanley to accept my invitation for hand-to-hand combat. I was locked in. I wasn't certain I'd win, and that meant he'd kill me. I'd become another sorry asshole on his resume. But I couldn't allow it. I was smarter and faster. I had more stamina. I believed that I had more to live for than Hanley. I reminded myself of everything I loved, of Rachel's senseless death, of Mick's uncalled-for beating, of Rex's demise and the fiancee he left behind, of Hanley's feeling of omnipotence, of Tracie the nurse practitioner with the special something, of Maggie, who was somewhere in New Mexico toasting her most recent public relations success. I thought about it all in an instant. Billy Hanley had to be stopped. Carla Granby had to be busted. Rachel Allen had to be avenged. I wasn't asking much of myself, was I?

"Let's do this," I said.

"Toss your piece."

"And you?"

A very large-barreled revolver spun through the air and bounced harmlessly in the clearing.

"Satisfied?" Hanley asked.

"Not really. I think you got more."

"Shit, Gracie, I didn't even need to bring my cannon along on this little hunt. If it'll make you feel better, I'll toss in my shirt. Ya know? Nothin' up my sleeve."

A moment later, a wadded up shirt joined the revolver in the clearing. It was an intimidation move on Hanley's part. He wanted to be all buffed up, flexing his pecs when we squared off.

Hanley added, "That's as far as I'm going. Let's see your piece."

I looked at the Glock so comfortably balanced in my left hand, then tossed it out near the old ring of fire.

"All right, Hanley. I'm clean. Let's go."

## *Chapter 26*

Hanley stepped up into the clearing, fully equipped with a condescending smile that told me I was out of my league, and began alternating a flex in his huge left and right pectoral muscles. The action made me think of some circus side show. I moved out from behind the felled tree and set a balanced stance with my left foot slightly in front of my right one. I remained on the balls of my feet. Hanley walked straight toward me, the smile bright enough to light the standing timber on fire.

"Tell you what, Grace. You either got some balls or you're nuts. Don't be beggin' me for a quick exit, 'cause I want to enjoy this."

I kept silent. I needed to focus on his every move. If he got me in close, I was done. I hoped he purely used his bulk in situations such as this. He stopped about six feet away from me and assumed the stance that I had and shadowboxed with lightning quick left and right hands. An untimely queasiness paid a rude visit to my insides. Hanley had boxing tools. Maybe that explained what a dim bulb he was -- all the blows to his head. But, somehow, the wattage cranked up in his smile. He looked like Dolph Lundgren in *Rocky IV*. And, as I recalled, Rocky kicked his ass. So, no intimidation. Quickness and snapping jabs. And street fighting when the time came. A layer of muscle-enhancing perspiration covered Hanley's upper body.

"So, Grace, do I have it right here? Left foot out front. Lead with the left hand and drop you fast with a right? I'm new at this, ya know."

"That's because you have to relearn it every day."

"Clever coming from a guy about to be beaten to death."

"What, no comment about how I'm a chicken egg and you're the whisk? Oh, that's right, you wouldn't know what a whisk was, even if it was shoved up your ass by Rex Steinman."

We began to circle counterclockwise.

"I told you. I ain't no fruit."

"Sure," I responded by stretching out the word in sarcasm. "You move like one. You like dancing to the Village People? I bet you'd be the construction guy, huh? A big hit at weddings."

"What the fuck are you talkin' about?" he asked truly out of confusion.

"This," I said as I snapped off three quick jabs to his square jaw.

The effect seemed minimal, and they were good, solid punches. He rolled his head a bit. That was all he offered.

"Nice jabs," he said. "Too bad you hit like a broad."

He fired out with a jab of his own, and I ducked it. He tried to follow up with a strong right hand, but I blocked it with my left forearm. And it hurt.

"Damn, looks like you got me all figured out," he said sarcastically. "Kinda like this Rachel Allen thing."

I shifted from counterclockwise to clockwise, feinted with a right hand and looped a left to his head. It rang his bell. I saw it in his face. But he shook it off quickly. We went back to dancing. The more we moved our feet, the better for me.

"You confirmed it all, Hanley," I said.

I wanted to waste as little time as possible on trading quips with Hanley. Physical combat, in whatever form, was much more taxing than most people imagined.

"Did I really?" he answered.

He rifled a jab to my midsection. Not a direct hit, but it sent a message to my entire body.

"I don't think so," he continued. "I said you were close. But what would you think if I told you that you forgot the key player in all this?"

I finally gained my breath.

"That you're full of shit. Carla pulled the strings. Steph was the messed up courier. And you were the muscle. Period."

I tried jabbing again, but Hanley merely flicked the punches off and connected cleanly with two jabs of his own. They hurt. I was in deep shit.

"What about Rachel's own brother, huh? You ever think that he was the one who called the shots in all this?" Hanley offered with a tone of superiority.

"No chance."

I knew Hanley was messing with me. Mick could not have been involved. Even if Hanley was the second person to mention it. It was not true.

"Okay," Hanley said. "Think what you want. You're the one with the answers."

He moved in quickly and pummeled me with a punishing combination, beating his large knuckles on my arms and head. It was hard to hold a guy off with that kind of size and speed. I finally juked and sidestepped away from the onslaught, drilling a right hand squarely into his left kidney. We each backed away. I felt a warm trickle down the left side of my face. I refused to acknowledge the presence of the blood and let it slide down my cheek.

"Need a Band-Aid?" Hanley asked with mock sincerity. "Or maybe a tampon, you pussy. The bleeding's just begun. Get used to it."

I had to maintain footwork and use my quickness. We resumed our pugilistic do-si-do.

"What do you say we get back to Rachel's brother? He knocked her up. His own sister. Sick bastard. So, he sent me to take care of her, 'cause she wanted the kid. Even if it had three heads. How's that sound? Carla and Stephanie thought Curt was the proud papa. Wrong. Yeah, incest is best, I guess," Hanley said.

"Hanley, only a sick mind like yours could dream that up. Then again, you're screwed up beyond belief. Maybe you actually knocked up your own sister. Maybe you're one of those rejects who couldn't handle adolescence and humped whoever or whatever you could. I think you're fucked up, Hanley. I know you're fucked up. You got a sister? Huh? Or maybe your mother? That's why you're with old lady Granby."

321

I knew I was pushing it, but I needed everything I could use. His smile mutated into a sneer. Quickly.

"You're a sick turd, Grace. You stink. You're nothing but a rotted piece of shit. You will die, asshole," Hanley said slowly and purposely. He accented the word "die."

He lunged at me in pure anger. It was a move elicited by emotion. It was good for me. As he ran at me, I stepped around to the right and hammered a right hand into the back of his head. The blow hurt my knuckles. I only hoped it had the same affect on his skull. He quickly wheeled around with a hateful fire burning up his blue eyes.

"This, I will guarantee you," he snarled. "There's no goddamn way you're walking out of these woods alive."

I ignored his conceptual malapropism.

"Was Mom a blonde, like you? Same blue eyes? Huh?" I needled.

Hanley walked toward me. His arms were down. His gaze locked on me. I kept shuffling my feet and kept my fists up. He didn't stop. I tagged him with three straight jabs below the right eye that halted him temporarily, but once he shook off the cobwebs, he started at me again. I shuffled backwards and connected with a solid left-right combo that I really threw my weight behind. Again, Hanley stopped briefly, now with his own cut spewing out blood from below the often punished right eye. He began to ball his hands tightly into fists. I guessed that he didn't feel a thing. I went lower and tried his midsection, but that was like striking concrete. I stepped back quickly. I was nearing the edge of the clearing, so I decided to dance around back toward the center. Hanley maintained his dogged pursuit.

"You son of a bitch," he finally spoke. "You think you know everything. You think you got the answers. You think you know what it's like. I'm tired of it. It's time I showed you how I felt."

Hanley wasn't talking to me. His blue eyes seared through me to a target familiar only to him. Hell, good thing I wasn't some kind of shrink, the way I elicited this kind of reaction from a few harsh words. I'd have to call the session over and run for my life. Not a bad idea at present. I concluded that asking if he wet to bed as a kid was not a wise choice. I stayed up on my toes. Moving. Moving. Moving. For someone who didn't prefer dancing, I was making a good show of it. Hanley remained steadfast in his pursuit. When I went left, he came at me. A move to the right, Hanley stayed true to his course. I knew I couldn't avoid him for much longer. He was intent on crushing me like a smoldering butt beneath his shoe. Maybe he'd talk to me if I led him down the path he initiated.

"Billy, I don't know it all. You can tell me the truth," I offered.

"Too late. I'm not taking it anymore."

"But why?" I asked.

"Because you're a lying, filthy, mean bastard who deserves to die."

Hanley was still not speaking to me. It was starting to creep me out. I had a buddy who was a counselor at some local lockup, and I thought that if, and when, I got out of this predicament, I'd ask him about Hanley's nut job behavior and what might or might not have been done about it in his time in the Pen. No wonder the guy was a psycho. And at that moment, my psycho. I would've preferred a rabid dog, or a jealous husband with a shotgun or some insurance scam guy holding a bomb. You can't always get what you want. I kept circling, careful not to trip over the extinguished ring of fire. I decided to make an attempt to push the button that would send Hanley into action.

"Well, Billy, if you think you got what it takes, then be a man. Kick my ass. Show me exactly how you feel. Weakling."

I tripped his switch. He bull rushed me with a fury and speed I failed to anticipate. He drove his massive frame into mine and sent me sprawling to the ground. Before I could gather myself, he had a hold of my shirt with both hands and hauled me from the ground with nauseating ease. He picked me up off my feet and looked into my eyes with the most hateful gaze I had ever encountered. Evil. Malacious. Unforgiving. Deadly. Then, he head butted me and released his grip simultaneously. I swore that I felt my skin split as the bursts of white light crashed around inside of my head. I knew that I landed on the ground, but I lost recollection of where I was. Then the blood spilled into my eyes as a reminder of the serious dilemma I faced.

Get away from his grip. Avoid the close combat. Gather your wits. Scramble away before he attacks again. Shake it off. Orient yourself. Do not allow this killer, this maniac, to snuff your life in the boonies, where animals will pick at your twisted and pulped corpse before anyone ever finds you. Fight, Holden. Fight, you bastard.

I rolled along the ground as I wiped the blood from my eyes in an attempt to avoid the clutches of Hanley. The blood continued to flow and I continued to move. My head cleared and I scrambled up to my feet. Hanley stood across the clearing, calm in his demeanor, fully expecting to kill me when the time suited him. He had plenty of time to snatch up one of the guns on the ground and cap me without effort, but I had a hunch he had forgotten about the firearms we tossed in treaty. With an iota of time to work with, I ripped my shirt into lengthwise strips and tied one around my forehead to curtail the bleeding. Hanley slowly approached. I needed to try a different approach than attacking him with jabs to the head or shots to the midsection. The knees. He came close enough for me to unleash a couple of jabs that didn't even connect. I followed with a slow right hand that he easily blocked with his left forearm, but I pivoted on my left foot where all my weight was settled and transferred the force into a kick with my right foot into his left knee right before he could deliver a lethal right hand. I was able to keep my balance as the force of my kick sent him earthbound. The pain registered in his face. I knew he was back to the moment. He would now refocus his effort on Holden Grace, not some demon from his past. I actually liked my odds better with Hanley in the present.

"Son of a bitch," Hanley screamed as he grabbed his damaged knee.

"Get up, asshole," I commanded.

Now it was my opportunity to grab a revolver or pistol and pop Hanley, but no chance was that the way this was going to come to a conclusion. Still too cold-blooded, and maybe my sense of revenge and self-imposed code of manliness figured into the equation. A bullet through Hanley's brain didn't seem a fitting end, unless, of course, there was no other option. But, he was gimpy, back to reality, and I was pretty damn ornery from the abuse he had dispensed on my body, so I wanted him to remember the punishment soon to be meted.

Hanley growled loud and long, as if it worked as an analgesic, and stood up, working hard with his arms and right leg to gain his balance. Once up, he placed little weight on his left leg. At least he had the brains to do that. I felt somewhat better about our encounter.

"I'm up. Now what's your plan? Kick me in the shin?" Hanley asked with no respect for the smart decision I made when I crumpled his knee.

"My plan? To beat you senseless... wait, can't do that. That happened a long time ago. When the doctor slapped you on the ass and scrambled your brains."

"A fuckin' comedian. Who kicks like a girl. Even on one good leg, I'll kick your ass."

"Well, don't fall down trying," I said.

Hanley limped toward me. He did one hell of a job disguising the pain that must have even tested his mettle.

"You gonna run? Or you gonna fight?" he sneered.

"You see me going anywhere?"

"Just to hell."

Hanley had a flair for the dramatic. And no doubt a bad habit of watching late-night movies on television chocked full of many more juicy lines. He moved in closer. I didn't back away. A left hand lashed out. It caught me above the right eyebrow, and it stung. He followed with another that I blocked with my right arm, and that hurt. Damn, he was quick for a huge guy. I ducked low and tried a left hand to his kidney but barely caught flesh, and that move opened me up to a thunderous overhand right that connected flush to my left cheek. I didn't just see stars. I saw supernovae. And I had no chance to remain on my feet as my brain sloshed around inside my skull like Jell-O in a jar. I knew I was in deep trouble. I was working on who I was and where I was when I felt a kick to my ribs. I covered my head with my arms and rolled along the ground to escape another foot to a tender place. It was that deja vu thing all over again as Yogi put it. I stumbled up to my knees just in time to catch another kick, this one to the left side of my face. The force of the blow sent me back to Mother Nature's floor. I could hear Hanley laughing. He stood above me, relishing the pain he delivered.

"Hey, Grace. Where're your jokes now, huh? Yeah, kinda hard to talk when you don't know where the hell you are. Get used to it, 'cause I'm bringin' on the hurt."

I managed to laugh. That line had to have been from one of those professional wrestling shows.

"You're bringing on what?" I asked.

"You heard me. And when I'm done squashing you into the dirt with the rest of the worms, I'm gonna piss on your dead body."

"But only if you can find your dick."

It hurt to talk... to breathe.. to just be. But I wasn't through. Hanley may have thought that I was finished, but he was gravely mistaken. I had landed next to the ring of rocks and secured one about the size of a softball in my right hand. I hoped Hanley was too busy puffing out his massive chest to notice.

"Tell you what, road kill, your sweetie won't have any problems findin' it when I put it to her," he said as he leaned in nice and close.

I swung my right arm up and caught him solidly above the left eye with the rock. Hanley grunted and tumbled to the ground to my left. His head didn't look right as the blood spilled forth, but he wasn't about to quit. He actually got to his knees, steadied himself, then stood up and smiled at me, holding my Glock.

He mumbled, "Just a scratch," and tried to wipe the spewing blood away.

I stood up, the rock still in my hand, amazed at Hanley's ability to handle such a powerful shot to the head. Most people would have been dead. He came at me, unstable, but purposeful, my gun shaking in his hand. He came in close and raised the barrel at me, and I drilled him again with the rock. This time in the left cheek. It was gruesome. The sound. The sight. The result. He crumpled. He was not going to hoist another weight, beat up another person, take up space in a correctional facility. Billy "Blue Eyes" Hanley, the Cadillac Man, was dead. And I vomited.

My head was still hanging when I heard someone approaching up the hill toward the clearing. I hoped that it was Jeffrey or David, because I had no strength left to take on any more assholes who wanted to waste me.

Before I turned to see who had arrived, I heard a panicked voice scream out, "Billy!?"

It was Ricky.

"Billy? Get up, man. Get up!"

Ricky ran over to Hanley's body and starting shaking him. He had ignored me to that point.

"Goddamn it, Billy. Get up! Billy! Jesus Christ. Jesus fucking Christ. Billy."

I thought Ricky was ready to burst into tears. Then, he focused on me.

"You fucking bastard. You fucking bastard," he bellowed. "You killed my brother. Goddamn you!"

He held a revolver exactly like Billy's and had it aimed at my head. Billy's blood had smeared on his shirt and hands.

"Now, I'm gonna kill you. Get up," he screamed.

I eased myself up from the ground. I saw his hands shaking, like it was a common theme out here in the woods, as if a constant tremor shook the earth.

"You got what it takes, kid?" I asked.

"You bet your dead ass."

Then, I heard the shot but felt nothing. I remained standing while Ricky jackknifed into the ground, the afterlife filling his eyes as he fell near his deceased brother, joining him in hell if that were truly the case. The reality of the situation finally choked the air out of me, and I sat down on the same downed tree as I did earlier, no longer prepared to fight. I was too tired. Too beat up. Too bloody. Too responsible for one body, maybe two, permanently hugging the dirt. A figure limped into the clearing. It was Jeffrey. He was sweaty and holding his piece.

I managed to say, "You got a flair for the dramatic."

"I prefer to call it good timing."

"I won't deny that."

Jeffrey stepped up to the two lifeless Hanleys and checked to make sure both were truly dead. He winced some when he saw Billy's crushed face.

"He ain't so pretty anymore, huh?" he mentioned.

"Got caught between a rock and a hard place."

"I bet," Jeffrey said as he walked up and sat next to me. "You okay? You don't look so great."

"Nothing time won't heal. What happened out there? The shots?"

"We dropped one, but David got winged. Must've been the guy I just took out. I made sure he was okay before taking chase. And, with the old knee not what it used to be, it took me a while to catch up. What do you say we get the hell out of these woods before we gotta answer too many questions?"

And we did just that. I snatched up my Glock, we walked back to find David, headed back to our vehicles and left the reforestation area a little lighter than when we first arrived.

## *Chapter 27*

With the help of Jeffrey and an angry and wounded David, I managed to work my Jeep out of the trail in the woods and back to civilization. As I drove much too quickly back to Skaneateles, I phoned the authorities and gave them an anonymous tip about gunfire near Apulia. When they wanted personal information, I hung up. The ride was much too far for a guy who hurt as much as I did. The bleeding had at least stopped from my forehead and face, but that didn't mean the suffering ended. I needed the longest shower of my life, a handful of analgesic, a cold beer and a body massage from a willing caregiver. I thought of Maggie but remembered that she was out of town. Maybe just as well. If she saw me in this condition, she'd give me the business for not being smarter. Then, I thought about Tracie from Dr. Russell's office. Not likely to happen. At least not now. Of course, there was Rachel's friend, Amy, who had the mean forehand and, chances were, two good massage hands. Wishful thinking. I needed to rest up, talk to Wade about Rex Steinman's death, then make a beeline for Stephanie Hendrix. With Billy Hanley gone, I wanted Carla Granby to trade her big estate in for the big house, and with an unstable Stephanie in the mix, Carla was in deep shit. I thought that Stephanie had a closer relationship with Curtis than she did with Carla. Of course, that might have been swayed by the future financial remunerations from Daddy. I needed Stephanie to roll on Carla, and I had an idea that just might make her do it. But what would dear Carla do now? When her hired hunk of steroids failed to come back to Cazenovia for some celebratory sex, sushi and champagne? Would she bolt? Would she contact Stephanie? She sure the hell wasn't going to call the police. Carla wouldn't panic. No chance. She might hope that we had killed each other. That would be the scenario to please her most, and she was just arrogant enough to believe that the stars would align for her and Hanley and I were now dead on the ground with our hands

329

wrapped around each other's throats. Sorry, Carla, despite many Hollywood portrayals, death is not that glamorous or convenient.

The sun was saying good-bye after another long day when I pulled into my driveway. Home never looked so good. Dorothy, darling, you were right on the button all those years ago. I pulled into the garage, went in the house and grabbed a beer from the fridge and headed to check my machine. Two messages. The first was from my buddy Mark looking to get some golf in. He said he could arrange his schedule to get out during a weekday morning. Mark was the friend who was a councilor at a local correctional facility. The second message was Maggie seeing how I was and wishing me well. She said things were going great in New Mexico and she'd call me sometime after she got home, and she asked me to give Mick her best. Her voice sounded upbeat, but I could hear the concern. Such an intuitive woman. I went back to the freezer and dug out a pile of ice just like I did on Saturday after Hanley rang my bell. This was a process I didn't want to get accustomed to. I didn't know if my icemaker could keep up, then I'd have to hit the local stores and gobble up their supplies. They'd be all giddy seeing me come in, my face all bloodied up from a most recent encounter. They'd have an ice account for me. Damn, I needed some sleep. I was punchy. At least I didn't have to concern myself about Hanley inflicting any more damage.

After a forty-five minute shower and two more beers, I felt somewhat more human. Then, I realized that I emptied my stomach in the woods and food actually sounded like a good idea, but so did sleep. It was nearly ten, and I was whipped, but food won out. I scrambled six eggs, using only two yolks, with low-fat American cheese, garlic and onions and some hot sauce. I added a couple of pieces of toast, sat down at the counter and ate quickly and in silence. I drained the last of my beer, set the dishes in the sink and headed to bed confident that no nightmares would abuse my brain due to my exhaustion. But I forgot one thing. I had just killed a man.

## *Chapter 28*

I couldn't do it. I lay prone, holding my breath, trying my best not to flinch a muscle. But I couldn't hold my breath any longer. I knew they'd see the movement and be on me in no time. I didn't know who "they" were, but I did know that they wanted me dead. I tried to hide myself by twisting up underneath a protective covering that I clutched in my hands. I held my breath again and waited. I didn't move. But I had to breathe. So it continued until I finally realized that I was caught in that state between dream and reality, asleep and awake with my sheet wrapped around my body like a boa. It took me a few minutes to gather myself, to understand where I was, to slow my rapid and shallow breathing, to stop sweating profusely and to pack the fear back away where it belonged. God, I hated when that happened. All too often with this case. I looked at the clock. Three-fifteen. So much for a solid night of sleep.

I unwound myself from the sheet, dragged myself out of bed and went to the bathroom. I then headed to the kitchen for something to drink. I grabbed a two-liter bottle of sparkling water and slugged it down. The carbonation forced me to belch. That brought me back to my world. Nice to be alive. I was still groggy, so I chose to give sleep another chance, but this time I opted for the sofa. For some strange reason, whenever I really had to sleep, the sofa offered the best opportunity. Maybe it was the safe feeling of the back of the sofa offering me protection from my nighttime demons. Maybe it was the comfort I recollected sleeping on my parents' sofa many years ago. Maybe I was a lunatic. Maybe I was no different from so many others. I stretched out, pulled a blanket over myself and quickly found that place where the body can recharge.

A chorus of birds, each one sounding like it practiced separate of the others, woke me up early, and I was thankful, even though my head throbbed, my body felt like one big bruise and my stomach protested. But there was much work ahead, so I needed to get to it. After taking care of feeding myself and dispensing of household chores, it was time for step one toward putting the final nail in Carla Granby's coffin. But one thing I had to remind myself of was that Stephanie Hendrix was far from an innocent bystander in this useless, murderous mess. She participated, on a lesser level, but I wasn't certain how willingly with Billy Hanley breathing his threatening hot breath down her nice neck. But she was pretty cool when I visited her. Was that the years of hardening herself emotionally and hardening her liver or the fact that she didn't really give a damn? Maybe when I set my final plan in motion, she'd surprise me. That would work well for me.

I first called Curtis Granby and told him what I had in mind. He knew about the firefight with Hanley and his sidekicks from Jeffrey and David and told me he was willing to help in any way possible. Very key. Then, I called Wade and spoke with him about Rex Steinman. He told me that Rex was not sexually molested. Someone simply snapped his neck. No prints. No witnesses. I revealed what Hanley had told me about Rex, and Wade questioned me as to how I ascertained the information. I told Wade that Hanley was just about stoned at the time. Wade let it go at that. Next, I called Stephanie Hendrix, who answered the phone, still sober in the morning hours.

"Hello?"

"Ms. Hendrix?"

"Yes."

She didn't recognize my voice. Then again, she wasn't a top notch private sleuth such as myself.

"This is Holden Grace."

"Mr. Grace."

"Holden, please. We've been through this."

"Yes we have. And you should have remembered to call me Stephanie. Or Steph."

"Fair enough," I acknowledged.

Score an early one for me. She stayed on the line.

"And to what do I owe this pleasure on a lovely Thursday morning?" she asked.

"I'm afraid this isn't a social call. It's business."

"That's a shame."

"More than you know. Things have gotten rather dire in the Rachel Allen case."

"What do you mean?" she asked, allowing a hint of panic to seep through her protective shell.

"I don't know how to say this, but I'm about to turn your father in for her murder. It all adds up. He had motive. Opportunity. The key to her apartment." I surmised about the key, but at this point, who cared. "He was the last one to see her alive." Complete line of bull. "I know he killed her, or had her killed, to protect his estate from a bastard child. His child."

I listened to silence on the other end. Is that possible, I thought as I waited for a response from Steph.

"That can't be true," she finally said.

"Sorry, Steph. I'm taking it to the cops. He's the guy. And you know what? He acts like he's absolved of any sin in this. Give me a break. I got him."

"I don't believe it."

"Believe it or not, you got no choice. It's a done deal. I just thought you deserved to know."

"Thank you, Mr. Grace. I have to go."

And then a discernible click and the silence that follows filled the earpiece. Not the first time a good looking woman hung up on me. It happened more than I cared for, especially when I was but a young lad and had no clue as to how to talk to or treat young women over the phone, let alone in person. And I knew that I wasn't the only gangly teenager afflicted with the syndrome, but instead of settling for being a member of the flock, wandering aimlessly through the male/female maze only to be sheered around the next turn, I set out to rectify my lack of understanding, common sense and social graces. Tall order for a young punk, but I excelled and the rewards boggled a young man's mind. In this instance, though, it was my adolescent

333

indignity prior to the behavorial revelation that gave me the inspiration to lay the false claim on Stephanie. Ah, yes, like falling off a bike, sabotaging sex, you don't forget how to screw up. Failure can be an adversary when applied properly.

I knew that Stephanie wouldn't call Carla about my accusations regarding Curtis, because Stephanie was smart enough to realize that was exactly what Carla would want to hear -- that Curtis was going to take the heat for Rachel Allen's disappearance and death. What Stephanie didn't know was that if she called Carla and told her about our conversation, Carla would see through the bluff. She knew I suspected her and Hanley. So, I picked up the phone, and chances were at the same time that Stephanie Hendrix picked up the vodka bottle, and punched in Curtis Granby's number again. He answered after one ring.

"Okay," I said. "Give her the call."

Then I hung up and paced the house, kicking around the odds of my sketchy plan realistically coming together. I had taken a lot of my eggs and placed them in Stephanie's loyalty-to-her-father-and-his-money basket. But I did save a few for a contigency plan, which I thought would involve Carla killing her daughter to protect herself and her wealth if Stephanie revealed my false theory, because Carla knew Stephanie would spill her guts. Drastic? Hell yes. Improbable? Hell no. Logical? Of course not. Did that mean I wanted Plan A to work? No question. But it was all based on a lot of conjecture. What a mess. Passion. Lust. Greed. Violence. All really for no reason. Because a group of dysfunctional individuals collided like a rack of billiard balls with some of them forever sinking into a side or corner pocket. Rachel Allen. Rex Steinman. Billy and Ricky Hanley. Not that the last two were going to be missed greatly by society, but a human life is a human life, and I didn't want another name added to the list. I wished I knew where Carla Granby was at that moment and what she was thinking. That's why I at least had Curtis send Jeffrey to keep an eye on the entrance to Stephanie's driveway.

The waiting had taken control of me by consuming me with unproductive thoughts, so I searched out my lob wedge, a handful of golf balls and headed outside with my cordless phone. I wasn't sure what kind of swing I'd muster with my myriad of bruises, but a painful golf swing sure beat no golf swing. I managed a few agonizing chips when the phone rang. I was thankful.

"Hello."

"Mr. Grace."

"Mr. Granby."

"I have placed the call and made the request as you instructed. She really is quite upset. You're certain this is the best solution?"

"It has to be."

"And why is that?"

"It's really the only one."

"I see." Granby paused. "Well, you've proven yourself quite able in a short time. Strangely enough, I have faith in you, Mr. Grace."

"Thanks, I think."

I took short swings with the club in my right hand, clipping the top of the grass. I winced with each swing but didn't stop. Maybe I thought I'd loosen up eventually. Say, in like a week or two when the bruises healed.

"So, is she willing to see you?" I asked.

Granby said, "I asked if I could visit her to discuss a grave consequence, and naturally she obliged. She is, after all, my only daughter."

"Yes she is."

"And you believe you can prevent her from serving prison time?"

"With her cooperation and the fact that Hanley was a psycho who was hard to say no to, yeah, I think it can happen. But she has to spill it all, and it's not going to be pretty or easy on you."

"Mr. Grace, I'll recover from my suffering. Perhaps Stephanie will. Perhaps not. It's a grim reality that she may

335

have stowed away with her other fears and pain. I hope it's not too late for her. Despite her involvement, I do not place the onus on her. She'll always have her father's love."

Granby told me what time he had arranged to meet Stephanie at her home, and I said I'd see him there, and we hung up. The more I interacted with Curtis Granby, the more I respected him. Here was a guy whose girlfriend and unborn child were murdered by an ex-employee in the company of his ex-wife and daughter, who initiated the violence because of their jealousy. I still had trouble comprehending it all, but Curtis, he rolled with it and kept pushing forward.

"Here's to you, Curtis," I said as I launched a high and long shot into the woods behind my home.

Then, I stashed my golf gear and readied myself for the confrontation at the Hendrix household.

## *Chapter 29*

I wasn't quite sure what to expect when I arrived at Stephanie's and Carl's home, so I mulled over the different possibilities as I made the now familiar drive down the west side of the lake, the weather debating on whether to stay cloudy or let the sunshine in. Maybe Steph would snap and shoot us all with a tiny revolver that she kept hidden at the bottom of her Bloody Mary glass. Maybe Carla was already camped out in Steph's house, having slit the throats of her own daughter and son-in-law with a razor-sharp platinum credit card, prepared to strangle Curt with a mink wrap and off me with multiple tennis forehands to the groin. The thought reminded me of *The Longest Yard*. Man, Burt was funny back then. Maybe Curt would finally get pissed off at his boozehound daughter and insensitive son-in-law and bust a vein in his brain and drop dead on the spot. Maybe it would all work out. Hell, it could happen. And that's what I hoped for.

I shot a quick finger to Jeffrey who sat in a white Taurus with the hood propped open across from the long drive that led to the Hendrix property, and he gave me a thumbs up gesture. I knew that meant Curtis had already arrived and was waiting for me somewhere along the drive. I pulled into the driveway and met up with Curtis just a couple of hundred yards down. He stood, what looked uncomfortably, next to his silver Lexus, dressed dapperly in gray slacks, a blue and white pin-striped shirt, black, blue and white patterned silk tie and blue blazer. His face could have been the poster child for rich man's anxiety. As Elvis said, "Caught in a trap." Like father, like daughter. I stopped, and he got in the Jeep in silence, and we drove that way to the circular drive.

Before we got out, Granby turned to me and said, "You are sure this is the wisest path to take?"

"If we had come to a fork in the road, this is the only way I would have chosen," I responded.

He nodded and stepped out of the vehicle. I followed him to the front door, where he rang the doorbell and we both waited. Stephanie answered. She had looked better on my previous visit. Her attire looked good -- snug cream pants and a red sleeveless button-up top with a wide collar -- but her face registered a weariness that looked like it had been sneaking up on her for a while and finally caught her while she wasn't paying attention. Her tired-looking eyes first registered on her father then flicked over to me in confusion.

"What the hell is he doing here?" she asked, her eyes still trained on me.

"I have asked Mr. Grace to join me," Granby answered.

"But he's the one ready to put you away," she said.

"Not necessarily the case," I chimed in.

"But you told me..." Then the light snapped on in her head. She knew I set her up. The accusation about her father was a ruse, but she still needed to hold her ground. Not give up anything or anyone.

"Doesn't mean it ain't gonna happen. I'm just saying there may be a chance for liberation. Depending on what we can find out here today," I said.

"Stephanie," Granby offered, "aren't you going to invite us in?"

Always the gentleman. Even under duress. Stephanie backed away from the door and we stepped in, Curtis before me. The foyer remained impressive, but instead of going through the French doors to the right when I visited earlier, Curtis led the way to the left into what I determined to be a study or a great room or just an incredible space that was carefully laid out with contemporary furniture and all the trappings to really make the room sing. Stephanie remained silent and dutifully followed where Curtis went. I was admiring what looked to be an original James Prosek watercolor of a trout-fishing scene when Stephanie broke her silence. Her words were not directed at me. In fact, they were spoken as if I hadn't been present.

"I don't want him here," she said.

This didn't seem like the same lovable lush I shared some meaningful poolside moments with less than a week before. That's what I get for not calling. We were all still standing. Finally, Curtis gave in and grabbed a piece of earth tone sofa. I lingered around the art. Stephanie remained on her feet, her arms folded tightly against her chest. Obstinate until the end.

"Well, my dear," Granby said eloquently, "Mr. Grace stays or I also go. Stephanie, I don't know if you realize this, but Mr. Grace knows the truth."

"The truth about what?" she asked with indignation clouding her otherwise attractive eyes.

"Rachel. My Rachel. And her disappearance," he said.

"Oh, so she's 'your Rachel' now?" Stephanie responded with a touch of venom.

"When Rachel and I were together, she was always 'my Rachel.' Not in a possessive means, but in that rare connection between two people, which rarely happens."

"It's called greed, Daddy. She wanted your money. Don't you think it was less than coincidental that she got pregnant? Huh? Gave her a nice bloodline to your fortune." Stephanie walked briskly to a stocked bar and started pouring her favorite drink. "Does anyone else want a drink, or am I alone here?"

I waved my hand in a "no thanks" gesture, because I thought it best to keep my mouth shut while the proceedings unfolded.

Granby said, "I'm fine, thank you. Perhaps you should refrain for the moment."

Stephanie whirled around, the bottle of vodka still clutched in her right hand.

"Refrain? Why should I refrain? Why the hell should I ever refrain? If I want a drink or fifty drinks to get me through the day, then that's what I'm gonna have."

"That's your choice, Stephanie, but we both know it's killing you," Granby said almost casually.

"Killing me? Ha, like there's anything left alive."

"There's always something to live for."

"Easy for you to say."

339

*Daniel Surdam*

"You truly think that? Honestly? When I know that my own daughter was in some part responsible for the murder of someone very special in my life and the child that we conceived?"

For the first time, I saw the ruthless ire rise in Granby like a pissed off grizzly that's had enough of missing the salmon springing from the water, and he turned the claws and fangs on his own daughter. Not that she didn't deserve it, but I felt strange witnessing the personal discourse building between the two.

"You believe that everything falls into my lap? I hurt every damn day from the hole in my life that Rachel filled. She was young. Assertive. Adventurous. Hungry. Many things that kept my fire burning after the disastrous divorce from your mother. Maybe she wanted my money more than she wanted me, but she never failed to show me how much she cared. So, I refuse to accept the fact that our relationship was purely based on financial returns. I loved Rachel Allen, and now she's gone."

Granby's tone softened as he finished speaking to his daughter. Stephanie had set the bottle down and now stared at the ice and vodka swimming together in the glass she held in her left hand. She turned away toward the bar and set the glass down. Her shoulders began to shake. Stephanie Hendrix knew that her world, which had revolved in a tenuous galaxy before, was hurtling toward the sun and was about to be fried to a crisp. I stood and watched. Curtis remained on the sofa. He looked down at his well-manicured hands but made no move to comfort his daughter. It was probably always that way. Not that he didn't love her implicitly, but Curtis Granby was the kind of self-made man who lived life by the code of pulling yourself up by the bootstraps when adversity hit home. I felt that he questioned that mindset at the moment, but he didn't know how to correct all the years of deprivation. I couldn't have been more uncomfortable if my boxer briefs twisted up in a knot.

Stephanie finally spoke, fighting through the tears, her back still to Curtis and me.

"Daddy, it's never been easy for me. Especially since the accident. I know you want me to be strong, but that's the same mistake Carl and I made. Be strong. Goddamn it. Why not be human? I hated Carl. I hated life. Maybe I still do. But the whole damn incident was conveniently tucked behind us. Like it never happened. Guess what? It did. I think my life ended that night, and maybe that's why I don't give a damn about killing myself with this stuff." She raised the vodka bottle and set it down. "Then, you and Mother divorce. And you take up with this Rachel, a young, beautiful woman." Stephanie turned around. The tears had been streaming down her face. "And I'm a young woman... and I'm a mess... a wreck. And I see what this Rachel gets from you. Not monetarily, but affection. And then she gets the gift of your child. And I'm there when she shares the news. Daddy, I was sick when I heard. It was like a bomb going off inside my head. I was crushed. So, I came home and called Mother. I wanted her to help my pain, and she said she'd take care of it. She told me to stay here, that she'd be by soon to pick me up. Carl was out of town, and I sat in the dark and drank. I wanted to be numb. It was my way. I couldn't have children and now my father's girlfriend was pregnant. It wasn't fair. So, I sat here and the hatred took over with every sip until Mother showed up. And she took me away. Said she'd look out for me. Unlike you. And Billy was with her. I didn't know he'd be with her. I thought he was away. Then, we drove up and waited on the road near your driveway. We waited for Rachel. Billy and Mother argued about whether we should wait. Billy insisted that we go to Rachel's apartment. We had a key to the building from Rex Steinman, and Rex was painting the apartment across from Rachel's and Billy had that key too. Billy said he could take care of her right there. But Mother insisted that we wait. She said she knew that the bitch was still hanging around your house, gloating about the baby. Mother said she knew. And she was right. When she drove out to the road, we cut her off, and Billy jumped in the car with her. We drove out to Mother's house. She said that they were just going to convince her to have an abortion. That was all. She was wrong. Billy got rough. Real rough. And he liked it. She wouldn't give in and she spit on him, and Billy kept hitting her. Harder and harder. And then she stopped breathing. Billy didn't care. Mother was furious that it happened at her house. They wrapped up her body in a sheet, tied weights around her and dropped her in the middle of the lake. Like they did it every day. Then Billy talked to me. He threatened me. Told me that I had to drive the bitch's car back to her apartment, go inside, do a couple of things, like call my own house and hang up. Then leave and walk away and they'd pick me up. Billy said I looked a lot like her and that any nosy asshole watching would think it was her coming home and leaving. Then they took me home. Billy told me to keep my fucking mouth shut for the rest of my life or he'd do a lot worse to me than he did her. So, I tried. I did the same damn thing that I did when I lost the baby. I shut down. I shut it out. I pretended it never happened. I was good when you came to visit me, Mr. Grace, wasn't I?"

I nodded.

"But that doesn't work in the end, does it? It doesn't work when you actually realize you have a conscience," she continued.

I was skeptical about her sudden turnaround. She had gone from a hardened rich socialite with a nice pool, better body and even better view of the lake to complete victim in Daddy's presence. I surmised that Curtis held the ticket for her behavior. He taught her to be tough, but when the master was around, she had no choice but to cave in to his authority. It was a lot of psychobabble better off left for the shrinks who thought they had all the answers. They'd need all of eternity for that.

"So, Daddy," she continued, "you know the truth. I didn't want Rachel to die. I was hurt. I felt all the old pain coming back. I'm sorry. God, I am so sorry."

Then the dam broke and the tears of liberation washed away her sin of ignorance as Curtis stood and held her tightly in his arms. I leaned against the wall admiring the moment and relishing the confession against Carla when my cell phone rang. I flipped it open without disturbing Stephanie and Curtis. It seemed a lot of history was being washed away with that one huge embrace.

"Yeah," I answered.

"This is Jeffrey. You got a visitor. Want me to stop her?"

"No, let her come. Just follow her down the driveway once she's well ahead of you, then put in a call to the village cops. Tell them it's a domestic disturbance." I gave him the number.

"Can do."

Jeffrey hung up. The visitor was Carla. I had to give myself some credit for posting Jeffrey out near the road. I guessed it was simply a matter of time before Carla paid a visit to her daughter, the only other witness to Rachel's murder, especially when Billy Hanley never returned. Stephanie and Curtis were still hanging on to each other, almost oblivious to my presence, when I gently nudged Curtis on the left shoulder.

He looked at me, slightly dewy-eyed, saw the expression on my face and instantly understood the implication of the interruption. He unclasped his arms from Stephanie and stepped back slowly as she continued to try to hold on.

He looked at her and said, "Your mother is on her way here. Mr. Grace is going to have to detain her in any way possible. You realize that, don't you, Stephanie?"

She nodded.

He continued, "And you realize that she will be coming in here fighting for her life. It's always been her way, and I'm afraid, in this instance, she will be less than cooperative. In fact, hostile."

"How do you mean?" Stephanie asked, startled by the seriousness of Curtis's tone.

I decided is was time for me to unhinge my jaw and put the brakes on the train of thought Granby had led down the tracks.

"Stephanie," I said, "your father's right. I have to keep your mother here. She has to pay for what she did. She used you. Billy Hanley used you. They both knew you were vulnerable

343

and took things too far. Maybe the plan wasn't to kill Rachel. Maybe they really just wanted to scare her into an abortion. But that doesn't matter. People are dead. Rachel. Rex Steinman..."

"What?" Stephanie gasped in surprise.

"Hanley killed him, because he knew too much," I said.

"Oh my God."

"Now you know too much."

"But...but...Mother won't have Billy kill me. I'm her daughter."

"You don't have to worry about Billy. Your mother's alone, and in order to save you, she has to go down," I said. "We have your confession. I have Billy's confession. The guilty truly must pay here."

So, the line was hokey. Stephanie wasn't in any condition to critique my verbiage.

"But, if what you say is true, shouldn't we call the police?" she asked.

"Taken care of," I replied.

"Then we shouldn't even let her in," she said, her mind suddenly racing knowing her life could be on the line.

"And how do we stop her?" It was my turn to ask a question.

"You can shoot her," she blurted out. "I know you carry a gun. When she comes in, shoot her, and I'll say you did it in self-defense."

Granby jumped in. "Stephanie, it doesn't work that way. You'd simply be practicing the same philosophy as before -- cover up what you can for as long as you can. You must stop thinking that way if you want to get on with your life."

"But, Daddy..."

"No, Stephanie. Mr. Grace and I will handle this."

I looked at Granby curiously when he said that. The old boy had something up his sleeve. I sensed it. I looked back to Stephanie, and did she ever look like she wanted a drink.

"Jeffrey is tailing Carla. He'll be right behind her. The police are on the way. And, most importantly, I won't let you get hurt. I have an image, you know."

She actually managed to smile, albeit briefly, because we heard the front door open and close. Enter the dragoness. She had the knowledge that Curtis and I were both there. Our parked vehicles gave that away. Now, she had to find us. I felt the adrenalin start to rush. This case was finally winding down to its last bitter note, and I had Carla Granby right where I wanted her. She had to have been so focused on saving her backside that she didn't care if Curtis and I were in the house with Stephanie. Maybe she felt an aura of invincibility having survived while her main man Billy and his brother and friend couldn't cut it. Carla still lived. In her mind, she deserved to live and thrive on other people's misery. Right now, she was strong. But not for long.

"Stephanie," Carla shouted from the foyer. "I know you're in here. With your cowardice father and that arrogant prick Grace."

Arrogant? Me? I'd settle with confident.

"I thought you and I were close, Stephie?" she continued. "I thought we had that special mother and daughter bond that no man can understand. No man!"

Her voice trailed away. She must have opened the doors to the right and looked around. I could see Stephanie shaking. Hell of a tangled web, darling. Curtis stood motionless, his face stern and unyielding. I knew Jeffrey would make his entrance soon, and I expected to hear sirens within minutes. I was really counting on that ancient aesthetic Tai Ming to help pull everyone through this. Or timing, as it were.

"Stephie, I know you're confused," Carla said, her voice getting stronger again, "but I'm here to help you. Your father and Grace only want to fill your head with lies. You know I'm here to protect you. Only I can understand what you feel."

Carla was at the doors to the study.

"Stephie?" she nearly whispered. "Are you there?"

Stephanie closed her eyes tightly, but the tears squeezed through like determined warriors fighting past a weak spot in the enemy line. I stepped over to Stephanie and put my body in front of hers. I felt the reassurance of my Glock. Curtis remained diligent and defiant in his stance. The doors swung open, and there stood Carla Granby in a black pinstriped business suit holding a small revolver. Her smile was indeed wicked, and she dressed appropriately for the occasion.

"Well, well, well," she said as she slowly entered the room, "what do we have here? A clandestine meeting of the Boobs and Fools Club? Curtis, so nice to see you again. You're looking well, except, of course, for that clenched jaw and the pulsing vein in your temple. But, then again, you never could handle stress very well. Hard to figure with a man of your professional stature. And, Mr. Grace, unfortunate that we couldn't spend more quality time together. I could've put you to good use. But my, how heroic we look right now. Shielding the damsel in distress. Too bad you can't pull your piece before I can pull this trigger."

Carla closed the doors behind her with her left hand, never diverting her eyes or her aim from my chest. She didn't appear very concerned about Curtis's presence. I surmised that if I had the same choice, I'd worry about me before Granby. Carla stepped up to the bar and saw the glass that Stephanie had filled with ice and vodka, snatched it up and drained a few ounces before setting it back down.

"Not bad, but I prefer a single-malt scotch. Isn't that right, Curt?"

He stayed frozen, but I knew it wasn't from fear, and I could bet that Curtis knew that Carla thought it was, and he had one up on her.

"What's the matter, baby? Too scared to talk?" she asked mockingly and walked close to him and put the barrel of her handgun under his chin. "Do us all a favor and don't shit your pants, okay?"

Carla pulled the gun away and quickly focused her attention back to me and Stephanie. Jeffrey, where are you, buddy? I didn't know how long Carla would continue her powerplay.

"Stephie? You don't need to hide behind a man. You can come out, dear," Carla said.

I held my right arm behind me and held Stephanie's hand. She squeezed hard. I didn't mind. It kept me in the here and now. Always a wise thing when someone held a loaded gun on you.

"Stephie!" Carla's voice was authoritative, like a mother speaking to a small child. "I need you to come to me, now."

Stephanie stayed behind me.

"Do you want me to kill Mr. Grace? And then Daddy? Do you want to be responsible for their deaths like you were Rachel Allen's?" Carla asked coldly.

Stephanie finally spoke. "No, Mother. I refuse to accept blame. I accept the role I played, but not the responsibility for Rachel's death. I'm not a bad person." Her voice was forced and shrill, fighting the tears, fighting the moment, fighting her whole screwed up life.

Carla quickly responded, "Ha, excuse me sweetheart, but we're all bad people. It's the way of the world. Go ahead, try to convince yourself otherwise, but we all know better."

"No, Mother. I will not come to you."

"Then, you leave me no choice. Whom should it be first? Daddy dearest or Holden the Hero?" Carla mused out loud. "Hmm, I think Mr. Grace for being so rude when he was a guest at my home. Then, you get to watch Daddy die last, groveling like the weak man he really is."

Carla aimed her gun at my chest, but before she pulled the trigger, the front door opened and closed and Carla briefly diverted her attention toward the French doors, which allowed Curtis Granby to pull out a small-caliber pistol from his suitcoat pocket and shoot Carla. Granby had the pistol poised again, but I leapt toward him and took him down hard just as Carla finished crumpling to the floor. Stephanie also folded to the floor, stunned by the surreal scene that played out before her. Curtis's and Carla's guns clattered away harmlessly. Jeffrey kicked open the French doors. I heard the sirens finally approaching.

"Oh, shit," was all Jeffrey said.

## *Chapter 30*

Mick, Maggie and I were sitting on my back deck on a splendid early-September Saturday afternoon soaking in the annual rite of the leaves telling the world that their time had come and they were at least going to provide some visual pleasure before taking that spiral fall from the branch to the ground. The SU football team had knocked off East Carolina earlier in the day, and I was glad for that. Small pleasures. Too easily forgotten. Mick still suffered from nightmares about Rachel, Rex, the beating he took and his parents, but he was working on dealing with his demons. He understood it wasn't as simple as ignoring them. He had good days, and he had bad days, but he was going to move on. I never questioned that. Maggie wanted to wring my neck when she returned from New Mexico and learned about the events that led up to the conclusion of the case. She wasn't just annoyed with me, she was irate, which led to a short cooling off period until Mick interceded and patched up the rift. I truly believed that helped as a healing aid for him as well as for myself. I was simply happy the entire ordeal was over. I learned a lot of things... about people in general, about Mick, about myself, about the mistakes that can be made during a case, and about a cold-hearted world that's not going to let you off the hook for very long. I also had a change of heart on certain matters, like when a grown man cries. When I first told Mick that the case was wrapped up, he wept openly, and I respected him for that. It didn't hurt to purge. It didn't hurt to express emotion. And it didn't hurt when I cried right along with Mick. Learning and growing are underestimated by far.

The two of us took time to hash out our feelings about what was revealed during the case, both about Rachel and Mick. There were some tough moments. But better tough early moments than regretful and awkward ones later. Mick found it difficult to accept the opinions shared about Rachel. I understood. I still struggled with the shock of the knowledge about his sexual preference, and he had a difficult time believing that I hadn't picked up on it sooner.

I had also followed through on my promises to Gary Howard and Amy Simpson and informed them of Rachel's death. Rachel's body was recovered from the depths of Cazenovia Lake, and the identifying process was another test for Mick, but the fact that he could properly lay her body to rest next to their parents served as a tonic, somewhat. I couldn't imagine burying a younger sibling alongside my mother and father while I was still young. Mick's courage was commendable. The mourners who showed up for the funeral were genuine in their concern. Those who didn't pay respects never had any in the first place.

Surprisingly, I found out from Curtis Granby that Officer Chad Houston was the one who tipped him off about my presence at Rex's murder scene. It seemed that Chad had made an influential ally in Curtis when he let him slide from a possible DWI late one night. Chad knew what he needed to do to accomplish his goals. Having Curtis Granby in your corner when you made your bid for the Secret Service could do nothing but help. I held no ill will. His phone call to Granby actually proved beneficial to the detecting process.

Jeffrey, David and I faced a barrage of questions from inquisitive law enforcement officers about the shootout in Apulia, but we were exonerated, I suspected, due to the lack of concern over the loss of three bad seeds. That and we had Granby in our corner much like Chad.

But, at the moment, on the deck, the three of us admiring nature's backdrop, we were good. We had new scars, but so did so many other individuals involved. We were contemplating whether I should put a golf green in the back left corner of my property when the phone rang. Maggie was closest to it, and she answered.

"Holden Grace residence," she said in a silky voice that touched me in all the right places. There was a slight pause, and then she said, "One moment please."

She cupped the mouthpiece and handed the phone over to me.

"It's Curtis Granby," she whispered.

I took the phone, stood up and began pacing the deck.

"Mr. Granby."

"Now, how many times must we go through this. It's Curtis. Please."

He sounded good.

"Sorry. Curtis."

"Much better. I trust you received the token of my gratitude for all you've done," he said.

"Yes I did. And, it was more than generous. It was... well, basically uncalled for."

"Nonsense. You deserved every penny."

"Maybe a few of them. How's Stephanie?"

"Doing well. She and Carl have seeked counseling. They're both very grateful. They appear to have taken their lives back."

"Always good to hear. And yourself?"

"Doing fine. At times, it's a challenge, but I'm okay. I've established a scholarship fund at Syracuse University in Rachel's name."

"Good for you."

"I want to thank you again for stopping me from pulling the trigger one more time. It served two purposes. You kept me out of prison, and you allowed Carla to live, and now she's away for a long, long time. Mr. Grace, if you ever, and I mean ever, need help with anything, do not hesitate to ask."

"Curtis, you can count on that. And, thank you again for your generosity. And tell Jeffrey and David I said 'hello'."

"Consider it done."

We hung up, and I returned to my seat to resume the golf green conversation and to bask in the warmth of quality time with quality people on a majestic day when all seemed right.